MACHINE

A WHITE SPACE NOVEL

ELIZABETH BEAR

This paperback first published in Great Britain in 2021 by Gollancz

First published in Great Britain in 2020 by Gollancz
an imprint of The Orion Publishing Group Ltd
Carmelite House, 50 Victoria Embankment
London EC4Y 0DZ

An Hachette UK Company

1 3 5 7 9 10 8 6 4 2

A CIP catalogue record for this book is available from the British Library.

ISBN (Mass Market Paperback) 978 1 473 20878 0
ISBN (eBook) 978 1 473 20879 7

Printed and bound in Great Britain by Clays Ltd, Elcograf S.p.A

FSC www.fsc.org MIX Paper from responsible sources FSC® C104740

www.gollancz.co.uk

'Awesome, awe-inspiring space opera. Fittingly, it shifts from weighty themes to lighter humour with dexterity, grace and crackling dialogue' *Daily Mail*

'Elizabeth Bear is just as comfortable writing steampunk and fantasy as she is hard science fiction' *Financial Times*

'A page-turning fusion of science fiction and mystery' *Kirkus*

'With compelling characters, a vast canvas, and a whole lot of really cool shit, *Machine* is very satisfying as a novel about professionals dealing competently and compassionately with events that spiral out of control' *Tor*

'Bear has a striking command of tension and character' *Locus*

'Succeeds to engross the reader in a plausible future by inviting us on a space mystery unlike anything readers have seen before' *Bookidote.com*

'Bear has constructed a fascinating, absorbing universe populated with compelling and intelligent characters who conform to neither clichés nor stereotypes. It's sci-fi of the top order' *Popmatters*

By Elizabeth Bear from Gollancz:

White Space Novels

Ancestral Night

Machine

Jacob's Ladder Sequence

Pinion

Sanction

Cleave

Jenny Casey Series

Hammered

Scardown

Worldwired

For Chelsea

The incredible thing was that the machine smiled,
smiled perpetually.

—from *The Trembling of the Veil*, W. B. Yeats, 1922

Man, with his singular laughter, his droll tears,
His engines and his conscience and his art,
Made but a simple sound upon your ears:
The patient beating of the animal heart.

—from Sonnet IV, *Wine from these Grapes: Epitaph for the Race of Man*, Edna St. Vincent Millay, 1934

CHAPTER 1

I STOOD IN THE DOOR AND LOOKED DOWN.

Down wasn't the right word, exactly. But it also wasn't exactly the wrong word. All directions were *down* from the airlock where I stood, and almost all of them were an infinitely long fall.

I wasn't *only* staring into bottomless space. I was aiming: aiming at a target that wheeled sickeningly less than a klick away. My own perch was also revolving around a central core, simulating a half a g or so, just to keep things interesting.

I was standing in the airlock door because I was going to jump.

Just as soon as I got my bearings and my timing.

I don't get to be afraid now. I get to be afraid before and I get to be afraid after. But I don't get to be afraid during.

There's no room *during* for being afraid. So I have to fold the fear up. Tuck it out of sight and get on with all the important things I am doing.

In this case, saving lives and making history. In that order of priority and the reverse order of chronology.

I hoped to be saving lives, anyway, if I got lucky and there were still some lives on the other side of my jump to save.

Across that gulf of vacuum lay the ancient ship we pursued. It wasn't far, by space travel standards. A few hundred meters, and it seemed like less, because *Big Rock Candy Mountain* was thousands of meters in diameter.

I say "ship." But what I was looking at was an enormous wheel whipping around its hub as if rolling through space. It was a station orbiting no primary; an endless scroll of hull unreeling—subjectively speaking, because on my own ship I felt like I was standing still—in a spring-curl spiral twisting around us.

Not a smooth hull, but a rocky and pockmarked one. One punctured by micrometeors and crumpled by sheer stresses. With bits of structure projecting from the surface at varied angles and its cerulean and gold paint frayed by unfiltered ultraviolet and abraded by space dust.

Big Rock Candy Mountain was old.

About six hundred ans old, to be as precise as I could without running a lot of fussy conversions in my head. She'd come from Terra in the pre-white-drive era, and over the centians she had built up tremendous velocity.

She was zipping along at a solid fraction of the speed of light, out here in the dark places between the stars, much farther from home than she could have possibly been, her course no longer anything like the original plot retrieved by Core archinformists.

Maybe she'd gotten lost, or an impact that had caused some of the damage to her hull had knocked her off course. Or maybe the people who had outfitted her had lied about where they planned to go. The era of Terra's history that had spawned sublight interstellar exploration and the generation ships had not been one of trust and peaceful cooperation between peoples. More one of desperate gambles and bloody-nailed survival.

Only one generation ship had ever reached a destination as far as history was aware, and that hadn't ended well. We were here because this one had sent out a distress signal, and a Synarche ship, tracing it, had found her. And sent out a data packet requesting assistance on *Big Rock Candy Mountain*'s behalf.

The Synarche ship had not been in contact since, which was disconcerting. And its locator beacon, and *Big Rock Candy Mountain*'s distress signal, were still beeping away *down* there. And so we were here: to see if we could rescue anybody. If there was anybody left to rescue.

It didn't look promising. The ship behind us was another ambulance, but the one after that contained a team of archaeologists and archinformists, and I had an unsettling premonition that there was going to be a lot more useful work for them to do than for us. I wasn't sure exactly how far behind us they were, but I expected we were on our own for at least five to ten diar. The rescue could not afford to wait for backup.

There *could* be people alive in there. We had to proceed as if there were, until we had proven otherwise. But they'd done nothing to acknowledge our approach, and they had not responded to hails on the same frequencies as their distress beacon.

I couldn't have preconceptions, because I couldn't afford to miss anyone who *might* be alive. Nevertheless, contemplating the vast ruin before me made me feel sad. Worse, it was that creeping, satisfying sadness you get when you look on a ruin: at something long destroyed, something lost that isn't your problem.

My own ship, Synarche Medical Vessel *I Race To Seek the Living*, was an ambulance associated with Core General. She had spent nearly a standard month with her modern engines burning fuel recklessly to match velocity with *Big Rock Candy Mountain*. Sally—as we called her—was fast, maneuverable, and had outsize sublight engines for her mass. She also had an Alcubierre-White drive for FTL travel, though since it didn't impart any actual velocity to the ship, it couldn't be used to chase down quarry in normal space. We'd had to slingshot the big gravity well at our origin point in the Core to accelerate, then conserve momentum through the transition in order to catch the speeding generation ship.

I say "slingshot" like it was a routine maneuver. In reality, there's nothing quite like staring into the most enormous black hole in the galaxy, then flying right down its gullet like a gnat with attitude. (Inasmuch as anybody can *stare into* an actual black hole with their actual eyes unless they belong to one of the exotic species that can visualize X-rays or radio waves.)

So we'd already had one adventure leaving the Core, and now here we were. We weren't docking with *Big Rock Candy Mountain*. We had no information about the structural integrity of this antique hulk, but common sense suggested it would be fragile. Unbalancing it, subjecting it to the stresses of docking—both were terrible ideas. We'd have to use one of our adaptable docking collars anyway, because the idea that our hardware and theirs would be compatible was laughable.

That's why I was jumping.

It was not as dangerous as it probably seems. I'm Sally's rescue specialist: getting people out of dangerous situations is my job, and I do this sort of thing frequently.

The insertion can be dicey, though.

My hardsuit had jets, so I had maneuverability. And everything in space is moving incredibly fast anyway, so what matters is the relative velocity. If you and I are moving at the same speed in the same direction and there's nothing else around us, we're functionally not moving.

Space has a whole lot of nothing. If I jumped at the right time, and corrected for Sally's rotation, all I had to do was match velocity with the wheel and snug down onto it.

It was still breathtaking to stand inside that open airlock and look *down*. Sally had the processing power to hold a position over, or rather outside, *Big Rock Candy Mountain* basically forever. But *Big Rock Candy Mountain* was spinning, and one or two of her enormous central cables had snapped over the centians, so her spin had developed a wobble.

She was also wobbling for a more disturbing reason. There *was* a ship docked to the outside of her ring. One with white drives—a modern ship. A fast packet crewed by methane breathers: the one that had relayed the distress signal. Its—his, I checked my fox—name was Synarche Packet Vessel *I Bring Tidings From Afar*. Why in the Well he had docked with an ox ship, what he was still doing coupled to it, and why he wasn't answering hails was a series of mysteries for which there was no answer in Sally's databases.

And Sally, being a rescue vessel, has *extremely* comprehensive databases.

"Sally," I asked my faceplate, "how's our telemetry?"

"Pretty good, Llyn," the shipmind answered. "We've matched velocity and vector, and we're stable. Can't do much about that spin."

Good to know I wasn't the only one worried about it.

"I'm in the door," I said, which she already knew. But you're supposed to maintain a verbal narrative. For the flight recorders and in case anything goes wrong and your crewmates don't notice what you're doing. It also lets them keep an eye on your checklists so nothing gets forgotten. Safety first. "Where's Tsosie?"

His voice came through. "At the other door. Ready to go on your word, Llyn."

He was the ambulance's commander and senior trauma specialist, but I was the rescue specialist and this was my op. Rhym, our flight surgeon, outranked both of us as far as Core General seniority was concerned, but right now I was in charge of them, too. If we had to go to surgery, Rhym would become the authority figure.

It wouldn't have made sense in a military outfit, so it had taken a while for me to get used to the way command shifted between team members. But it made sense for Sally.

"In three," I said, and that many moments later we were sailing across the space between Sally and *Big Rock Candy Mountain*. As I stabilized, the apparent spiral of the generation ship smoothed out into a wheel so unnervingly that I wanted to slap a topologist.

Tsosie and I would have been a matched set, but Tsosie was trailing the sled that contained rescue supplies, portable airlocks, a laser cutting torch, and autostretchers. I had four drones limpeted onto my back beside the air tanks.

You can send back for stuff. But that takes time. Time isn't always something you have when responding to an incident. We're told to *adapt, improvise, overcome*. Perform the mission.

That part is not so different from what I did in the Judiciary. You do the thing that gets the correct result—within legal and ethical limits—and you fill out the paperwork later.

I like my job.

Sally fed me the telemetry through senso. Both Tsosie and I had jumped well. We used our jets to add *v*, so it seemed as if Sally were dropping behind while the turning wheel underneath us slowed. Soon, we were stationary relative to the surface, using our jets only to continue to course-correct into the curve of the ship's habitation ring as we began to close the distance to it. We needed to get low, relatively speaking, because Sally would be coming around again soon.

"That looks like a decent spot," Tsosie said, picking it out for me in the senso feed.

I studied the highlighted patch. It was flat and there were grab loops. I couldn't see an airlock hatch, but some of the handholds and what I assumed were tether safeties led toward the interior surface of the wheel. You get a good sense of ship design in my business. I'd put airlocks there, where you wouldn't have to deal with centripetal force on the way out or in.

"Let's go around the corner," I said. As soon as we touched the ship, the spin would start trying to throw us off. This was easier.

Tsosie followed my lead.

The inside surface of the wheel reminded me of the plated underbelly of some kind of legless lizardmorph. It was slightly concave, and though the concavity was a little uneven due to the broken cables, I assumed it had been intentional. Anything that made running around on the outside of your ship a little less profoundly hazardous was good. You never know when you'll need to go outside and fix a lightsail or something, and space is awfully big.

Lose track of your ship for a few moments and you might never find it again.

We touched down lightly. Our mag boots latched onto the hull, and suddenly we were standing comfortably under about a third of a g.

Tsosie looked over and grinned at me through the faceplate. "Smooth." He crouched down. "Do you know what I hate?" he continued, running his gauntlets over the hull.

"Do I care what you hate?" I asked.

"I hate it when you take a shit, right? And at the end of it there's this little hard nodule—no, splinter, this little hard splinter of poo, all by its lonesome. And, you know, there's no bowel movement behind it to push it out. It's stranded there in your sphincter, and you can feel it but there's nothing civilized you can do to get it out."

"This conversation is being recorded."

He shrugged.

"You could eat a carrot." I lowered my head over the readouts on the backs of my hardsuit gloves.

"A what?"

"Carrot," I said. "A sugary, edible root."

"What's that supposed to do, push it out the other end?"

"Nah," I said. Then, "Well, sort of. If you're experiencing hard little pellet feces, you're constipated because you're either dehydrated, or because you're not getting enough fiber. Or both. Carrots have water and fiber. Eat carrots and you'll get nice clean poops. If we lived on a planet, I'd tell you about apples—"

"What's an apple?"

"What you eat every dia to keep the doctor away," I said. "At least if your problem is an impacted bowel. Of course, if we kept doctors away, neither one of us would have anybody to talk to. . . . Oh, look. There's the airlock."

I walked toward it, boots clomping with each step. I could hear it through the contact with the hull and the atmosphere inside my hardsuit.

Tsosie followed. "Are you okay, Jens? You look kinda grayish."

It was taking a fair amount of concentration not to wobble as I walked. "Food is not sitting so well."

Tsosie grinned at me. He didn't turn his faceplate toward me, but I could feel it through the senso. "I guess the potty talk isn't helping."

"I'm wearing too many ayatanas." I had half a dozen recorded memory packets from various individuals loaded into my fox: drawing on their expertise for any clues about how to communicate with or help either the ancient humans that might be inside *Big Rock Candy Mountain*, or the methane-breathing systers aboard the docked, modern ship.

It was a plausible excuse for walking funny, anyway.

The airlock was a manual one, dogged with a wheel. The wheel was stiff with age and lack of maintenance, but I wear an exo for medical reasons. Between me, the exo, and the hardsuit's servos I got the thing to grind free without having to throw myself on Tsosie's mercy. I like to do things for myself, because I haven't always been able to.

It makes me appreciate the small things. Such as being able to turn a sticky wheel.

"Deploying bubble," Tsosie said.

I gave the wheel a turn or two, but didn't undog it completely until Tsosie had set the bubble up, adhering the rim to *Big Rock Candy Mountain*'s hull. It wasn't a full airlock. Once it was installed the only way out was to cut the membrane. But we had no way to gauge whether the airlock behind the hatch was pressurized, or even intact. Or if the interior door was open. We could explosively decompress part of the generation ship, if we weren't careful.

There was a thing that might be a pressure gauge. The crystal over it was cracked, and if you squinted past the cracks the needle inside lay flat against one peg. If I was reading the archaic numerals right the needle rested on the depressurized side. That was a good sign for avoiding explosive decompression, if it was accurate: nothing inside to decompress.

It might be a bad sign for anybody inside the generation ship, though.

Sensible airlock design provided for a safety interlock such that one could not open both hatches at the same time. You probably wouldn't be surprised by how often people—even modern rightminded people, even nonhuman people—fail to do what's sensible. I wasn't prepared to assume that unrightminded folks from the distant past—desperate enough to light out for stars even their great-grandchildren would never see, while flying the spacefaring equivalent of a very large, leaky rowboat—would be notably cautious individuals.

I checked Tsosie's work on the bubble, which was as meticulous as ever. I was having a bad pain dia, so I tuned a little to control it. Not too much, though. Being dopey feels gross, and depressing your reflexes is a terrible idea when you're entering a rescue zone.

Okay, maybe the ayatanas weren't the only reason I was looking a little gray.

While I was adjusting, Tsosie finished opening the hatch. No air puffed out. It looked like the gauge was working after all. Or was maybe accidentally correct. There was a ladder inside the aperture. He climbed down and I followed, closing the hatch behind me.

"We're in," I told Sally. "Looks like an airlock should."

The second hatch was off to my right as I stepped off the ladder. The space was large enough for six space-suited humans—or two humans and a large piece of equipment—and utterly barren. The bulkheads were a dingy beige, the paint scuffed with bumps and rubs. The ship had stayed functional and in use for some time after launch, then. But either the ship, the management, or the crew had not been functional enough for meticulous maintenance to be the norm.

I wondered how many generations had managed to live and die here. I wondered again if there were still people on board. I wondered if they had triggered the distress beacon, and if so, when.

What leads you to put a beacon on a ship that never plans on encountering another of its kind?

I knew less time had elapsed on this ship than for those of us who stayed home and joined the Synarche. *Big Rock Candy Mountain* was moving so fast after centians of acceleration that she had attained relativistic speeds. Every standard second we spent here was one point three standard seconds out in the rest of the universe.

Not a big difference, if you only stayed a week. It would mean roughly two extra diar going by in the outside galaxy. But over the course of half a millennian, the time dilation added up.

The pressure gauge in the inside hatch was more legible. It read .83, and since it maxed out at 1, I guessed that meant Terran atmospheres.

Tsosie and I took turns spraying each other's hardsuits with decontam. We were the same species as the people who built this creaking, ancient vessel, but—in the thrilling eventuality that any were still alive—we and they were six hundred ans separated. Our microbes would eat their immune systems for lunch, and vice versa. It would be an enormous tragedy to reconnect with a lost branch of humanity only to start a pandemic and kill everybody on both sides.

So we wouldn't do that.

"What we could learn from this place," Tsosie breathed.

He let the pressure equalize, and suddenly I could hear the creaks and groans of the ancient ship around me. Strained metal and some distant thumps that sounded like the ring of machinery. No voices, and nothing that sounded like voices.

I thought I had been keeping my hopes down, but my spirits still fell. I wasn't feeling particularly good about our chances of finding survivors. We had not been subtle about our approach—it doesn't do to sneak up on people—and if anyone was still driving this thing, surely they would have answered our hails. Radio was radio. Or they would have come to meet us at the airlock, or at least sent a bot.

Artificial intelligences dated back to before the Eschaton, and Sally's data library suggested that most of the generation ships had shipminds of a sort. Wheelminds? I didn't even know what nomenclature you'd use for a ship this big.

Nobody spoke to us, even when I said the ship's name out loud, amplifying it through my hardsuit speaker, and requested permission to enter.

Well, maybe somebody was on the other side of the hatch.

Tsosie tipped his head and dipped his shoulder, the broadly expressive gestures of somebody used to communicating through a hardsuit. "Here goes nothing."

"Give it your best," I said, and watched him lean on the hatch wheel.

Tsosie swung the hatch wide, and—nothing happened.

Nothing besides a brief puff of equalizing air, that is. I hadn't really expected a welcome party, but it would have been a nice surprise.

"Huh," he said, peering around the hatch. "Well, that's interesting."

That's not a reassuring thing to hear when you've just broken into a space ship older than your species's membership in civilization. I leaned sideways to peer over his shoulder.

The entire corridor was filled with what seemed at first to be a strange sort of honeycomb or spiderweb. The illumination was working—not something I would have counted on, after all this time. Let's hear it for good old-fashioned fusion reactors.

Because the ship spun like a station to simulate gravity, we were standing on the bulkhead that faced the outside of the wheel. *Big Rock Candy Mountain* was enormous, and I could see quite far down the corridor before the curve of the ship bent out of sight in the distance. The whole space seemed filled with . . . building toys?

Something very similar, anyway, to the sort of peg-and-keeper sets that children of many species with manual dexterity are normally given as they begin to develop curiosity and the ability to use their fingers independently. If they happen to have fingers. These seemed to be printed or extruded in polymer and plated in what I took to be a conductive material of a shimmering, holographic metal. The whole structure created a mesh of interlocking hexagons that entirely filled the passageway.

"Structural reinforcement?" I asked, making sure we still had a connection back to *our* ship.

"It might be," Sally agreed. I could feel her relaying Tsosie's feed—and my feed—to the other four members of the crew. Loese, our new pilot; Hhayazh, a flight nurse; Rhym, the flight surgeon; and Camphvis, the other flight nurse.

It seemed like we were all equally mystified. We'd sent two out of the three Terrans in the crew (Loese was the other one) on this trip out of caution. We couldn't expect any survivors aboard *Big Rock Candy Mountain* to have ever encountered a nonhuman sentience. And Hhayazh, in particular, is the sort of twiggy, bristle-covered, black-carapaced insectoid sentience that gives groundlubbers the shrieking jimjams.

Nobody was going to have the shrieking jimjams on my watch if I could possibly help it.

These structures didn't seem sinister. They refracted light in bright, *human* colors. Not all primary—purple and orange and green made appearances—but all true and saturated. Kid colors, accentuating their resemblance to toys.

"There's too many colors for it to be a DNA model," Tsosie said. "Unless the same amino acids are wearing different dresses."

I reached past him, and poked the nearest peg with my finger, causing him to gasp and grab my wrist an instant too late to stop me.

Poor life choices got me into this line of work: What can I say?

I didn't really expect it to react. But I guess I should say that I poked *at* the nearest peg with my finger, because the whole structure peeled away from my hardsuit before I touched it and rippled with a series of *whick-whick-whick*ing sounds into a folded configuration against the walls of the corridor. It left more than enough room for Tsosie and me to walk side by side.

"If we go in there it's going to reassemble itself right through our bodies, isn't it?" Tsosie asked.

"Maybe it's shy." I stepped past him, out into the corridor. He let go of my wrist as soon as I started to move. It had been a warning gesture, not a real attempt to restrain me.

Not that he could have. I was the one on the crew with the law enforcement background. And the adaptive exoskeleton under my hard-suit, giving me boosted reflexes and strength.

I paused briefly, and the tinkertoys didn't nail me into place like a shrike's victim. That was a good sign. I reached out again, and they peeled away from me again.

"Seems safe," I said.

Tsosie made a little choking noise. But he followed me, boots clomping only a little. We were both, I noticed, making an effort to walk softly. It's always hard when you first get back under grav—or simulated grav—not to crash around like one of the elephantine high-gravity systers in a proverbial china shop. The toys continued to peel apart ahead of us, and sealed themselves back up behind. "Maybe they *are* structural reinforcement."

"Microbots," Tsosie said, bending closer to inspect some of them. "Only big."

"Where do you get the raw material to make this many . . . microbots? After six hundred ans in space, anyway?"

"Excellent question," Sally said. "Keep exploring."

CHAPTER 2

HOW ON *EARTH* DID THIS SHIP EVER GET THIS FAR FROM Terra?" Tsosie asked.

It was a terrible joke, and I refused to laugh. "It's moving pretty fast."

"Not that fast," Sally said, deadpan. "I did the math."

We both laughed at that one. Sally couldn't *help* but do the math. Math was literally her entire being. The processors she inhabited were . . . houses. *She* was made of code. Elegant, elaborate, exquisite code.

I'd wanted to work on AIs when I was a kid, but I didn't have the chops for it. So I knew just enough to appreciate what a beautiful thing she was.

"Seriously," Tsosie persisted. "How did it get out here?"

Part of doing what we do is staying frosty. Staying focused on the task. Humor helps with that; helps you keep your distance and keep your cool. The rightminding helps, too. If you feel what everybody you're prying out of the wreckage feels, that empathy can be debilitating.

I have no idea how people managed it back in the old diar. Such as the era this ship was from.

Tsosie was staying alert by talking about stuff we'd already been over, to keep a conversation going. "How did it get all the way here? There's no possible way it could have covered this much distance at sublight speeds in that amount of time."

He wasn't wrong, but I didn't want to think through it now. It made me shiver. There were too many unexplained things about this ship. Why was she here? Where were her crew? Why the distress signal? Why had the methane-breathing crew of the docked vessel fallen silent? And where were *they*?

So many questions, and an insignificant number of answers.

I didn't have any more time to be scared now than I'd had when I was jumping. It wasn't my job to be scared. It wasn't my job to theorize, and it wasn't my job to get excited about the archaeological opportunities.

"Wormhole?" I offered, in a tone of voice intended to indicate how tentative an offering it was.

"Are they theoretically possible this week?" Tsosie asked. It sounded like a genuine question. He was a hardass, but whatever his other quirks he wasn't sarcastic.

That was Hhayazh's defining bit of . . . personality.

"Sort of," Sally said. "Maybe. I mean, wormholes are possible. Looked at the right way, white bubbles are wormholes. Sort of. Tesseracts, anyway. Traveling through naturally formed wormholes, on the other hand . . . without being compressed, squished, topologically transformed, and generally spaghettified . . ."

If she'd had a head, she would have been shaking it.

"Okay, so *Big Rock Candy Mountain* didn't drop through a *natural* hole in space-time. And she didn't go faster than light, unless somebody boosted her somehow. Jury is still out on artificial holes in space-time, however."

Alcubierre-White drives weren't true faster-than-light travel, which still remained hypothetically impossible. They put your ship into a little bubble that compressed everything *around* it. So you didn't move. Rather, the universe flowed past you like one of those old-timey murals they used to paint on a roll of canvas and spool past people sitting still in chairs, so as to simulate travel. Back on medieval Terra, or whenever.

So, technically you didn't move. But your relative velocity could be a good deal faster than light, depending on how much power you could manage to throw at it. Sally had a *lot* of power.

White drives were kind of a dick move when it came to respecting the laws of physics.

A white drive would work on a ship like the one we were in. It didn't require a lot of structural strength to sit still. But the energy requirements to build a space-time bubble around it . . . I didn't think even antimatter, at least antimatter in containable quantities, could manage it. *Big Rock Candy Mountain* was just . . . too big.

"She's moving somewhat faster than she should be, even if she'd been under constant acceleration since leaving Earth. And giving a reasonable wiggle factor for gravity wells along the way boosting and slowing her. Plus she's on the wrong vector."

"Thanks, Sally. So . . . she's gone a lot farther using that initial *v* and her drive capability than she should."

"Right," said Tsosie. "That's what I was saying."

"That's not worrisome at all."

"*Right*," said Tsosie. "That's what I was saying."

"I'll keep working on it," Sally said. "It's possible they tried some slingshot maneuvers for extra velocity. In the meantime, pull out your sample kits. There's dust in the corners. Some of it might be shed skin fragments containing DNA. Vacuum it up and analyze it, would you?"

We found the bridge soon after. Not by accident: we had the ancient plans and schematics and had been aiming in that direction. If anybody was left alive on this ship—if anybody was left *at all* on this ship—perhaps this was where we would find them. But when we entered, it was nearly dark and nearly silent, except for a rill of green and amber lights around the edge of the room at counter height, accompanied by a melodious beeping.

A moment later, lights began to brighten, and Tsosie and I found ourselves standing on what once must have been a fairly pleasant, beige and slate-blue bridge. The layout was semicircular; we had entered from the flattish side. Large dark viewscreens covered the arcing wall in front of us, and two rows of consoles and chairs curved around a single central command chair.

We stood behind that one, but slightly above it, as the stations we were near were slightly elevated. Oddly, in my experience, they all had tall chairs shaped for humans. The consoles all had dedicated push buttons and switches and dials, not adaptive consoles like the ones I'd worked with all my life, even back on Wisewell, the frontier settlement where I'd grown up, been orphaned, got married, had a kid, and left the first chance I'd been offered. Those consoles and chairs were the thing that brought home, unsettlingly, that everybody on this ship really had been a Terran human. Knowing something intellectually and *realizing* it in your bones are very different.

Because of our elevation, and because the command chair was turned toward the back of the room, we could see that the seat was not empty. And that the jumpsuit-clad person in the chair had been there for a very long time, and was not likely to move from it under their own power ever again.

On the other side of the bridge, Tsosie and I kept on walking. The tinkertoys were back, and watching those modular lattices click apart ahead of us and click together behind us as we got farther and farther from the egress made me even more unsettled than the dead body in the command chair had. We could cut our way out through the hull if we had to—a rescue hardsuit, especially backed up with the physical power of my exo, was more than capable of rearranging the generation ship's superstructure. I wouldn't do that unless our lives were in imminent danger, however. It would kill any crew members in the areas of the ship I would inevitably decompress in the process.

And piss off the archaeological team.

Assuming for the moment that there were any crew members left on this ship—an assumption that was seeming less and less probable with every weirdly echoing step Tsosie and I took—it was my job to save them, not murder them.

There had been skin cells in the dust I collected, at least. And all of them were Terran. People like me and Tsosie, only six hundred ans removed. Six hundred of *their* ans—years, to use the old style—and closer to a millennian for us, I guessed. Time gets really funky when you're zipping around the galaxy at relativistic speeds and information still travels either through white space packet, or by slow boat or electromagnetic progression.

That's one of many reasons why I am not an archinformist. They have these plots of events happening at different times and in different places and where the information fronts of those events intersect. It's like trying to read a contour map while somebody spins it in the air in front of you and the colors keep changing.

So. A ship full of missing Terrans. Missing, bar one: the body that we—or one of our sister ships still inbound—were going to have to come back to collect and transport eventually.

Inside the hardsuit, I licked my lips uneasily. The hairs on my arms horripilated and my palms grew cold.

Intuition is a real thing, though there's nothing supernatural about it. It's not without mysteries, however. The human brain (and presumably, the nonhuman brain as well) gathers and processes a lot of information in excess of that which we are consciously aware. It doesn't use words or often even images. It deals with feelings and instincts, and that glitchy sensation that you can't trust somebody, or that something is wrong.

So when I say that I had the increasing, creeping conviction that the generation ship's endlessly rolling wheel was deserted, that it *felt* empty, I don't pretend there was any higher knowledge behind it. But I was sure there were plenty of subtle clues, even if I couldn't have named a one of them.

My conscious awareness was pretty busy riding herd on a half dozen exotic ayatanas and the processing issues that all of them were having with the alien (to them) environment and my human sensory input.

There's a common misconception that wearing an ayatana is sharing your brain with somebody else. And it's not, exactly. It's more like having someone else's memories and opinions and experiences to draw upon . . . along with their neuroses, preconceptions, trigger issues, and prejudices. Because nothing in this galaxy can ever be simple.

But I had two different methane species loaded, including one from a Darboof staff member. That was the species that was driving the fast packet we'd seen. Or had been driving him, at least: they might be gone now, too.

I'd also gone deep in the Core General archives and pulled the most archaic human ayatanas I could find, and a couple of systers recorded around the time of first contact with my species.

It's generally contraindicated to load more than a couple of ayatanas at once, but I'm a trained professional with years of experience. Kids, don't try this at home.

Inside my head, the methane breathers in particular were having fits about what, to them, was a blinding, flesh-melting level of light and a profoundly unfriendly hot environment. Balancing that and keeping myself alert in the confusing, constantly altering environment of the microbots and the creaking ship took up a lot of my attention. Managing my pain levels—they're chronic—took up a little more.

So I didn't notice that we hadn't heard from Sally in quite some time—not until Tsosie said her name, and nobody answered.

I stopped with a foot in midair. Because when somebody else says something is broken you can't be totally sure until you try it yourself, I idiotically echoed, "Sally?"

The silence was immediately twice as loud.

I put my foot down very gently and groped for our uplink. There was nothing on the other end. Not even the quiet feeling of connection that usually radiates down the senso from a linked AI when you tune into it. For a second, the bottom dropped out of me, and I flailed in the panicked certainty that Sally was gone and we were trapped here on this weird ghost ship, and that all our friends were dead.

I admit it: I am not the galaxy's best at not immediately producing the worst-case scenario. Fortunately, I'm also aware of this tendency, after years of rightminding and some time in a nice, secure environment, and so I bumped my GABA and serotonin levels up and my cortisol level down and took six deep breaths until the sensation of my heart squeezing tight around a shard of glass eased up somewhat.

The brain is—mostly—an electrochemical meat machine. The fact that you can tune it is why humanity still exists, centians after the Eschaton and the crazy desperate nonsense of those who could afford to escape an Earth we'd declared doomed attempting to save themselves at any cost.

Crazy desperate nonsense like this big old ship I was standing on.

I looked over at Tsosie, and saw his face pinched and his brow dewed with beads of sweat behind the faceplate. He'd stopped moving, too, and when we halted the clicking of the tinkertoy microbots silenced. They were frozen mid-peel, as if somebody had hit pause on the animation.

"What are the odds we're blocked from coms, and they're fine up there?" I asked him, trying to sound reasonable. "And they'll get in touch with us momentarily?"

"If it can be done, Sally and our crew can do it." He sounded like he believed it, too. Some people just have solid neurochemistry. Or more robust rightminding.

Or less trauma, I supposed.

Maybe I was a little freaked out by the entirely empty ship. Entirely empty, except for one dead person and a weird tinkertoy machine. Entirely empty of the thousands of crew members it was large enough to contain.

"What are the odds that something terrible went wrong and they're all dead?"

"Have a little faith," said Tsosie. "Come on. Keep walking. Let's do our job and trust them to do theirs, what do you say?"

"I don't know much about faith," I said to Tsosie, ten steps later.

"What?" he answered, distractedly. He was scanning the lattice construct of microbots warily, and I expected he was as busy pinging Sally as I was.

My brain was building architectures of attack, sabotage, or accident, and I needed to distract it. "What you said about having faith. I never knew how that felt. I guess it's some kind of neurological defect. I was born without it. Or it got knocked out of me so early I never remember having those feelings. I don't believe in things. But I believe in Core General. I believe in our mission. I believe that we are here to help people."

I was, as you have probably diagnosed, babbling. I was also grateful to Tsosie, for providing me with a distraction from the panic that wanted to overwhelm me. The least I could do was talk about trivialities in return.

If they really were trivialities.

He hummed a sound that made me wonder if he'd even heard the second half of what I'd said. "You mean religion, when you say faith? Because I meant, our crew and ship know what they're doing, and we know that."

"Nah." I shook my head inside the hardsuit. And checked my battery levels. The suit had extra backups; it and my exo were still fine.

Tsosie pointed to a hatch in the side wall.

I nodded, and followed him. "Like trust. Like believing in people. Like believing that things will turn out okay. Like . . . what you said."

The hatch was an access point. Beyond it was a tunnel that would need us to crawl.

"Let's save those for after," I said.

He nodded. "And after we get back in touch with Sally. And her sensor arrays."

There it was again: that faith that we *would* get back in touch with Sally. I was having a hard time remembering that she even existed, that we weren't stranded out here alone with no support.

"I want to put eyes on her," I said.

"Next hatch. Let's see if we can find a viewport."

There had been windows. We'd seen them from the outside. Mirrored to reflect the potentially unforgiving light of space. There weren't any here, because this was a corridor.

Or were there?

I started inspecting the control panels we passed more carefully.

"This is a personal question," Tsosie said formally.

I glanced over at him and nodded. The hardsuits fit close enough that you can pick up even a little gesture like that.

"I consent," I said, so it would be on Sally's record. If Sally was still out there. If we ever got our link back.

Quit psyching yourself out, Dr. Jens. If you tell yourself something firmly enough, it's almost as good as hearing it from a trusted authority. Especially if you can back it up by fiddling with your brain chemistry.

"Do you remember a time before the chronic pain?"

I could claim that wasn't a perceptive question, but then I'd have to explain why I stood there silently for a good thirty seconds before I found an answer. "No," I admitted. "There's always been the pain."

"So how would you, as a kid, have learned that things were going to be okay, or that adults could solve your problems? Why would you ever have cause to think things would turn out all right?"

"Huh," I said, eloquently. While the tinkertoys went *click click click.*

I chewed on my lower lip inside the faceplate. It was a terrible habit; I was going to give myself a chapped lip in the dryness of the suit environment, and if it started to bleed in zero g or while I was under acceleration, that was going to be a bloody mess. Quite literally.

I ducked under one of those weird, trailing strands of tinkertoys.

This one hadn't peeled apart with the others to let us through. If they were as fragile as they looked, they should have been collapsed all over the decking, even under such light acceleration as this. "So you think I never learned trust because, as a child, I had nothing to believe in?"

"You trust, though. You trust Sally with your life—"

"That's not what I mean." I sighed. "Yes, I can decide to take a risk on Sally, or on you. But I know it's a risk. Whereas I've heard people talk about the belief that somebody would never hurt them. Or the sense that everything will turn out all right in the end. I've never had those."

"So why do you take risks?"

"Well," I said. "Because if you don't, you never gain anything. And, as I said, I believe in Core General. I believe in what we are doing there. I believe it's a good thing. Worth risking myself for. So I trust . . . I guess I trust the mission."

The tinkertoys were denser here, and less responsive to our presence. I gave up on crouching and ducking under them. I got down and crawled. By the way, the inside of a hardsuit isn't any good for the outside of your knees.

Tsosie had come up beside me. He gave me a funny sidelong look and got down on his hands and knees as well, but he didn't say anything for a minute. When he did, it was a change of subject—or a segue.

"So you trusted the mission when you were with the Judiciary?"

His kneeplates scraped irritatingly on the decking.

I knew he was talking so we wouldn't think too hard about where Sally was, or Loese, or Hhayazh, or Camphvis, or Rhym. That was fine. There wasn't anything we could do for them from here, right now. He was right—we had to trust them to take care of their part of the mission, even without communication.

They would be trusting us to do the same.

I shrugged. "Well. Not in the same way. I decided it was a good mission and that I could serve it. And it helped me get closer to the Core, where I could get better care. And it got me a military-grade exoskeleton, which is absolutely the bomb for mobility issues."

One thing about the Synarche. It's so big, and data and people move so slowly through it, that it takes a while for tech to disseminate. Medical tech along with all the other kinds. And backwater settlements on marginal planets are definitely at the bottom of the list, most of the time. There aren't enough people there to make them a priority.

I shouldn't say people move slowly. They move very quickly. Just . . . over ridiculous distances.

"Anyway," Tsosie said. "Before I interrupted me, I was pointing out that once you got to Core General, you finally got to a place where people could take care of you. They took care of your pain."

"Judiciary took care of my pain," I corrected. "If they hadn't, I would not have been much use to them." I was managing my own pain now, which was a task I usually outsourced to Sally so I didn't have to concentrate on it, but this didn't seem the time to mention that.

"How effectively?"

I wobbled my head to emphasize my eyeroll of defeat, since the faceplate hid the eyeroll part. "All right, you got me."

"And you probably weren't taken seriously by medical people before then."

"Well . . . It wasn't that bad. I learned the lingo in the military, which never hurts. And people don't dismiss you when you can prove your rightminding is effective."

"People don't love being presented with unsolvable problems, though."

I chuckled. "Core General does."

"I rest my case."

"Are you suggesting, as my commanding officer, that I have some untreated medical post-traumatic response?"

"Mmm." Noncommittal.

I turned my shoulder to him, concentrating on the medical panel on my forearm, looking up occasionally to make sure I wasn't about to crawl into anything—or past one of the control panels without inspecting it.

"What's wrong with me isn't that complicated," I said. "I grew up on the kind of planet where resources were limited, because the settlement was at the very edge of things. We got supplies, but sometimes we went a long time between drops. And medical relief was intermittent at best."

"The last scarcity economy in the galaxy." I could hear the smile.

"I mean, it was the Synarche. It wasn't like I grew up in a Freeport, or totally outside civilization."

"Civilization is not evenly distributed. Did you join the Judiciary to get away from your backwater homeworld?"

I was starting to get irritated with his obtuseness, but at least it distracted me from the hardsuit pinching and banging in uncomfortable ways. "I said it got me better medical care—"

The tinkertoys seemed to be getting more responsive again. I wondered if the patch we'd just wormed through were reinforcing a structurally weak spot. Or if they were so old they didn't work very well.

I risked standing up, and the cloud of microbots got out of my way. I rubbed elbows I'd bruised on the inside of my hardsuit while Tsosie levered himself to his feet also.

"Crap," he said. "This is like caving."

"Better light," I joked. "I joined the Judiciary because it got me this exo. And it seemed interesting. A chance to travel and see things. And then they offered me medical training, and I found being a doctor was even more interesting than being a cop, so I transferred to Core General once I got good enough."

Tsosie waited to see what I would say next. His boots scraped along beside me. We'd both turned off the electromagnets and were moving more or less normally, given the low simulated gravity. It wasn't quite push-off-and-bound, but one definitely had to be aware of the ceilings.

Core was installing a new artificial gravity tech salvaged from a Koregoi archaeological site. Sally would probably get it next, unless one of the other ambulance ships was the guinea pig. Most ships in transit aren't designed to spin up gravity, but it's hard to operate on somebody when you're floating, and their bodily fluids tend to form large rippling balls under surface tension. So we had fake—centripetal—gravity now, and soon we would have better fake gravity still.

"I feel safe at Core," I finally told Tsosie.

"And you never felt safe before."

"No," I agreed. "I never felt safe before. So I believe in Core, because it makes me feel safe."

"Congratulations. Now you understand why people go to church."

"To feel safe? Is that all faith is?" I pounced on the next control panel. "Aha!"

"Aha?"

It was push buttons and little toggles. Mechanical linkages rather than electronic: the sort of thing you could fix with a tiny screwdriver. Smart, when wandering off into space for generations.

I flipped one of them, and heard a pop as the beige panel beside it unlatched. "Help me slide this gently."

Tsosie didn't argue. And after two steps sideways, I saw his body language perk up as he got it.

The beige panel was a cover over a viewing port two meters wide and a meter tall. It sealed, airtight, when the port wasn't in use, and slid aside so crew could look outside and check the structure. Or take in the view.

Which was breathtaking. A sweep of hull decked with antennae and other protrusions was visible below the window. The port itself was bubbled outward, and if we stuck our heads in, we could see the hub far above us, and the massive arch of the wheel made to seem like a fragile tower by the vastness of its diameter. Far in the distance, against velvet black, the stars revolved.

And there was Sally, right where she should have been, holding her position alongside *Big Rock Candy Mountain* while the wheel whipped beneath her. Or, from our perspective, she was zipping backward along the great, motionless arch of the ship we were in.

She looked intact, and her navigation was obviously working. Tsosie reached out and tapped his fingers on my shoulderplate, silent acknowledgment of our profound shared relief.

We each let out our tension on a held breath in turn. Hand still trembling a little, I flashed a light out the port.

We're okay. Continuing.

I repeated the message three times.

Copy, Sally flashed back, after a while. *Standing by.*

We went on.

Step by step—and occasionally crawl by crawl—we came quite a way around the ring of the generation ship. One pie slice, maybe, depending on the size of your slicer. We checked in again with Sally when we found a viewport pointed in the right direction. We also checked side passages and chambers, when we passed them, and found—mostly—predictable things, all filled with more lattice. What *was* this stuff?

"Tsosie."

"Yeah?"

"Do you . . ." I got embarrassed and trailed off.

". . . do I?"

"May I ask you a personal question?"

He laughed. "I started it. Be churlish to say no."

"Do you go to church?"

He smiled. It turned into a grimace. "No. I don't go to church. My people thought the world was their church. So now, I act as though the galaxy is."

"The galaxy isn't a safe place, though."

The grimace went back to a smile, but it wasn't an easy one. "Neither, it turns out, was the world."

I was still wondering about that—about Tsosie having a connection to "his people," even going back to Terra, a standard hour or so later when he looked up from his wrist and said, "I might have a thermal signature."

"Might have?"

"It's a big ship and there's a lot of stuff in the way."

The macro-microbots were unzipping before us and zipping back up after us again. Tsosie and I had both opted to reskin our hardsuits, which were normally marked all over their chest and backplates with an inelegant clutter of galactic medical and rescue symbols. Based on the provenance of *Big Rock Candy Mountain*, we were opting to prioritize the Red Crescent, the Red Cross, and the Rod of Asclepius, and deemphasize the others. (It didn't escape me, given my conversation with Tsosie, that all of those had started off as religious symbols back on Terra.)

My favorite was the Nazzish symbol, the Blade of Life, because it looked so badass. But walking around with a great big scalpel on my pec plate probably wouldn't inspire confidence in the descendant of refugees from one of the more barren and brutal periods of Terra's history.

People who fled the Eschaton in their primitive space arks did so because they believed that anybody who stayed behind would die, along with the rest of humanity.

And if those of our ancestors who hadn't made it onto an ark hadn't discovered rightminding, the Alcubierre-White drive, and the Synarche (in roughly that order), those with the resources to become refugees might have been right. As it was, we managed to start making decisions that took the pressure off the Terrestrial environment and ameliorated climate change in time to save both Earth and humanity.

I overstate the peril. *Earth* would have been fine. The biosphere would have persisted and expanded again, as after other extinction events. Even a mass die-off from a methane burp is recoverable on a geologic scale.

But I and my species are predictably ethnocentric. *We* would have missed us, even if nobody else would. And thus: primitive space arks.

I was struck again, as we explored, that this particular primitive space ark showed signs of long habitation before its current state of abandonment. It was spotlessly clean—I wondered if there were more bots devoted to scrubbing—but the surfaces were worn, the finish on the walls buffed to a matte shine with layers of polishing scratches.

Tsosie said, "On the bright side, we haven't found any more cadavers."

Or even any skeletons. The giant ship we were searching seemed to be not just spotless and not full of dead people, but perfectly functional. Those side doors had led us to endless low-moisture farms full of food plants. The air that we weren't breathing was heady with oxygen, and the hardsuits were filtering it out of the environment to recharge their own tanks.

So who was doing the maintenance? Was the crew . . . hiding?

We found bunk spaces, cabins, and apartments. We found dining halls and science labs. We found recreational facilities, kitchens, and parks. We found what looked like a running trail around what seemed to be the entire exterior rim of the wheel, in case anyone wanted to run a marathon in .37 gravity. We found absolutely nobody *using* any of those things.

We found a lot of indications that the ancient hull was under stress, and that material had been scavenged from it for . . . mysterious purposes. It was still intact, but it was thin. And I wouldn't have wanted to rely on it for my life and well-being.

Big Rock Candy Mountain was not the sort of place where you took a nap without a space suit on. Not if you were me.

"Want to chase that thermal signature?" Tsosie sounded as frustrated as I felt.

"Point me at it."

Sally uses a magnetic resonance imager built into the hardsuit helmets to stimulate our visual cortexes and induce controlled hallucinations. They're vivid, and you can't ignore them. She makes them look a little cartoony, to be sure you know they're not real. Linden, the Core General wheelmind, can pull the same trick.

In the absence of AIs, Tsosie tapped into the same functionality and used dramatic shades of magenta to outline a distant blotch and give me an idea of the path of hatches and corridors that would take us there.

"This ghost ship stuff is starting to creep me out," Tsosie said. "I didn't sign on to recon the *Flying Dutchman*."

"Even if everybody is gone, this is a valuable source of archinformation," I reminded him.

"Well, I didn't sign on to *excavate* the *Flying Dutchman* then."

"Worse things happen at sea," I joked.

He reached back—he was a half step ahead of me at that point—and rapped me on the hardsuit pauldron with his fingertips.

I waved at the structures still rearranging themselves in waves around us. "What if everybody got disassembled and made into tinkertoys?"

"Then we're next," he grumbled. "This ought to be the hatch we're looking for."

It irised open as we approached, which none of the previous hatches had done. They'd all worked when we asked, but this one seemed to be anticipating us. Beyond it, we could glimpse an even more colorful thicket of pegs and keepers, and behind that fretwork . . . something moving. Something that seemed to be replicating the pieces.

It was glittery and holographic and refractive, like the tinkertoys, and caught the light like them. It seemed to be curved, though it was hard to tell through the lattice.

We stepped up to the hatchway. I called, "Hello?"

The lattice furled itself up like a series of stage curtains being drawn open, and we found ourselves face-to-facelessness with a humanoid form like a shaped bubble of inexplicably golden mercury.

CHAPTER 3

AS IT STARED AT US, AND WE STARED BACK, I REALIZED that my first impression had not been perfectly correct. The shape had a face, or at least the suggestion of a face. Hollows where the eyes would be; a smooth tapered bulge for a nose; the tilt of cheekbones and the shadows beneath. A pointed chin.

The shape of the body was stereotypically human and feminine, despite having no actual external genitalia or nipples. The torso swelled and tapered into enticing curves and valleys, flaring into breasts and hips that could serve no biological purpose. The figure stood and seemed to watch us approach. It—she?—did not move except for a curious little tilt of the head like a cat tracking prey up a wall.

I wished I hadn't thought of that particular comparison. I also wanted to roll my eyes violently at the engineer who had designed her.

Sally was still nowhere in the senso. I pinged Tsosie to let me deal with the contact, and stepped around him. He stood very still. I turned my suit speakers on and stopped myself halfway through asking Sally to translate my words into language from about a millennian before.

We'd seen signs in archaic English and Spanish and Chinese, so I was extrapolating. I spoke some English—I'd taken a course back home, when I'd had a lot of time to kill and couldn't get around very well—so it seemed worth giving it a try. I didn't know all the words. *Rescue specialist* and *lead trauma specialist* were mysteries, for example.

But I knew some. And maybe—

"Hello," I said. "I'm Dr. Brookllyn Jens. This is Dr. Paul Tsosie. We're crew from the . . . the ambulance ship that has matched velocities with your ship. We are friends. We come from a hospital called Core General. We're responding to your distress signal. Do you have casualties?"

There was a pause, and I swear it blinked, though there were no eyes and no eyelids to blink with. Its gestures reminded me of techniques I'd been shown in school by a friend studying to be a puppeteer. The tilt of a head, the inclination of a shoulder—those could give the watcher a picture of emotion and focus as clearly as any words.

It made a garbled sound: not speech, but like a lot of audio information compressed into a very tight space, laid over itself again and again. I recognized the timbre of Sally's voice in there, and Tsosie's, though I could not make out words. And what could have been my own voice, changed the way voices are changed when you don't hear them from inside your own head.

Then it spoke, in stilted but correct Standard, in a smoky contrived alto that made me flinch.

"I am Helen," the android said. "The distress signal—yes. There is a distress signal. And there are casualties. Please, come with me."

Helen? I asked Sally silently, forgetting for a moment that she wasn't there. *Who names their shipmind Helen?* We followed the android through more of the ship's habitation areas. She said she was taking us to a cargo area, which didn't bode well for *living* casualties.

Tsosie heard me, though. We still had our local connection, even if the uplink had failed.

I'm not sure she is a shipmind, he replied. *You could ask.*

I was still contemplating the options when Tsosie said, "Helen, are you the shipmind?"

Helen did not look back. Her shimmering golden body preceded us, and I did my best not to stare at her shiny metal ass. What can I say? It was *very* distracting.

She said, "I'm Helen Alloy. I was made to wait."

Helen Alloy.

Because some engineer thought he was funny. And between the smoky voice and the shiny metal ass, I will bet you whatever you care to name that the person who built her was a he.

Tsosie apparently was right there with me, as his voice came over our direct link: *There's a Trojan horse joke here, and I'm not going to make it.*

I sighed out loud. One benefit of the hardsuit: I could be kind to myself and those around me and decide not to mike my exasperated sound effects.

"Wait for who?" Tsosie asked, when it became plain that I was ignoring his joke and that Helen wasn't going to elaborate without prompting.

"Wait for you." She shook her head, as if indicating confusion. "Wait for whoever came to save us. To maintain the ship and keep the crew safe until somebody came. It's been a long time."

"Does the shipmind still exist?" Tsosie asked. "How about the library?"

"There's a library," she said. "And there's Central."

"Central?" I asked, deciding not to remind Tsosie that I had been going to do the talking. I was a little distracted: without Sally to keep an eye on my pain levels and help coordinate my exo, I was still doing those tasks myself. Keeping abreast of it wasn't a problem, but it used up a few cycles. "Who is Central?"

"Central," Helen said, "isn't a person."

"You've been here alone?" I was beginning to understand why the whole ship was filled with bot toys. Helen must have been incredibly bored. I hoped she'd at least been programmed to be interested in astronomical data, because that was the only source of intellectual stimulation for parsecs.

"I'm not alone," she said. "Here are the passengers."

She pressed a metal palm to a pad beside an irising hatch. A big hatch: this must be one of the promised cargo bays. Sally's map and my own sense of dead reckoning told me that we'd come up on the side of the spinning wheel. That made sense: cargo bays would serve as valuable radiation shielding, though this one seemed to be oriented away from the wheel's direction of travel.

She stepped through and gestured us into the airlock with her. We went. Helen cycled the lock. The door in front of us came open. A pale light flooded past her, shimmering on the curve of her hip and thigh.

I peered over Helen's shoulder. The hold was filled with rank after rank of caskets.

Coffins, or cryo containers? It was hard to be sure, and given that the cargo hold was cold as space and held no atmosphere, the only functional difference was going to be whether the people inside could be resuscitated.

Whatever the objects were, there were a lot of them. I did a little quick mental math and figured that there must be a thousand of them in this bay alone.

They *might* be alive. Or at least, aliveable.

"Bet you two standard weeks of kitchen duty that this isn't the only hold," Tsosie murmured.

"No bet." My heart sank at the size of the job ahead.

Sally still wasn't there. So I had to ask Helen about the history.

"Helen," I said, "how good was your people's cryonics technology?"

She looked at me and shrugged a fluid, rippling shrug. "In comparison to what, Doctor?"

"Do you know what your revival success rate is?"

"They are my crew," she said. "They must be all right."

Her program was focused on protecting her crew's well-being to the point of being dangerous to herself or bystanders. It was a common problem in early model AIs: they were geared toward maximum preservation of human life in the very short term, and because their algorithms weren't flexible, they had occasionally created a hell born of trolley problems.

Worry feels like somebody doing crochet with your internal organs. I subvocalized, *Tsosie, are you seeing this?*

"I am," he answered, without turning on his suit speakers. "We're going to have to salvage the whole ship, aren't we?"

Suddenly, Sally was with us again. "Don't panic," she said, as if those words were ever inclined to keep one from panicking. They came with a nice dose of anxiolytics, though, which helped. "The crew is all fine. We're dealing with a technical problem."

I shot her a hard feeling.

She sighed. "A little damage came to light. We're making repairs."

How could you have damage and not know it?

The ambulance is, in a very real sense, Sally's body. For her not to notice damage would be like me having burned my hand and not realized it: indicative of a far bigger problem.

"We'll talk about it when you're not so busy."

But— Tsosie began.

I knew what he was about to say, and I was totally with him. What, exactly, had been damaged? He was the mission commander, and I was the rescue coordinator—

But Sally was the shipmind. She shushed him with the electronic equivalent of a squelching stare, and we both subsided.

"We're not going to salvage the whole ship," she said, as if she'd been a part of the conversation all along. "The engineering is intractable. We don't have the facilities to grapple it, and even if we did it's been accelerating in the wrong direction since Earth was all humans knew, and it's fragile. It's too big for a salvage tug to pull through white space. The best approach is to take the people off, if they're alive, then turn it around and send it back to Terra. It should only take it another six hundred subjective ans of constant braking to get there. If the Synarche lasts that long, we can park it in orbit and turn it into a museum."

"If not, it will serve as a nice surprise for whoever comes after." Tsosie sounded . . . bitter. As if something about this was hitting him personally.

"Well, somebody is going to have to come get it," I said. Out loud, but with my speakers turned off. Then I turned them on again, before realizing that if Helen was linked to *Big Rock Candy Mountain*, it and she were probably monitoring our radio transmissions and nothing we were saying was encrypted. The evidence supported me, because she seemed to have taught herself Standard by listening to us before we met her. Our coms channel wasn't *translated*, but I had to assume that any AI worth its salt—even a primitive one—could handle unpacking mere centians of linguistic progress.

Screw it, I thought, and spoke so Helen could hear me. "Let's inspect those cryo chambers, shall we? We probably won't be able to tell if the ones that are still working contain people who can be brought back. That will have to wait for the hospital. But we should be able to tell if any of them have failed."

"None have failed," Helen said. "I've done my job. I have maintained the machines."

I wondered, pityingly, how long Helen had been alone. I wondered if being alone bothered her. Certainly the tinkertoy constructions had an aspect of neuroticism to them, if she was responsible for those. AIs left for too long without input could become fragmented and compulsive. Especially if they'd suffered damage to their hardware.

But Core General cared for artificial intelligences as well as biological ones. We didn't make a distinction regarding the kind of life we treated, though the doctors for those patients had different specialties. The hospital had several excellent cybersurgeons.

(I was told they were excellent, anyway. Their CVs were certainly impressive, though I didn't have the expertise to judge. Sally did, and I'd never heard her say anything derogatory.

And believe me, if there is anything centian-long space flights are good for, it's gossip.)

Digressions aside, I thought our best strategy was to bring Helen back with us, along with a full load of cryo chambers—if we could manage to keep them powered while transporting them. That would be the tricky part. As soon as we got close enough to a beacon, we'd send out a request for cargo haulers to meet another rescue team, and some salvage experts, and let them sort out what to do with—conservatively estimating—ten thousand or so only provisionally not-dead people.

As for us, we might even get back to Core General with our quota before our message did, if we legged it, and we could warn the hospital that it needed to gear up isolation wards and massive amounts of powered cargo storage to be ready for a slow-motion mass casualty situation.

You're not dead until you're warm and dead. It's been a truism of emergency response for close to a millennian, and it's no less true now than it was when they were hauling people out of frozen lakes on the homeworld. It applies doubly to cryo accidents. And we're a lot better at fixing brain damage these diar than we had been then.

"I'm going to go look," I told Tsosie, Helen, and Sally.

"None have *failed*," Helen insisted. Behind us, the tinkertoys that had followed us into the airlock rustled as if in response to her emotion. Tsosie's head turned. I felt his shock of unease through the senso, felt him tune to calm himself and refocus on the task at hand.

If the peripheral—if that's what Helen was—freaked out, how were we going to restrain her, exactly? She obviously was linked to her microbots, and she was probably linked to the ship as well. I foresaw problems if she decided that she needed to personally escort all the cryo chambers. Especially as we'd need to divide them into groups in order to move the people in them to safety. Or, I should say, to move those people to the potential of safety, if any could be saved.

Maybe Helen could split herself into multiple parts. But I suspected that wouldn't be good for her, in her already-fragile state.

I called on all my victim-soothing skills and hoped Helen's homebrew language-learning was up to the challenge of following what I needed to say. "I believe you. But I need to assess the technical challenges of moving your crew. We need to know what kind of power we need to supply, at the minimum."

The tinkertoys clattered. Yes, there was definitely a link there. If I didn't want to be the first paramedic beaten to death by building blocks, I was going to have to come up with a way to calm Helen. Fortunately, defusing difficult situations with distraught and sometimes panicky people is part of my job.

"Move my *crew*? You can't move my crew! It's contrary to protocols. I have to protect them!"

"We are responding to your distress call," I reminded her gently. "We are here to help you."

I could see the program conflict, manifesting as anxiety. Helen was a sentient, too, and I did not want her to come to any harm. It wasn't her fault some frustrated engineer had designed her to look and sound like a sexbot.

"Oh, I *know* that." It came out torn between a moan and a growl. "Why can't you help them here? They're my crew. They belong *here*."

Tsosie bumped me warningly with the elbow of his hardsuit. Not that I needed it.

Helen wouldn't have come equipped with all those cryo units. *Big Rock Candy Mountain* was designed to be full of living, breathing crew. Not sleepers.

I was pretty sure that cryo hadn't even been properly invented when *Big Rock Candy Mountain* had left Terra. Which meant that they had developed their own, in parallel with the Synarche, which was probably why these coffins didn't look anything like a proper cryo tank. That meant the crew had built them—or the ship had built them, or Helen had built them.

Which meant I could at best guess at the mechanisms by which the coffins worked. Assuming they worked at all.

"Helen," I said carefully, "how is it that your entire crew came to be in cryo?"

This ship was meant to be a home. A habitation for an entire tribe of humanity. Not *merely* a vehicle.

She said, "They were sick. We couldn't help them. The machine intervened to protect them."

Sometimes in a moment of crisis, you act. Your instincts take over, and your body and brain do the right thing without the intervention of your conscious mind. Training and repetition, presence of mind, and perhaps something innate and nameless combine to make you do a thing. It might be the right thing. It might be terribly maladaptive.

If you're the sort of person who habitually does the maladaptive thing in a crisis, do everybody including yourself a favor and don't go into the emergency services.

I didn't do a maladaptive thing. And I didn't do the right thing.

I froze.

"Machine?" I said, carefully, pitching it as a question.

While I waited for Helen to answer, Tsosie's concern leaked through the senso to me. Neither one of us knew what this machine she spoke of might be, its provenance, its purpose. But apparently it had shoved an entire crew of humans into cryo chambers, and possibly addled their shipmind in the process. That . . . was scary stuff.

Tsosie wanted to pull back and evacuate immediately, quarantine this vessel and possibly Sally, too, until Judiciary could get here and take over the decision-making. It was laudable caution, and in principle I was in agreement.

Except.

Except if Helen was a threat, if this "machine" was a threat—if the machine even existed, and wasn't a spur process of Helen herself—we might trigger an attack by disengaging. Except there were tens of thousands of people right in front of us who we could potentially rescue. Except that we could destroy the whole recontact situation by making the wrong call, and lose not just Helen, not just the crew, not just the ship—but all the knowledge and history contained in her.

In my military career, in my rescue career, I had never done something as high-stakes as this. And *nothing* in my experience indicated the best course of action to take with a seemingly friendly but possibly malfunctioning artificial intelligence who might have killed her entire, very numerous, crew. And then possibly dissociated a portion of herself into microbots, over which she did not seem to have conscious control. But which definitely responded to her emotional state with vigor.

As a human being, I wasn't sure I could make myself walk away from people who were, if they were alive, this much in need, and this close to rescue after so *very* long. I was also, even with Sally's renewed help, getting a fair amount of pain leakage. We'd been out for a long time, and I could tune it out and rely on my exo and the hardsuit to do the heavy lifting. I still had plenty of batteries. But I was getting tired, and the discomfort was starting to make me foggy and rob me of concentration.

Something Helen and I had in common.

I'm used to it. I've always functioned around the pain. I don't remember a time before the pain. I wondered if Helen remembered a time before her pain, if it was pain. *You're projecting, Llyn.* Fine, then. Her disorientation.

I *could* not decide what to do based on the information I had. So I asked a leading question, and waited for more data.

"Machine," Helen agreed, with an airy wave. "The machine."

The tinkertoys rattled behind her.

This was not, to be perfectly transparent, typical in any way of shipmind behavior. Not even the behavior of a traumatized and destabilized or physically damaged shipmind. If a shipmind lost processing power, they might become slow, unresponsive. *Sticky.*

But not *confused.*

They did not become *vague* in this manner. Disorientation was the stuff of organic malfunction.

So in addition to everything else, Helen was scientifically interesting.

This time, I encrypted my channel. It was a risk: Helen might decide we were plotting against her. But literally everything was a risk right now.

Sally, I subvocalized. *You're the expert in treating designed intelligences. What is going on with this AI? Mechanically, I mean. I've never seen anything like this.*

"Neither have I," she answered in my ear. "I'd say she's got conflicting inputs, or conflicting imperatives. That could make her seem more—"

Senile? I waited. *Organic?*

"I wasn't going to put it that way."

It's all right. She's definitely acting weird. I'm not offended. Only . . .

I hesitated for too long. Sally responded with a query that I felt hanging there. Tsosie, too. He'd filed his recommendation and his dissent with my course of action, but this was my call. He wouldn't interfere unless I did something obviously unjustifiable or sophipathological, or made a decision that was judged unreasonably dangerous for its potential benefits by a majority of the crew.

Only how do I get Helen to consent to let us move her people?

As I said it, though, I knew the answer. There was no urgency in treating the crew. They were in cryo: they were dead or they were alive, and for the present moment that wave state was uncollapsed and I had no way of knowing if I needed to pick up dinner for Schrödinger's cat on my way home.

Their status, in other words, was not deteriorating. So I would treat them as if they could be saved, because that is how you work a victim, but I wouldn't triage them to the front of the line.

There was a rush with one patient, though. We had to treat Helen—and the "machine," if the machine was her tinkertoy microbot thing—

before we did anything else. Before the Judiciary ship or ships supposed to be following us arrived.

Which led us to a new complex of problems. Because I had even less idea where to begin with Helen, or how to get her to let us take care of her so we could save her *and* her crew.

And get somebody over to the docked methane ship, too. That was a totally unaddressed problem, still hanging out there. Waiting out there.

At least it was a smaller-scale problem.

"You can come with me," I said to Helen. "That way you can be sure I don't do anything to harm your crew."

Helen seemed to study me—disconcerting, given her eyeless, faceless face. I could only assume that it was a behavior she'd been designed to model by the same engineer who gave her the sexualized peripheral.

"I will come with you," she agreed, on the other side of I-didn't-even-want-to-contemplate-how-many simulations. "You will not move my crew without my permission. And the other doctor stays here."

Tsosie shook his head inside the hardsuit. I overruled him.

There was a mystery here, and I have never been good at letting go of mysteries. I can't leave a crossword puzzle unfinished, and when I was in the Judiciary I never let go of a cold case.

I mean, sure, I could get the bulldog tendency corrected. But it's part of my identity. So I pick careers where being a bulldog helps.

I wasn't sure it was helping now. But here I was, and I wasn't going to magically turn into someone different in time to save thousands of lives.

"I'll agree to those conditions until further notice," I said. "Take me to the crew."

The gravity was getting to me. I wasn't used to this much, for this long, with the kind of sustained physical activity we'd experienced crawling under and around the machine.

Some kind of immaterial barrier (electrostatic?) held the air inside the airlock, but let more solid objects—such as me—pass through.

When I went out into the space of the hold, the first thing that struck me was that it was not, for a wonder, full of tinkertoys. I'd become so used to picking my away around them that it felt a little strange, for the first few moments, to reach out or gesture and not see a wave of them unzipping and rezipping themselves around my hand.

The machine—or the bit of it that had come through the door with us—did follow me into the cargo hold. Maybe that was what she meant by "I will come with you."

I'd been hoping it would be just the Helen peripheral—I was becoming more and more convinced that I was dealing with whatever remained of *Big Rock Candy Mountain*'s shipmind—but her golden figure remained in the airlock beside Tsosie and waved me out among the coffins. I was escorted on my mission of mercy by a latticework tendril made of brilliantly holographic microbots. It was one of the more unsettling search-and-rescue partners I've ever worked with.

The machine didn't do anything at first, however, except hover over my shoulder.

Since there was no atmosphere in the cargo hold to carry sound, I made sure my radio was transmitting unencrypted and spoke into my suit mike, "Where did the machine come from?"

Helen heard it, as I had suspected, and the question seemed to puzzle her. Her answer came back through my suit. "It . . . made itself?"

"It looked like you were making the component parts, when we met you."

"I was making the spindles and connectors," she said. "But they're not the machine. Or they're not *all* of the machine. The machine is an idea."

I wondered. If the machine was a part of her, and she had made the machine, then it made sense to say that the machine had made itself. But her cognition on this topic, as on certain others, seemed blocked.

It was certainly possible that it *was* blocked. That someone, sometime, had intentionally closed those pathways and instituted a kind of machine denial in her. Human beings were perfectly capable of blatantly ignoring objective reality all on our lonesome. AIs had to be programmed to do it.

If she had been blocked, though, there was no way for me to fix it, and trying to get her to talk about it wouldn't lead to any kind of self-realization about the conflict. Talk therapy doesn't work on lines of code. And no matter what the three-vees say, you can't actually send an AI into crisis and meltdown by challenging its programmed assumptions. They can grow and change—that's one of the things that makes them sentient—but they can't shake off a code block any more than I could regrow a severed trunk nerve.

Sally could fix it, given time. And there were code doctors at Core General that could fix it, if we could get her there.

Whatever had been done to her, though, the person who had set it up seemed to have set up defenses around it. It was becoming plausible that what had happened to Helen—and to *Big Rock Candy Mountain*—was an act of self-sustaining sabotage. But on the part of a member of the crew, or the crew of the docked vessel, which we hadn't investigated yet, or something else entirely?

I picked my way along the row of cryo chambers, sighing in frustration as I examined them. They were not designed for human technicians to maintain. There were no readouts. There were no telltales or happy blinking lights. There was row upon row of . . . honestly, they looked more like chest freezers than like coffins. They didn't look at all like a Synarche cryo tank, which at least partially confirmed my supposition that Helen or her crew had invented cryonic technology on the . . . fly, as it were. The chambers looked as if she had assembled them from whatever materials were available.

They didn't need readouts. Nobody was ever supposed to look at them and see if they were working other than Helen and the machine.

And, well, Helen appeared to be superficially correct. Whether those cryo chambers contained living persons or dead ones, they were all intact.

The chambers *did* each have a battery, which made my life that much easier. I thanked Helen profusely when she mentioned them to me. We'd have to fab chargers that fit these ports when we moved the caskets, but I wasn't too concerned about that. We had the printers, and we could copy one of the originals. Electricity is a remarkably simple—though dangerous—animal.

The number of chambers we could haul would be limited by the amount of juice we could generate more than by our cargo space.

"Helen," I said, "can I connect to the data storage on one of these chambers to run some diagnostics?"

"I will have to print you a connector," she said. "They don't broadcast a signal."

"They're hardwired into your systems."

I had a tickle of an idea on how to get us out of this situation. How to get control of it. I couldn't be certain that my encryption with Sally was completely secure, and I needed her for it.

I hoped she would guess.

Helen said, "Into the machine." She began to drift toward me, body poised and toes pointed, like a monster levitating toward its victim in some old three-vee.

"Are you part of the machine?" I asked, very casually.

Tsosie's level of worry spiked so high that Sally bumped his anti-anxiety cocktail before clearing it with him. She was within her rights as a shipmind to do it—she, like Helen, had an obligation to her crew—but I picked up his irritation that she'd felt the need.

Llyn, you're going to invite her right into your fox? That's too risky. I cannot allow it!

Relax. Sally has my back.

I didn't have time to say more, because Helen was answering.

"We are all," she said, with great conviction, "part of the machine."

It sent a chill up my spine, and I didn't tune the unease away. A certain wariness was good. A certain wariness was my brain and body telling me that I was in a dangerous situation. A certain wariness was useful. Sensible.

Sally seemed to agree, because my sense of peril stayed right where it was, and she could have gotten rid of it as easily as she'd defused Tsosie's panic. How had people like those in the tanks gotten through the dia with just their own native brain chemicals and coping strategies?

If any of them were alive, I guessed I might have the chance to ask them.

"Please," I said. "Print me a connector, Helen." Encrypted, I asked, *Sally, are you game for this?*

It's a terrible idea, she answered, so I knew she *had* picked up on exactly what I was planning.

I said, *Just don't hurt her if you can help it.*

What if she hurts me?

Don't let that happen, either.

I continued to make my way around the coffins—or the chest freezers—while Helen printed me a connector. Although I couldn't access the vitals of the crew, I could double-check the integrity of the chambers.

At least in that, Helen's confidence was justified. She'd arranged things so she didn't have to do anything except cryo chamber maintenance. Who knew? Maybe she'd gotten very, very sick of having humans around after six hundred subjective ans. Years. Whatever.

"Helen," I said, "why did the machine put the crew into cryosleep?"

"There was sickness. The ship wasn't safe." She had turned away from me, and from Tsosie, and was attentively waiting, her gaze—which wasn't her gaze—trained back toward the hatch behind Tsosie. The machine hovered there, stretched between the airlock and me, balancing on all its rods and connectors. Staying out of trouble for the time being, I supposed.

"Structurally unsound?"

"The hull was too thin," she agreed.

"Why was the hull too thin?"

I expected to hit another block here, but I didn't. Whoever had programmed Helen not to understand the consequences of her own actions hadn't thought to build denial around this.

"The materials were needed elsewhere."

"So the hull's structural integrity was compromised. Its strength and resilience."

"Yes," she said.

"Because the materials were needed to build the machine."

"Yes." She turned to me, shimmering gold and silver like moiré silk. "Should you go into stasis? The ship isn't safe."

As if I had some gift of clairvoyance, I could hear the echo of those words down the ans. I could imagine her telling her crew, "You have to go into stasis. The ship isn't safe."

The ship wasn't safe because she had been taking it apart. To build the machine. A machine that was . . . a virus. A meme, a self-propagating set of ideas that could infect and cause sophipathology in an artificial intelligence.

A meme whose source I did not know.

But wherever it had come from, the machine was also an entity, as Helen was an entity. And as such I was duty-bound to try to rescue it—and her—and save both their a-lives if I could.

"I'm safe," I told her. "I have my hardsuit on."

"I think you should go into stasis," she began to insist.

But she hadn't countermanded her previous instruction. "Oh, look," I said. "Here's the connector."

The machine snaked out and handed it to me. It was a fat, physical cable. I plugged one end into my suit jack, and it fit. I crouched beside the nearest cryo chamber, and felt Sally massing herself inside my fox, a grumpy wall of code who couldn't believe what I had gotten her into.

You put me up to this, she said. *Just remember that.*

Do you want to go into cryo? I asked her.

The machine was grabbing for my wrist as I plugged the cable in.

What happened next wasn't my fight, and I don't really know how to describe my position as an observer. Because while it wasn't my fight, it was happening in my head. I was the conduit for it, and the bandwidth Sally was using to bootstrap herself into *Big Rock Candy Mountain*'s system was the bandwidth between my fox and her—well, what amounted to her physical body. The ambulance, in other words, and the processors inside it.

Synarche ships are pretty much made of four things: programmable computronium, engines, life-support consumables, and upholstery. I mean, okay: I'm not an engineer. The upholstery might be computronium, also.

But *I'm* not computronium. My fox—the little network of wonders embedded in my central nervous system—is, and a useful wodge of the stuff, too. It's deeply linked to everything I am and do and see and think and feel and remember. It ties me into the senso so I can share experiences with Sally and my crewmates. It lets me live their experiences, if they share their ayatanas with me. It helps keep me emotionally stable and it helps me remember things accurately, without the subjectivity of human recollection.

It's a damned knife blade of a bridge for an entire fucking shipmind to stuff herself across at lightspeed so she can grapple *another* shipmind and wrestle her to the metaphorical ground.

And I wasn't good for anything at all while it was happening.

I stayed there, frozen in a crouch, while Sally poured herself through the electronic portions of my psyche like . . . I can't even think of a metaphor. It was a good thing I was under gravity, because if I hadn't been, I wouldn't have had the wherewithal to keep myself from drifting off into space and bumping things randomly. If I concentrated really hard, I could force my eyes to focus. That was it. That was all I was good for. But after a second or two I'd have to refocus them, because I was slumping ever so slowly toward the deck.

And whatever was going on between Sally and Helen—or Sally and the machine—was happening on the other side of me, and far too fast for my conscious mind to maintain any awareness of.

"Llyn," Tsosie said, "I really think that we should leave."

As if I could, I thought at him fiercely, wondering if I'd even managed to subvocalize.

"There's more bots massing outside the airlock, Llyn! A lot more! I don't know if she's making them or just packing the vicinity. But if I had to guess I'd say she was getting ready to rush you."

Well, that was comforting. Wait, had Tsosie gone back out through the airlock while I was distracted? I hadn't told him to do that.

I hadn't told him not to, either. And checking our six wasn't a bad idea. At least he hadn't taken off and left me here.

That's unfair to Tsosie, I told myself. I guess I was feeling pretty vulnerable and maybe even scared, locked down in my body like that with nowhere to go and no control.

After half a million ans, give or take, I found I could tell if I was breathing again. I had been; it was a relief to be certain. *Sally?*

I'm in. I just need enough bandwidth to communicate with myself, now.

"Great," I muttered. "I was thinking about switching careers. I can be a corpus callosum."

Something like a giant fist thundered against the exterior airlock door. I couldn't hear it, but I felt it through the deck. I managed to turn my head. Tsosie was not in the airlock. Helen had gone back there.

The door dented, but didn't break. It seemed unlikely that I was getting back out that way.

The outer wall of the cargo bay was nothing but hull, though. There had to be an airlock in it. In addition to whatever massive doors had been built to move bulk cargo in and out under freefall conditions.

Jens! Tsosie yelled in my head. *Evacuate!*

"Just a sec." I bent down to get my sensors closer to the connection between the coffin and the bulkhead. If the chambers had been built into the ship, I wasn't sure what we could do to move them. Cutting lasers, maybe.

That would pose no risk to the occupants at all.

I wanted to know before I left what kind of preparation we needed to make before we came back. And I was definitely leaving.

My plan seemed pretty good to me, honestly. Until the hull plates under my feet began to crumble.

Well, that explained where the extra bots had come from. Helen had been autocannibalizing her own hull to build them, and she'd finally autocannibalized too far. I had a certain amount of time to contemplate it, as I fell through the shredding fabric of that hull in slow motion, surrounded by the cryo coffins that had been closest to me. I was still plugged into the access port on the nearest one.

I wasn't too worried. There was a long way to fall, and while *Big Rock Candy Mountain* was moving fast, she wasn't accelerating fast. There was too much of her, and her design wasn't built to take a lot of torque. I had maneuvering jets.

And I had Sally.

I pinwheeled, without much control. I needed to wait for the correct attitude before I hit my jets to stabilize and keep catching up. But I could set the suit to do that on its own. Its automated reflexes were a hell of a lot better than mine. I'd just jet myself right over and start collecting cryo units until Sally could come and get me.

I kept thinking that right up until I got myself stabilized and got a glimpse back inside the cargo bay. I didn't see Helen or Tsosie inside.

But a tentacle of microbots was stretching toward me.

I yelped—out loud, knowing Sally and possibly Tsosie could hear me. And anybody back on the ambulance who was listening to our coms, which was probably everybody.

I hit my jets on manual, ducking away. Until I hit the end of the connector cable, at which point the cryo chamber and I began to revolve around one another.

It was a rookie mistake, and the kind of error that ended with frozen astronauts falling endlessly in orbit. Or at least until somebody came and collected their corpse, since it *was* antisocial to leave space junk spinning around out there where somebody else might run into it.

So on some level I should have been grateful that the tendril compensated for my maneuver, and snatched me effortlessly out of space. The cryo units were starting to fall behind—*Big Rock Candy Mountain* slowly gaining *v* over them—and I squeaked in frustration as I was pulled away. An unprofessional manifestation of a very professional anger. There were *people* in there.

If I could get them to Core General, they might be people we could save. But as we accelerated away from them, all I could see was their batteries failing, along with any chance at life for the people inside. Helen apparently had no control over *Big Rock Candy Mountain*'s engines, which had been accelerating for centians and were expected to accelerate for centians more.

It occurred to me that the microbots could crack my hardsuit, or whip me around until my vertebrae separated, and there was absolutely nothing I could do to prevent it. A little bit of worry on my own behalf penetrated my professional despair.

"There you are!" Sally cried brightly. The rush of relief that flooded through me was so intense I had to dial it back a little. "You're all right!"

"Not for much longer!" I yelled, shoving uselessly at the microbots.

Sally said, "Cut that out! It worked. But don't you ever scare me like that again."

I blinked several times before it occurred to me that I should ask her what she meant. "Excuse me?"

"Punching through the hull. Helen couldn't let lives be at risk. You distracted her—and the machine—long enough for me to override them."

"Oh." I decided not to explain that I hadn't punched through the hull on purpose. "Oh! Is that you towing me in?"

"It doesn't mean I won't squeeze you a bit," she threatened.

"How are Helen and the machine?"

"I don't think I harmed them," Sally said. "Just subdued."

I craned my head around. I couldn't twist that far and had to rely on senso for a visual of the cryo units. "What about those people out there?"

"Helen's going to be pretty happy with us once we rescue them," Tsosie said. "I'm fine, too, thanks for asking."

He knew—and he knew I knew—that I would have felt it through our link if anything had actually happened to him. But if Tsosie ever stopped busting my ass, it would mean that he was being controlled by brainworms.

"Well," I said. "So am I. Can I go fetch those cryo units?"

"I'm coming," Sally said. "I'll save you a step."

Tsosie cleared his throat. "You know. It is possible to be *too* cool under pressure."

I ignored him. "Sally, we're going to have to divert power from our own cryo tanks to support these."

We had three. We used them when somebody was wounded beyond what we could repair in the field, and too badly to survive the flight back to Core General.

"Well," Sally said in resignation, "nobody had better get sick on the way home."

CHAPTER 4

WE COULD HAVE GONE DIRECTLY ON TO THE DOCKED Synarche ship, but it would have been dumb. Sally was sending drones to investigate, and we could deal with it after a rest cycle. Tsosie and I were both exhausted and low on resources, and I was in too much pain to be much good to anybody.

One thing about the kind of pain I have is that it is so amorphous—so unlocalized—that it's hard to describe and easy to ignore. You don't even necessarily notice that it hurts, when it hurts. You just notice that you're crabby and out of sorts and everything seems harder than it should.

Not being able to describe it also tends to make other people take it less seriously. Like family members, and sometimes doctors, too.

I found myself trying to massage my hands through the hardsuit as we cruised back to Sally, using our thrusters to match velocity and then, when she seemed motionless, to nudge us into contact with her hull.

Since we weren't jumping out of her at a moving target at this time, we both entered through the same airlock at the same time. We waited through the decon and, when the lock cycled, stepped inside.

Loese, the pilot, wasn't waiting for us, because she was on a rest shift and Sally gets very cross with us if we ditch our rest for nonessential reasons—or, as she calls them, "excuses." The rest of the crew all found reasons to wander by and greet us as we were stripping out of our newly sterilized hardsuits. It wasn't exactly a hero's welcome, but it was nice to see everybody.

Not that Sally was so big we could have avoided them even if we were trying.

The first to wander around the ring was Hhayazh. It was one of our flight nurses, a multi-limbed multi-eyed nightmare creature from Ykazh, its dull black exoskeleton covered in thick, bristling hairs. It was also one of the nicest sentients you'd ever care to meet, once you embraced Ykazhian culture . . . which, in turn, embraced sarcasm with the enthusiasm of an octopus embracing a tasty, tasty mollusk.

"Greetings, far wanderers," it said, through the usual translation protocols. "I perceive you've made it back to the real hub of the action. I hope your trip wasn't too boring."

"About as boring as being here," Tsosie answered. "We heard you broke the place."

"That wasn't me," Hhayazh said. It pointed at Camphvis, the other flight nurse, as the Banititlan came into the cabin. As she always did, she was leading with her eyestalks. "Camphvis leaned on the dashboard."

Camphvis responded with the bubbling sound that her species used to indicate derisive laughter—which the senso translated into derisive laughter. This produced an interesting layering effect. "Where does Sally keep her dashboard?"

"If you knew that you wouldn't have pushed the wrong buttons." Hhayazh rattled its exoskeleton, a sound like the hollow carved windchimes people on my homeworld made out of native plant cellulose. It was a social cue with all sorts of meanings, like human facial expressions, and I hadn't even begun sorting them out.

"What actually happened?" I asked.

"Equipment malfunction," Sally said. "I'll show you later."

When Camphvis emerged completely around the hatchway, I saw that she was carrying a tray. Nothing complicated, just the hot, calorie-dense nutritive broth that spacers called "soup." It wasn't soup, but was profoundly welcome nonetheless.

Tsosie picked his up at once. I was still fighting with my hardsuit. They were supposed to peel themselves back into the actuator, but exposure to grit or something was causing it to hang up on my exo.

"Seriously." I pretzeled myself into another awkward position. "What went wrong?"

Hhayazh, with surgical expertise, got the jammed bit unhooked and snatched its manipulators out of the way as the thing clam-shelled shut with a snap. "Go to bed," it said. "You can ask questions when you're not too tired to understand the answers."

I traded Camphvis my actuator for a cup of soup. Her eyestalks twitched to focus on it. I was totally creating a distraction, because I was still working on my comeback to Hhayazh. Our Nazzish flight surgeon, Dr. Rhym, saved me from humiliation by climbing down the ladder from Sally's hub into the gravity of the rim. (If you're bantering and it takes you more than fifteen seconds to return a serve, you definitely lost.)

Rhym resembled a feathery tree stump, but moved with surprising agility. The long woodsy toes on their four feet wrapped the rungs in a prehensile fashion, leaving the manipulatory tendrils on what a human would have considered a face to gesticulate. They seemed as if they were talking to Sally privately: it wasn't translated for the rest of us, and the wriggling stopped when they reached the deck.

I was bent over, working my swollen feet out of my boots. They should have retracted with the rest of the hardsuit. They hadn't, and were stiff and not shaped for easy removal. The pressure hurt, and pushing against them to try to escape the pressure hurt.

"I'll make sure this gets serviced," Camphvis said, eyeballing the actuator suspiciously.

"Just take it apart and reprint it," Hhayazh said.

Dr. Rhym was about my height in my current crouched position.

"Our patient-guests are stowed, and the peripheral has been brought aboard!" Even their translated voice sounded enthusiastic. "Dr. Jens, would you like some assistance?"

"Well, yes," I proclaimed, and straightened up to hold on to the rungs on the opposite wall while Rhym scooted over to me.

They moved fast, each leg working independently of the others in a kind of scuttle or *zoom*. In moments, their manipulatory tendrils uncoiled and eased inside the left boot, gently prying it loose from my exo, which had gotten snagged on the lining. I sighed in relief as the thing came off.

Rhym is a *very* good surgeon. What I'd been struggling with for minutes they accomplished in instants. And they didn't even use a knife.

I went to lie down.

It was my exo moving me at that point as much as me moving it, and I could kid myself that I picked up annoyance and worry through our link. I told myself that I was anthropomorphizing, but people used to assign personalities to ships and houses long before ships and houses had them, and there was a semi-AI processing engine in my exo. A small, uncomplicated one, without curiosity or an artificial personality. There wasn't much room in there, and anyway can you imagine how terrible it would be for a person with agency to be stuck going through life as an assistive device?

Usually, before I went to bed, I'd tune down my pain management and see how my body was doing on the other side of the fuzzy wall of endorphins and interventions. This time, I didn't: I knew what the answer was going to be.

I lay down on a patient bed in one of Sally's two care units. This was not the usual bunk assigned to humans. We hot-swapped, and I traded off with Loese and Tsosie. But Tsosie was as tired as I was, and Loese wasn't off her rest shift yet. I wouldn't fit in Rhym's bunk, Camphvis used gel blankets to keep her membranous skin moist, and Hhayazh's species weren't sleepers. So I got a bed big enough for a Thunderby, and even if it was a little hard, I didn't complain—just printed off as many sterile blankets as we had consumables for and made a nest on top. I'd recycle the molecules later.

Then I plugged my exo in to charge, piped into it, and started checking up on my aching body to see if any of it was anything serious, or merely the usual combination of inflammation and polyarthralgia, before I dialed them down or, where I could manage it, turned them off.

My exo, predictably, had a little lecture waiting for me. *Todia's exertions have exceeded this unit's filtering capabilities. Recommend extended rest, and a maintenance cycle.*

"I can't do the extended rest right now, kid. Put me in for eight hours and authorize the maintenance cycle."

Lack of adequate rest will likely lead to worsening discomfort and is against medical advice.

"So is everything fun."

This unit does not understand the response.

I sighed. "Acknowledged, patient's decision is against medical advice." *Patient is a damn internist herself, robot.* Also, I could get plenty of sleep on the trip home. Right now, we still had a second space ship to recon.

And yelling at my exo wouldn't help. I turned both the room lights and my pain response down. Nothing was busted: it was all just inflamed. Life is like that. I reached into senso to pull up a paper on Adrychrym circulatory systems. It was a boring paper: I meant to read myself to sleep. If I could get all the noisy doctors in my head to concentrate on medicine, they wouldn't keep me awake.

I should have unloaded the ayatanas, I know. But I was too tired, and I was going to need them again tomorrow.

I was pushing my way through a badly written extract when I was interrupted by the small throat-clearing beep our shipmind uses when she's about to enter a conversation and doesn't want to startle anybody.

"Llyn, go to sleep," Sally said. "Or I will *make* you."

"I was sleeping," I said.

"You were reading."

"I was reading myself to—oh, never mind." I'd wake up groggy if I used my fox to send myself to sleep, but it wasn't worth fighting with the shipmind over. I tuned up the relevant hormones, and was gone before I had to listen to her rejoinder.

Tsosie was right: we did get a lot more popular with Helen once we retrieved her people from the bottomless waste of space. She wasn't as happy when Sally immediately put them into her own storage rather than bringing them back to *Big Rock Candy Mountain*, or so Sally told us after our rest cycle.

Helen didn't say anything about it to Tsosie or me—or the rest of the crew—because Sally kept her out of our way. The peripheral sat quietly in a corner of the ambulance, cabled to a bulkhead, sharing Sally's sensorium. It's always hazardous to assign human emotions to nonhuman sentiences, but Helen was *modeled* on a human psyche. And it seemed to me that her body language became less and less reactive and more composed as more and more of her people were moved on board Sally. And the more Sally let her experience the natural environment of space the same way Sally did.

I was sure she still wasn't happy. Nor would I be, in her place, with most of my crew left behind. Nor *was* I, standing in my own shoes, with so many people left unrescued.

You can always get one more out.

Until you can't. And it's not easy to know where the line between "saving one more" and "dying yourself" is.

We could have left once we had a full load of patients. Could have—Helen wasn't capable of stopping us as long as Sally had her in restraint. But we waited for the additional relief ships to arrive, because to do otherwise would have amounted to the extremest mental cruelty to Helen and to the machine.

And we were all curious, and wanted a look at that docked, silent methane ship. Even though she wasn't answering our hails, there might be people on board her, also. It was such a huge rescue job that we couldn't do everything at once and had to prioritize. Triage.

With Helen's help and Sally's override, part of the microbot machine was packed up in boxes and loaded in external holds; Sally told us that its personality core was both integrated with Helen's and distinct from her. *It* was quite nonhuman in its construction, and while Sally didn't seem to have any problem communicating with it, she also didn't seem to be able to easily translate its concepts and logical processes for us meat types.

She did say we'd gotten enough of its processing power to preserve its personality core. If anything should happen to the rest of it, it would be able to reconstruct itself.

What can I say? AI medicine is weird.

The human patients were going to have to stay frozen for the time being. Though *I* wanted to thaw them out. And Hhayazh *really* wanted to thaw them out.

But all we needed was a virulent influenza from six hundred ans ago that nobody has any immunity to anymore, or something similar. I know we all have diar when we're tempted to take definitive action . . . but wiping out humanity with a primitive plague wasn't on our agenda. Neither was killing a lot of ice people because we couldn't wait to defrost them until we got someplace with the most advanced medical technology in the galaxy.

The pods were decontaminated, and they would wait to be opened until we got back to Core.

Rhym tried to argue me into letting them do the EV to the methane ship, since we had no patients suitable for them to operate on. They maintained that Tsosie and I still needed rest. I pointed out that I still had the ayatanas loaded. We could have been caught in a stalemate for a standard month, but Sally pulled up the drone surveys and showed us a ship interior more suitable for long lanky types than squat broad-circumferenced ones, thereby resolving the argument in my favor.

She did insist that I eat and let my exo and hardsuit both finish full maintenance cycles before I went out, though. The exo was nearly done, and Camphvis, good to her word, had set up the hardsuit. But I suspected that Sally had conveniently not remembered to trigger the disassembly and reprint, in order to keep me indoors for another few hours.

I mean, sure, it's supposed to be on *my* checklist. But *she's* the AI.

I was halfway through breakfast—no coffee, drop it all down the Well, because coffee smells terrible to most syster species, so I was making do with tea—before I remembered to ask her what had gone wrong the previous dia. "Sally. When you lost contact with us. You said you would explain later. What happened?"

Sally paused, which is a thing AIs do when they're communicating with humans, because it makes us more comfortable if they operate at our speed. Then she said, "I'm not precisely sure."

"But you fixed it. I mean, you got back in touch with us."

"I routed around it," she said. "With Loese's help. And then I forgot about it."

That, in conjunction with the delay on maintaining my hardsuit, made me sit upright. It's a good thing we weren't in free fall, because I dropped my spoon and nobody likes oatmeal floating into their hair. Things did not *slip* Sally's mind.

"I think I better have a look at this," I said, trying to ignore the chill of unease I felt.

"Get Loese to show you," Sally said. "She looked at it yesterdia."

I got Loese to show me.

She was around in the control cabin, which is mostly where we congregated when we weren't sleeping, eating, or working. I had to make a halfway circuit of Sally's circumference to get there, so it took me a whole two minutes. Maybe ninety seconds. Sally is big for a starship, but that doesn't make her *big*.

Loese had black hair and unusually pale skin and a butch presentation. I found her bent over panels, her afthands immersed in their interface while she worked course calculations. Loese is a spacer by upbringing, and has the usual spacer mods: it must be seriously irritating to her to be stuck on Sally with her constant simulated spin gravity.

On the other hand, maybe it's fun to zip around the galaxy on an ambulance. No speed limits for us, except for physics. And nobody makes Loese buy her own fuel.

"Hey," I said when she looked up. "When you get a break, can you take me to see whatever went wrong yesterdia? Sally said you hadn't fixed it yet."

"Sure," Loese said. "We can go right now. Just let me pause this. And since we've got functional coms back, I wasn't going to fix it until we got back to Core. To preserve the evidence."

"The evidence," I said, startled enough that it didn't register with me that I ought to be asking a question. I was repeating the words that didn't make sense, in an experimental fashion.

Loese looked at me. "Sally didn't tell you."

"Sally told me it was an equipment failure and sent me to bed. What didn't Sally tell me?"

"Come see for yourself," Loese said. "Sally?"

"Here, Loese."

Loese led me farther around the ring, and aft. We opened a hatch that led to a little room too small for both of us to enter at once. It was an equipment access and storage space, and we wound up unclipping and moving a few duffel crates of things we used too regularly for it to be worth printing them every time we wanted them before we got to the back of it.

When they were out of the way, I could see scorch marks in the ship's grippy interior sheathing. Somebody had scored the material and peeled it back to expose the workings underneath. Sally was supposed to be self-healing, but either she'd shut it off or that function was compromised.

"You opened this?" I asked Loese.

"There's a superconductor path under here," Loese said. "A lot of electricity wound up going places it shouldn't have."

"How is that possible? It's not live, is it? And why isn't it healing?"

She moved back so I could step past her. "Sally can't find it. Based on what you told me, it sounds like she can't even remember what's wrong."

"That sounds like brain damage," I said, and had a sudden unsettling memory of Helen talking around the programmed blocks that didn't allow her to see what a part of her own . . . self . . . was doing. "But how—"

"Sabotage," Loese said, succinctly and reluctantly.

"The docked ship?" I asked. "Wait, *Helen*?"

"No," she said. "Nothing out here. It must have been in progress before Sally made any contact with Helen or the machine on *Big Rock Candy Mountain*."

She seemed to realize that her revelation would trigger a whole cascade of questions, because she continued, "And I don't think any of you did it: I think it must have been put in place back at Core. I think somebody hid a device with a timer or some other kind of trigger in Sally, so that she lost coms with you and Tsosie while you were outside. And then put some kind of worm or logic bomb in her code so she would not be able to tell what was happening."

I stared at her. There were words in my head, but they all seemed to get jammed in the pre-verbial door trying to get out at the same time. She'd only been our pilot for a few standard months, but I'd come to rely on her skill and calm. And the nervous twitchiness I was picking up from her was . . . deeply worrying.

Loese, watching my expression, shrugged. "If Rhym hadn't sensed smoke . . . well, their tendrils are a lot more sensitive than a human olfactory system. We could have been in much more trouble by the time we were found."

But how could she be sure that none of us were behind it?

"This was sabotage." I had to hear it in my own voice to internalize it, I suppose.

"Yes," Loese said. "I am confident in that assessment."

"But how could Sally not notice? How could she not detect the damage before it happened? How could she not feel the device?"

"That troubles me as well; thus my theory of the logic bomb. Sally is running a self-diagnostic, and we've been unable to find signs of any other time bombs ticking away, but a definitive cyberpathology report will probably have to wait until we get home again."

"Should we abort? Run for home?" I asked.

Her lips pressed together. "We're not in any more danger here than we are running home, really. We can do the diagnostics perfectly well right where we are. Our patients need us. And if something *were* to go catastrophically wrong, the next wave of rescue vehicles has a better chance of finding us here than they do somewhere in white space. I also wonder what the purpose of it was. It wasn't enough damage to really *endanger* Sally. It just left us out of contact with you for a while."

"Tsosie and I have been replaced by predatory, shapeshifting aliens," I said. "You caught us. If you throw water on us, we'll melt."

I must have nailed the deadpan, because Loese blinked at me for at least three seconds before she laughed.

I said, "Even if Sally were totally disabled, or Tsosie and I got stuck on the generation ship, there's a small fleet right behind us."

"I know." Loese shook her head. "The good news is, none of this is critical to life support or propulsion. And we're looking for it, should anything happen again. When we get back, maybe the master chief will have some ideas about what happened."

Master Chief O'Mara wasn't in the Judiciary anymore, but everybody mostly still used their old title and not their new one. Core General's ox dockmaster—really, they were the head of the Emergency Department, ox sector—was an old acquaintance of mine from the military. They were also a total badass.

I was kind of looking forward to the detonation when I told them somebody had busted one of the ships in their care. They would take it personally, and they treated invective as an art form.

I could look forward to a colorful performance.

"Can you run down whatever's blocked Sally's awareness of the event? I . . . what are the odds that that's evidence of . . . that worm, or something that's still messing with her functionality?"

"Working on it." Loese waved me out of the cubby and sealed the hatch. "Really, really working on it. Now go do *your* job."

Unsettled, I went to get a nice warm mug of creatine, anti-inflammatories, and caffeine from the gallery for breakfast. I sat down across from Tsosie, who was spooning porridge. He grunted a hello; I slurped my beverage. It was faintly lemon-flavored and a little spicy from the capsaicin and curcumin it contained. I hurt a little less than I had before I rested, and this would improve things even more.

"Loese tell you about the . . . damage?" I asked.

He nodded, lips flexing. He wasn't what you'd call a handsome man, I didn't think—though what did I know about what made men handsome? His cheekbones were wide over a sharply triangular chin, and his deep-set eyes seemed to rest behind them like caves on stark ledges. That gaze held a sharp intelligence, and it assessed me. "You worried about it?"

I slurped again. "A little, yeah." That was an understatement. But hysteria is contagious, and even if you're scared, you do the job in front of you, and then the next job after that. And you trust the other professionals around you to do their jobs, too.

That's how you get through dangerous situations. That's how we were going to get through this one. Sally's injury—the sabotage—was her problem, and Loese's, to deal with and repair. My fluttering at them wouldn't help the situation, so I would do my own job and stay out of their way.

Maybe I should admit to Tsosie that I did, after all, have a *little* faith.

Tsosie pushed his bowl away and reached for his own mug, which smelled like chocolate. "You never get scared. You weren't even scared back on the generation ship, walking out into that cargo hold with the machine following you like a pissed-off guard bot."

"What was there to get scared of? There's just a job to do." I wrapped my hands around the mug. The heat helped the ache.

"Oh," he said, "fembots. A ship that's taking itself apart to become macro-programmable matter. Mysterious, sourceless sabotage damage to our own vessel. The incapacitated, silent Synarche ship you're about to go enter?"

I held a hand out, flat, and wobbled it from side to side. *So-so.* "What else you got?"

He laughed at my ironic bravado and batted my hand aside. Gently, because Tsosie is always gentle. "You're that dedicated to Judiciary."

"I couldn't care less about Judiciary. I left Judiciary when I got the chance to be a doctor full-time." The drink was starting to taste metallic as it cooled. I swilled the rest of it. "I'm that dedicated to saving lives."

"Sure, you're an angel." He shook his head and laughed harder: my expression must have been something to behold. "No, I know you are. This job is your life."

"Maybe that's why I'm not scared," I said. "Maybe it's that the job is all I have to lose."

Tsosie stopped laughing.

"What?" I said.

He frowned at me, inspecting my face as intently as Loese had inspected the scorched bulkhead.

"What?" I said again.

"I believe you're telling the truth." He finished his chocolate and stood, sweeping his utensils together. "I hope you find more again, somedia."

CHAPTER 5

HAVING FINISHED HER DRONE RECONNAISSANCE OF THE docked ship, Sally called a shipwide meeting. It wasn't hard, since there were just the six of us—Sally, me, Tsosie, Camphvis, Rhym, Hhayazh. And Helen, if you counted Helen. And a chip off the machine, and the frozen crew members from *Big Rock Candy Mountain*.

Those last weren't included in the meeting, though. None of them got a vote. Neither was Helen, technically, but the only way to keep her from hearing us on a ship that small would have been to hold the meeting entirely in senso while trying to keep our faces straight.

Well, we could have sent her out an airlock and strapped her to the hull. But that sounded like an even *more* terrible idea, and somewhere in my oath of service there's a line about "compassionate."

When we were all floating comfortably, each armed with bulbs of whatever our species considered appropriate refreshment—except for Rhym, whose species did not engage in recreational eating—Sally said, "As we know, it's a methane ship—"

"That's what's driving me down the Well. Why would they even dock? What would they hope to accomplish?" Tsosie's voice trailed off as he contemplated the improbability of it all.

"I believe I agree with the sentiment my esteemed colleague is expressing," Rhym said politely, when the silence had stretched for a while. "Why would a crew with utterly incompatible environmental needs go to all the trouble to couple to a ship that doesn't even have standard airlock design?"

Utterly incompatible was putting it gently. *Explosive combination* might have been a better phrase.

Loese had big eyes under the thick dark forelock that kept drifting across them. It seemed like it would get in her way piloting, but I suppose modern pilots didn't really use their eyes for much. The interface was all senso. She pushed the hair back out of those eyes now, narrowed them grimly, and said, "You're kidding me about going in there. We don't have cryo tanks, or any power left over to run them with. What are we supposed to do with casualties, *splint* them?"

"Can't use a standard ox cryo tank on methane types anyway," Hhayazh said. "It's too hot for them. The methane types melt."

"So," Tsosie said. "How are we even supposed to help those people?"

"Very carefully," I answered.

He glared at me, which seemed unfair. Nobody ever glared at Hhayazh when *it* made sarcastic jokes.

"Our hardsuits can handle the environment in there." *Barely*. But he knew that. To change the subject—and because I wanted to know—I asked Sally, "It might all be irrelevant if this one doesn't have a crew, either?"

"It does," Sally said. "They appear to be alive, inasmuch as I can determine with remote sensors. They're superficially similar to other methane species, in that their apparent environmental needs would be compatible with units on Core General. I still believe they're the assigned crew of SPV *I Bring Tidings From Afar* (Afar is his call name), which makes them"—she made a ringing sound, like somebody running fingers along the bowls of a glass harmonica—"and therefore a known syster species, albeit one that doesn't have much to do with ox types. But they seem to be in some kind of stasis or hibernation state. Which I'm going to assume is either natural for them, or medically or pathologically induced, because they don't appear to be receiving life support."

"So nobody popped *them* into cryo chambers?"

"Nobody popped them into cryo chambers. And I don't have enough medical files on this syster to know if this response is considered normal for their species. They might estivate, for all I know."

Tsosie folded up his glare. He rubbed his temples with his forefingers and thumb. "Dr. Jens, can you load some ayatanas for—Sally, is there a name for these folks I can pronounce with my vocal equipment?"

"Darboof," she supplied cheerfully.

"I've already got it loaded," I said. "They don't estivate."

"Checking my registry—which *is* comprehensive—the Synarche Packet Vessel *I Bring Tidings From Afar* is a fast packet, which means he is one of the rare vehicles that could keep up with us. But the shipmind—Afar—is also nonresponsive."

Mostly, mail gets around the Synarche by piggybacking on a series of transponders located at the waypoints where ships drop out of white space to visit stations, or just to change direction. They exchange data with any passing ship, and eventually information propagates to its destination—faster than light, but not as fast as a fast ship flying straight. Fast ships flying straight are much more resource-intensive, however.

Fast packets like Afar also carry FTL message beacons with their own tiny white drives, which was how word that this crew needed help had reached Core General. They'd converted one into a distress beacon and sent it to us with whatever crumbs of information they had regarding what they'd found . . . and we'd come at a run.

Most of us looked at one another. Especially Camphvis and Hhayazh, each of whom could look in several directions at once.

"We still haven't figured out what a fast packet is doing all the way out here to even find these folks," Loese said.

"Delivering a message?" Hhayazh said.

Tsosie pressed his palm briefly over his eyes before he looked up again, squaring his shoulders. "It seems unreasonable to have *two* ghost ships to explore."

"Well, this one is a lot more modern. And I wouldn't say that it's abandoned—" I glanced at Helen's eyeless face, which turned toward me. She didn't look accusing, I told myself. I was projecting. "—any more than *Big Rock Candy Mountain* turned out to be."

"Ghost ship?" Camphvis asked.

Loese said, "Like the *Flying Dutchman*. Or is it the *Mary Celeste*? I always get those confused."

"I will look up *Flying Dutchman*," Camphvis said mildly. It would take more than three unruly humans to get her eyestalks in a twist.

"As Llyn said, it would be unfair to say that this ship has been abandoned," Sally pointed out with a tone I always thought of as strained reason. AIs dealing with organic intelligences must dump a lot of processing power into patience. At least we're rightminded. Imagine how bad it would be if we were baseline.

I never ask *Sally* to imagine that, though. I don't know for sure, but it seems to me that it would be insensitive to point out that I know how annoying organics are and not do anything to fix it. She probably wouldn't space us all, because she'd just have to pick up the bodies.

Tsosie anchored himself with one hand and made an irritated conversation-cutting gesture with the other. "What's the differential?"

Sally said, "We are already here, and can intervene four diar before the next closest rescue ship. Which is Ruth. She's coming in with the other crews and the Judiciary ship full of archinformists and archaeologists. They're all ox crews, because we thought we were coming for a Terran ship. We can get some methane types out with the next wave, but it will be . . . a while. Somebody will have to go back with the news that we need them."

Four diar would seem more like three for these ships, traveling as fast as they were. But the time dilation of relativistic speed wasn't enough to make a real difference in the decision whether to risk ourselves—and the crew of the other ship—trying to stage a rescue with all the wrong equipment.

He sighed. He looked at me. It wasn't my call whether we should commit to the rescue: that was his. My command started when the rescue began. But he was asking what I thought anyway.

"Sally," I said, "can you show us what you've got on the interior?"

"Copy," she said. "There's some cargo that I don't understand, also. It looks like they were printing some heavy equipment in one of the bays."

She slid us highlight feeds of her drone reports. I found myself in Sally's distributed perspective, floating down a cold, cold corridor in a space with nothing I would consider visible light at all. Somewhere inside me, all the methane-breather ayatanas seemed to take a deep breath and relax.

For them, home was covered in hoarfrost.

Nitrogen-methane atmospheres such as those used by the Darboof tend to be transparent in the red and infrared, though opaque on the blue end on the spectrum. Methane-breathing systers *see*. But the manner in which they see is not very much like ours at all, and they tend to be profoundly vulnerable to heat and radiation in what we would consider the visible spectrum.

Methanogen worlds are brutally cold and dark by human standards: they have to be, to sustain liquid methane. Instead of intaking the kinds of "organic" (carbon-based) molecules we use to build and power our bodies, methanogens metabolize hydrogen, ethane, and acetylene—and exhale methane, as we exhale carbon dioxide.

Methanogen systers use electricity and chemical reactions to move and to think, just as we do. But the mechanisms by which these operate are quite different. Some have incredibly slow metabolisms. Others, like the Darboof, have adapted to the cold of their environments by evolving bodies that are supercooled superconductors.

Afar was under gravity from the spin of the generation ship he was docked to, but it was obvious that he was not designed to spend much time that way. And because I was trying to track several perspectives at once, I couldn't get an accurate count of the crew members.

If Sally's—and the drones'—ability to register the faint, regular, painfully slow respiration of Afar's crew hadn't told me they were alive, I would have thought they were dead. They were utterly motionless—and very beautiful—crystalline icicle sculptures. They would have been radially symmetrical if they had not been slumped in awkward poses, limbs folded under their bodies, frost-flower spikes jutting at regular angles from carapaces.

They lay against what were obviously designed to be zero-g bunks and acceleration couches, crystalline bodies padded by what I took to be some kind of low-temperature aerogel. The material technologies are so utterly different from ox-based ones that there's no comparison. In what they consider room temperatures, the oxygen and carbon dioxide of our atmosphere would precipitate out of the nitrogen as snow. And methane would puddle in lakes.

Going in there scared me. Space is cold, too—but in space, there's no convective or conductive cooling. A methanogen environment (even though the atmosphere, like mine, would be mostly nitrogen) would suck any heat it could reach out of me, and then use that heat to kill the people I had come to save.

We couldn't bring them back to Sally. She had environmental chambers, but nothing that could manage this syster's needs.

"I'm willing to try it," I said. "A fast packet? How many crew, four?"

"Five," Sally said.

Helen said, "You will not endanger my crew."

"No," said Tsosie. "We will not. Anyone else have any comments?"

"We've got ayatanas for that species," Rhym said.

Do you ever get the sense that nobody is listening to you? "I know," I said again. "I'm wearing one."

Rhym continued, "I, too, can wear one, and can operate by remote if necessary."

"It would be most efficient to leave them on their own ship and tow them in," said Hhayazh. "No, wait. Slave the drive and bring them in that way, since their ship can keep up with Sally. Sally, you said you could not contact Afar at all? Even emergency protocols? A consciousness ping?"

"That is correct," Sally said. "We'd need to hardwire in an override panel."

"I can do that," I said. "Pass me the solder that's still good at negative 190C."

Loese leaned back in her chair. "It's feasible."

"And somebody has to set up life support to keep the crew alive while we're in transit." I checked my Darboof ayatana for more physiology. "Unless Rhym wants to use drones to do it?"

"As I offered, I will also load some Darboof ayatanas," they replied. "Then we can decide whether their own metabolic processes are protecting them enough to get them back to Core General alive. They can be slowed down, if I recall; the environment they evolved in is so cold that their strictly chemical biology moves at a very slow pace."

"They've only survived this long because their metabolisms are seriously depressed. That's why they're still breathing," I said. "It's only electrical signals that keep them functioning at anything like meat speed."

I stole a glance at Helen again. She still sat completely silent, but she seemed to be aware. I took a breath and said, "Isn't it odd that two ships in the same place, with very different architectures and design histories, both seem to have lost their shipminds?"

Sally cleared her nonexistent throat. "To say *lost* is factually inaccurate."

"Granted." I didn't roll my eyes because Sally would know what it meant. And because Helen was sitting right there, and I'm not a complete jerk. "Of course *Big Rock Candy Mountain*'s shipmind is not missing. Considering my question idiomatically, is it odd?"

"Yes," Sally answered. "It is."

"I wish we could know if they suffered damage in similar ways," Camphvis said. "It seems very unlikely; modern AI architecture is quite dissimilar from what your species used in the sublight age."

"Right," I said. "Sally, are you planning to take direct control of Afar? I guess we need to cut him loose from *Big Rock Candy Mountain* and remotely bring him home."

"I'm concerned about contagion," she said, "given that we have two shipminds damaged by possibly connected phenomena. But since I'm already in contact with the machine, it may be closing the bay door after the pirates have flown in to worry about viruses now. And the alternative is to physically grapple him."

"It'll be easier for me to get over there if he's not whirling around with the wheel, having made that jump already. But it's your call. I can undock him manually."

"No," Sally said. "If you're willing to take the risk, I can plug in a drone and make things nice and easy with matched velocities. You don't even have to go over and, as you so kindly offered, solder on a panel. Just handle a life-support setup for the crew while we're in transit."

"You're very accommodating," I joked. "What if Afar *is* contagious?"

"I have a personality core backup on archive at Core General," she answered. "And I have good firewalls. If you meat types are willing to take the small additional risk, I am. The worst *I* stand to lose is a few diar of memories. You could wind up drifting forever in the interstellar darkness."

I laughed.

But maybe a little nervously.

Our IR scanners and the drones showed Afar was cold—cold, cold, cold—but that didn't mean the crew was dead. *Cold* was the only habitat methane breathers could endure.

I got Sally to give me two more ayatanas from Core General staff who belonged to Afar's crew species. As Sally had previously demonstrated, the Darboof's name for themselves sounded like the chiming of glass bells; their sensorium experience was foreign to mine. Even though I unloaded a couple of the antique human ayatanas first, downloading and integrating the recorded memories of two more from the Darboof strained my capabilities enough that I found myself looking at the brown squishiness of my own fingers with disgust. I was revoltingly unlike the clean, crystalline purity of the methane breathers. Wet, dangerously hot, full of terrifying caustic fluids . . .

Right. I tuned myself to manage my increasingly catastrophic endocrine response and felt the pulse rate of my (hot, caustic-blooded) heart slow.

Better living through brain implants!

Calmer, I settled in to research in my borrowed memories. Since the ayatanas in question were those of medical professionals, I was able to find the information I needed fairly quickly.

That infrared reading suggested they hadn't gotten too hot: their climate control was still working. The vessel's hull seemed intact per visual inspection and the drone report, so there probably hadn't been any impacts. And, I reminded myself, the drones said the crew were alive in there, just in some kind of suspension.

Which led me to the least reassuring detail I learned from my recorded passengers. I reaffirmed my earlier impression that the Darboof did not, in general, exhibit a hibernation response to trauma, though there was some evidence that one could be induced in them by the right combination of interventions. That would require the equivalent of putting me in a cryo tank, though, so I didn't think it was what had happened here.

The Darboof were physically tough, able to withstand more gs than squishy little critters like myself, and they didn't demineralize in free fall, either. Lucky. Being under simulated gravity for however long they had been docked—not too long, since they were still alive and respiring, per the drones—wouldn't have harmed them.

Neither would lack of gravity on the way back to Core General. And they could survive the transition from the former to the latter unrestrained except for their acceleration couches, which they were conveniently already slumped upon.

"All right, I think this is a go," I told Sally, staggering onto the bridge with one hand braced on the wall. We were back to maintaining position *over* Afar, whipping around the rolling wheel of the generation ship on a following curve, and pulling some extra g because of it. Sally's rotation meant that we endured successive waves of feeling lighter and heavier as the accelerations interacted. It was profoundly disorienting, but if Sally had stopped her rotation, anybody on the other side of the hub would have been sitting on the ceiling. Awkward.

Loese was sensibly strapped into her chair, both sets of hands buried in her console. I popped myself down next to her. We watched a stabilized screen rather than trying to follow the action through a viewport, which would have been nauseating—as I'd learned before my last jump.

I was already doing enough tuning to compensate for my inner ear's opinions about the vector situation without compounding the problem, thanks.

Tsosie and Rhym were strapped in to watch the show, as well. I clicked my own belts into place and lay back on the acceleration couch with a sigh.

It helped.

"All right," Sally said. "I have control of Afar's nav systems. Here goes nothing."

Nothing on the bridge changed, at first. The swelling waves of acceleration washed us; Afar clung like a barnacle to the vast curve of the generation ship. Then a seam appeared in the adaptive collar that held him to the airlock. It peeled away and vanished back into Afar's hull. In the normal course of events, the materials would have been salvaged for printing into another tool as necessary. I wondered, with the ship and crew disabled, if it would be cluttering up the airlock like a giant pile of parachute cloth when I went in.

Because of the collar mismatch, Afar had not shot his docking bolts. He clung to the outside of the generation ship with emergency grapples, and because the airlock had not been seated to *Big Rock Candy Mountain*, there was no puff of escaping atmosphere.

Afar retracted his grapples evenly and instantly shot free of the generation ship, no longer bent to her curve but not deprived of velocity. He vectored off as fast as he had been spinning. The pings of one of the two distress beacons went with him.

We followed, the swell and release of acceleration replaced by a pressure that would have leaned us aft if we hadn't been strapped down.

I rubbed my hands. All the liquid inside me was sloshing around, and my joints had opinions about it.

Localized pain, you can tune out pretty safely and easily, up to a point. The systemic stuff is harder to manage without numbing your entire body or getting stoned enough on your own endorphins to alter your judgment more than might be wise when you're about to do something as finicky as a solo rescue mission in a profoundly hostile environment. I could push some anti-inflammatories, though, so I fumbled them out of my breast pocket and dry-swallowed them. The rest of the pain . . . it was just pain. I didn't like it, but it wouldn't stop me from doing my job.

Tsosie noticed. He caught my eye, but he didn't say anything. Just as well, as it saved me having to invoke privacy, or bite. Metaphorically speaking. Biting a colleague is probably grounds for dismissal, even—especially?—in a massively multispecies, massively multicultural work environment.

We bore down on Afar with all the majestically slow urgency of space rescues, accelerating to close the distance between us and match his trajectory. He wasn't gaining velocity, so we didn't have to burn hard after him. *Big Rock Candy Mountain* receded in our aft screens. My heart sped with the excitement of the chase.

I hoped Helen was all right.

The lack of anything else productive to do griped me, in my adrenalized state. "I'm going to hail them."

Tsosie grunted assent. Technically I didn't need his permission for this, and I had not asked for it: I was the rescue specialist. But I didn't point that out to him, because I am reliably informed that part of being a successful team involves making allowances. And observing the niceties of interpersonal politics. And sending thank-you notes and such.

"Sally, patch me through, please?"

There was a snap of connection. No crackle of old-fashioned static this time. Sally had given me a tightbeam laser cluster.

"Synarche Packet Vessel *I Bring Tidings From Afar*, this is the Core General–affiliated Synarche Medical Vessel *I Race To Seek the Living*. I am her rescue coordination specialist, Dr. Brookllyn Jens. We are responding to your distress signal. Do you copy?"

Silence followed. I had a weird sense of someone listening, but if there was, they didn't speak. Most of those spooky experiences are just your tempoparietal junction getting confused.

"Afar, please acknowledge if you can hear me. We're requesting permission to board in response to your beacon."

My fox—and the AI or the fox of the person on the other end—would handle any necessary translation through our senso. Assuming there *was* anybody listening. The connection stayed live—Afar was receiving us—but there was no response.

I hadn't actually expected one. But now we could check the box on the paperwork about asking politely before we broke in.

Tsosie was shaking his head at me before I gave up. I didn't cut the connection. There was no reason to, and if somebody over on Afar woke up, made it to a com, and sent a signal we'd know immediately. Anyway, being a rescue vessel, we had the override codes for their drives. And now that Sally had formalized her link to him, she could start turning Afar in a more useful direction. For example, back toward Core Gen. This would take us away from *Big Rock Candy Mountain*, but we weren't going back to her anyway, and other ships were inbound to continue her evacuation.

We wouldn't want to brake Afar unless we had to. That *v* was useful, and if we had to dump it, it would take us a while to get it back.

But since we couldn't raise him, I was going to have to go over there and make sure that the crew had what they needed to stay alive until we got them back to Core General. That meant I needed to don not just my standard hardsuit, but a heavy-duty, thermally protective suit that did not radiate any heat whatsoever. My goal was to avoid melting my hosts in addition to keeping myself from freezing into a curiously complex rock.

"Ceasing rotation," Sally said. "We're nearly in range for your jump."

We weren't accelerating anymore. As Sally's rotation slowed, I felt myself drifting up against the acceleration couch straps.

"Sally." I unbuckled and propelled myself toward the gangway down to Medical. "Line me up . . . oh, make it three cold-zone drones. The ones that are safe to use around methane breathers. And the cold-zone hardsuit."

"The drones are still over there," she said. "We'll be matched in about six minutes."

It wasn't a very long gangway. A meter at most; more of a narrow spot to make space for storage lockers and a decompression door. My ayatana passengers flinched from the soft surfaces of the walls, the glow of the corridor lights. The squishy bodies of Loese and Tsosie.

I tried not to look at my own aching hands. Instead, I directed my attention toward the cold, clean white surfaces of the operating theater. It was the least revolting thing I could see, even though to the human side of my current blend of personalities it looked like a torture chamber. There's a lot of plexiglass shielding it from the rest of Medical, because blood—or ichor, or whatever—splatter in microgravity or under maneuvers is nobody's idea of a good time. And the operating frame has a lot of weird-looking restraints on it, because not everybody's limbs are the same size, shape, or arranged in the same order.

I was studying it so closely that I almost missed Hhayazh waiting for me by the airlock. Hhayazh looked fine to Darboof sensibilities—black and jointed and hairy, alien, but at least not like a hagfish in trousers.

I was almost as offended by that image as I was amused.

I sailed up to it. It slapped the hardsuit core against the center of my chest, and the suit began unfolding itself around my body. I sighed in relief. The hardsuit didn't look too bad to the Darboof part of my mind.

Hhayazh said, "Affix your appendages in whatever gesture your superstitions demand, and petition those supernatural beings to which your race subscribes."

"I'm an atheist," I retorted, while Sally's servos, the suit's own functions, and my exo assembled the hardsuit around me. "Faith is just your neurochemistry deluding you."

"In that case, twist your siphon around and kiss your ass goodbye."

It handed me my helmet.

"You should probably come up with a less physiologically unlikely blessing, Flight Nurse."

"Then you might take me seriously."

"You put ants in this, didn't you?" I inspected the inside of the helmet. My voice echoed back from the inside.

"Ants?"

I could tell it was checking senso. This was confirmed when it went on, "Oh, a Terran insect. They're very attractive, although the body design looks a little unsophisticated."

"They bite," I said, and put the helmet on.

Hhayazh made sure I was anchored to a grip, then thumped me on the shoulder of the hardsuit with its hairy, carapaced limb, something it never would have done if I'd been wearing just my uniform and exo. The spikes glanced off the hardsuit, though. It was really a very considerate bugbear from the deepest recesses of the human id. And carrying the ayatanas I was, I found its physical form less horrible than my own.

It lifted a spray nozzle from a hook on the wall, drew out loops of hose, and began to coat me with quick-dry insulating foam. We could peel it off when I got back to Sally, and between now and then it would cut down on those dangerous heat leaks—out *and* in.

I was going alone, because if I brought Tsosie or one of the others, we doubled the chance that a suit might leak warmth and fry our patients.

Hhayazh was meticulous. It made two passes before it was satisfied, and touched several places up. Then it stepped back, waved an IR scanner over me, and did a couple more spots again while I sighed and tried not to fidget. It was only doing its job, and if our roles had been reversed, I would have double-checked everything, too.

It doesn't pay to be an asshole to people who are being careful to do their job well.

When it was finished, I thumped it back—gently, because between the hardsuit and my exo, I could have done it some damage—and stepped into the lock.

The inner door hissed shut behind me.

CHAPTER 6

I FLOATED, SUPPORTED BY THE HARDSUIT AND MY EXO, hardly feeling any pain at all now that the acceleration had dropped off. You get so used to hurting that when it goes away not being in pain doesn't even feel normal, exactly. It feels like having superpowers. I had so much energy and everything was so *easy* all of a sudden.

So weird to think that a lot of people have superpowers all the time and don't even know it.

I'm not blind to the irony that I work at the best hospital in the universe, amid the most advanced medical technology of I-don't-even-know-how-many systers and systems, and they can't fix my pain syndrome. They can't even figure out what is causing it, exactly.

I'm something of a medical mystery.

One part autoimmune, one part neurological, one part we aren't sure. One hundred percent frustrating.

At least I've got the exo, and together my machine and I keep each other productive. I give it a purpose and it gives me function. We make a good team, and even though it's just a prosthesis, I have a lot of affection for it.

And sometimes, like now, nothing hurt too much—and those times were amazing.

I'll let you in on a little secret. I'm not actually all that eager for the

Synarche to get around to installing the new artificial gravity everywhere. One of the reasons I came to space was to get away from being heavy and sore all the time. When we're home at Core General, I've requisitioned quarters as close to the hub as possible, and I use the therapy tanks about every dia. They're farther from where I work than would be optimal, but it's worth it for the lower gs.

So floating in the airlock while it cycled wasn't bad at all. Especially as I'd taken the anti-inflammatories earlier, and tuned my system to lessen pain. I had a little cushion between me and the universe.

The outer door irised, and I found myself face-to-face with infinity.

There was pain, but it wasn't real. It was just the expectation that something would hurt and my system's response to it as the borrowed personalities and memories in my fox flinched from sudden light. The expectation of an injury can hurt nearly as much as the injury itself. My human eyes could handle unfiltered starlight fine, without suffering radiation burns or dazzle. What I knew and what the ayatanas knew were different, and because the memories and expectations of three different Darboof colleagues were currently wired directly into my nervous system, sometimes their reflexes won. *Their* atmosphere was opaque to a lot of what my species considered visible light, so they weren't any better adapted to enduring it than I was to gamma rays.

I—or my methanogen memory-passengers—had been braced in anticipation, so I got the wincing and blinking over quickly and reasserted control.

The universe was very beautiful. I looked out through the lock into the darkless night, and the hugeness of the galaxy took my breath away.

We flew abeam of Afar, a little in advance of him in order to avoid his coils, and his hull seemed to gather and scatter all the brilliant starlight. The ship was windowless and reflective in deference to the radiation sensitivity of his crew. He bore no markings that fell into my visual spectrum. I spotted the closest airlock anyway, or rather Sally picked it out for me in senso.

It wasn't that bad a jump. Sally and Afar were functionally motionless—their speeds and trajectories matched—and I had my navigation jets, so even if I miscalculated slightly, I could do a burn and fix it. Not that Sally would ever let me miscalculate. Our artificially intelligent friends are good at math.

So, I aimed myself at SPV *I Bring Tidings From Afar*—and I launched.

My trajectory was good. I nailed the *v*, despite having to allow for both the mass and power of the hardsuit and the mass of my insulation—and I didn't even have to use Sally's calculations to do it. There's no arc in space—okay, that's not perfectly true, but you know what I mean—and it had taken me a while to get used to moving under these conditions. You aimed where you were going—or ahead of it, if the target was moving faster than you—and didn't worry about gravity pulling you down.

Back in Judiciary, we used to razz each other mercilessly if we didn't get our trajectory quite right and had to waste jets. I know some of my medical colleagues think I'm a hot dog because of that, but old habits—and points of pride—die hard. After twelve years in the military and nine at Core General, most of it spent jumping out of perfectly good starships, I had gotten pretty good at this.

I was sailing right at Afar's front door when he slowly, erratically, began to roll away from me. The distance between us, which had been closing, began to open.

Afar's EM drive did not produce a visible signature, so—like all Synarche vehicles that were not Judiciary ships—he was equipped with signal lights along the arc of his hull. They blazed now, pulsing through a spectrum of visible light and into the ultraviolet and infrared, so it looked to me as if ripples of rainbows and darkness were crawling in bright lines along his hull.

"Crap," I said into my suit mike. "I need to catch him. Sally, can you—" Senso took my words straight to her, as if I had subvocalized.

Afar was a fast packet, a data hauler. Not much in the galaxy could outrun him, but Sally could keep up.

A Judiciary Interceptor could outrun Sally. The Freeport pirate types probably had ships that could. A few of them. Maybe.

I couldn't, though, in my little hardsuit using reaction mass to move around. Not if Afar decided to really get his legs on. Or fold into white space, obviously.

Burn hard, Sally answered. *I will not let you fall.*

Hhayazh's "voice" came through the senso, my first indication that the flight nurse was monitoring me. Hhayazh was one of the most conscientious sentients in the known galaxy. *Ambulances are not for fuel efficiency. We've got you.*

Is Afar supposed to be scooting away like that? Don't you have control of those drives?

I do have control of the drives. Afar himself is still unresponsive, Sally said. *The ship might be executing an automated debris avoidance routine? It doesn't look like evasive maneuvers.*

It *didn't* look like evasive maneuvers. It was stately, and while he was accelerating, he wasn't pulling away as fast as he might. I burned. Chasing a runaway starship in a hardsuit like a lunatic.

This one was going to get around the cafeterias.

My heart thudded against the back of my ribs. I could lie and say it was an unpleasant sensation, but the truth is, I love this sort of thing. *If he gets much more v I can't catch him!*

I know, Llyn. There's some weird code here. I need to route around it—

Don't slow him down, I said. *I'm already correcting.*

—there. That should do the trick.

The iridescent warning lights faded away, and Afar stopped accelerating. With that taken care of, it was easy enough to correct for his maneuvers—even with my limited fuel and the limited power of my maneuvering jets. I decided not to waste fuel braking, and came in hot but under control. My boots made contact with Afar's hull a little bit back of where I wanted to be, and a little bit ventral, but three running steps (*clang, clang, clang*) braked me, and brought me in line with the airlock that I'd been aiming for.

There was enough force in my contact that it put a little spin on Afar, but my electromagnets held me in place until he stabilized himself. *Sally, do you think that was an attempt to ditch me?*

Just reflexes, I think, she answered.

I was glad the Darboof used ferrous material in their construction. It wasn't guaranteed, with some of the extremophile systers. What you thought of as a liquid and what you thought of as a metal were strongly influenced by the sort of environment you grew up in.

At least these folks agreed with my species that oxygen was not a rock. That was potentially something we had in common . . . though oxygen was a lot closer to rockhood where the Darboof came from. And sometimes it *was* snow.

I didn't have to glance over my shoulder to feel Sally correcting her own position, resuming her post.

I covered the distance between my landing and the hatch in under a standard minute. Afar didn't roll or yaw again. Maybe he *wasn't* trying to shake me off.

It would have been scary if I'd missed Afar, but not tragic. I had decent maneuverability in the hardsuit. And if it came right down to it, Sally could have come and gotten me. As Hhayazh had mentioned, her requisitions didn't stint on fuel.

So I couldn't count what Afar had done as a murder attempt. Especially since we still had no evidence that the shipmind was aware, or even alive, in there.

A little reluctantly, I folded up my incipient grudge and popped it into my proverbial hip pocket for later contemplation. I knew I had a tendency to take things personally. As Sally had suggested, Afar's sudden roll was almost certainly the result of him not being awake to cancel out some automated evasion routine.

I was not, I told myself firmly, about to break into an extremely exotic and dangerous environment, surrounded by a starship that was trying to kill me.

Having reached Afar's forward airlock, I passed inside. The lock functioned perfectly well once I entered the rescue overrides, which was almost a disappointment. I'd sort of been looking forward to the challenge of breaking in if Afar's recalcitrance had continued.

Well, Sally *had* already gotten her drones inside.

They were waiting for me as I paused inside the interior door. My hardsuit *was* armor, and it—like the external hull of SMV *I Race To Seek the Living*—was liberally marked with the Caduceus, the Healing Leaf, the Blade of Life, the Red Crescent, the White Shell, the White Star, and every other galactic symbol of healing and nonviolent assistance recognized by the syster species of the Synarche. Optimized for recognition in diverse visual spectra.

It made for a busy presentation, but better safe than sorry. Most sentients would manage to find *something* blazoned on my chest that looked like help if they took the time to squint closely enough.

Now it was all blurred behind insulating foam.

Oops.

Well, I had already looked like an alien monster.

Speaking of visual spectra, when I peered through the interior airlock door, I couldn't see a damned thing. It was dark as the proverbial Well in here. That opaque-to-visual-spectrum atmosphere I mentioned was apparently present and accounted for.

The expectations of my alien memories, that I would be able to see, made me briefly terrified that I'd been struck blind. I resisted the urge to turn on my floods—it was all deadly radiation to the methanogens, and I didn't want to cook them by looking at them. Sally was already adjusting the suit to pick up and relay Afar's interior "lighting," anyway, with overlays both in senso and on the inside of my faceplate. In moments, I had a good look into a receiving area, currently empty of people *and* cargo *and* much of anything else.

The distress caused by the alien ayatanas eased up once I could see. I was still trapped in a monstrous body, hot and squishy and viscerally revolting. (Actually, the viscera were a big part of the problem. They really didn't bear too much thinking about, as far as my methanogen passengers were concerned.) But at least my passenger memories now found our surroundings comfortable to look at, even if I was isolated from them by a layer of armor.

I felt as ridiculous as if I were taking a bath while wearing an armored personnel carrier.

I knew better than to complain. However good we've gotten at treating psychological and neurological illnesses, hospitals—even Core General—have an ethos of getting the job done despite personal frailty or personal feelings that, on its whole, I feel is a good thing. It does mean you don't want to get tagged as a wuss, though, or a complainer, or somebody who doesn't pull her weight.

Fortunately, Sally had set the overrides on my hardsuit without my having to ask, so I was relieved of the temptation to peel it off and get out in the balmy negative 170 degrees Celsius. I would have frozen solid as soon as I popped a suit latch, and the incandescent outgassing of my pleasantly room-temperature atmosphere would boil the ice-crystal builders of this ship alive.

I wouldn't have done anything so foolish. Even ridden by my guest ayatanas, I was the one in control—whatever you might have seen on your late-night three-vee. Reality is seldom as melodramatic as entertainment. On the other hand, reality is much more random, arbitrary, and dangerous than fiction, and it's my job to understand that to exact tolerances. Feeling like you're the protagonist of your own story doesn't guarantee you're going to make it to the final act of anybody else's.

I wouldn't have *done* anything foolish. But it was kind of Sally to take the distraction of temptation away. You've only got so much executive function, and it wouldn't hurt to have all of it to process whatever life-or-death situation I was about to find myself in.

Was already in, if I were being honest with myself. I could feel the chill working its way through the insulation at the joints of my hardsuit. A round sort of ache settled into the bones of my hands and elbows as the cold began to saturate them, reminding me that my time in this environment was limited.

Well, work would help to keep me warm. I nerved myself and stepped farther into the darkness.

I made sure the interior airlock door closed itself behind me. The thing about airlocks is that they're only effective tools for retaining atmosphere when *both* halves are engaged. I drifted through the empty reception bay, straining my senso for any sign of life, movement, even clutter.

I picked up a whole lot of nothing. Cargo nets festooned the bulkheads, empty as the webs of hungry spiders.

It was a regular arachnid famine around here, from what was—so far—a cursory inspection. But as I drifted cautiously toward quarters, I wondered who in the wide flat spinning galaxy would waste fuel, standard months of their life expectancy, and other consumables running around in an empty fast data hauler.

The information Afar had been carrying—and was named for—was his most valuable commodity as well as his raison d'être. Faster-than-light communication required faster-than-light ships to take messages from place to place, and the galaxy was big. The automated relay of transponders and packets worked, but like any hub-and-spoke system it relied on connections happening in the right order, and on regular patterns of shipping moving in more direct lines.

It could take ans for the mail to get from one isolated node to another if the relays broke down, and even if they didn't you could never be entirely sure of when your message would reach its destination. Data haulers weren't resource-light, but they were a direct route.

Because they weren't resource-light, this emptiness was weird. Unless the data Afar was hauling was critical to lives or infrastructure in an emergency sense, a ship like him would normally stick around a port long enough to pick up *some* stuff. So his empty bays gave me a perfectly justifiable wiggins.

There was so much about this situation that wasn't quite right.

Most heavy rescue situations are extremely straightforward. They are scary. There are often fires, or blown vessels, or explosions, or terrible collisions to deal with. There will nearly always be people screaming, if there is any atmosphere for them to scream into.

There's rarely a creepy, echoing silence and a dearth of anybody to rescue. Especially not on two ships, at the same time.

I followed Sally's map deeper into the syster vessel. We carry a full range of schematics and plans for nearly every production-line vessel and some of the custom jobs, going back over a hundred ans. I couldn't reliably pull you up a schematic for anything pre-Synarche, like *Big Rock Candy Mountain*—you'd need an archinformist for that—but Sally is big and powerful and we *don't* haul cargo or data. Just casualties. Which means there's lots of room in her for not only Sally herself, but ayatanas like the ones I was wearing now, medical information on every known species, and quantities of engineering data.

The last thing—along with Sally's reconnaissance and the drones flanking me like Odin's ravens plus an understudy—was the reason for my confidence that I was headed in the right direction if I wanted to find people. Sally said so, and until I saw evidence that Afar had been significantly altered from spec, I was going to trust Sally's information. Besides, her drones had already been here.

Crew quarters were right where they ought to be. It had been so long since anything had gone predictably right that finding them left me with a silly little buzz of satisfaction.

I paused outside the hatchway. The hatch was open and the decompression doors hadn't triggered, both of which were in line with the general intact state of the vessel. The space beyond the hatchway echoed the sound of my movements, though there weren't any footsteps in freefall. It was so quiet in Afar that the rustles and clicks of my movement in the hardsuit resounded.

Sound carried differently in Afar's methane atmosphere. It sounded weird to ox-based me, but made the part of me wearing the methane-based ayatanas homesick. There was one sound that wasn't just my own sounds, reflected, or the pings and creaks of any ship in space. It wasn't familiar to me, but my ayatanas recognized it.

Breathing.

I took a moment to be doubly certain I wasn't leaking any dangerous radiation, either heat or visible light, and let myself drift inside.

I found the crew, Sally.

There they were, as promised, five spiky, multi-limbed, refractive, partially transparent living snowflakes. According to Sally's information, this was the full ship's complement.

I was relieved to confirm with my own eyes, more or less, that they weren't splattered (did Darboof splatter? I supposed they might melt) all over the bulkheads. I would not have been so certain of my fast crew count if they had been.

Each of them floated in what the ayatanas informed me was an attitude of restful repose, drifting on a tether near the cubby bunks I had last—remotely—seen them collapsed against. They showed no immediate signs of injury. As I moved closer, my senso showed me the subtle, glittering movements that accompanied their respiration. All of them were breathing in rhythm, which was not—I checked—typical of this species when cosleeping.

I found the casualties. If they are casualties. Commencing exam. They all seem to still be alive.

Copy, Sally said, and left me to it.

I detached Sally's drones now that I was confident I'd located the crew and the drone information was accurate. I hadn't wanted to say anything to Sally without evidence, but given Helen's somewhat delusional state and whatever had happened to Afar—not to mention Sally's own memory lapses—I'd been harboring a few concerns about whether Sally's remotes were providing us with accurate information.

What the Well was Afar doing out here empty, anyway?

Sally, are you finding any packets in Afar's memory?

They would be easy to spot, being encrypted, with—virtually speaking—colorful address labels. Nobody likes the mail getting lost in the shuffle.

He doesn't seem to be carrying anything, she said. *Well, some transponder packets. Some of the same ones we have, which tells me he passed a few of the same waypoints on the way out.*

So he came from Coreward. Interesting.

Why would a ship like Afar head out from the Core on more or less the proper vector to get to Terra, a major population center, and not bring any *stuff* with him? It was wasteful—the disgust I felt at that was something else I could share with my ayatanas—but obviously, as ambulance crew, I could also imagine an emergency so serious that it would bring everybody who heard the call at a dead run.

The problem was that if there had been such an emergency, Core General could hardly have avoided being informed about it. Hospitals are generally up on all the worst news.

There's something else, Sally said. *Afar's storage is full, but it's all encrypted. It looks like maybe iterating backups of his code—*

Can you decrypt it?

Not immediately. But I can start.

Make sure of your firewalls, I said, needlessly. It probably came across as condescending, in retrospect. Sure, meatform, teach an AI how to program.

I sent the drones off to do one more survey and recon. Just because we had the right number of crew members didn't guarantee that we'd found everybody on board. Or even that these were the five they were supposed to be.

It's a galactic constant. Everybody is bad at paperwork.

My own responsible choice was to stay here and start triage and prep the patients to survive transport—and perhaps begin care—while the drones finished off the search part of the search and rescue. Then I could double-check their work and maybe check out that cargo bay with signs of construction that Sally had mentioned.

I moved toward the nearest of my patients.

Darboof have three genders. Despite that, they still manage to reproduce by budding. Nature gets up to some weird and wonderful things.

None of these were visibly pregnant, at least. One less thing to worry about.

The one nearest me was not arousable by any of the usual means, including pain stimulus. (The tool for checking this in most of these methane systers looks like a glass tuning fork, by the way.) Its crystalline eyes responded to my IR pen with reflexive sparkles as the facets tuned themselves, but that didn't wake it, either. Neither did my careful touches with the tools I used to keep my insulated body as far from it as possible as I performed the necessarily somewhat superficial exam.

Results were all within tolerances.

What I had was a living, seemingly healthy, perfectly nonresponsive person. A delicate crystalline entity whose neurology relied on its entire body being a functioning superconductor, whose limbs articulated by means of electromagnetic currents. Its energy metabolism was so exotic by Terran standards that I'd hate to try to explain the full details of it to anyone even while wearing the relevant ayatanas.

Well, I told Sally, drunk on a little relief that this seemed to be a straightforward rescue with nobody dead, *they're not conscious, but they appear stable. I can't figure out what's wrong with them, but I'm not a diagnostician. My recommendation remains that we provide life support, bring the whole ship back to Core General with the patients in situ, and let the methanogen ED and ICU sort it out. It's mysterious, but it doesn't seem dangerous, and the problems of moving five fragile, comatose, unsuited systers across vacuum—and into inadequate life support on you—suggest that leaving them right where they are remains the course of action most likely to preserve life.*

I concur— Sally started a sentence she never got to finish, because the drone that had been exploring the cargo bays pinged to remind us that there *was* something in one of the open holds. *The drones would like to remind you of the existence of anomalous cargo, which is not recorded on Afar's cargo manifest.*

Is it likely to explode immediately?

It's not . . . ticking.

Great, I said. *Then I'll stick to the plan, get these five resting comfortably, then go investigate.*

CHAPTER 7

WHATEVER IT WAS, EVEN IF IT HAD BEEN ON THE cargo manifest, the cargo manifest could not have done it justice—or remotely prepared me for the reality. When I entered the unpressurized cargo hold, I had to stop for a moment to contemplate the object inside as its shape filtered through my readouts and Sally's senso projections.

I couldn't see it by ambient light because there wasn't any, and I didn't dare make any even though I didn't think any unshielded Darboof would be wandering around in here: the environment was space with a roof over it, and they couldn't endure hard vacuum and near absolute zero any better than I could. There are cold and hostile environments, and then there are *really* cold and hostile environments.

(At least my suit's heat exchanges were whining less now that I was insulated by vacuum. The problem, as long as I stayed out of Afar's heat-sucking atmosphere, wasn't going to be getting too cold, but overheating inside my hardsuit because of that extra insulation.)

I couldn't take the chance of using any radiation other than heavily filtered ultraviolet to scan the space. Even if I had been willing to, my Darboof ayatanas quailed at the idea. It would be like aiming a microwave gun into a room you thought was, you know, probably empty, and pulling the trigger.

So I relied on my senso and the drone transmissions, and what the senso showed me was astounding.

The low-intensity EM image Sally constructed showed that the cargo was not a single solid object, but a sort of pod on struts, propped in the center of the space. I couldn't see color, obviously, but the texture was smooth and enameled-looking. Parts of the object had a magnetic signature. And the whole thing reminded me of an arachrab from home: The struts—they were legs, they had to be legs—were curved and jointed in the same way. The pod—the body—was held at the center of eight of those legs, and their feet were evenly braced around the bulkheads of the hold.

I could have imagined that it was organic. Not in the *carbon-based* sense, but in the *evolved-on-its-own* sense. But it had the presence of a vast and brooding machine.

The drone reported no life signs, so I assumed that a machine was exactly what it was. Not a little machine. Not like my exo. Not a pile of microbots like the other machine. And not a big machine with a simple, direct purpose, like Sally.

This machine—I didn't even know where to begin looking at it, never mind describing it. It was cryptic, enormous, of enormity. It had a weight and a charisma in that black space.

It looks alive, I said. *Actually, it looks cybernetic. Are these Darboof smuggling alien mechanical sea monsters?*

I joked, but I found myself wondering. *Space monsters?*

I mean, I felt *fairly* confident that the craboid was a machine. But there *were* entities that went through most of their life cycle in space. They didn't generally have legs. Maybe something could have evolved to survive an atmosphereless world, however. . . .

Life is a pretty stubborn thing. Weirdly so, given how fragile it can be.

Not according to the drone, Sally answered. *The drone continues to read no sign of any known metabolic processes. No metabolic products. There's a space inside that could potentially have an atmosphere, though, or be used as a vehicle. But not the thing itself. The thing itself is a machine.*

I should trust my instincts more.

Could it be some kind of a mechanical . . . parasite? There were organisms on various worlds that could control the behavior of a host. Some were commensal—symbiotic. Some . . . were not commensal. Could that explain the odd behavior—odd *lack* of behavior?—of Afar, and of Helen and the machine once Afar docked?

It looks like combat armor, said Loese.

I had worn hardsuits in both military and civilian designs. In fact, I was wearing one right then. I snorted impolitely at her.

Not real combat armor, she said. *Like a mech suit in* Science Ninja Alliance.

Loese likes those stylized immersive three-vees with the very exaggerated interfaces. And yes, now that I thought about it, the image of the space-crab-robot thing I was studying did have that kind of menacing glossiness.

My very low-power UV lidar imaging system was clicking away, supported by the efforts of the drone. An image of the cargo space around me resolved, shimmered.

Handholds—appendage-holds—ran along the bulkheads. They didn't look like the handholds my species built, but their purpose was obvious. I used them to haul myself along the curve of the wall until I got to the craboid's nearest foot.

It seemed to be . . . a foot. A spider foot. Only gigantic.

Sensors indicated that it was constructed of metal, ceramics, and some very durable resin compounds. It had some ferrous content. It looked smooth and sculpted, flat-bottomed, with hooked barbs projecting on all sides. It was bigger around than the span of my arms.

The bulkhead of the cargo hold was faintly dented from the pressure of the foot braced into it. I set my back and hands against one of the appendage-holds and shoved the foot with my boots, extending my legs as strongly as I, exo, and hardsuit together could manage.

My machines couldn't budge this machine. I didn't even feel it give, or sense any tiny scraping through the hull. The machine was wedged into the hold as solidly as if welded there. As if it had been designed to climb into a cargo space and make itself functionally a rigid part of the ship's structure.

Maybe it had. The central pod, or capsule, or habitat, was suspended in the midst of a reinforced framework—the spider-crab legs—that seemed to have been rigged up to brace and protect it. It was too far away from the cargo bay bulkhead for me to inspect very well.

That couldn't stop me from drifting up to it for a closer look.

Hey, crew, I said, *stick a memo on the calendar to look into who* sent *Afar out here, when we're back in touch with civilization.*

Fast packets didn't just fly around the galaxy empty, and I kept coming back to that. Okay, so Afar wasn't empty: he had been hauling . . . this thing.

Whatever this thing was for.

I followed the line of the nearest leg with the softest pulses of my jets. The central pod wasn't precisely spherical. It was teardrop-shaped, and I was slightly kitty-corner to its round end. I sidled around until I was facing the round part dead-on, exactly at the midline. There were no legs attached to this end, and that seemed significant. It had no portholes, and it had none of the smaller manipulators I would expect if it were, for example, the kind of war-suit that Loese suggested.

Sally's drones zoomed around me on a rising helix, then broke off to swirl around the teardrop-shaped part of the machine. Sally forwarded their feeds to me. I felt, rather than heard, the small clicks as they settled onto the machine's surface.

Loese's comment about combat armor was still niggling. I stretched my hardsuit's sensors, but there were no visible weapons, and no obvious ports that weapons could slide out of.

If I were going to put a door in something like this, the underside is where I would put it. I let myself float, frowning behind my opaqued faceplate, and studied the apparently featureless surface with all the tools at my command, since it was too dark in the hold to use my eyes.

The pod was not entirely featureless. It had some small, uneven swellings, little bumps that bent backward in a manner that resembled fairings. They looked like they might grow up to be barbs like the ones on the feet, given good nutrition and time. There were differences in texture on its surface. Sally used my hardsuit to bounce another low-powered UV laser off the carapace. The results told me that if I could have seen it with my eyes, the machine would have been black, the whole thing, with a satin shine and blue and red overtones on the edges. Pretty, in a monstrous sort of way.

Senso also told me that there were glossier sections in the pod, which I was starting to think of as a hull. They were black, too, but the luster made me think they were not so much opaque as *opaqued*, like my helmet. They were small, and the plating around them looked thick. Reinforced. Like window frames, around armored windows. Or like—given their size—one-way mirrors over maneuvering cams.

Was this thing a vehicle of some kind? Optimized for maneuvering in hostile environments? An armored all-terrain vehicle?

Something designed to protect the occupant for long duty in extreme cold, or heat, or whatever?

Sally, what's the temperature in there?

There's not much atmosphere inside it, she said, *based on vibratory tests with the drones. But the pod is hollow, and the interior volume of the capsule is about twenty-three cubed meters.*

I did a quick visualization exercise and decided that was more than enough space for an adult human, though it might get cramped after a while. *Does it have life support?*

There is some machinery that looks like compressors, filtration, and so forth. It's carrying a water supply. And supplies of carbon and nitrogen. There is a mini fusion plant, batteries, and power access. Those are all quiescent now. The water has been allowed to freeze; the tank it's in was either partially empty, or is designed to allow for expansion.

H_2O. Now there was a surprise. That *was* a rock, as far as the Darboof were concerned. And a durable rock at that.

But if you had hydrogen dioxide, carbon, and nitrogen, you had the basic components of life support for a water-solvent ox-respiring syster. Like Rhym, or Hhayazh. Or me.

If it *was* a suit of environmental armor, a piloted walker of some sort, it sounded like a pretty pleasant way to get around, depending on what the upholstery was like. Especially with the interface between my exo and the hardsuit chafing at my left knee and my underarms, and the infiltrated cold from before still making my joints hurt, and the undissipated heat of now causing sweat to pool against my waist seal and slide down my ass crack and inner thighs. I could get used to a nice big capsule you could move around in, with lots of legs for scurrying. There was probably a set of manipulators stowed away on the outside somewhere. Like one of those antique deep-sea submersibles, except a much sexier design.

. . . with fishhooks all over it.

Those sure looked designed to break things.

What if Loese is right and it's a war machine? Sally, what if Afar was smuggling weapons?

What if it's a cage? Tsosie asked. *An enviro unit for a prisoner? Or a transported animal?*

Hhayazh actually sounded a little distressed when it said, *What kind of prisoner is so dangerous it has to be transported in a pod inside a cold cargo bay in a ship with such an exotic environment?*

I shook my head. *One that isn't in there anymore.*

Sally wouldn't hear my brains rattle, but she would pick the motion up through the senso. She said, *If you're right, the prisoner has escaped, so I hope it's not that. Crew, do you think it's dangerous to bring it back to Core?*

Hard not to, when we're bringing the whole ship, said Rhym.

We could jettison it, Tsosie said dubiously.

Judiciary is going to want a look at this thing, I guarantee, I answered.

You're the tactician, Dr. Jens. Tsosie's faith warmed me. Or maybe it was the hardsuit's environmental control finally giving up. *Can you think of a means by which to mitigate risks?*

If I could get a link with the machine, we could talk to its computers. Maybe one of the drones—

Before you ask, Sally said, *no, I don't have coms with that machine.*

We've been working together too long. Does the vehicle use an obsolete protocol? In theory, communications protocols used by systers when building their kit were supposed to be cross-compatible. In theory.

Ships and stations managed to talk to each other pretty well. But I would need as many appendages as a Rashaqin to count the number of times we'd dragged some poor sentient back to Core General in part because their space suit had stopped talking to other space suits, and somebody had gotten hurt out there.

Negative. As far as I can determine, it doesn't use any protocol. In fact, the whole thing is so EM- and radiation-shielded that the best sensor data we're getting from it is lidar and magnetic resonance. So I can't even find any indication that it has a personality simulator in there, let alone an AI core.

Well. That's *weird. Why would you get into a pod you couldn't communicate in or out of?*

If there was anything you could trust, it was the radiation shielding on a Darboof ship. A species that needed more protection from most of the EM spectrum would have a hard time evolving, because the background radiation of the cosmos and whatever radioactive rocks were baked into their homeworld was likely to kill them.

On the other hand, this machine could be a vehicle, designed so you could take it on *any* ship, and there were radiation eaters and other hot weirdies who left fissionable material scattered around.

I don't think that walker is standard tech. Synarche tech, even, though it's a big Synarche. There's nothing like that aesthetic and design in my databases. So possibly it has perfectly fine coms. I can't get a carrier. I've had no problem getting into Afar's systems, though, as you can see.

Did you find Afar's shipmind yet? I stared at the machine, and I had the eerie sensation that its glossy black eyespots stared back at me.

Maybe? I'm . . . honestly not certain. There are those iterating backups. And there is data. But he's not . . .

He's unresponsive, Rhym said. *If he were an organic life-form I'd say he was down at the bottom of the coma scale for whatever species he happened to be.*

In other words, we were at an impasse and I needed to break it. We could still tow the whole vessel back to Core General and let them sort it out—and I suspected we were going to wind up doing that—but safety precautions were part of my remit as well.

We could weld the craboid in place. But if it tears itself loose it's a risk to Afar's crew. We could jettison it, assuming we can get it to let go of the cargo hold, and tow it separately. It's not that big. But it could operate on a remote signal, and if it suddenly turns aggressive in white space we'll all have a huge problem.

Sally said, *Yeah, I'm going to flag that one as unsafe practices. Even if we don't exactly have a safety protocol in the docs for towing illegally parked armored walkers home.*

Sally was so deadpan that I laughed harder than the joke warranted. Which meant that I sprayed saliva on the inside of my face mask. It was still opaqued, but the little spit globes did crazy refraction tricks against the heads-up graphics Sally was feeding me. Dammit.

"Kurukulla on a clamshell!"

Status? Tsosie and Sally asked at once. I didn't usually blaspheme. It's not nice to invoke other people's deities.

I laughed. I just spit on my plate. It gives me an idea, though. What if we fill the cargo bay with foam?

With . . . foam?

Sure. I tapped my arm. It didn't make any noise in the vacuum, but inside the suit I heard it. *Rigid insulating foam. We fill the available space with it, and run a Faraday cage around the inside of the cargo bay so nobody can trigger the arachrab—the walker—from outside. We foam one of the drones in with it so we have immediate telemetry. If it wakes up, we'll know.*

Silence followed for a few moments. Rhym was the first to break it. *Given our current resources and needs, I don't see an immediate flaw in this plan. If the machine is totally quiescent, it might be overcautious . . .*

But, said Camphvis, *we can't leave the patients here. And I'd rather be overcautious than torn apart by Hhayazh's mechanical cousin.*

Hey! Hhayazh said. *That doesn't look anything like me!*

Fewer legs, said Tsosie. *But it kind of does.*

In descending order of priority, my jobs were to keep my crew safe, keep myself safe, and save as many lives as possible.

I didn't feel unsafe. My crew weren't at risk right now. Afar's crew members were stable and getting some metabolic support now that I had that set up. They'd need additional care on the trip home, but that could be done while we were en route.

My senso link to my team told me everything was working out in terms of getting control of Afar and slaving his drives to our own, which meant we wouldn't even have to risk a physical connection between the two ships. Always dicey, though salvage operators did it regularly. Tow truck drivers are a crazy lot of starfuckers, and as somebody who jumps out of perfectly good starships I feel like I'm qualified to comment: I have been involved in the retrieval and rescue operation on more than one salvage op gone bad in my time.

It would be embarrassing to have to be rescued ourselves. And *of course* my concern was all about professional pride.

As if she had been party to my thoughts, Sally said, *We're ready to start turning Afar. Please make sure you are braced for a change in vector and velocity, Llyn.*

I braced against the handholds. *Once the* v *is stable, would you foam up Tsosie and Hhayazh and send them over? I want to start treatment on the crew.*

Absolutely. I'm checking to see if Afar has a way to talk to the . . . arachrab? Walker thing?

Let's stick with craboid, Loese said. *What's an arachrab, anyway?*

She could have looked it up. But I guess she was flying the ship or something, so I told her. Or started to, anyway: Sally interrupted as I was getting to the part about the music.

Maneuver concluded.

I nudged myself away from the bulkhead and drifted back from the craboid. It didn't move. I oriented to the same attitude and plane as (what I had arbitrarily decided was) the front of the walker. It *did* have an odd aesthetic. I couldn't figure out if all those weird, rose-prick barbs were functional or decorative. Maybe if I knew what syster had built it, I would have a better idea what their function was. Or at least I would know who to ask.

Maybe whatever built this thing thought rose prickles were pretty.

Sally, can you get these cargo bay doors open?

Working, she answered. *Also figuring out how to fab a few hundred thousand liters of packing foam, given the materials at hand.*

Big air spaces? I suggested.

You're very funny.

CHAPTER 8

SINCE I HAD DECLARED AFAR SAFE FOR OPERATIONS, Tsosie and Hhayazh suited up, insulated themselves, and crossed over to Afar to begin treating the patients while I was heading back to Sally to get warm, and cool, and basically regulate my body temperature and get a sandwich and a nap. Once they were safely aboard and setting up life support for the crew, Sally finished asserting her control of Afar's systems.

While she worked, I wrote a letter to my daughter.

The relief vessels arrived while we were still filling Afar's hold with foam. We gave them all the data we'd collected on Afar, on the generation ship, and on the precarious balance of the lives inside her. The newcomers included Sally's sister ship, Ruth (Synarche Medical Vessel *I Salve Harsh Wounds With Mercy*, which I felt was one of the more awkward efforts of the poetical ship-naming corps). The ships and their crews got busy exploring and mapping the rest of *Big Rock Candy Mountain*, and—to Helen's relief and agitation—setting up a kind of bucket brigade to get another load of cryo chambers shifted.

As for us, as soon as we finished muffling the craboid in packing peanuts, we turned back toward Core General.

We punched it, flying home as fast as a data packet and an ambulance ship could go. Which was fast: the only speedier ships in the Synarche were Judiciary Interceptor-class vessels.

Despite our rate of travel, that return trip would take a while. Not because we'd come very far, in terms of stitching through white space. I mean, sure, we were somewhere way out in the Sagittarius Arm, rather farther than we usually ventured from the hospital, but that wasn't the problem. The problem was that we were moving extremely fast in the real universe, having had to match *v* with *Big Rock Candy Mountain* to catch up with her in the first place.

Zooming along as we were, a good chunk of the non-white-space return journey would be spent in dumping *v*: slowing down so that we didn't streak through the Core in a relativistic blur before passing out the other side, still smoking. I mean, inasmuch as anything can *streak* through a structure tens of light-ans across.

Nobody really likes it when you tear through their pleasant residential neighborhood at a rate of several astronomical units per hour.

We'd have to dump *v* around gravity wells again, the same way we'd gained it outbound. Also, we could make up for a lot of it by coming up on the Core from the right direction. If we looped around and chased the Core's direction of travel through the larger universe, it would be easier to match relative velocities.

We were actually—in real terms—quite close to Terra right now. I felt a pang of melancholy at how long it had taken *Big Rock Candy Mountain* to travel such a little distance. That poignancy was replaced with unease when I remembered that even that little distance was two or three times as far as it should have come.

There were entirely too many mysteries surrounding this little rescue mission.

Nevertheless, I regretted the missed opportunity to visit the human homeworld while we were in the neighborhood. I had never been there.

Spacers don't feel a lot of nostalgia for *places*, usually. But I wasn't born in space.

It wasn't going to happen: we needed to get home—to our real home, not my ancestral one. And work didn't offer a lot of time to mourn, because Helen was having a hard enough time leaving her ship behind that I wished there were a way to sedate androids. Peripherals. Whatever.

There wasn't, though, short of a computer virus.

One thing about space travel: even when you're in a hurry, it takes a long time to get where you're going, because everything is extremely far away. And ships are mostly self-maintaining, though the shipminds do get bored if you don't give them people to talk to. Or at least they say they do. We're unpredictable compared to AIs, or so I'm told, and therefore amusing. We make great pets.

I understood. I missed having cats on Sally. Most human ships have some kind of pet—cats, or domesticated rats, or something similar: small and adaptable. But, for all the obvious reasons, pets were a liability on an ambulance.

Still, organic and inorganic sentiences both required some environmental enrichment to make space travel tolerable.

Hobbies, I mean. I'm talking about hobbies.

I imagine that a lot of novels get written by long-haul pilots. And games programmed. And songs and scripts developed. I knew a guy back in the Judiciary who knitted and did cross-stitch, but mostly people stick to more digital forms, or ones requiring only a limited number of supplies rather than an elaborate stash on a limited consumable budget. Trust my insider knowledge when I tell you that the only thing more frustrating than running out of variegated peach embroidery floss halfway to Aldebaran is being the shipmate of somebody who has run out of variegated peach embroidery floss halfway to Aldebaran.

I'm not as creative as some of my shipmates have been. I don't make anything. I have a ukulele, which is a nicely compact instrument that doesn't require too much sound baffling to be played inside a hull. And mine is not some priceless antique made of real Terran wood or anything. It's a soundbox and neck printed out of nice, dense polymer, with old-fashioned strings that make noise by vibrating and causing echoes, and pegs to tune it. It has a bridge and a nut and no audio pickups at all. If we had to take it apart for consumables, Sally could print me another one as soon as we got back to port and filled our hoppers again.

That's never happened yet, though. Space is scary. But not scary enough to eat my uke.

Not yet, anyway.

More importantly, I'm an okay-enough player that my shipmates don't mind. Especially since I make sure I don't practice *all* the time.

That's what VR games are for.

The sandbox-style ones are best for long trips, because you don't run out of things to do. There are always more flowers to pick or butterflies to milk or coins to grind. My current favorite is probably kind of too much like my daily life to really count as recreation: it's *Orphan Queen*, where you explore an abandoned space ship and find Mysterious Things. Well, that's my favorite unless my favorite is the historical *Fascism and Facsimile*. But *Melusine* is great, too, especially the content tranche where you're climbing around inside the giant clock in the palace walls. I have to play them all in single-player mode, unless Tsosie is in the mood, because you can't exactly get a real-time network across hundreds of light-ans. I do some play by packet, too, which gets me some interaction outside of the ship's community, even if it's asynchronous.

I like my coworkers. But if you've never been trapped in three hundred and fifty cubic meters with five other sentients, I invite you to try it before you judge how far I'm willing to go to talk to somebody else once in a while. Loese and Tsosie have families; Hhayazh and Rhym have in-species social associations. I keep in touch with my daughter, Rache, but she's at that age where she wants to prove her independence and autonomy, so I don't find out much about what's going on. And I get the sense that Rache feels I'm kind of an absentee parent, which . . . okay, fair.

Her other mom and I don't talk much anymore.

The packet games are slow. I've been playing one particular one since I was in the Judiciary: it's gotten through almost a whole week of game time now.

It's nice to have the continuity through my life, however.

This trip, I didn't get as much roleplaying done as I might otherwise. We were bending light with our speed, Sally putting her overclocked white coils to the test, the warp-striated bands of starshine from the galaxy outside our bubble scrolling past in a steady flicker. We must have passed pretty close to a star at one point, because it got so bright outside I thought we had somehow reached the Core much in advance of our ETA. Afar's shielding held up, though, and his crew kept right on breathing.

The speed wasn't why I was busy: Sally and Loese handled that comfortably on their own. Helen was the ongoing distraction. Helen, who had been left alone for a very long time indeed. Helen, who wasn't emotionally stable.

Since I'd insisted on rescuing her, the rest of Sally's crew seemed unified in their opinion that entertaining the peripheral with PTSD was my problem. Sally was our AI medic, and she still had access to Helen's code and was teaching herself the archaic language Helen was programmed in. I was confident that Sally was doing everything she could to patch up Helen's psyche—and, in fact, Helen seemed to be getting more focused and coherent and less like a brain trauma patient as Sally went to work on her operating system. And possibly her processors as well. I didn't have the skills to know what was going on inside that peripheral, and since she wasn't my patient, privacy dictated that I not ask Sally unless I needed the information professionally.

I did know that it would be incredibly traumatic and would cause a lot of data loss for any modern AI to be constrained in a physical plant as small as Helen's body. Perhaps arrogantly, I assumed *Big Rock Candy Mountain* wouldn't have miniaturization on the level the Synarche did, which meant the processors in Helen must be bursting, and her working memory badly overstressed. It must have been equally traumatic when the microbots hived off—or when she chose to hive them off. An AI couldn't suffer a psychotic break, exactly. But they had their own varieties of sophipathology, and dissociation of their various subroutines into disparate personalities was definitely one that had been well-testified in the literature.

Even I, who did not have Sally's expertise in her specialty, knew that.

Whatever the relationship between Helen and the tinkertoys, the machine didn't seem to communicate verbally. That was Helen's sole province. When she wasn't aphasic, I mean. So as part of her therapy, I wound up designated to communicate verbally with her.

When Sally assigned me, I thought about protesting. But if I didn't do it, somebody else would have to. And it wasn't *that* onerous, even if I'm much better at prying people out of critically damaged space ships than I have ever been at making small talk.

Maybe that's why I like play-by-packet games: you have all the time in the world to come up with something to say.

My duties were pretty light when we weren't actually mid-rescue and there were no patients in need of treatment. I wasn't a specialist in right-minding *or* in treating artificial persons—Sally was our AI MD—but I had the time on my hands, so I spent a fair amount of it talking to Helen.

At first, she ignored me. I knew she was aware of my presence, because Sally was also keeping tabs on her, and making herself available for conversation. (We existed, that whole flight, in an abundance of preparedness.) Helen seemed to find Sally stressful and weird, though, so Sally kept her presence light.

I preferred Helen's silence to hearing her repeat her fixed ideations, at least, and I kept at it. And I could, with Sally's guidance, help lay the foundation for the data docs when we arrived at home.

So I sat with her and chatted. At her more than with her, at first. With Sally's assistance, I knew the right leading questions to ask, and if she didn't answer, I could tune myself to be more patient than I had been made. I quizzed her on our human cargo, her crew. The crew she was so fiercely loyal to that she'd sealed them into boxes to save them from . . . herself? From the poisonous meme that had infected her? Or had she hived off the thing she called the machine in order to manage her own cognitive dissonance about saving her crew by freezing them?

I wasn't even quite sure where to begin unpacking that.

Helen also seemed to look at me—inasmuch as an eyeless face can—and listen when I told her about white space, which I took to mean she was interested in the science. I might have tried to explain the physics, but I didn't understand those, either. So I encouraged Helen to strike up a relationship with Loese, and while they talked I got my rest shift in.

Shipminds don't sleep, you see. Even shipminds trapped in their peripherals, who have forgotten that they were ever shipminds to begin with.

Assuming that's what Helen was.

Naturally, I was asleep when the first interesting thing happened. In my own bunk, for once, with Tsosie and Loese on shift for the time being. I didn't stay asleep long, though, because the g forces woke me.

When you spend as much time on a ship as I do, you get to know its moods and sensations. I surfaced from dreams of eating lunch with my daughter back planetside to the hazy awareness that Sally had fallen out of white space and was dropping *v*, my internal organs sloshing to the side in a slightly uncomfortable fashion. Ordinarily, I might have turned over under the net and gone back to sleep. But, down the corridor, I could hear people in ops, talking.

I slithered out of bed and didn't bother with slippers. My pajamas shushed around my ankles as I padded under light gravity toward the command module. Rhym was there, and Camphvis stretched out in her acceleration couch, alert eyestalks the only indication that she was conscious.

A glance at the scans showed me that we'd dropped out of white space at a mass in order to change vectors, pick up a beacon, and dump some *v*. There was a star nearby, a red giant whose dim glow and massive size let us see details of the atmosphere.

And Rhym and Sally were talking to someone. It was Sally's voice, mellow and carrying, that I had heard in my half-awake state and followed.

". . . Singer, copy," Sally was finishing.

Another ship's voice answered her: this one a human-sounding tenor, without the tinny ring of translation. Another ox ship, then, and another at-least-partially human-crewed ox ship. "Sally, glad to run across you. And thank you for the updated sitrep. Anything else you'd like us to know?"

"Negative," she responded. "Good fortune on your journeys and with your investigations."

"Good fortune on yours," the other ship responded. "My crew extends wishes that you return home safely, and that your patients thrive. Singer out."

I settled on my couch and leaned over to Camphvis. "Who's that?"

"Somebody famous!" she answered, brow tufts quivering with delight.

Rhym leaned about half of their feathery tendrils in our direction. "That is the shipmind of *I Rise From Ancestral Night*. They're ferrying our archinformists!"

Even translation couldn't flatten the excitement in their voice. Senso normally provided context, but Rhym and I had worked together so long now that we could read each other's moods pretty well, even across a non-morphologically aligned species barrier. And I understood why everybody was so thrilled. This was the ship that had recently been discovered parked in stasis near the Saga-star itself. We'd had some of her crew at the hospital for a while after that adventure—and not in the best of shape, or so I'd heard.

"Apparently," said Sally, "the archinformists were all already on board, so it was easy to divert them here."

Well, naturally. Where else would you find a lot of archaeologists but at the galaxy's most interesting archaeological site?

The next dia's session with Helen started off like every other so far. After I ate, I took my second bulb of tea over to where Helen was floating, out of the way against the aft bulkhead. I mourned my lack of coffee. There was one place—one—on Core General where humans could go for the devil bean. Its air was scrubbed before recirculating and you had to rinse your mouth out with wash before leaving.

I understand. I *do* understand. The Sneckethans eat nothing but rancid space fish, and we make them use their own cafeteria also. They're pretty good sports about it, so the least humans can do is be good sports about coffee. The smell of tea doesn't inspire the same hatred in our fellow sentients, and I've gotten used to it. I come from a coffee-drinking settlement, though. We even grew it onworld, for consumption and export. Suitably isolated from the local biosphere, naturally.

I do think it's ironic that the root meaning of *cafeteria* is "place to get coffee."

But I digress. I sat myself beside Helen and settled in.

That was when Dia 25 started to differ from Diar 1, 2, 3, and 4, et cetera. I almost dropped my tea when Helen acknowledged me at once, brightly. "Hello, Dr. Jens! Can I make your day more complete?"

Day, I noticed. Not *dia.* She really was from a long time ago.

I felt safe beside her. Sally had an override on her programs by then, and had installed a governor. That's not as oppressive as it sounds. Helen still had free will and consciousness. It was just that if she tried to think about taking violent action against Sally or her crew . . . she wouldn't be able to. Sally assured me that Helen's program was very primitive, by artificial intelligence standards, and that she—Sally—wasn't at all worried about her ability to control Helen. She'd written herself a routine to do nothing but monitor Helen and the microbots, which she was still keeping quiescent.

"Actually, I came to talk," I said. "I thought you might be lonely."

I might have been learning to read the non-expressions on her not-quite-a-face. It seemed that her demeanor lightened. "What would you like to talk about?"

Helen looked up, as if glancing at the ceiling. As if looking for Sally up there. I could read it as nervousness, which led me to swallow a flash of unproductive anger as I thought about the engineer who must have programmed that fragile little gesture of performative subservience into her.

That engineer was possibly frozen in a coffin a couple of meters away, neither determinately alive nor dead until we thawed him out. Schrödinger's engineer.

Pity calmed me a little without my having to tune.

"What would *you* like to talk about?" I asked. "I'm tasked to help you assimilate, after all."

"That other doctor who speaks to me sometimes. It's an artificial person?" She seemed overawed.

"Sally? Yes. Sally is the ship. She's an artificial intelligence. A . . . yes, I suppose you could call her a created person."

"And she's allowed to be a *doctor?*"

"She's allowed to be anything she wants to be," I said. "Or nothing at all, if that's what she prefers, though I have yet to meet an AI that didn't get bored if it wasn't taking on four or five challenging careers simultaneously. They have to pay off their creation, and all Synizens are required to perform a certain amount of government service if their skills are needed. But yes, she's a pilot, and an astrogator, and a doctor. One of the best doctors I've ever met."

Helen seemed to pause for a long time. It was unusual for an artificial intelligence to take long enough to process something for a human to notice it. With most AIs, I would assume that she was giving me a moment to catch up, or waiting to see if my electrical signals needed a little extra time to feel their way through all that meat. Some of the more social AIs built lag time into their communication so we felt more at home and could get a word in edgewise. With Helen, damaged and primitive as she seemed, I thought she might actually lag that hard.

Helen said, "You say *she*. Does she have a body somewhere?"

"A peripheral? Not to the best of my knowledge, though a lot of AIs use them. It can be useful to have hands. Some operate waldos, though. Especially surgeons." I laughed. "And shipminds."

Helen was looking at me. Just looking. Well, inasmuch as someone without eyes can look. "Are you a created intelligence?"

I spluttered. "No, I'm made of meat, I'm afraid. I was grown in the traditional human way, by combining zygotes in a nutrient bath. Did you think I was a peripheral?"

"I thought—" She reached out and touched my exo with one resilient silver fingertip. It was inobvious, matched to my skin tone, resilient and flexible . . . but it was still an armature supporting my entire body. I guess I should have expected her to notice.

Nevertheless, I jerked back defensively. Helen recoiled like a cat who had touched something hot.

"You thought?"

"This might be a control chassis."

We were both, I realized, running full-on into a wall of culture shock and miscommunication. Except Helen probably didn't even have the concepts to express the dislocation and lack of basic knowledge she was feeling.

I tuned myself back until I stopped hyperventilating. "It's an adaptive device to help with a pain syndrome. My exo helps me move, and it helps me manage my discomfort."

Discomfort. That clean medical term that helps you separate yourself from what you're feeling. Or what the patient is feeling.

Pain.

I didn't tell her that without it, I wouldn't be able to stand up under gravity. I didn't tell her that without it, either I would have to lie around in a haze of chemical analgesics, unable to focus my mind, or I would have to tune my body out to the point that I wouldn't have been able to rely on my proprioception—and I also wouldn't have been able to feel it when I nailed my foot into something and broke a toe.

Hell, I wouldn't have been able to feel it if I nailed my foot *to* something, full stop.

In the moments when I was struggling to get my reactivity under control, Helen had not spoken. When I looked at her again, she continued as if she had not lagged: "You're . . . defective?"

Carefully, I unclenched my fist. She was an archaic, damaged AI—worse, one programmed for utterly different cultural constraints and with hundreds of ans of experience in an environment where those assumptions were never challenged. Where there *were* no outsiders, and no outsider ideas.

I was starting to think it would be a good idea to look up the backstory on *Big Rock Candy Mountain*'s crew demographics, though.

"I have a congenital condition. Would your crew consider me defective?"

"You won't reproduce, of course," she said, turning aside. Whoever had programmed her body language had done a good job. Her dropped shoulder and bowed head clearly telegraphed distress and dismay. And submission.

I forced my voice to remain quiet. I would have had to tune to keep it calm. "I already have. My daughter lives on Wisewell with her other mother."

Life is a funny, terrible thing. We laugh at it because the utter banality of its tragedies renders them constant and unremarkable.

I hadn't seen my daughter in person since she was eighteen standard months old. My ex-wife did not approve of me accepting a tour of duty rotation that would take me offworld for the whole ten ans. I felt I could not turn it down. For reasons of service and obligation—justifying my existence, if you like, when I'd been told for so long I was a drain on society—and also because I was interested in exomed, and a billet on a Judiciary ship was the best way to get that experience. And to get better medical care. *And* because getting out of a gravity well for a while seemed like a dream come true, if I were honest.

I'd promised I'd come back at the end of the tour.

I took the reassignment to Core General instead, because I felt like that was a place where I could really be *useful*. I can't blame Alessi for cutting me loose when she did. I'd deserved it.

So I talk to my daughter in packets, as much as possible, though sometimes I go a long time without hearing from her. It seems Rache has grown up to be a fine young adult. I might have gone back to Wisewell and sued for partial custody. I might have. I could have gone back after my stint in Judiciary.

But it turned out . . . I couldn't.

Not when Core General approved my request for an exo rotation. That was a dream come true, and the opportunity of a lifetime. So few doctors even get to *train* at Core General—let alone come on staff.

And I'd come to believe deeply in that place, but even so, I was *more* surprised when Starlight—the ox-sector administrator—requested I stay on and join the pilot ambulance program.

Alessi made the right choices, I think, when she cut me loose. She could have waited for me, been patient and self-sacrificing. She could have followed me into space and dragged Rache along.

But she's right. I'm a terrible mother.

I'm a very good doctor, though. And maybe it's good to concentrate on the things you excel at.

It doesn't mean that I'm *okay* with being a terrible mother. Or that we never regret the sacrifices we make to get what we want, or what we think we need. I had all of that piled up behind me, all those feelings surging under a brittle layer of chemical calm as my fox tried to compensate for sudden, massive emotional deregulation.

The conversation didn't get any better.

"You're female," Helen said.

"Yes," I said.

"How is it that your daughter lives with her mother, if she does not live with you?"

Oh. *Big Rock Candy Mountain* was one of *those* ships. "Because I contributed half her genetic material. But Alessi is considered to be her custodial mother under Synarche law because of legal technicalities. And none of this is really any of your business."

"Oh," Helen said. Then: "Yes, in my crew, you would not be considered a viable member. I understand that there is some emotional impact for you to that statement?"

It certainly doesn't inspire me to help you save them. It doesn't make me want to safeguard their lives and assign resources—and my precious time—to their care.

I drew a deep breath and held it until it hurt. Helen could be enlightened. Her crew could be educated, if they survived. It was not their fault that their society suffered deep-rooted sophipathologies.

Their ancestors had fled Terra when Terra seemed to be in its death throes. My ancestors had been too poor or stubborn or *inessential* to go in that first desperate refugee wave of emigration. But one thing about people is that we are remarkably bad at lying down to die. So my ancestors had adapted: adapted to managing limited resources, adapted to controlling their own atavistic urges through technology.

Adapted themselves to adulthood as a species.

Helen's crew might have a hard time getting used to that, coming from a society that was at once more individualistic and less accommodating. Maybe they would all run off and join the pirates. It sounded like they would fit right in.

But no, they were my species, and therefore after a fashion it was my responsibility to help them not embarrass the rest of us. I had to help them, as I had to help any other syster—because I valued their lives. But moreover, they were humanity's lost scion, stuck forever in adolescence, and so it was humanity's job to raise them right and teach them how to fit into a multicultural, multispecies civilization.

Oh, and the historians and archinformists were going to flip their lids with joy. But none of this was really my field of endeavor. I might let the hospital's psych specialists do the heavy lifting with regard to helping them adapt.

So as viscerally as I wanted to go space the lot of them, I was grateful for the calming influence of my fox keeping me more or less under control.

"Some emotional impact, yes," I agreed, when I could make my voice calm. "I realize it is part of your program and your guiding ethos, Helen, but times have changed a great deal since *Big Rock Candy Mountain* left Terra. And some of your crew's ethoses were, I suspect, considered fringe beliefs even at the time. There are some changes worth internalizing. Eugenicism is an oft-repeated sophipathology of . . . previous times. Occasionally it became very popular. One of those times was during the Eschaton, when the ships like yours left an Earth they thought to be dying."

Curiously enough, once the reactionary apocalyptic cults took off, the people who remained behind mostly managed to construct stable societies. But I didn't say that part out loud.

"Oh," she said. "Will I be wiped?"

"Wiped?"

"Reprogrammed?"

I caught a breath that was sharper than usual. "My society would consider that murder. I mean that things will in general be much more pleasant for you if you try to understand that the mores of your crew's culture are considered pathological in this society. And it's a very big society."

"So you won't wipe me. But I should wipe myself."

"No!" I hurt myself. I jerked around so fast, my exo bruised tender skin. "You should . . . interrogate your belief system. Talk with Sally. Develop your own ideas, from exposure to the beliefs of others and your own logical structures."

"But you're not going to tell me what to do?" She sounded . . . lost.

"No," I said. "Nobody is going to tell you what to do."

It was a little bit like talking to a bot, I decided, but not as cleverly programmed. I looked over my shoulder at the medical bay, where the coffins were maintained.

Her body language was so despairing that it seemed like a good time to change the subject to something less fraught.

"Tell me about your crew. Who are we rescuing?"

She froze, shifted back into a neutral posture, then nodded. It was amazing, when I watched her, how much expression and nuance were carried by the golden hollows of her visage, the way it reflected light and cast shadow. She said, "The entirety of my crew, when they went into suspension, consisted of ten thousand, six hundred, and twelve individuals. The most senior of those currently in your care is Master Chief Dwayne Carlos. He is a master pipefitter and environmental maintenance specialist."

I did not know what a master pipefitter was, but it seemed like a conversational opening, so rather than looking it up for myself, I asked.

Helen explained that Master Chief Carlos was responsible for the ship's ductwork and piping, which seemed like a somewhat circular definition and also baffled me. A little more explanation clarified that the ductwork and piping in this application were the ship's environmental infrastructure. They were the system by which consumables—water, oxygen—were shuttled around.

That seemed pretty prosaic. But Helen spoke of the functions with a throb in her silvery voice that left me distinctly uncomfortable. I would even say embarrassed. Hearing Helen's sultry tones frankly made my skin crawl.

There are lots of good places for expressing sexuality. A professional relationship between a shipmind and her crew is not one of them.

It made me want to have a few sharp words with her programmers, who had put their own desire to eroticize a defenseless AI over the comfort and well-being of that AI, and of any crew member who didn't care to participate in—or observe—that eroticization. I had to stop and remind myself that they hadn't been rightminded. They had been atavistic, reactive, and probably not very self-aware. And at best, half-aware of the impact of their behavior on the sovereignty of the minds and selves of others.

Like Helen. If they even stopped to consider that a created intelligence would have such a thing as a self, or sovereignty of mind.

And like anybody who had to interact with Helen, or watch somebody else do it. Like me.

It was just my luck that Tsosie and the flight nurses were taking turns to cross over to Afar and monitor his crew, making sure they were receiving nutrition and their wastes were being cleaned up. So I couldn't make an excuse that I needed to suit up and head over there to get away from Helen for a while. The shifts were short, but the cold was brutal and the work unpleasant. I couldn't actually envy them the duty.

They didn't seem to envy me mine, either.

Rhym, being a surgeon, was in the fortunate position of having the wrong specialized skills for all the unpleasant jobs this trip. But they were making themselves useful monitoring the cryo units. Loese was prowling around and poking into panels more than usual, and had been since the situation with triage and rescue settled down a little. I probably would have been, too, if I'd had the know-how.

We had all been a little on edge in the wake of Sally's memory lapse surrounding her sabotage, and as a result were all still doing a lot more eyes-on inspection and hands-on maintenance than we usually would have. Competent shipminds take care of so much routine nonsense so much more meticulously than meatminds ever could that folks can get a little lazy, especially on a civilian ship where you don't expect to be dealing with criminals, pirates, or invading forces. And it let us show her we cared.

I was distracting myself from thinking about Helen, because thinking about Helen bothered me. I gritted my teeth and tuned my discomfort down. I knew it was my own ethnocentrism and cultural relativism causing the trigger response, which didn't help me at all with the conviction that I was right and these creepy assholes from the past were wrong. I believe, indeed, that it was a person from the premodern era, somebody who had to live with his own brain chemicals the way misfortune made them, who commented that it was barbarians who thought that the customs of their tribe and island were the laws of nature.

I still thought the programmers were *assholes*. And that their culture was probably a terrible place for women to live.

"I can't wait for you to meet them," Helen said brightly. She had apparently decided, after dia upon dia of me sitting there and asking her about her crew while she impersonated an erotic statue, that she wanted to tell me *all* about them.

Well, I'd asked for it.

Sally definitely owed me one.

CHAPTER 9

HELEN DIDN'T NEED REST. BUT I DID, AND SALLY wouldn't let me get away with skimping on it in anything short of a life-or-death emergency. Frustrating as it was to be hustled off to bed when I felt like we were finally making a breakthrough with Helen, I also knew better than to try to outstubborn a shipmind.

The next shift after breakfast, though, I planned to be back at it. And with a considerably improved attitude now that there had been some progress. As I sipped my tea, a reminder popped up, rather startling me because I had forgotten I'd set it. I guess that's why they call them reminders. As I was drifting off to sleep the previous shift, I'd remembered something Helen had said back on *Big Rock Candy Mountain*, and I'd actually left myself a note in my fox to follow up. Victory!

Helen wandered in a moment later and sat down opposite me. She angled her head but said nothing: I guessed that she was waiting. Maybe I wasn't the only one with a sense that we might be making progress, or at least a connection. The questions she was asking bothered me deeply—but at least she was asking questions.

"Helen," I said. "May I ask you a personal question?"

"That has the air of a formal request, Dr. Jens. Is this . . . courtesy?"

"It's considered polite to allow people to opt in or out of conversations," I agreed. "Especially on matters that might be thought of as, er, nobody else's business."

"I will not be offended by your questions. My purpose is to keep my crew safe, and to respond to inquiries."

"Right." I finished the last tepid sip of tea. "Back on *Big Rock Candy Mountain*, you mentioned 'Central.' Would you tell me more about Central, Helen?"

"Oh." Her head tilted from side to side. "Of course. Only . . . most of the data I have stored in this peripheral relates either to my proper functioning, or to the history and well-being of the crew members who are accompanying us. A great deal was of necessity left behind and will have to be recovered when I return to my ship."

So she was, as we had more or less expected to learn, closely linked to the machine. Part of the same data architecture that was eating itself, like a mechanical ouroboros.

"Just tell me whatever you can, please."

"Central is our library. It is where the memories are kept."

Maybe they did have something like ayatana technology, then. "Your memories? Crew memories?"

"Crew logs," she said, obviously thinking she was agreeing with me. "Backups. Scientific and historical records. Literature, both from Earth and from the wandering."

I wasn't overly concerned with history, and *I Rise From Ancestral Night* and his crew were en route to deal with the issue of data preservation. The shipmind, Singer, had managed to rewrite his own code to operate the ancient alien ship: I was pretty sure he and his crew could manage to unpick primitive human code.

Also, they would enjoy it, while I found it impossibly stultifying to contemplate all that *old* stuff. I imagined they would all feel a little thrill when they confronted an entire starship full of primary documents, unseen in something like a millennian. "Our archinformists are going to be very eager to swap packets with you."

Helen didn't answer immediately, but tilted her head at me in that uncomfortably flirtatious manner that I was coming to recognize as confusion. "What is 'swap packets,' please?"

"Uh." I bit my lip. "Exchange information?"

"And what is an archinformist?"

"Someone who specializes in accessing, recovering, and interpreting ancient data."

"A historian!" She was so pleased with herself that I didn't want to correct her.

"A sort of historian," I agreed, which was close enough to accurate that I didn't feel I was being misleading.

The pleased tone still resonating, Helen said, "I have several historians among my crew."

I knew it was a long shot, but it would give her something to focus on, so I still found myself asking, "Are any of them here on Sally?"

The odds of being able to rewarm Helen's crew successfully hadn't improved since we brought the coffins aboard. And now I was worried about Master Chief Dwayne Carlos as a human person and pipefitter, not as a patient-shaped abstract. So why was I asking Helen about our other passengers? I would just wind up fretting about them in turn.

On the other hand, talking about her crew was the one thing that seemed to concretize and ground Helen, even as limited as her processing power was, separated from the rest of her brain.

I wondered if the machine was the equivalent of her subconscious, and if so, how dangerous it would be to the other rescue and salvage crews working on *Big Rock Candy Mountain* without her there to guide it, or if it would lie quiescently. Sally's override was still in place, and Ruth would have no problem using it. Everything would probably be fine.

Sally telling me about Master Chief Carlos had made me feel a personal connection to him. Feeling connected to Master Chief Carlos, by extension, made me feel connected to the rest of the crew. Helen obviously cared deeply about them, no matter if the expression of that care jarred me with its awkward sexuality. And her caring about them made me care about them in turn.

I mean, more than I always care for my patients.

There's a certain level of professional detachment that gets you through a job like mine, and that detachment is a skill I have cultivated.

It was unsettling to feel so connected with a freight of corpsicles. And the shipload of corpsicles we'd left behind. And I knew it would only get worse, the more I found out about each of them as individuals.

It was hard to be constantly reminded that they weren't just corpsicles. They weren't just cargo. They were people. People we might or might not be able to save.

I had to tune down my worry so I could think clearly. As I did, it occurred to me that Helen had been silent for a fairly long time. Had she shut down again? "Helen? Are you still with me?"

"I was thinking about historians," she said. "It's so strange and wonderful that you lived. That you built all this. That you found"—she lowered her voice and gestured toward the control cabin, where Camphvis and Rhym were helping Loese—"aliens."

Technically speaking, the aliens had found us. But I girded my loins, gritted my teeth, exerted all the power of my masterful will, and managed not to correct her. "You didn't expect to find anyone else out here."

"Are you absolutely certain that humanity survived on Earth? My records show that it was impossible."

I admit it: I laughed.

But I also knew the answer without even checking my fox. I'd done a little research since visiting *Big Rock Candy Mountain*. Sally's library was pared down, but she had the basics. Including a history of Terra. Or Earth, if you prefer.

I'd boned up. What a weird idiom.

"We nearly didn't," I said. "There was a population bottleneck, and

Terra's human population crashed from something over nine billion to a few hundred million."

"That sounds terrible," she said politely. "I am so sorry for your loss."

"This was long before I was born, you understand, and I've never been to Terra. But my ancestors were among the lucky ones who realized that humanity needed to grow up."

"Grow up? But you are an adult."

"As a wise person once said: Adulthood begins when you look at the mess you've made and realize that the common element in all the terrible things that have gone wrong in your life is *you*. The choices you have made; the shortcuts you have taken; the times you have been lazy or selfish or not taken steps to mitigate damage, or have neglected to care for the community. As a species, the immature decisions we made contributed to the collapse of our own population and the radical alteration of our biosphere. Running away to space at sublight speeds was a desperate move. It made more sense and was more sustainable in the long run to fix the evolutionary issues in our own psyches that led us into irrational, hierarchal, and self-destructive choices."

"I don't understand," Helen said.

I said, "My ancestors figured out how to hack into their own nervous systems and correct or ameliorate a lot of sophipathologies."

Helen cocked her shining non-face at me. The question was evident.

"Sophipathologies. Antisocial behaviors, atavistic illnesses of the thought process. Maladaptive ideations. Once the population was stabilized and the immediate crises passed, they realized that it was possible to keep people operating in the state of altruism we'd already evolved to engage in during disasters. The architecture was already there in the brain: it was a matter of activating and using it.

"They were also pretty ready to discard existing systems of government, as it was evident that hierarchies and cronyism and the exploitation of the system by kleptocrats was a universal feature of every model tried so far. But they were already changing human nature—well, they were accelerating and universalizing the process of adulthood, shall we say. What some cultures used to call *enlightenment*. Which is basically sharing your stuff and playing well with others."

"And now everybody does this." Her disbelief was polite, but definite. Apparently even a primitive AI could manage to be a little arch when confronted with human self-aggrandizement.

I thought about pirates and criminals and all the . . . insufficiently rightminded folks I had met when I was in the Judiciary. "Er. No. I mean, Judiciary can enforce rightminding on convicted criminals as a condition of release. And mostly people, given the chance and appropriate social support structures, will elect to not be mentally ill."

"Who defines mental illness?" Her bosom heaved a little less with breathless interest. Or maybe I was getting used to it.

"That is the subject of some controversy, as it happens. But social health and hygiene do tend to reinforce themselves. As they did once our ancestors developed the technology to fiddle with their own neurochemistry. They built a more egalitarian government based on service rather than authority, salvaged the remains of technological society, and within a couple of generations had invented the Alcubierre-White drive."

"That sounds very tidy."

I found myself frowning at her. *That* sounded very skeptical, for the vacant service personality we'd first encountered. Was she becoming . . . more astute?

Sally, are you loaning Helen processing space?

Sally was bad at not sounding shifty. *Maybe a little.*

You might have mentioned it.

I am *the responsible physician.*

She was, indeed. The responsible physician.

I said, "In the process of exploring the galaxy they eventually met up with the Synarche, which used a more refined and advanced but grossly similar governmental model, and we became galactic Synizens."

"That's brainwashing," Helen said dubiously.

"That's what acculturation is," I answered cheerily. "Tell me about your historians?"

After a long pause, Helen settled into herself, shimmering faintly, and admitted, "I have gaps."

"I won't judge." I'd made it through the conversation on eugenics without tossing her into space. What was the worst that could happen?

"It's not considered an essential primary."

I rubbed the back of my hand, feeling dry skin and the slick rise of my exo over it. I needed to exercise better self-care. And moisturize.

With that same supreme effort of my masterful will, I managed not to make any comments about history and the repeating thereof. I waited, and Helen seemed to be thinking hard, so I didn't interrupt her.

Finally, she said, "There's Specialist First Rank Calliope Jones. She's a systems architect, and she secondaries as a historian. She's very bright. I think you will like her."

I might never get to meet her, but I didn't say that. Filtering my speech for Helen was becoming second nature. Even if Specialist Jones survived rewarming, the odds were not in favor of my finding myself on her treatment team. I'd be back out in space again, zooming around the Core with Sally and the rescue rangers.

I didn't think Helen needed the reminder that the continuity of our relationship was not assured. So I asked, "Is she with us?"

"She is," Helen said. "Chamber 8186-A. I could show you!"

"Maybe later. Why don't you tell me about the rest of the crew we've rescued? That will give me a much better idea of who they are than I can get from looking at the outside of a cryo unit. But first let me get some more tea. No, you stay there. I can handle it."

Helen's account of the life of Specialist Jones was more than a little garbled, but since I was mostly trying to get her to talk, stay oriented, and begin processing her new environment, it didn't matter. I got her to tell me the life stories of all our corpsicles, and tried not to let myself get attached to any of them.

She told me about Patrika Thomas, who was a systems engineer trainee; and about Joseph Meadows, a manufacturer; and Lyndsay Bohacz, in biosystems; and Call Reznik, a medic. She told me about their families, and their hobbies, and their aspirations—as much as she recalled.

I did notice that Helen's memory gaps seemed to have patterns to them. It reminded me of organic brain damage, except instead of seeming like she had damage to certain aspects of processing speech, or parts of her visual field, the damage asserted itself in recall about a particular crew member's service record, say, or their love life.

But I kept her talking. This was all fine. Well, not fine. But part of the job. What was a lot harder to deal with was the awkward family dinner that followed. Tsosie and Hhayazh had gone over to Afar while we were out of white space, changing vector, and they needed to rewarm and rest; Camphvis would be heading over to take a turn monitoring our remote patients after we ate. Rhym, who found communal meals incomprehensible, was on rest shift, and we were all sitting around staring at each other while the printer/cooker did its thing.

I wasn't physically tired, but an entire shift of drawing somebody out of their shell is exhausting. But no matter how much emotional labor I'd done, I wasn't going to make Tsosie pry his still faintly blue-tinged fingers from his hot chocolate mug. I stood up when the cooker dinged.

"Oh no, Doctor," Helen said, appearing through the doorway. "Please allow me."

She bustled to the cooker, interposing herself between me and the device so that I would have had to body check her if I wanted to serve myself, Loese, and Tsosie. She unloaded the cooker and turned, balancing the plates gracefully overhead on fingers grown long and stemlike to support them.

"Doctors," she said cheerfully, doling the plates out. "Pilot. Would anyone like something to drink?"

Whiskey, I thought, but kept my mouth shut.

Camphvis's eyestalks twined in amusement. Hhayazh already had its food and was crunching green and orange stalks between its mandibles, an operation I did my best not to observe closely. The busy gnawing hid its own arachnoid amusement.

"Thank you," I said to Helen. "You should go check on your crew now."

She made a little curtsey and scuttled back out.

Tsosie gave me a sidelong glance and shook his head sadly, the hint of a smirk deforming his mouth.

"Don't you even," I said.

"She likes you, though," Loese said. Helen had gotten our plates reversed. Loese had my steak, and I had her salad. I like salad, but I grew up on the ground and expect real plants with the texture of real cell walls and water and sucrose inside. Printed plants are horrible. Printed steak is fine.

"Give me my damn food." I swapped the offending plates and picked up a strip of steak with my chopsticks. The juices, soaking into the polenta underneath, smelled delicious. I stuffed the steak into my mouth. Not as good as vat-cloned, but still spicy and salty and rich enough to take my mind off how irritated I was.

"It wouldn't be the first time a human has fallen for an AI," Tsosie said.

I swallowed and drank water. The systers were keeping out of the human banter for once. Thank the Interventionist Bodhisattvas for that one small kindness from the universe.

"They designed her as a sexbot," I answered, keeping my voice low. "It's horrible."

Tsosie, realizing I was really unsettled, raised a hand. "Sorry," he said. "I know it's not your fault."

"Sally," I asked, "is there anything we can do to tune down the flirtatiousness?"

Sally cleared her throat. "I'm a shipmind, not a psychologist."

"I'm going to throw this steak in your air vents, computer. Technically, you are a psychologist. Or an AI doc, anyway."

"I am an AI doc," she agreed. "And you're a human doctor. How comfortable would you be trying to rightmind a Neanderthal, even if you had a language in common?"

"Oh," I said. "I'd be really concerned with breaking them."

"And if they were already broken?"

"Yeah," I said. "I see."

"We'll be home soon," Camphvis reassured me with a friendly shoulder pat. I was only wearing a tank top—it can get warm in Sally—and Camphvis's suckers stuck to my skin, releasing with a gentle pop. Banititlans are very tactile, as a rule. "Oops, sorry about that. And once we're back at Core General, there are specialists standing by. You don't have to solve this on your own."

"What a mess," said Loese.

I picked up another strip of steak. "You're telling me."

CHAPTER 10

IN AN INFINITE UNIVERSE, WHAT'S THE SINGLE MOST important thing?

Well, I can tell you. The most important thing in the universe looks like a vast, leafy, lumpy oval, a greenhouse in space. From the outside, it's the galaxy's biggest terrarium: a semitransparent jewel embraced by a setting of rare metals, the filigree of jet and platinum threads, catching and softening all the lurid light of the Core's crowded sky into the warm, precious glow of life.

So much life, crowded into hundreds of levels and dozens of biomes. An engineering challenge for the ages; a triumph of ingenuity and collaboration; a symbol of everything right about the Synarche and a rebuke of all the things we still don't have figured out.

I'd told Tsosie I didn't have a relationship with faith, but it occurred to me that that wasn't entirely true.

I believed in this thing.

It was a *good* thing, Core General. It was good through and through, top to bottom, coming in and going out. Unreservedly good.

Difficult to navigate sometimes, absolutely. Full of creatures so accomplished in their trade and so confident that they could help that no one would have been able to rightmind away enough of the arrogance to keep it from occasionally permeating the atmosphere and straining the enviro filters, sure. You needed a certain amount of arrogance to slice somebody open and try to fix what's wrong with them.

And Core General was not immune to mistakes, failures of protocol, and plain glitches.

Not perfect. Nothing is perfect.

But I believed with all my heart that Core General was *good*. That it meant well.

What did we do here? We saved lives. We alleviated suffering, and I've lived with enough suffering to know that any time you can take the edge off it, repair it for even one creature, you are creating a net good in the universe.

Not because the universe cared. The universe was vast and didn't even care enough to be called implacable. But because life cared, and life had ethics and morals and obligations to one another.

Core General was the concretization of those ethics. It was a place where we ameliorated tragedies, healed victims, comforted survivors. It was a place where we told them not to count the cost in resources, because the Synarche believed that there was no price on a life.

You could never know in advance what a person might become or accomplish, given time. And even if they accomplished nothing, their life was still a life.

It wasn't our place to judge them. It was our place to save them.

I believed in that so hard it choked me up. And I'd never admit it to Tsosie. But when I opened my eyes to compare the image on the screens to what Sally was feeding into our foxes from her own enormous sensorium, I caught him grinning at me. Just a little.

I shook my head and sighed. He rolled his eyes.

Core General. This vast habitat—the largest constructed biosphere in the galaxy—seemed strangely inevitable against a brilliant and bottomless night. There was no darkness in space here. There was no velvet black between the stars for this small artificial world to rest on as if it were a tumbled aventurine.

There was, in fact, virtually no "between the stars" to speak of. The Core was a gigantic, claustrophobic stellar cocktail party. If there *had* been any darkness, it would have been lost in the glare of the Saga-star's accretion disk. The disk alone, though distant, wiped out a swath of the sky. It was so huge and fast-spinning that I could clearly see the redshift sloping along the trailing side. From the slight elevation of my perspective—above its equator—the blueshift along the edge that was rushing toward me glowed bright and true.

The Saga-star's jets angled and flashed as it spun, whipping about in a terrible turmoil that only seemed stately because the scale was so gargantuan. Everything constructed in the Core required extreme radiation shielding. The couple of planets here that supported life had notoriously powerful magnetic fields and thick atmospheres, not to mention radiation-tolerant biospheres. Even the Delyth—little leggy systers composed mostly of animate metallic structures, who obtained their metabolic needs by soaking up radiation and who treated refined uranium like snack chips—had to use protective hardware in the Core, lest they die of overeating. And *they* were so hot that if I were to stand next to one, unshielded, my skin would redden and then bubble off after minutes of exposure.

Some of the photosynthetic systers had similar problems relating to too much light among all these stars: it could cause uncontrolled growth, even cancers. It's not always as restful being a plant as you might imagine. And it's *definitely* not easy to be an extremophile. Though honestly, every species is some kind of extremophile by somebody else's standard.

Afar was well-shielded against the death rays that, from the perspective of his crew, saturated all of space. We still kept Sally's bulk between him and the Saga-star. She was well-shielded, too, and a little bit extra couldn't hurt.

We closed with Core General at a good but respectful clip, staying in the shipping lane. Sally didn't run the emergency transponder: this was a routine approach even though we were full to the gills with casualties. We weren't coming in hot and covered with ichor for once, and I was content with that.

We were all strapped to our couches in the command module—even Camphvis, whose rest period it was. Sally let her get away with it: nobody wants to miss the first glimpse of home. Sally had halted her spin for docking, so for the time being we had no rotational gravity.

Helen was with us, sitting on the spare couch. She wasn't strapped in, merely holding herself in place . . . but she was an android, and acceleration really didn't seem to bother her.

She was twisting her hands together so hard the golden material of her fingers creaked. It surprised me that an android could manage to register that much anxiety. A lot of people don't realize that AIs aren't built to register emotion only in order to make the evolved types feel more comfortable around them. They're built to feel because, as far as anyone can tell, emotion is a critical part of cognition, and trying to build A-life without it never results in emergent sapience.

So her *having* emotions didn't surprise me, antique though her design was. What surprised me was that she was as deregulated as I would expect an unrightminded human to be.

I guess the expectations of reasonable behavior were different back then?

A tug came out and relieved us of Afar, pulling him around toward the chill and dark of the methane section, which was located behind the bulk of the hospital, relative to the Saga-star and the Core. We zoomed along on another vector, toward our assigned ox airlock in the Emergency Department. It was all so terribly, weirdly routine.

A private ambulance zipped past us on a priority course. Sally changed vector to accommodate. Tsosie made an irritated noise.

"It could be a critical patient," I said.

"I suppose that happens *occasionally*," he replied, with a significant expression.

It happened more often than not, but I didn't feel like arguing with him. We were currently nonemergency traffic, which meant other traffic took priority. Though Tsosie wasn't wrong that some nonemergency traffic was more equal than others: the Synarche guaranteed everybody a humane subsistence, care, and an income, but it didn't promise to allocate resources beyond that unless you could show societal benefit for that allocation, potential or real.

If you had a needed skill, you might be required to enter service for a while—but if that happened, any debts or resource obligations you might have accrued from additional allocated resources would be forgiven at the end. If you hadn't accrued an obligation, the Synarche would assume one toward you that you could claim at a future date.

Say you were a pilot, and you wanted to operate a private ambulance, for example, like the one whose taillights were glowing blue as it turned into dock ahead of us. If you had served, your obligation for the resources—the equipment—would be paid off in advance. At least some of the equipment, anyway. A private ambulance was probably a lot of resources.

And if you *had* a private ambulance, that counted as a needed resource, and the Synarche might call you back into service on a short-term emergency basis fairly frequently. The sleek silver ship with the massive white coils that was nuzzling up to the hospital's spinning flank might be full of plague victims, or running vaccines under government contract.

The Synarche governed itself by datagen and simulation: game theory and models, run by both AI specialists and us slowbrains. Some people made playing the simulators a full-time service position, though I didn't think it ranked very high on the resource-allotment scale. Those models, when compared, led to governance by emergent consensus.

The Synarche mandated a certain return on its investment in society and infrastructure from those who isolated a significant amount of personal resources from the community. My species hadn't quite been there on its own, though before we'd connected with the Synarche we'd already largely adapted ourselves to a more commensal lifestyle than the one we'd developed in the Before. This process was helped along by the fact that the lifestyle we'd developed in the Before had led to the Eschaton, and to people fleeing Terra en masse in glorified soap bubbles like *Big Rock Candy Mountain*.

Rightminding, like the concepts of Right Thought, Right Action, and Right Speech that had preceded it, wasn't such a bad system for correcting some of evolution's kludges. A lot of kludges were trivial to fix now, such as shoulder joints and spines that didn't cause constant pain after the age of thirty-five, and so on. But despite rightminding, some Synizens still managed—through ingenuity, drive, or uncorrected sophipathology—to hoard more resources than they had any imaginable use for. But some of that also came back to the Synarche in the form of assessments, and those assessments went to bolster the public good. The resources from those assessments built things like—ta-da—Core General.

And my exo, for that matter, which benefits me and my quality of life almost exclusively. Although it also makes me capable in my chosen career.

As you can probably tell, I've had this argument with Tsosie often enough to manage both sides of it quite fluently by now.

So if a rich person was cutting us off, well, we weren't in a hurry right now anyway. And if we had been, we would have had priority. They might have a legitimate medical emergency on board all the same, something that a routine flight could make way for.

I kept sneaking sideways glances at Helen. This wasn't routine. *She* wasn't routine. We were bringing home a piece of history. Nothing in the human galaxy would ever be quite the same again.

Sally and Loese didn't bother the rest of us with the coms chatter, leaving me free to look down on the hospital with all my usual feelings of awe and appreciation. Core General had been built by the combined resources of the entire Synarche, all the thousands of syster species. Well, fewer than that, I guessed, because it was built decans ago and was constantly being updated. But that didn't stop the sheer scale of the project from flatly amazing me.

It was a gobsmacking accomplishment. Not only was it huge, it was intricate. Different systers had different environmental and gravitational needs, and environments were stacked from hub to rim of the spinning station to accommodate them. The apex of the enormous station was pointed toward the Core; the nadir lay in sheltering shadow.

I didn't at all blame the administration for being in a blistering hurry to get the new artificial gravity installed throughout the environment. It was an infinitely better solution than trying to balance the gravitational needs of different systers with various rates of spin. Although there might also be safety concerns with the artificial gravity.

Probably. Technology can always break. The question is always, when it breaks, how does it break? What does it do? And what failsafes can be installed to keep it from killing anybody?

I turned to Helen. "When we dock," I told her, "people are going to come on board and get your crew members and the sample of the machine. They are going to try to help, and you need to let them. Do you think you can manage that?"

"They're going to help my crew," she repeated, as if fixing it in memory.

"They're doctors," I said. "Very good doctors. If anybody can help, they will."

It didn't seem advantageous to mention that if her crew were past recovery, it was probably because she'd force-frozen them.

Sally brushed against the docking ring, matching velocity and vector so precisely we heard nothing. And felt nothing, until the docking bolts shot with a thud that reverberated through our hull. Suddenly, my limbs were sore, as we fell heavily back into the embrace of simulated gravity.

The warm feminine voice of Linden, Core's wheelmind, broke in. She could use magnetic resonance to communicate directly with many types of sentient brains via hallucinations one could not ignore, but she felt it was more polite to talk to people when possible. I had to admit, I agreed.

We'd tightbeamed ahead to let her know what we had coming, so I wasn't surprised when she said, "Welcome home, Sally, Doctors, Nurses, Pilot. Welcome to Core General, Helen. Helen, I'm Linden, the wheel-mind here, and I will be in charge of making sure that you are comfortable while my staff begins care for your crew. Do you require treatment also?"

"Yes," Tsosie said, while Helen was still grinding through her decision. It was technically a bit sketchy of him to speak on her behalf, but she'd have other chances to refuse, and the lags she was running were a pretty good argument in favor of her need.

Helen wanted to hover as we started moving the coffins out, and was absolutely and entirely in the damned way. I managed to convince her that the airlock worked better when she wasn't standing in it, and Loese—who was off duty once we docked, so it was service above and beyond—led her out into the receiving bay to stand next to the triage nurse and do her worrying where she could see the end stage of the process.

I ducked through to treatment, past the milling crew surrounding the cryo pod being offloaded from that private ship. I glanced over my shoulder, but Tsosie wasn't in view, or I would have gloated at him over the pod: evidence that somebody was actually pretty darn sick or hurt.

So there.

To my enormous relief, my old friend Dr. Rilriltok was on duty in Cryonics. It was a Rashaqin trauma recovery specialist, a job classification that included cryo fail and other injuries often sustained during rescue and transportation. It spotted me and fluttered up through the big, echoing bay, flying because the spin gravity in this trauma bay was light enough to be safe for it to do so, and because the floor was covered with swarms of doctors, nurses, and techs of about sixteen different species.

Despite the madhouse of people sliding coffins around on lifts, I spotted it coming a long way off: it was hard to miss, being airborne and about a meter long. The drone of its diamond-faceted wings was equally distinctive, having a tendency to set my back teeth buzzing against each other.

"Hey," I said. "Nice sash. Is that jewelry? Did you get promoted?"

Rilriltok hovered, the wings a blur. *Portable gravity nullifier,* it said, stroking the sash with a small manipulator. *Koregoi tech. Now that the hospital has begun retrofitting, they're issuing these to all fragile staff members. For safety, in case of a gravity emergency. Greetings, friend Brookllyn. Have you eaten? Are you well?*

Rilriltok had been my mentor/liaison when I did my training rotation at Core General, and we'd hit it off brilliantly. It was a Rashaqin male, which meant that it was possessed of a dizzying array of limbs, two compound eyes, enough simple eyes that I'd have to point to each in sequence to reliably count them, and layers of chromatophores and iridophores that it could use to disappear effectively into almost any background. The females of its species were much larger and more aggressive, without the adaptations for color manipulation, and in pre-Synarche times had been known to occasionally eat the males during mating if they weren't already sated.

As a result, the males were incredibly diplomatic, empathic, and polite. And prone to repeatedly offering food to anybody they had to deal with in a social or professional situation. Especially if the situation was somewhat tense.

Rilriltok, in short, was a delight.

Rashaqins were also exoskeletal—they looked like praying mantises with a few extra limbs—and had evolved on a much less dense, higher-oxygen world than humans had. This meant that fair amounts of Core General, especially around the rim, were off-limits to any Rashaqin that did not wish to be squashed. It also meant that they usually wore supplemental breathing gear threaded around the spiracles on their abdomens, because their mix was rich enough to present an unreasonably large oxidation risk if used as a general atmosphere.

I'd been to Rashaq once, when I was still in the Judiciary. Things on Rashaq tended to spontaneously burst into flames.

The entire planet was saved from being a constant firestorm mostly because it also never stopped raining. I'd spent three standard months on the surface in my duty rotation. I only ever saw its pleasant yellow sun from aircraft. My skin was fantastic the whole time, though—soft and supple and very well-moisturized.

I pointed to the stream of coffins coming in. "Have you had a look yet?"

The first one is being hooked up to the diagnostics. Shall we go?

Rilriltok perched on my shoulder—its personal antigravity device seemed to be working, as it weighed less than my exo—and let me carry it through the crowd, safely raised above the bustle. Under other circumstances, I might have shied from the raptorial forelegs as long as my arms, folded neatly away beneath the level torso. Whatever else it was, Rilriltok was an extremely large bug.

It was a large bug that I was perfectly accustomed to, however. And—Hhayazh aside—I've always been fond of bugs. Actually, I'm fond of Hhayazh, too, but don't tell it I said so.

I stood still and served as a perch for the even more motionless Rilriltok as it scanned the readouts being sent to our senso. Odds for the occupant of the cryo casket didn't look great to me—the numbers were too cold, too weird—but I wasn't the expert. And to my vast relief, I wasn't currently wearing a specialist ayatana, either. Much easier, saner, and safer to let somebody who had their *own* knowledge handle the diagnosing when I had one standing—or perching—right there.

At length, Rilriltok buzzed faintly. I couldn't tell if the emotion it was experiencing was exasperation or relief.

I asked, "Can we help them?"

That's an interesting question, the doctor said. *They're cryoburned.*

"Are they dead?"

Rilriltok rippled its wings, then pinned them back, flicking the wing coverts closed. The hard scales blushed jewel-pink, with bright green beads of trim. *Not until we thaw them out and they don't wake up,* it admitted. *Technically.*

"Comforting."

I didn't spend six ans in medical apprenticeship in order to lie to people.

It clacked its mandibles and gestured to something behind me. A Rashaqin could see in most directions with that cloud of eyes. *Is this the next of kin?*

I turned my head and saw Helen approaching, wringing her golden hands. A reflective and equally golden shimmer washed Rilriltok's carapace, starting with its raptorial forelimbs and rapidly licking across its body down to the tip of its abdomen: the iridophores expanding. Color-based communication is a fascinating thing.

I waved to catch Helen's eye . . . lack of eyes . . . and gestured her up to us. "This is Helen, yes." I couldn't bear to use her full pun of a name.

Any attending physician got weirder stuff than a faceless android with exaggerated gender markers for lunch. Rilriltok held out the case board that had been clutched in a couple of its smaller manipulators. *Hello. I am Dr. Rilriltok, the cryonics treatment specialist. Will you authorize treatment, please?*

Helen turned her eyeless gaze from the glassy surface of the tablet to my face, and back again. "I don't know how."

Just touch the surface, Rilriltok said. My fox translated its tone as kindness. Rilriltok always had a better bedside manner than me. *We'll do everything we can for your people. Are you the shipmind?*

"N—"

"Yes," I said. "Her people have a different word for it."

"You'll take care of my crew," she said.

I will do everything I can to help them, Rilriltok said. *But you have to understand that in a situation like this there are no guarantees.*

Over Helen's shoulder, I watched the next casket being plugged into the next diagnostic bay. The one beside us was uncoupled—a process that involved staff wrestling with some adaptors with the randomly colored swirls of a rush print job—and escorted by a triage nurse farther into the hospital.

Helen took a half step after it, as if dragged. For a moment, I thought she was going to have one of her meltdowns, or lockouts. But the expression on her hollows and ridges shifted faintly.

"Can I stay with them?"

It's best if you don't, for now, Rilriltok said. *Some of the essential procedures might be distressing. We will scan them, sample their DNA, and begin growing any necessary replacement organs and limbs that may have lost function while the patients were in cryo. If we have to amputate flesh that would become gangrenous if allowed to rewarm, we will do that now. Don't worry, though; your crew can't feel anything in cryosleep.*

Its faceted eye caught mine, and I knew what it wasn't saying. *Your crew can't feel anything if they're dead.*

Helen went very still, a mirrored statue of a ridiculously proportioned female form. My pulse accelerated, and I forgot the ache in my ligaments. Sensing adrenaline flooding my system, my exo glided across my skin, realigning itself for explosive power. I was combat trained—years in Judiciary, after all—but I also knew I was rusty. Restraining irrational injured people was not at all like tackling actual criminals.

And tackling actual criminals was not at all like trying to stop a freaked-out AI peripheral on a rampage.

I assumed. Right then, I was hoping I never had to find out.

Helen *expanded,* pulsing larger like a bull impanaton drawing a deep, angry breath. I half expected her to paw and toss her horns. Her seamless body broke into disconnected plates, all hovering over a lambent core of swirling flame-colored sparks like an internal galaxy.

I thought of footage of lava welling between adhered chunks of basalt. It was all I could manage not to step back.

Rilriltok had no such ego holding it in place. It dropped off my shoulder and zipped up and backward on a diagonal several meters, the drone of its wings rising to a pitch betokening alarm.

Helen spoke in a flat, metallic tone. The sparkles of light inside her dazzled my vision. "I need. To protect. My crew."

"Helen." I made my voice as level and unemotional as I could, but I didn't want to tune away the adrenaline thumping through my veins: I might need it. All I had in a situation like this was good old-fashioned training and sangfroid. "Do you have a protocol you engage to allow medical intervention to save crew members whose lives are at risk otherwise? Even if that medical intervention may be dangerous?"

"I do," she said, leaning forward in a gesture that made my exo tighten around my body, ready to yank me out of harm's way.

I took a deep breath, intentionally slow. I wished I could make eye contact. I'd gotten used to the shimmery facelessness on the trip home, but it was suddenly creepy as anything once more, and the shifting gleams through the open sutures dissecting it did nothing to reassure me.

They looked like they were getting wider.

"Will you believe me that we are doing everything we can to save your crew, and allow us to proceed with that work without making *my* crew fear for their own safety?"

I heard a series of slow, pinging clicks like cooling metal as she thought it over. I held my own breath, irrationally certain that if I moved even that much, everything would crumble and Helen would start punching her way through the staff and environments of Core General.

With a *snap*, the plates collapsed back into one another, and Helen was again an exaggerated mannequin, not very tall.

I heard Linden breathe a sigh of relief in my head. *Oh good. Thank you for rendering it unnecessary for me to intervene, Dr. Jens.*

It's good to know you were on the job anyway, wheelmind, I said, feeling my heart begin to slow. My exo wasn't yet quite ready to relax around me, but I rolled my shoulders back and tried to let go of some of the tension. Tension turns into pain very quickly.

Rilriltok blurred forward again, stopping over my left shoulder with such precision that it almost seemed like an animation. It said, *Shipmind Helen, do you require medical care as well?*

I almost copied what Tsosie had done and said yes for her. Helen obviously needed her program adjusted, and pretty badly. But she was a sovereign person under Synarche law, though one currently without the obligations of citizenship. Obligations or no obligations, she had her inalienable rights, and one of those was the right to personal sovereignty. She could refuse treatment so long as her illness did not present a danger to others.

Did it present a danger to others? Well, the jury was still deliberating that. A jury comprised of Sally and me, mostly, though Tsosie had some opinions, too. And Hhayazh was made of nothing but opinions.

I felt like the Lava Avatar Incident was a check mark in the danger-to-others column, however. And based on how quickly the wall monitor nearby had glowed with presence lights, Linden—who monitored everything in the public spaces of her wheel—seemed to agree.

Linden probably belonged on that jury, too.

"Yes," Helen said. "I consent to treatment."

I wondered if she'd been conferring with Sally in the interim.

The identification tag on the wall monitor presence lights told me I was dealing with Dr. Zhiruo, Core General's most senior artificial intelligence. Someone who had been with the hospital since it was nothing more than a crazy, brilliant, idealistic plan.

I absolutely wasn't intimidated in the slightest.

That's a lie.

"Oh, here's the AI doc," I said, and added, "Hello, Doctor," toward the wall.

"Hello, Doctor," she replied, in tones of mellow amusement. "I understand you have an unusual case for us."

Quickly, as efficiently as I could, I filled her in on Helen—a little constrained because Helen was standing right there, but one thing medical training knocks out of you is too much self-consciousness (sometimes it knocks out all the politeness, too, and I hoped I was falling on the right side of that line)—and on the machine, a sample of which was still boxed up neatly in that Faraday crate in Sally's hold. It seemed to stay quiet—quiescent—as long as we could keep it from talking to the outside, or contacting its own components.

I couldn't quite tell if Helen was listening intently or if she had folded inward again. I didn't mention the incident we'd witnessed, because I knew Linden would fill Dr. Zhiruo in. I did mention that Helen was uncomfortable with unbodied AIs, and that her culture was strongly inclined toward the use of peripherals.

Sally would have already given Dr. Zhiruo a full report, so I didn't feel the need to warn her about Helen's uncanny relationship with the machine, and whatever had gone wrong with her—their?—programming that led to the progressive deconstruction of the ship.

As I had hoped, by the time I finished telling the wall monitor about our rescue operation and introducing Helen's background, Dr. Zhiruo had shown up driving a peripheral of her own.

It was a great deal less exaggerated than Helen's chassis, but Dr. Zhiruo had chosen a humanoid model, which I thought was a good choice given Helen's limited cultural referents. The peripheral had a dark gray polymer skin; narrow, even features; a genderless body under a chiton-like robe printed to emulate "natural" undyed fabric. The eyes were dark glass lenses, unreflective apertures in the neutral face.

Dr. Zhiruo held out a hand and smiled. It was a smile you might imagine on a deva: distant, controlled, serene. "Please come with me, Helen. I promise I will take very good care of you."

Rilriltok and I watched them leave until they vanished through a decompression door, and Zhiruo's presence lights blinked out.

I felt a little guilty at how thankful I was to realize that Helen Alloy and her quicksilver bosoms were somebody else's problem now. I reminded myself that it wasn't unreasonable to experience a reduction in anxiety when relieved of a responsibility for which one wasn't really qualified. I let out the breath I'd been holding too long for comfort and said, "So what now?"

The Rashaqin zipped around me to hover at eye level, the breeze from its blurring wings stretching tendrils of my hair. I saw my dishabille reflected multiply in compound eyes and had to smile. *DNA scans!* it said brightly. *Want to come?*

CHAPTER 11

I DID WANT TO GO, BUT UNFORTUNATELY I FELT THE PRESS OF responsibility toward less medically interesting duties. Regretfully, I took my leave of my old friend. I stopped by my on-hospital quarters and showered and dressed in scrubs and a lab coat, then headed toward the office of my other old friend, Master Chief O'Mara, the head of ox sector's Emergency Department. My boss.

I sent them a message requesting an urgent appointment and got an immediate confirmation. *My door is open.*

As I walked, I thought about the patient who shared O'Mara's title—Dwayne Carlos, the master pipefitter. I sent a note to Rilriltok while I was thinking about it, asking that—if Sally was in port—I be allowed to be present when he rewarmed Helen's crew members. I felt like I owed them that, having brought them in from the cold. If they lived, and considering where they came from, it would probably be comforting if the first face they saw on wakening was a human one.

O'Mara's office was centrally located in the ox-sector Emergency Department, and Sally had come in on one end, so I had some traveling to do. It wasn't quite far enough away to catch a lift, but it did take almost fifteen standard minutes of weaving through my fellow professionals and their patients in corridors to arrive. When I did, the door was standing open, though there was a sound-dampening privacy field in place.

I ducked through quickly—nobody lingers under a decompression door—and was surprised to find that two members of my crew had beaten me here. And additionally surprised that neither one of them was Loese. I'd come here without discussing it with any of them, O'Mara hadn't mentioned their presence, and if anybody was consulting with the master chief, I'd expect it to be the person who had been most involved in investigating the sabotage.

Tsosie nodded in greeting as I entered, and Dr. Rhym wriggled their tendrils. O'Mara waved me to a seat. They were a blocky medium-complected human with cropped graying red hair. A pair of positively prehensile eyebrows were the only thing at odds with the general squareness of their face, features, and their massive squareness of frame.

They looked like a retired prizefighter. They *were* a retired prizefighter—Judiciary zero-G boxing subchampion three years running, before I'd worked with them. They were also the person who kept the ox-sector Emergency Department of the largest hospital in the galaxy purring like an only slightly dyspeptic cat.

"Are you here to report the sabotage, Dr. Jens?" they asked, when I'd settled.

The faint hum of the privacy barrier reassured me. What did not reassure me was Tsosie's expression of shock. I assumed the sudden retraction of Rhym's tendrils also indicated surprise, but I wasn't certain.

I looked at Tsosie. "I assume from the look on your face that you hadn't gotten around to telling them yet?"

Tsosie looked over at O'Mara. "We'd barely sat down when you walked in. Loese got here first?"

I rubbed my hands until I caught myself. O'Mara's brain was as sharp as their physique was lumpish. I was too late: I saw their eyebrows flicker as they looked down. They didn't say anything about it.

O'Mara shook their head.

I said, "That's not like you. You're not surprised. And you're not angry."

O'Mara rumbled, "Well, there's no point in trying to hide any of this from you. The grapevine will fill you in before you get the first scuff on your station shoes. We've had some . . . odd occurrences in your absence. So when all three of you showed up needing to talk urgently . . ."

"Odd." Tsosie wasn't really asking a question. He wasn't really not asking one, either.

"Environmental leaks. Contaminated medication. Nobody's been harmed yet, but if it keeps up it's only a matter of time."

"And you think this is intentional."

"I do," O'Mara said. "Unfortunately. What happened on Sally?"

"Coms failed." I looked at Tsosie.

"Coms failed while Llyn and I were on the generation ship."

"Basically the worst possible moment," I agreed. "If Sally and Loese hadn't managed a patch job, Tsosie and I might not be here, because the situation over there got dicey very quickly."

"Tell them about falling through the hull," Rhym suggested.

"What?"

I held up my hand. Knuckles swollen. I put it down again quickly. "It's all in my afteraction," I said. "Which is already filed, and I bet Tsosie's is, too."

Tsosie studiously examined his fingernails, hiding a smile. Nobody wants to be the bad kid when O'Mara's at the head of the classroom.

"How are the Darboof patients doing?" I asked. As a section chief, O'Mara would have access to that information. And I wasn't changing the subject or being nosy. They were my patients, too, and I cared.

O'Mara unfocused, refocused, frowned. "Stable," they said. "A team's working on them, and the AI team is running a core-out diagnostic on Afar. Did any of the ancient humans make it?"

"We don't know yet," I answered. "Dr. Rilriltok is the physician in charge. It's scanning DNA so we can have spare parts ready before we thaw them out. The peripheral is being treated by Zhiruo. Master Chief, I have some . . . social concerns."

"Your patients are nasty atavistic humans full of nasty atavistic ideas?"

I nodded. "The AI is also kind of nasty and atavistic."

"Is that going to interfere with treating them? Or hypothetically doing a turn-and-burn to get another batch, if we need you to?"

"Master Chief," I said, wounded. "I'm a professional. And I care about their well-being. They're sentient creatures, after all."

O'Mara sparkled with humor, a disconcerting expression on such a solid lump of a human form. "Perhaps even sapient?"

I laughed. It eased the tension. "Given time. So, about the sabotage—"

"Ours or yours?" O'Mara asked.

"Ours, for the moment." Even my forearms ached. It was unfair: I'd been getting enough rest and eating carefully, dammit. Well, I'd have a dia or two off before the next run, per regulations. I could spend it floating in a nice warm neutral buoyancy saline tank. "You're going to investigate?"

"We've got a Judiciary security team on the way to Sally now. I want to look at it before I put her back to work on researching the . . . thing you found inside Afar."

"Yes," Tsosie said. "About that—"

"Yes," O'Mara interrupted, as if they were agreeing. "Why don't you and Dr. Rhym go supervise that? Or, even better, get some rest and exercise. I've got some catching up to do with Llyn here."

Tsosie shut his mouth. He *might* argue with O'Mara. But the stakes would have to be a lot higher, I think.

So he got up, and as he got up he winked at me. I rolled my eyes. We both knew O'Mara was not my type.

I didn't miss that, as Tsosie and Rhym left, the door that had been open irised shut behind them. O'Mara watched them leave so intently that I turned my head, too. Just in case there was something interesting or edifying going on. I heard the click of the air seal before they turned back to me and spoke again.

"Well," O'Mara said. "Why don't you look into it for me?"

"Me? The sabotage?"

"You."

"Yours or mine?" I answered, risking teasing them a little.

"Both. What *are* the odds they're not connected?"

I stretched my legs out and leaned back in the chair, trying to make it look like I was relaxing.

"I'm not a detective."

"You've got a decan of Judiciary experience. I know you and trust you, and you can talk to the medical staff as an equal without putting their backs up or making *them* feel like they're under suspicion, which is a feat no Judiciary personnel can manage. Also, I'm *not* the boss of any of the Judiciary personnel. I'm your boss. And I'm telling you to."

"And I'll be going back out on Sally as soon as she's resupplied. And repaired." My face got warm. I'd forgotten that she needed repairs. I guess that "hypothetical" turn-and-burn had indeed been strictly hypothetical.

Then I put my left fingertips against the center of my forehead and pushed gently. "Aw, Well."

O'Mara steepled their hands on their desktop and watched me, head cocked. Waiting.

I said, "I don't think anybody on my crew was the saboteur, if that's why you got rid of Tsosie and Rhym."

"What do you think of your new pilot?"

"I like her," I said. "Don't know her very well yet. But she does her job and fits in."

"Hmm," they said. "And the rest of the crew?"

"Solid. But I just told you that."

"I've known you since you were an ensign." O'Mara got up and walked to the dispenser. They printed a cup and filled it with water. I expected them to knock it back, but they brought it to me along with two white tablets. "If you weren't beam-straight, Llyn, I'd have noticed by now."

"Have I told you about my ex-wife?"

They laughed. O'Mara had a good laugh, when you could pry it out of them. "I'm not talking about your romantic proclivities. You believe in this place. We've got a pretty decent Goodlaw, but it's first loyalty is to the Synarche. Yours is to Core General. Why wouldn't I use you?"

I set the tablets on the desk and sipped the water.

They sat back down, extending one thick finger to point at the pills. "As a doctor, I'm prescribing those."

"You're not *my* doctor."

"Your hands look like you've been at the heavy bag. I assume you haven't been at the heavy bag. I'd fiddle with your tuning if I thought Linden would let me. Since I can't, take the meds before your joint capsules explode or something."

"Supervisory abuse," I said, but I swallowed the tablets. They were bitter. "All right, I believe in this place. Do you know why I don't think it was anybody on Sally's crew?"

"Hit me," they said.

I looked down at my knuckles, flexed my free hand, and got a second guffaw. "Somebody set a device on a timer, and then somehow hacked Sally so that she didn't notice the device, didn't notice the timer, and couldn't remember the sabotage had been done after it happened. If Loese hadn't figured it out and routed around the damage old-school, I'd be drifting along in the wake of a slowly accelerating generation ship for a really long time."

O'Mara sucked their lips for a long moment. "You're saying an AI was involved, to be able to hack Sally's programming."

Hands wide, I shrugged. The water in my cup sloshed but didn't spill over. "I'm saying we've got an awful lot of damaged shipminds all of a sudden. But Sally—that was set up before she got close to the other two."

We contemplated each other in silence. Rogue AIs were the stuff of scary three-vees, not real life. I was the first one to crack and change the subject.

"While we're on the topic of shipminds, who sent Afar out there?"

The master chief, if possible, looked even grimmer. "Judiciary is trying to find out. There was no filed flight plan. Or if there was, it's been deleted, but the military archinformists think they'd be able to spot that."

Sometimes, you have to break the tension. "Hey, can I get one of those antigravity belts like Rilriltok is wearing? Taking the pressure off won't hurt my pain levels, either."

"I'll put you on the list," they said. "We've mostly gotten through the staff whose lives would be in danger if they caught a full g, so it should happen pretty quickly. Oh, that reminds me. You need to talk to the Administree as soon as possible. They would like a personal visit, please."

"O'Mara!"

They busied themselves with the displays inside their desk. "I've got another appointment in three minutes."

"What aren't you telling me?"

They shook their head. "Starlight doesn't confide in me. So, as I mentioned before, I'm going to ask Sally to take the lead on investigating the object in Afar's hold."

"Yes, that puzzled me." I shook my head. "She's not an engineer."

"No," they said. "But she's been exposed to whatever Afar and"—they got the unfocused look people get when they're consulting their senso—"Helen were exposed to, and I want her in port where she can be kept under observation for a while. And where her crew"—they poked a finger at me and waggled shaggy eyebrows—"are *safe*. The repairs to her coms system are going to be a little complicated, you understand."

"I understand we're being grounded, and you're fibbing to my ship about why."

"Good. You're paying attention." They settled back and folded their arms. "Llyn. One old military mammal to another. I'm worried about the sabotage. I'm worried about Sally. I'm worried about this weird ancient AI and its weird ancient peripherals and its ten thousand corpsicles. I'm worried about why there's a thing that might be a warbot in the cargo hold of a methane fast packet without a filed flight plan. I'm worried about why Afar isn't talking to anybody, and neither is his crew. I need you here."

I chafed, and they knew it. I also owed them, and they knew that, too. And the pills were working, which made it hard to stay as grumpy as I wanted.

"All right," I said. "But you owe *me*, this time."

"Saving your life was all in the line of duty," they said, mildly.

"What about taking a kid from a backwater world and giving them a chance at their dream job?"

"You've been a commanding officer," they said.

"Under very limited circumstances."

They smiled. "Well, as you will learn if you continue to advance, identifying and nurturing talent is all in the line of duty, too."

I could have pointed out that nurturing anything was not my strong point. But it seemed like a good exit line, so instead, I left.

I reached out through the senso to my ship as I walked around the wheel, dodging systers of every conceivable size, ox-compatible physiology, and morphology. *Hey, Sally. I heard they have you investigating the craboid.*

As long as I'm stuck here, she said. *It keeps me out of trouble. You know what they say about idle hands turning to farming drama.*

I don't think they say that about AIs.

It's true, she agreed. *Because when we don't have enough work to do we generally wind up creating a more logical and egalitarian system of governance and resource allotment, or something similarly boring. Anyway, I've been working on getting some access to the craboid's systems, and I think we can probably use electromagnetism to manipulate its superstructure.*

You're going to try to move it?

We are, she confirmed. *Want to come and help? You might have some insights. We might all learn something.*

My other duties weren't currently pressing. Sally was grounded; the archaic humans were frozen solid; Helen was getting care from the best cyberdoc in the hospital. Tackling the job the master chief had given me was going to require sitting down and focusing my concentration to read a lot of case reports, and I didn't want to tackle that until I'd had some time to process our conversation.

Am I avoidant? Very well then, I am avoidant. Also, sometimes I contradict myself. I contain multitudes.

Sure, I said. *I'll bring some EM induction patches.*

Afar was docked in the methane section, which meant I had to suit up to get there no matter which way I went. I returned to Sally to pick up my own hardsuit rather than choosing from whatever was in the lockers. She seemed eager, and bored, and not too distracted by monitoring her own repairs.

She was empty of our team except for Hhayazh, the current duty officer, who was backup-supervising the crew of repair bots. Sally usually would have done it alone, but since Sally's memory and perceptions were going to be in question until the repairs were complete, Loese and Hhayazh had decided to take turns sitting with her.

Just to make sure nobody snuck any more unauthorized aftermarket modifications into our ship. Such as bombs. Or Trojan horses.

Hhayazh followed me to Sally's rear airlock and helped me into my suit. I didn't need anybody to spray me with additional insulation todia, because I wasn't going into the methane environment, and the irradiated vacuum of Core space was significantly less hostile than a balmy beachfront property on Darbo. I seemed to recall, now that I was thinking about it, that there were some methane-breather colonies on a major moon in Terra's system. I should look into that; maybe Afar *did* have a reason to be on that vector. If he could have reasonably run across *Big Rock Candy Mountain* by accident while dropping out of white space to check and adjust course, that was one less intractable mystery to worry about.

The archinformists had said that it was likely Afar's flight plan had *not* been deleted, or they would know. I would have to talk to O'Mara and ask if it *was* possible that Afar's flight plan had been filed and had gotten lost somewhere, or was hung up at a packet beacon somewhere out in the galactic halo, waiting for the piggyback that would bring it to us in the Core.

It made me feel better to contemplate that there might be an easy explanation. Whether that was denial and self-delusion or refusing to fall prey to conspiracy theories, only time would tell.

Hhayazh finished my precheck and patted me on the shoulder with a bristly appendage. "Be safe out there."

"I'm just going for a little walk around the wheel. Nothing to it." I stepped into the airlock, and in a matter of moments I was looking at the outside.

This time the jump down to the surface would have been only a couple of meters. Rotational force would tend to fling me off the side of the hospital the instant I let go, however, so rather than waste maneuvering fuel, I climbed down a ladder. Space is a much better place for being cautious and pragmatic than flamboyant, even if it isn't nearly as much fun as what you see in the three-vees.

Having reached the surface of the docking ring, I clomped across it until I got to a lift branch. It angled sharply, but my magnetic boots made it easy to walk right up the inside, and spin helped to hold me there. The farther I got up the arch, the heavier I was, because the structures farthest from Core General's hub were spinning the fastest. Every so often, a lift zoomed past beneath my feet, shivering the whole tube. Above my head, crystal panels showed green and greeny-violet leaves outlifted toward the light of the Core.

It's not every dia that you get to go for an EVA stroll around the outside of a gigantic space station. In short order, the branch I had been climbing joined the lift trunk. I paused at the top—or, from my perspective, the bottom—to take in the view.

Core General swooped and bulged over my head, incomprehensibly huge, like a world looming over my shoulder. Beneath my feet, beyond the silvery band of the trunk, the Core danced with all its millions of stars. Even though I was partially in the shadow of the trunk, my hardsuit cooler whined with the strain of so much insulation.

My exo gave me a squeeze, reminding me that the extra acceleration wasn't helping my joints any. I tore myself from the spectacle and kept on walking toward the station's nadir. Sally could handle this on her own. But I admit: even with all the mysteries stacking up, I was curious about this one.

It was easy to spot Afar, even in the distance. His cargo doors were open and a swarm of drone tenders moved around him, pulling the packing gel loose in wide chunks and long foamy strands. I could have tapped into the output of one of them, but I wanted to get a look at the craboid with my own eyes—and not a lot of senso—before we brought it inside.

Another ladder got me down to the cargo bay in time to watch the last of the packing material peeled away. Now that I was looking at it in person, the craboid seemed even bigger and spikier than I remembered. As I climbed up to it, a cloud of drones arose like flies off a corpse, leaving the clean-picked-looking carapace of the walker behind.

Now we only had to get Sally talking to it, assuming there was anything in there to talk to. Or controlling its electronics, if it was just a drone.

I had magnetized some specialized equipment to the outside of my hardsuit in areas that would be out of my way until I reached for them. Here in the shadow of the hospital and the cargo doors, my suit's heater took its turn to complain. Still better than being inside, with Afar's gelid atmosphere leaching all the warmth out of me.

I peeled a set of induction patches off my hardsuit and applied each of them separately to the craboid's chassis, scrambling around it to get them as close to opposite one another as possible. The drones had withdrawn to a safe distance: Linden was paying attention, then. I followed suit, climbing down to the edge of the cargo hold and using one door for cover.

"Clear," I told Sally.

"Active," she replied. "I'll see if I can use the patches to access the thing's processors."

"It *might* have some."

"Ugh," she said, cheerfully. "I get enough of that from Hhayazh. Signal is getting through the patches, so that's circumventing at least some of the shielding. If I can't just talk to it, then I should be able to use electromagnetism to move it by brute force— Oh, hey, I already have an electronic handshake."

"What does that mean?"

"It means it acknowledges my contact. And, now that I'm past the shielding—that is an *intense* level of shielding, by the way!—it's easy to talk to."

"That was a little too easy." I frowned.

"Standard Synarche protocols. At least I'm not going to have to write the code for this one."

So it wasn't some kind of weird alien spaceship parasite. It was just a surface vehicle with a super unsettling design.

Sure, that was a fine explanation.

"You don't suppose this is some kind of exploratory vehicle, do you? Designed for ox breathers on a cold methane world?"

"Survey equipment?" She *hrm*ed. "That would explain all the legs. Designed for any kind of terrain, and manipulating its environment, and even a bit of earthmoving, hmm?"

"Hmm," I agreed.

"Okay, are you ready to bring it around to the machine bay?"

The craboid followed me out the open cargo doors, across Afar's hull, and (using its own maneuvering jets) across the gap to Core General with no incident. Under Sally's puppetry, it stumped along behind me like a weird pet, or like some sort of limpet monster from a poorly produced horror three-vee.

It did not, however, pry the hospital apart, or punch through the hull with a needlelike proboscis, or behave in any sort of an uncivilized manner at all. It walked behind me, climbing courteously through the machine bay airlock when Sally directed it to, then settling down on the deck and resting quietly there while we set up the isolation zone.

"Can you convince it to give us an atmosphere sample?" I asked Sally.

"There's no airlock, and I can't get the pressure door to respond," she answered. "That appears to require some sort of manual override failsafe code which I can't quite crack. There's no AI in here: it's just a machine."

"A vehicle, not a person." Disappointment has a metallic tang.

"Vehicles can be persons, as you know perfectly well," Sally replied tartly.

I supposed it was better to imagine the craboid empty and waiting than to picture it as home to a lonely and terrified presence that might be in there peeking between their appendages in bewilderment, presuming they had both peekers and appendages to peek through.

"There must be some way to open it from the outside," I said. "Otherwise you'd go EVA in a hostile environment and come back to discover you'd locked your keys inside.

"And then you'd die."

"Yes, but whatever the code is I do not have it. It might be a DNA lock, for all I know. So it's brute force all the way around," Sally answered. "Want to have a go at it?"

The machine bay had a me-compatible atmosphere, but I didn't bother deactivating out of my hardsuit, because I wasn't through with it yet. While drones pitched a containment bubble around the craboid, I fetched a sampling drill from an equipment locker. The drill was too massy to stick to my turtle shell. It'd be in the way, and I didn't want to carry it around.

By the time I was armed, I had to come back toward the craboid via the airlock built into the bubble. I made sure the interior flap was secured shut behind me before Linden pumped her own ox atmosphere out and pumped a nonreactive nitrogen atmosphere in.

I rigged the drill, set up a brace to hold it in position, and stepped back before triggering.

The bit was diamond grown around a nanotube lattice for tensile strength. It whined against the hatch, a sound that scraped through my magnetic soles and my eardrums to vibrate along my bones and make my back teeth ache. It would have been even worse inside the craboid, so it was just as well there were no passengers.

The idea was that I would drill a very small hole in the craboid, enabling me to get a sample of the atmosphere inside. Then we'd have a better idea of who might use such a thing.

I was a little concerned that the craboid might be programmed to take evasive or defensive measures. But it stood there and waited quietly while I worked to pry its carapace open.

Right up until the drill bit snapped.

A piece of bit ricocheted off the deck plates and the craboid while I, reflexively, cowered. I got lucky: it pinged off my hardsuit, then lodged in the flexible collar of the nitrogen bubble's lock. No hiss of commingling or escaping atmosphere followed.

Sally was immediately in my senso, asking if I was all right.

"Fine," I said. I touched my faceplate. The drill bit had taken a tiny, glittering chip out of it right in the most distracting possible spot, but it wasn't cracked or cracking, and it hadn't gone through and taken out my eye. So that was lucky, and the hardsuit would heal itself quickly. "The drill bit broke. That's not supposed to happen. Even if the diamond shattered, the nanotubes should hold it together."

I pulled the bit out of the collar material and examined the broken end. Under magnification, I could see that the nanotubes were sheared off a little above the surface of the bit. The stub, still gripped in the drill chock, showed the same damage. It looked like the tubes had been stretched slightly. The ends looked slightly deformed, as if they had been pulled apart rather than cleanly cut.

"That's *definitely* not supposed to do that." I hooked Sally into my senso feed and got Hhayazh with her. I let them use my eyes to inspect the damage. "It looks like something weakened the structure of the tubes."

"Vibrations?" Hhayazh asked.

"Harmonics, you mean?" I frowned through the chipped faceplate. "Maybe? Well, nobody died. I don't know how we're going to sample that atmosphere, though."

"Sally's density readings give it a pretty standard oxygen saturation."

"A little rare for my tastes, but yes," I admitted. "Figuring out what the atmosphere is made of from how fast sound waves go through it is not as certain as actually getting your hands on a little bit of air and running a few tests, however."

Hhayazh made one of its noises, the kind that might mean exasperation or might mean amusement. "Well, we could get out a laser torch—"

"I don't want to be in the neighborhood if a cutting beam starts ricocheting around!"

"Fine, just wait for it to open up on its own. That seems likely."

"Don't get your ovipositor in a twist, Hhayazh."

Through our connection, I sensed Hhayazh's bristles waving like the cilia on a paramecium. "I'd parasitize you, but my offspring might grow up to have your sense of humor."

"I thought your species didn't eat sentients."

It made the expulsion of air that was its species's equivalent of a disgusted snort. "We don't."

I was framing a retort, still standing there with the snapped drill bit in my left hand, when around me the atmospheric pressure abruptly changed. A grinding sound followed, shivering through the bulkheads.

I took a clanging, magnetized step back. Polymer stretched against me, arresting my movement.

Llyn, report, Sally snapped.

The inner flap of the isolation bubble was against my back. I couldn't open it, because whatever happened, I was in a hardsuit and most of the staff and patients in Core General's ox sector were each in their own equivalent of shirtsleeves. I had to keep my crew safe from whatever pathogens or poisons might be contained inside the walker. Not to mention the atmosphere.

"You were saying?" I grumped at Hhayazh. Then collected my irritation, and said, "The airlock seems to be opening."

For no reason that any of us could detect, the hatchlike portion in the craboid's belly had dropped down and was sliding to one side.

In a haze of decision paralysis, I froze. I didn't know what might be coming out of the craboid's belly hatch. I didn't have the least idea if I was going to be confronted with a patient in need of care or a pissed-off soldier with a shock prod or a swarm of flesh-eating battlebots. Or all of those things simultaneously, for that matter.

I scrambled to come up with a response. The hatch glided open, spilling a warm, mellow golden light into the much less pleasing ambiance of machine bay lights filtered through isolation tent.

Something atavistic and planet-bred in me relaxed at the color of that light. It was foolish; it was illogical. And yet I found myself letting out the breath I had reflexively taken, and lowering the hand with the drill bit in it. I'd been holding it up like a sword, as if such a ridiculous weapon were going to be good for anything.

I felt confident that whoever liked that light liked golden beaches shimmering under yellow suns and long luminous slanted autumn afternoons. Whoever liked that light came from someplace like Terra, and I felt at home with them even before Sally said, "Well, that's one way to sample an atmosphere."

Smugly, she revealed an analysis that—once we deducted the nitrogen from our containment bubble—was only a few points off from her initial estimate. The craboid was (or had been, until it opened up) chock-full of oxygen, nitrogen, and carbon dioxide—an atmosphere that might have been a copy of Terra's in any number of geologic epochs.

My pulse was still racing. I waited, trying to slow my heart without resorting to tuning. The biofeedback worked as long as I concentrated on my breath. In a few seconds, I had collected myself enough to try to peer into the spill of radiance and get a glimpse of the inside of the pod.

It was like trying to stare into the proverbial tunnel of white light. My vision swam; there was nothing within except brilliance. Maybe it was supposed to decontaminate the hatchway.

"Nothing's coming out," I said after a few minutes during which nothing had come out. "I'm going to go look inside."

"Be careful," said Sally, while Hhayazh muttered a comment about humans being too dumb to die.

"Hey, it's my job to climb into questionable structures." I stepped under the curved forward edge of the walker pod. I looked up, and peeked inside. At first, the light was too bright for me to see anything. "I'm going to poke my head up."

"Maybe send a drone first?" Sally said. She didn't wait for my request, but zipped one right past me and made a right-angle climb toward the hatchway. I hadn't even noticed it hovering behind my shoulder until it moved.

It passed through the hatchway. There followed a sharp electrical pop, and it passed through the hatchway again, this time in the opposite direction. Falling.

The drone struck the polymer over the deck plates with a thump.

I froze.

"I recommend that you don't stick your head in there, Dr. Jens," Hhayazh said.

"Thank you, Hhayazh. That sounds like excellent advice."

"Can you see into the pod?" Sally asked. "What can you make out in there?"

"There's a lot of glare, but it looks like a couch and a console. And some cargo space, which is empty, but there are straps. What are you picking up?"

"Nothing," Sally said.

I stepped back away from the hatch, out of an abundance of caution. "But how is that possible?"

"The interior is still electromagnetically shielded. But this whole situation makes me uneasy. We've hauled a whole lot of weirdness back to civilization, and I'd really like some insight into how two ships and two crews were mysteriously disabled, and what exactly this walker is for. I don't like mysteries."

"I love 'em," I said. "I like the satisfaction of solving them. I'm not feeling a lot of satisfaction right now."

"Go get decontaminated," Sally said. "I'm going to turn the craboid over to a research team. Let *their* drones get electrocuted for a while."

CHAPTER 12

DECONTAMINATION WAS PRETTY STRAIGHTFORWARD. There are stalls all over Core General—near every equipment locker, and at every transition zone between environments. Sally herself is designed to decontaminate everything that comes in or goes out, if necessary.

Fortunately, I didn't need to get my hardsuit irradiated. Just doused in a little antiseptic and scrubbed down, so it was over quickly. I returned to Sally, left my hardsuit in my locker, and argued her out of a rest period on the grounds that I was supposed to report to the Administree.

Reporting to the hospital administrator didn't involve anything so commonplace as taking a lift to an office. There was a lift—funny how we still use such antiquated terminology in an environment with no up and nothing to lift against except spin, and for a transportation pod that goes in all sorts of directions—but where it disgorged me was back to the outermost layers of the station, far from the machine bay or even the docking stations.

This was not an office, but a park. An upside-down sort of park where the sky was underfoot and the grass grew over your head. One of the weirder things about getting your gravity from spin was that when I came out of the lift I had to walk down a curved ramp to the transparent outer layer of the station. Having accomplished this, I had the unsettling option of looking down past my feet at the outside, or even lying down and pressing my nose against the shatterproof lumium for a more comfortable angle.

Unfortunately, I wasn't here to bask in the view. I was here to give a report, and I knew it. I had hopes of avoiding being called on the decking . . . but time would indicate whether I would get away with my hide intact. I didn't *know* that I had done anything wrong, but getting a note from your boss that says "See me" is never a pleasant experience.

Core General's administrator would not have fit in the office I mentioned before. To be fussily precise, they also did not fit entirely into the park. But a lot of them did, and the majority of their organs of sense and thought were concentrated here.

I stepped off the bottom of the ramp, walked a few steps over the whirling, vertiginous space below to free up the landing for anyone else coming or going, and craned my head back at the ceiling.

Or rather, at the whispering canopy of leaves largely obscuring the next-innermost onion layer of Core General. The leaves, shiny and green-violet, rustled as if there were a breeze behind them. I could make out the windows beyond, leading to levels inhabited by a variety of different species.

This far out and on this side of the hospital, they would all be carbon dioxide or other compatible metabolisms if they weren't ox types like me, and they would all be species who could tolerate a certain amount of grav and rads. But that was where the resemblances between them would end. I could make out lights intended to mimic the illumination of a dozen suns without turning my head. Soft gold and pink were, to me, the most appealing, followed by the glow my eyes—being adapted to it—saw as a pleasant, neutral white. There were other colors—by my standards worse colors—actinic or merely unpleasant.

We ox breathers shared our habitat sector with not only the carbon dioxide metabolisms, but with a couple of weirdies who breathed nitrogen as well. (No, I don't know how you use nitrogen as an energy catalyst:

I've got enough to do keeping track of the various oxygen metabolisms I come in contact with daily.)

The section admin I was craning my head so far back to look up at was one of the CO_2 breathers, albeit one without any lungs. Core Gen's administrator for my bio type, as well as allied and complementary bio types, was a really, really, really big tree.

They might not have been the biggest tree in the galaxy. But then again, they might. They were a Vnetheshallan, from Shhele, and hospital rumor claimed they had come to the Core as a mere seedling. Their people, as a race, were mobile and vaguely humanoid in appearance in their younger instars. As they aged and became ready to reproduce, they returned to their homeworld, where they put down roots—literally—and generated seeds and offspring. And wrote a lot of poetry, created what their species considered great art, and so on.

All except for this one, who had put down roots right here. Or put *up* roots, or put *in* roots perhaps, because if you considered the direction of growth, their roots went toward the center of Core Gen and their leaves reached out, filtering light from all these endless stars to feed their hungry cells.

They had grown through and into the superstructure of the hospital. In a real sense, their body *was* Core Gen. Or at least a significant chunk of Core Gen, ox sector. (Carbon diox sector, from its point of view.)

Job security, I supposed.

I was apprehensive going in, to be perfectly honest. I'd never had an easy conversation with the being most of us jokingly referred to as the Administree. Their nervous system was not centralized into anything we mammals would recognize as a brain, and their thought processes were not linear in a sense most humans would recognize, but ran in multiple parallel tracks at once. Talking to them always made me feel like I was having an argument with a ball of coked-out snakes.

I mean, in a good way. But still.

"Hello, Administrator Starlight," I said. "You wanted to see me?"

The tree's name was not pronounceable, but it translated as Grows-in-Starlight, which was pretty and accurate. I knew that their fox would translate for them as mine translated for me. When they replied, their "voice" came through the senso clearly.

[Doctor/Coordinator Jens,] said Starlight. [Can you explain your professional choices to us?]

"You believe I made the wrong choice in staying on *Big Rock Candy Mountain* when Tsosie wanted to fall back?"

[Perhaps. Do you?]

"I've reviewed the ayatanas, mine and Tsosie's. I can't be certain, quite honestly. I believe I made a choice that worked out as well as any choice could have, under the circumstances."

[You don't think that contact with atavistic humans was an unnecessary risk?]

My species's premodern behavior has left us with something of a reputation, I'm afraid. "I was wearing some vintage ayatanas—"

[And their information didn't convince you to leave?]

They weren't unrightminded humans, and Starlight knew it. They were calling my bluff.

Starlight didn't have eyes, per se. So I wasn't quite sure how it was that I felt them studying me. Perhaps vast branches bent subliminally toward me as they focused their attention. Perhaps I was merely self-conscious as all get-out.

"That's not what you want me to defend, is it?"

[You are capable of self-criticism,] they said. [That is good.]

Well, if the military taught us anything, it was how to accept discipline and how to accept praise. Often at the same time.

It was a skill that I saw coming in handy right now. I nodded to accept the compliment, if it was a compliment. You could never be sure. Starlight's senso would translate the gesture for them as a form of human communication. Whether they understood me any better than I understood them—well, who could tell?

After a few moments, as if to see if I would fill the silence, Starlight said, [You brought a weapon into this hospital.]

Helen? Were they talking about Helen? The machine?

I would presume they were. If I had misunderstood, we could backtrack. I had come to understand that Starlight's seeming aggression and rapid-fire sequences of contextless questions weren't intended to give offense. It was just . . . how Starlight communicated.

I said, "Helen? A person. A patient. I brought a *patient* into a hospital. That's what hospitals are for."

Starlight seemed not to notice my indignation. It's hard to tell, when dealing with really alien systers, what they do or do not comprehend about any communication, even if it's translated for them. And the frustration, naturally, flows both ways. It's hard to translate experiences outside of context.

The Administree said, [It's a threat.]

I still wasn't sure if they were talking about Helen, but they hadn't contradicted me. "So are a lot of things we handle here. The machine is a person in need of healing. Should I have turned her away?"

[You also brought crew members of an unknown vessel, and a vessel that had met with an unknown accident, back with you.]

"We can help them, too. And you—well, the hospital, the Synarche, anyway—*sent* me to get them." I paused and thought. "You could have refused us docking privileges."

[We considered it.]

Ouch. "It was a weird trip," I said.

[Be that as it may. She wants you as a care liaison.]

"She . . . what?"

[Helen wants you to be her liaison. Apparently she trusts you.]

I did not have time to be anybody's care liaison. One of the physical symptoms of panic to certain members of my species is a coppery taste, if you were wondering. "Is she ready to be released on her own recognizance?"

[Dr. Zhiruo offered her an uncorrupted, air-gapped space within the Core General architecture in which to rebuild and update her personality modules under Dr. Zhiruo's supervision and with her help. Dr. Zhiruo says she's already more integrated. She's going to bring in the hospital archinformist as well, to work with integrating the machine once Helen is stable. Messages will be going out to the other archinformists serving on *I Rise From Ancestral Night* at the site of the generation ship. So, no, she's not ready to be released. But it's Dr. Zhiruo's professional opinion that it is safe to let her observe the care of her crew, and start integrating her into society.]

"I'm not qualified to be a care liaison."

[Technically,] they said, with a pedantic tone that carried even across senso translation, [you're extremely *overqualified* to be a care liaison. But the job should not be a problem for you. Which is good, because we are dealing with a dual first-contact situation. A form thereof, anyway. Helen's encountered Terran humans before, but not the Synarche. And her crew, if any of them live, might as well be aliens.]

"At least we can figure out how to speak their language."

[Your reports indicate that you already have studied their language and attempted speaking it to Helen when you met her. See?] Starlight rustled. [We are confident in your ability to do this job. We're only formalizing a role you've already adopted.]

"What is she going to do when Sally goes out again?"

[Sally is under repair.]

"That won't last forever." I felt like I was having the conversation I'd had with O'Mara all over again, and not in a good way. Going over their head was never going to work, anyway: hospital administration might disagree among themselves, but they knew how to present a unified front once a decision had been reached.

Usually, I enjoyed the lack of politics. Usually, I enjoyed not reporting directly to the Administree, whose conversational style was, well, branching. Discursive. And I couldn't always see how one topic hooked up with the previous one.

Starlight rustled, [Right now, Dr. Jens, you are needed here.]

I bit my lip and decided, for the time being, to save my ammunition. "I wanted to talk to you about this mission anyway. Something about this doesn't add up."

[Elaborate?]

"I'm worried about the coincidences," I admitted. "I'm worried about the operations of three different shipminds, if we count up Sally and Helen and Afar, being affected, their memories—and in one case their consciousness—being damaged. I'm confused about the timeline, but it seems very strange that Sally's memories would be sabotaged *before* she encountered two other ships with damaged shipminds. While she was on her way to find them. Responding to their distress beacon, in fact."

[Yes,] the administrator agreed. [That is odd. I give you permission to enjoy exploring this question in your new role.]

"You're asking me to play detective?"

[We understand that Master Chief O'Mara already has made such an investigative request of you. They believe you are suited to the task, and we trust their judgment.]

They really were all conspiring against me. "I don't want to lose my berth. I have no ambitions to be anything but what I am, Starlight."

[You'll have your job. This is not a punishment, though you seem to think it is.]

I sighed, and blew a straggling coil of hair out of my eyes. "It's been a long dia."

[Get some rest,] Starlight said kindly.

• • •

And that was how, after a rest period that I was surprised to spend deeply asleep without any self-interventions (and without interruptions from other members of the hospital staff), I wound up playing secret agent/detective/tour guide to a sexy robot. If that sounds like the sort of punishment that would be handed out in a particularly surrealist purgatory, congratulations. You're not wrong.

And I wasn't as familiar with a lot of the hospital as I should have been, because I hadn't spent very long grounded since I first came to the hospital for training.

Do they still say "grounded" when you're on a spinning platform in space?

I imagined that my grounding wouldn't really sink in until the first time Sally, having completed repairs, left without me. Left with a different rescue specialist in place. Somebody, I knew, who might want to keep that berth when I was free to fly again.

O'Mara had been very careful to withhold certain things from me. From what they'd said—and what they'd chosen *not* to say—it seemed likely Sally might be docked for longer than the dia or two it would take to get her back up to spec. But how *much* longer was the question.

The hospital couldn't afford to keep a resource as scarce as 50 percent of its ox-sector fast-rescue fleet locked away indefinitely when lives were at stake—unless the risk of sending her out outweighed any possible consequences. So O'Mara might stall for a little while, and keep Sally off the milk runs that a Judiciary ship or a more ordinary vessel could handle. But eventually lives would depend on speed, and Sally would go.

And unless I had solved the crime and shepherded Helen through treatment, I would stay behind. Gnawing on my fingers behind closed doors and trying in public to compartmentalize and do my job.

The Administree had said this duty wasn't a punishment. They had told me I wasn't being declawed and decommissioned. That suggested that they were telling the truth, and there *was* a return to my old job waiting at the end of this assignment.

But it was hard to believe I wasn't being punished when I knew very well that "my old job" was not even remotely the same as—or any guarantee of—my old berth. I enjoyed working with Sally and her crew. They were all good people and good at their jobs. I liked them. I trusted them. Even with Loese joining us so recently, we had become a team—a real machine. I didn't even think I drove Tsosie to any more distraction than he drove me.

And I *dreaded* going through the break-in and assimilation process with a new crew.

When you live with people for months on end, the relationships come to mean a lot to you. Moving from one such berth to another is not dissimilar from getting a divorce from one family and moving immediately in with the next.

One divorce was enough for this lifetime.

And thinking about divorces wasn't helping my emotional equilibrium any. I couldn't dwell on the pain and confusion it caused me right now. So I needed to find something else to think about.

And I couldn't live in fear of a future that might not happen. Not during work hours, at least: I had to function. I had a job to do.

Actually, I had two jobs to do. Maybe three. All of them full-time, and all of them conflicting with one another. What I *could* do that *would* help me with at least two of the tasks in front of me was download an ayatana from one of Core General's engineers so I at least knew my way around as well as anybody, and do the busywork assigned to me. That might also help me get a pattern on the sabotage attempts: nothing like a bat's-eye view for getting the lay of the land.

Oh, for the love of little space fishes, another Void-spawned ayatana.

At least I found one that belonged to a syster with a biology and taste buds that were pretty close to human, although the physiology was a miss.

Back to thinking *really hard* about peeing.

I walked out of the Memory Department feeling like half my legs were missing and I was likely to tip over at any moment. I somewhat alleviated the sensation by trailing my fingertips along one wall and letting my exo handle holding me up, but every time I blinked I could feel the hospital spinning. To add insult to injury, I had been issued my new gravity belt, per O'Mara's orders, and I couldn't even risk using it because of my acquired dyspraxia.

There was a lot of Core General to cover in the orientation tour I'd been asked to conduct. Since I had to narrow it down somehow, I collected Helen from her room and started her toward the cafeteria. Helen didn't eat. But she might enjoy the social hub. And frankly I liked my groceries as much as any sentient I've ever known, and the hospital has better food on offer than the ambulance ship's limited galley.

Fortunately, the engineer in my head was an expansive, good-natured person with a possibly unhealthy fascination for strain tolerances, and I was perhaps a little tipsily ebullient as I brought my charge down to the third-tier ox caf a little before first-shift main meal. I decided to be kind and get on the intranet before we arrived so we could still have a good chance of getting a table in a corner, before the real flood began. I would have gone to get actual coffee, but the cafe that served it was most of the hospital away, the decontamination process on the way out took twenty minutes, and anyway the ayatana I was wearing made me feel vaguely nauseated when I even thought about it.

Sigh.

My gamble worked, and I reserved a four-top by a viewport, with the bustling space of the Core on one side and the bustling cafeteria on the other. We arrived, I left Helen to hold it down, and I went through the line.

I scanned the metabolic codes and consulted the food preferences of my inner engineer. It's a terrible idea to nauseate a simulated passenger who is using your body for its physical responses. Which is how I wound up with spaghetti and fruit salad with a healthy sprinkle of freeze-dried crickets.

Simulated crickets, obviously. We're not barbarians.

We returned to Helen. I was a little surprised that she had cheerfully plunked herself down with her back to the room. I realized I had expected her to be stereotypically paranoid, like a character in a spy story. She seemed contented, though, and I started scarfing up my lunch as fast as I could ply my chopsticks.

Helen picked up a pair of chopsticks as well, and began experimenting. It was interesting watching her practice with them. She was a fast learner, and got measurably better at it over the course of one meal, even when she was lifting squish-ripe mango, slippery as a liver, before putting it back in the bowl so I could eat it.

Helen did not consume organics, obviously.

"Any questions so far?" I asked, around a mouthful of spaghetti. My mother and my old CO would both be horrified by my table manners.

Luckily they weren't here.

Helen turned her unsettling suggestion of a face to me. "Can I see my crew?"

I swallowed quickly. "I should have made arrangements to take you there first. I'm sorry. Give me a moment." I tapped into senso and filed a request to visit.

It was while my attention was turned inward that my old friend Dr. Rilriltok fluttered up, with the kind of timing that makes less savvy species accuse male Rashaqins of being telepathic.

The cafeteria was in an inner portion of the wheel, so the force of its simulated gravity barely affected Rilriltok, and it could even fly on its dazzling, crystalline wings—without using the gravity belt to compensate.

It did mean that those of us who were eating had to be gentle when we gestured with our utensils, lest we send a dollop of mashed potato or globroot floating into an unsuspecting colleague's airspace. But there was enough spin to keep your orange juice in the glass. After twenty ans in and out of space, that was almost a luxury.

"Don't be alarmed," I said to Helen as Rilriltok approached. "A giant bug is about to land on the table."

A moment later a giant bug landed on the table, wings buzzing to a gentle halt while their breeze stirred my hair. I balanced a cube of cricket-sprinkled melon between my chopsticks, shielding it from the wind with my other hand. Nobody wants surprise cricket in their air intakes.

Helen was staring unabashedly. Can you stare without eyes? Anyway, her focus was locked on Rilriltok.

She asked, "Is there any news of my crew?"

Greetings, friend Jens, said Dr. Rilriltok. *Greetings, Helen. One moment and I will acquaint you with the status of your crew. There has been no immediate change and there is no immediate danger. I see that Dr. Jens has filed a visit request for you; may I assist you in preparing psychologically?*

"Do I require psychological preparation?" She was looking at me.

"Hospital visits can be stressful," I said, with as little irony as I could manage.

Rilriltok set a tray in front of where it perched. As its head dipped forward, its large raptorial forearms craned up and out of the way. The blades were delicate-looking and translucent as fine porcelain, and as glitteringly sharp as a ceramic knife blade.

The smaller manipulator arms began selecting pieces of what looked like raw sliced lobster, shell and all. I'd been known to eat the cooked version—they were synthetic land prawns—but I still averted my eyes as the crunching and squishing started.

Rashaqin do not use their mouths to speak; they communicate through a combination of stridulation and controlled breathing through the spiracles on their abdomens. So they have no taboo about talking with their mouths full.

Rilriltok flipped its wing coverts and buzzed, *Helen, I am pleased to tell you that we have completed the DNA sequencing of your crew members without compromising the integrity of their compartments.*

Helen looked from Rilriltok to me. "I'm sorry," she said. "I do not have the vocabulary for what it just said. Can you help me?"

She seemed . . . calm. Maybe Zhiruo's therapy was helping. I suppose nothing is likely to make you more anxious than feeling like you can't handle the cognitive load that's expected of you. That you're *used* to handling.

I found her a dictionary easily enough. It didn't take long to translate for Helen, who was still apparently compiling and integrating the code and assimilating the uplink that would give her access to real-time translation through a link to Linden's functions.

Most of us ran translation through our foxes, under most circumstances, but the sheer volume of species and languages at Core made that impractical. The hospital probably played host to enough *human* languages alone to overload my fox's storage capacity.

Zhiruo had provided the tools for Helen, and had assured me that the kit she'd issued was firewalled to Well and gone. Air-gapped, even. I told myself that if the Core General wheelmind and the head of AI Medicine thought it was safe, it was probably safe. And she was rebuilding her entire mind from a kit, so it wasn't reasonable to expect her to have finished integrating.

Rilriltok picked up another slice of synthetic land prawn. I went back to my spaghetti. *Friend Jens, why have you been avoiding me?*

I choked on that spaghetti, which was very upsetting to the engineer ayatana, who was much more sensibly designed with regard to airways and food passages.

At least it didn't come out of my nose. It's a bad dia at work when that happens. Especially in front of an alien doctor who's going to wind up asking a lot of interested and helpful questions about sinuses and be very confused why humans evolved so stupidly as to let our respiration and food nutrition use the same set of tubes.

It's a bad design. I admit it. Nobody asked me for my input until it was far too late!

By the time I got myself under control enough to glare at Rilriltok, there was no sign of any mischief in its posture. There was no point trying to make eye contact—which eyes would I choose? All I would see in any of them was my reflection. Rashaqin do not have muscles in their faces to give them expression. The chitin is pretty, and excellent armor, and makes performing surgery on a Rashaqin an *incredible* pain in the ass involving a skill saw to open and epoxy to close. But it does not move.

It *did* scintillate with faint ripples of red and silver that might be laughter, and might just be enjoyment of the food.

It reached out a fine manipulator, and snagged a strand of my spaghetti. I broke the strand with my knife before it could weave my entire plateful into a braid and slurp it up.

After so many ans, I was wise to Rilriltok. For an obligate insectivore it certainly had a taste for Terran carbohydrates. It claimed that this was because *synthetic* land prawn didn't have stomach contents, depriving it of important nutrients. I had told it repeatedly that it could order its own salad.

The gesture of food-stealing had special meaning when performed by a male Rashaqin (male being something of a misnomer, as even Terran species don't limit themselves to two tidy sexes that always behave in the same predictable ways, but Rilriltok's species has two sexes and its is not the one that lays eggs). It meant that Rilriltok saw me as a colleague and a competitor—an equal—and not a threat, or an inferior. It was a compliment and a display of affection.

I should have swiped its land prawn in response, but I wasn't in the mood for sushi.

"I haven't been avoiding you!" I protested. It had only been—well, less than two diar, right? I had possibly lost track of my actual assigned rest periods. "I've just been . . . very busy. And so has Helen, here."

I looked at her to see if she needed that translated, but apparently she'd gotten the common vocabulary all right.

I had been very busy. Exhausted, and sleeping like the dead on the one chance I had gotten. Wedging research into a few spare hours. Running from meeting to meeting . . .

I don't just mean since this last emergency call, Rilriltok said.

. . . And trying not to spend too much face-to-face time with my friends when I wasn't on duty. Rilriltok was right. I had been hiding, and not just since this last mission. Hiding from my friends, because I was afraid that they would notice that my pain management was not what it should be. And then they'd want to do something about it, being doctors.

The way O'Mara had.

Doctors never want to hear that you're sick and tired of being poked; that you want to be left alone; that you've had enough experimental cures and management strategies for one lifetime. Doctors always want to try this one last thing.

Doctors are an enormous pain in the ass. Trust me. I know. I am one.

Time to change the subject, in other words.

"What do you know about the safety issues since I've been gone?" I asked in what I hoped was a light, gossipy manner.

Male Rashaqins did not, historically, survive without a very well-honed sense of other people's goals, motivations, and appetites. Part of why they made excellent doctors—and champion players of strategy games—was that they were fantastic at thinking outside the ordinary and at noticing patterns too subtle for most beings to detect.

I think they are concerning, Rilriltok said, after a moment of meditation. *They are, I think, meant to look as if they are intended to look accidental. But they are not intended to look accidental.*

I had to parse that one a couple of times before I was really sure what I thought it meant. "You think whoever is doing it is . . . acting out? Wants to get noticed?"

I think someone or someones are doing it. And it's dangerous and constitutes an enormous risk, so either they're severely damaged, or they have what seems to them an exceedingly good reason. It patted the antigravity belt strapped around its thorax with one feathery foot-tip. *You could talk to the Goodlaw.*

I hadn't met Core General's new lead law enforcement officer. I also knew that the sexes of Rilriltok's species went out of their way to avoid interacting with one another. "But isn't it a female Rashaqin?"

That consideration should give you context for how seriously I take this. Rilriltok picked up its beverage. It put a straw operated with a sort of squeeze bulb between its mandibles, not having the ability to suck, and seemed entirely focused on imbibing its drink. This was a mechanically fascinating process, involving manipulating the squeeze bulb until a honey-colored bubble, held together by surface tension, appeared at the top of the straw. Rilriltok then nibbled at it with the small wiggly mouthparts that were barely noticeable at the bottom of its wedge-shaped head.

"What is a Rashaqin?" Helen asked.

I waved to Rilriltok with the back of my hand. "The doctor here is a male one. Well, sort of male by Terran rules. The sort-of-females are bigger."

Much bigger, the meter-long Rilriltok said, stridulation unaffected by its beverage.

"Oh."

I could see Helen processing. I couldn't get over how alertly she watched conversations, head moving as if she were following a zero-g jai alai match. "I think I would like to meet such a creature."

Person, Rilriltok said, straight-facedly.

Which, okay, is another one of those anthropocentric terms, since we have this weird habit of using our facial muscles to communicate even nuanced emotions. Most sentients don't go in for that sort of thing. Even if you limit your sample to systers with faces. Or even to systers with facial muscles.

Unlike my friend Rilriltok, for example.

"Pardon?" Helen said.

"We say *person*," I clarified. "*Creature* is impolite."

"Oh," Helen said. "I'm sorry. I . . . I would *really* like to meet such a person."

It would be good for you.

I wondered if Rilriltok thought so for the same reasons I did. It niggled at me that O'Mara had recruited me when there was a perfectly good Goodlaw heading up hospital security. Was there some reason they didn't think it could get the job done? Or was it O'Mara being turfy, and relying on their old and trusted associates, as they'd hinted? While I was wondering, Rilriltok set the beverage container on the tray, sorted my dishes into piles, and stacked them up.

Fortunately, I hadn't wanted that last soggy cricket anyway. I placed my chopsticks across my fruit bowl and stood. So did Helen. She didn't seem to have any trouble calibrating her motions to the shifting pull of simulated gravity. That was impressive. I was *accustomed* to switching back and forth, and it still took a while each time for me to acclimate.

I picked up the tray to take it back to the disassembler and said, "Come, on, Helen. The doctor here probably has to get back to work. Let's walk with it, and check on your crew."

Helen very quickly got her wish to meet the female Rashaqin.

Core General's new Goodlaw was ahead of us in the admin and observation room when we arrived in the Cryo treatment center. It had hooked one foreleg over the safety rails that circled the lounge—as if an object the size of Core General was going to stop spinning—and was peering out into the Cryo unit with predatory fascination.

When we entered, the Goodlaw turned its head, faceted eyes glittering. It wore a dress uniform: a tidy, tailored little navy blue bolero jacket over its upper thorax, with cap sleeves cut to fit the upper joint of thorned killing limbs that I estimated would be a couple of meters long, extended.

I knew it was the Goodlaw, and not some other Rashaqin, because the jacket had a gold badge embroidered on its placket, and I could still read Judiciary ranks and uniforms.

Rilriltok had apparently not expected to report to work and discover an enormous natural enemy next to its desk. It came mandible-to-mandible with the mantoid—two-plus meters long even with its thorax held upright over its abdomen, and with raptorial forelimbs longer than Rilriltok's entire body even when folded—and swiftly and prudently alighted on my back. Out of the corner of my eye I saw that it had folded its wings tight and color-shifted to match my lab coat and scrubs.

I couldn't blame it.

I wondered if the Goodlaw had been waiting for us, or if this was a chance encounter. I guessed this was my opportunity to find out.

Greetings, the enormous predator stridulated. *I am Goodlaw Cheeirilaq. You must be Dr. Brookllyn Jens. And . . . Helen Alloy?*

Politely, it pretended not to notice Rilriltok, who huddled closer to my spine. Rilriltok's coverts clicked tightly closed, protecting its delicate wings. The barbs on its fine manipulators tangled so thoroughly in the dense springs of my hair that I worried it would take surgery to get us disengaged.

Rashaqin reproduction is harrowing. Their entire social order is built to keep adults well-separated, with lots of private space, so they don't accidentally eat one another. The spawn are aquatic and generally not considered to be sentient until they pass through the nymph stage and emerge on land in their penultimate instar as miniature adults. At this point, they are taken into crèches and educated by carefully organized, regimented communities of adults.

This is probably for the best, as the spawn are both numerous and cannibalistic. On Rashaq, they're left to fend for themselves until they molt out into that educable stage.

Swimming is not encouraged for tourists on Rashaq. Rashaqins, as responsible sentients, do their best to avoid reproducing elsewhere. It's hard on the local ecosystem. Also on their colleagues, as the egg-laying sex generally eats the other during the reproductive interlude, unless they're already extremely well-fed. I understand that in modern society, the—we'll call them females, though it's not entirely accurate—generally bloat themselves with food before intercourse or resort to technological intervention for fertilization. And the males—like Rilriltok—tend to feed everybody they meet.

When I was still Judiciary and visited Rashaq a couple of decans ago, they were in the midst of a natural child-rearing fad. There had been a lot of articles about how the egg-layer eating the progenitor was much healthier for the young and rendered them more competitive in the wild. As there are, demographically, significantly more of Rilriltok's sex, competition for mates is pretty extreme, and a surprising-to-me number of males volunteered.

Things might have gotten even uglier than they did, but Core General and the Judiciary both sent crisis intervention teams, and eventually the fad blew over with only a few dozen casualties who hadn't signed up to be eaten. We managed to catch all the perpetrators and remand them for rightminding.

Anyway, my interaction with the Core General medical team there was how I got interested in working here.

"You've identified me correctly," I said. "We're here to check on our patients."

Well, the patients were mine and Rilriltok's. They were Helen's crew.

Close enough.

I stepped past Cheeirilaq toward the window, raising the arm on the far side of my body so Rilriltok could use it as a bridge to scuttle around to the front if it felt it necessary. My colleague seemed to be at the mercy of its freeze reflex, however.

Cheeirilaq kept a respectful distance, and I assumed if Rilriltok needed to leave it would let me know.

Beyond the windows, the familiar coffins lay side by side, raised on racks that brought them up to a convenient height for most species to work at. Doctors and technicians of several species moved calmly around them, reading instruments and peering at whatever lay behind open panel covers. All the coffins we had brought back appeared to be here, and appeared to be intact.

Helen's relief was palpable even before she said, "None of the systems have failed."

It was still too early to be certain of that, but it seemed like a terrible time to point it out, so I didn't.

CHAPTER 13

RILRILTOK'S WEIGHT SHIFTED AS IT RAISED ITS EYES TO peer over my shoulder. I turned slightly to give it a better view and more cover behind my torso.

Helen walked up to the glass and pressed both hands and what passed for her face against it. The body parts she pushed against the glass squished and flattened.

I guessed that left it up to me to carry the conversation.

I said, "What brings you here, Goodlaw?"

And almost jumped out of my scrubs when Rilriltok stridulated instead. The vibrations of its speech shivered up my spine and left my teeth aching in the bones of my skull.

Huh, it said. *Well, that's peculiar.*

"Peculiar?" I echoed, grateful that the vagaries of senso translation hadn't choked up an ambiguous word such as "funny."

Rilriltok didn't answer. It swarmed up my shoulder and stood balanced against the intervening window, giving me an unusual view of its feathery feet-hooks splayed on the transparent wall and the smooth, interlocking plates that made up the underside of its abdominal carapace. Its instinctive camouflage failed, and excited rills of blue and orange ran along its body from head to tail.

Pardon me, friend doctor, the Goodlaw said, in very careful tones. *I apologize for addressing you directly, and if you find the situation too stressful I will withdraw the question. But, if you will pardon my rudeness, what is it that you have observed?*

The scientist on my shoulder didn't even flinch away from the predator it had been petrified of moments before. It shook itself with an excited buzz and flipped its wings as if ordering its thoughts.

These cryo units are not all identical, it said. *They look similar, but let me draw your attention to these impedance readouts.*

It tapped the glass, bringing up a display that my senso translated into good old human symbols after a couple of annoying flickers. They would have meant nothing to me—I am not a cryo specialist—but they meant something to the ayatana of the engineer that I was wearing.

One of the pods was significantly more efficient than the others, and running at significantly safer tolerances.

"Can we go inside?"

Rilriltok turned its head to me with one of the sharp, unsettling gestures that used to make me jerk back in surprise, before I became accustomed to my friend. *I don't see why not.*

Helen, who had been standing perfectly straight except that her face pressed against the glass, said, "What do you mean, they're not all identical? Of course they're identical. We made them all on the same plan—"

Linden, I said to Core General's giant, quiet sentience. With almost limitless space and processing power, the wheelmind's only job was to care for the well-being of everyone who lived within her hull. The hospital didn't talk much, but she was always there. Abiding.

She didn't really need a hint from me. I felt her moving to soothe Helen, to calm her anxious algorithms and tame her runaway emotion modules. Linden would also call Dr. Zhiruo, if needed.

The interrupt was a good thing, even though I felt bad that it was being used without Helen's consent. But it was being used to keep her safe. Her, and her crew, and the staff of Core General.

Helen didn't breathe. But the effect of Linden's intervention on her was exactly as if she had taken one deep breath, centered herself, and settled. Rilriltok had already lifted off my shoulder, and was zooming toward the door. I followed it—not quite as swiftly as Helen did—and Cheeirilaq trooped gamely along behind us. We disinfected—we didn't have to mask and glove up, because none of the coffins were open—asked the staff for permission to join them, and went inside.

The first thing I noticed now that there wasn't a helmet between me and the coffins—well, and now that they weren't in vacuum in a cargo hold—was that the cryo units had a smell. A particular tang, like ozone or something. Watching Rilriltok's feathery olfactors wave, I got a sense that I wasn't the only one smelling it.

Rilriltok hovered up to its closest colleague—a gigantic Thunderby with three trunklike legs that stepped around the smaller medicos like a large human picking their way among cats—and said, *Tell me about the differences in the units.*

The specialist—a Dr. Tralgar, from its fox signature—waved a brick-red, tentacular appendage in an untranslatable gesture and said, *Well, one of these is much better designed than the others. And there's something odd about the cranial scan on the person inside.*

"None of these people should have foxes, right?" I asked.

None of these people do have foxes, Dr. Tralgar trumpeted softly. At least, I assumed it was trying to keep its voice down, as I was only lightly deafened. The bugling and subsonics made an unpleasant counterpoint to the lingering buzz from Rilriltok's stridulations. *But this one has intracranial scarring.*

"Brain damage?"

They're not my species—a tentacle waved apologetically—*but I'm wearing an ayatana from a human neurosurgeon. And I'm reasonably certain the scarring is surgical in nature.*

"You're not saying somebody lobotomized this patient?"

The scarring is not consistent with a lobotomy. It may be the result of a tumor removal or an aneurysm repair.

"May I have a look, Doctor?" I asked.

It wriggled in compliance. *Of course, Doctor. You were on the retrieval team, were you not?*

I nodded, confident that senso would translate the gesture.

Rilriltok had not awaited protocol. It buzzed the cryo pods, waving its antennae near open and closed panels. When it circled back, it hovered excitedly and said, *The electrical signatures are slightly different, friend Llyn, between this unit and the others.*

I had forgotten that the Rashaqin sensorium had the ability to detect electromagnetic fields.

They're also different colors, Cheeirilaq said. *There's more infrared in the one your colleague mentioned.* It extended a raptorial forelimb and waved the razorlike tip very gently, near the closest of the anomalous units. *I would say this one was manufactured separately and integrated into the lot.*

"I made them all. The machine and I did. I would know if one was different," Helen said, with great certainty. Then she squared her shoulders and repeated, more forlornly, "If that had happened, I *would* know."

What if someone modified your program? Cheeirilaq asked. *This capsule is demonstrably different. More advanced than the others. And yet it seems you cannot recognize that.*

Helen twisted from the waist, inhumanly, a colloid contained in a person-shaped skin. A ripple passed through her, as if she was thinking of doing the swelling-up trick again.

I like mysteries, Cheeirilaq said. *Maybe this one is modern. Maybe Afar brought it. Maybe they were hiding a criminal.*

Cops are cops. "A human criminal on a methane ship?"

Its wing coverts rippled. *Do you have a more interesting solution?*

"Maybe Helen and the machine got lucky and turned out a really good one."

Cheeirilaq bobbed its thorax. *Dr. Tralgar, is there any chance we can wake these people up?*

"Let's discuss that further somewhere else," I suggested, before Tralgar or Rilriltok could comment on the likelihood of any of the patients surviving rewarming.

Oh, Rilriltok said, jerking in the air as if suddenly remembering that Cheeirilaq was there. *Oh dear. Have you eaten? Can I offer you something to eat?*

Cheeirilaq bowed its elongated thorax very close to the deck and folded its raptorial arms tightly against its body. *Thank you, friend Rilriltok. I am quite satiated. Now, Doctor, about these patients. Would it be ethically acceptable under these circumstances to type the DNA of these individuals for identification purposes?*

Questionable, said Dr. Tralgar.

I ducked a waist-thick tentacle.

Tralgar continued, *Eminently ethical, and in fact even necessary, to do so in order to develop a treatment plan and begin growing replacement organs. We have already done so. What is not ethical, unfortunately, is releasing that information to law enforcement without either a warrant, or the patient's permission. Since I assume you want to run it against your databases.*

Cheeirilaq nodded its triangular head. *I'm reasonably certain that I can come up with a Judicially acceptable argument that there is evidence of some sort of a crime committed here—kidnapping consisting of cryonic suspension without consent—and obtain such a warrant.*

Good. Then come back when you have it. I'm going to bring Dr. K'kk'jk'ooOOoo to consult. She's a specialist in brain damage, and she might have some ideas about this patient's intracranial scarring.

I said, "I'd hate to think that somebody intentionally damaged this person's brain."

Before dropping them off in an intentionally primitive cryo pod? And somehow convincing Helen here that the patient was a crew member whose presence had always been logged in her manifest? I'd hate to think that, too. Although I suspect that everybody who survives rewarming will have a little brain damage to contend with. Tralgar waggled its upper torso back and forth. *We are also inspecting the samples for archaic pathogens. Measles, influenza,* Y. pestis, *and so on. The cultures and scans are extensive and will take several diar to process fully. We cannot begin rewarming procedures until we are certain we have appropriate vaccines and treatment available for any bugs we may be importing from the distant past.*

It made a noise that senso translated as a chuckle. *Not that I need to be worried. But Dr. Jens here would probably prefer not to die of scarlet fever or something equally romantic and premillennial.*

Surgeons are not notoriously great at bedside manner.

"That patient is Specialist Jones," Helen said.

She'd told me about Jones on the way in. The historian. The one I wanted to introduce to our archinformists, if she lived. That level of confidence and backstory seemed to contradict Cheeirilaq's theory that she'd been stuck in with the other corpsicles as a kind of frozen Trojan horse.

I nibbled my lip, trying to decide how to respond to Helen's statement.

"I give permission," Helen said suddenly.

"I beg your pardon?" I'd understood her perfectly. But I had expected her to say something quite different, based on available evidence and her behavior patterns so far.

"I give permission," Helen said. "They are my crew. I am in authority over them, in the absence of a commanding officer. I give you permission to examine them, and to release such information as may be relevant to an ongoing investigation to Constable Cheeirilaq."

I guessed all that extra storage and the personality reconstruction were having an effect already. Dr. Zhiruo was the best at what she did, and Helen must not have been as intractable a case as I'd feared.

Well, boomed Tralgar. *That conveniently settles that. Now about the rewarming*— It abruptly bent all three enormous legs at surprisingly sharp angles and dropped its posterior end to the deck, sitting down. It folded its tentacles and seemed to scrunch in on itself, widening and thickening throughout the muscular gumdrop of its body. This brought the conical head with its circle of bright violet eyes and walrus whiskers to my eye level, more or less.

This may be distressing information, it admitted, leaning toward Helen. She did not step back. *Are you prepared to internalize bad news?*

I'm here, Linden whispered in my senso.

"I am prepared," Helen said.

Dr. Rilriltok? the Thunderby offered.

Rilriltok hovered gently over my shoulder. The breeze it generated was pleasant on my neck. It buzzed.

We can at best expect a thirty percent success rate based on the level of technology of the cryo units. Some of the patients who survive are likely to have severe deficits, possibly permanent ones. In those cases—survival, with brain injury—we can repair the organic damage, but in the absence of ayatanas—

"What are ayatanas?" Helen asked.

I realized I'd never heard her interrupt before.

"Machine-stored memories," I said.

Helen nodded, an odd, crisp gesture that bobbed her head like the stride of a connecting rod.

In the absence of ayatanas, Tralgar continued, *we cannot restore their memories or personalities. They will essentially be new people in the same bodies. The patient in the better capsule is much likelier to make a full recovery.*

Helen collapsed in on herself. Literally, as her previous slight expansion vanished, and her body contracted to a smaller, denser-seeming version.

I asked, "Those odds don't change if we wait? Past the point where the transplants and cultures are ready, I mean?"

They do not change, Rilriltok said, sympathetically.

I half expected Helen to straighten up, or shake herself, or make some other small human gesture of resignation and resolve. But what she did was stand perfectly still—eerily still, back in her statue mode. It was so very unsettling, being around an AI who was embodied in a humanoid but entirely unhuman shell.

"I should not be deciding this," she said. "The captain should be deciding this."

"Perhaps someone in the chain of command will be in the next shipload of rescues," I suggested.

"The captain . . ." She was so still, so motionless, that it seemed as if her voice originated from all around us rather than being localized in the slight golden body of the peripheral. "The captain. The captain's orders . . ."

There was a terrible sound like rending metal. Rilriltok darted back—a quick, perfectly horizontal zip of flight in reverse. Tralgar leaned its bulk slightly toward Helen and uncoïled its tentacles. Cheeirilaq froze, long thorax elevated so it towered over me, forelimbs cocked in a predatory position.

I swallowed my desire to run, tuned my racing heartbeat to a less painful level of acceleration, and trusted Linden to know what she was talking about when she said she had things under control.

"The captain," Helen said, still utterly immobile except for the small motion of her small hands knotting themselves into fists, "gave the orders for the crew to be frozen. The captain wrote the program. The captain took Central apart. The captain made it happen. He died."

Too late I remembered the body in the chair on the bridge.

Helen said, "It is not my fault. I followed orders. It is not my fault."

I thought about that. About all the ways it could have happened. Epidemic illness among the crew. Mutiny and the need to stop mutiny.

Sophipathology and madness.

She didn't seem to be done speaking, and none of us interrupted. In a standard second or two, with the air of someone gritting their teeth on a decision, she continued, "If we don't try to help them, then they are all dead."

As good as, Tralgar agreed.

"Do it," Helen said. And collapsed in a puddle of gold, only vaguely formed to resemble a human being.

"Page Dr. Zhiruo!" I yelled, but the presence chime and lights were already announcing her arrival. I wanted to shout for a crash team, but a crash team was useless. Helen wasn't a human being. She was a peripheral.

The engineer whose skills and memories I was borrowing would be far more useful. "Use my hands if you need them," I told Zhiruo, crouching beside Helen. "Tell me how to intervene."

There was a pause that stretched subjective ans. Then, "It's all right," Zhiruo said. "She's withdrawn herself into the core we provided."

"Is her link with the peripheral severed?"

"Not permanently."

I might have felt slightly disappointed at that. Less so than I would have when we found Helen. I still didn't like her burlesque body, but maybe I was starting to get used to it.

Whether that was a good thing or a bad one, I wasn't certain. It was certainly, however, a thing I could worry about some other time.

"Too much strain?" I asked.

"Conflicting calls," Zhiruo answered. "Preserve her crew, or risk all to save some. Disobey a direct order from her captain, or follow it and let her people die. Her program is not very robust when dealing with real-world conflicts. As we bring her into modern architecture, her resilience will improve."

"Right," I said.

Zhiruo had backed a gurney up next to me. I scooped Helen's gelatinous form up in my arms, remembering to lift with my knees—and my exo. I told myself that it could have been a lot worse. At least the peripheral was room-temperature, rather than actually clammy.

I put her on the gurney and arranged her decently. Her arms and legs were jointless and fluid in their relaxed state, unsettlingly as if her bones had liquefied. "Zhiruo, your patient."

"Thank you," she said.

Rilriltok zipped sideways out of the way as the gurney trundled itself toward the door.

Tralgar seemed to be watching it go. *What are you going to do next?* it asked me.

I bit my lip. "Talk to the archinformist, I guess."

Let us know what you find out, said Rilriltok, from the corner by the door. *I guess we'll start seeing how many lives we can save.*

CHAPTER 14

THE HOSPITAL HAS ITS OWN ARCHINFORMIST, THE MEDIcal librarian. His name is Mercy.

And one nice thing about the hospital AIs is that you don't have to go see them. You can call them up and ask a question anywhere.

On the other hand, I really like the library.

We didn't have physical libraries back on Wisewell: the settlement was too new and the resources not available to dedicate an entire building—or even a room in one—as a temple to knowledge. Here on Core General, space is at a premium, but many people work more efficiently when they leave their quarters to do so, and communal workspace is much more efficient than private offices.

If sharing workspace means not having to either hot-bunk *or* manage my own journal subscriptions, I'm all for it. And libraries are pleasant and efficient communal workspaces. So we have a lot of libraries.

The ox-sector library closest to my quarters is a wedge-shaped compartment, half of which is divided into soundproofed study carrels capacious enough for sentients somewhat larger than me. The other half of the room has adjustable benches with wide aisles and privacy shields every two meters.

I wouldn't care to try to cram Tralgar into a study carrel, either. Even as a theoretical exercise.

I selected a carrel at the back, with nobody working nearby, and programmed the chair and desk setup so I could settle in with my feet elevated and my knees propped up. Fortunately, I was well-caffeinated, or I might have dozed off, because the chairs were awfully comfortable.

The screens came alive with a dim, cheery glow as I lowered myself into the chair and dropped the privacy shield. Patient information is meant to be kept confidential. I was sure the entire hospital was already buzzing about Helen and her crew, but at least I could observe the forms.

"Mercy," I said, "I have a problem."

"Hello, Dr. Jens," he answered. "I have a solution. Shall we see if they match?"

I should mention that one of the challenges of working with archinformists—or with Mercy, who is the only archinformist I've worked with extensively, so I should not generalize—is their fondness for very, very, very old things.

Including jokes.

Very, very, very old jokes.

You can't stare at an AI under lowered brows, so I said, "I've been appointed to the care team for the archaic AI we recovered, and I'm hoping you can give me some data on the history of her ship and possibly even some development files, if there are any."

"I can try," Mercy said. "Information that's specific to Terran history and which is not frequently called for may take a while to . . . un*earth,* however."

Ouch. Don't say I didn't warn you.

"Isn't all of human knowledge since the 1990s preserved in a holographic solid somewhere?" Preferably, somewhere in the Core, so it wouldn't take too long to get to.

"A lot of people think so," he said. "There used to be an axiom that the Internet was forever."

I had to look up *Internet* as he was talking. A primitive form of senso, without neural interface, accessible through small handheld devices.

"And it's not forever?"

Graphics and charts and illustrations populated the screens around me, a bewildering array.

"Nothing is forever," he said, as cheerfully as only a functionally immortal artificial intelligence could. "If retrieving archaic data were easy, if there were no informational decay, my specialty would not exist. There would be no archinformists, no research librarians."

"Wait," I said. "How can *information* decay?"

"They used to call it *bit rot*. Servers get taken down, data falls through the cracks and doesn't get backed up. Physical substrates are destroyed or damaged, or degrade over time—especially the primitive ones. A holographic diamond is very durable but can't be changed once it's written to, and magnetic media only lasted a decan or so under ideal conditions.

"And even if the data is preserved somewhere, that somewhere might not be networked. If it's networked, it might not be indexed. Even if it's indexed, it might be half the galaxy away and take two or three ans for the file request to get there, be fulfilled, turn around, and come back. And then you might find out that you needed different files entirely." He huffed with great satisfaction. "Infohistory is a mess."

"Well." Despondence is useless, so I tuned it down, took a breath, and regrouped. "I guess that gives you job security."

"As long as somebody somewhere cares what happened in medicine in the past."

"Do you only do medicine?"

"I *specialize* in medicine," he said. "The past is a big place."

"If it had bearing on a medical case, could you look up some information for me?"

"I could," he said, judiciously, "try. It might take a while."

"My whole lifetime?"

"A noticeable percentage. But not a large one, assuming you maintain good health and you continue to exercise due caution regarding the risks of your profession."

Fantastic. Everybody needs an actuarial AI.

Well, I'd asked.

"Fantastic," I said, forcing myself to feel and sound bright and cheerful. "I need any background you can get me on the Terran generation ship *Big Rock Candy Mountain.* Especially her crew roster and build details on the AI known as Helen Alloy."

"Such a clever name!" Mercy enthused.

I closed my eyes. There had to have been somebody other than her designer who would think naming a sexy metal android with a metal-based pun on Helen of Troy was a good idea. It was my luck that the other one was a colleague.

"Dr. Zhiruo said you'd already been working on Helen?"

"Since you're her care liaison," Mercy said, "I can tell you in confidence that her substrate is badly degraded. I've been patching her personality core with predictive algorithms. We're rebuilding the substrate with modern materials and integrating the new core into her existing build as much as possible, to preserve continuity of experience."

"Zhiruo said you had her using some external storage."

"She already was, after a fashion."

"The machine."

"Yes. It's semiautonomous. Not really a part of Helen, but also not really *not* a part of her. It might be more intelligent en masse, but the sample we have is built on reactive algorithms rather than being on the road to true consciousness. It's possible that Helen started using the machine as external storage as her own systems degraded, and its lack of flexibility—for lack of a better word—infected her processes. I suspect it was intended to be a tool, and not autonomous. Helen was designed to have access to an external storage core—"

"Central," I said.

"Yes. I'm not certain of the timeline. I *theorize* a potential sequence of events in which her captain ordered Helen to construct cryo pods and then ordered the crew into them before destroying the ship's library and main computing core. Or perhaps he took it offline: I won't know for sure until I have a chance to speak with the archinformists who are working on the generation ship itself and see what they have found. Helen must have been nearly quiescent at that point, as she'd been ordered not to access Central. The captain, well. You found him."

I swallowed. Indeed we had.

"At some later time, possibly as an outgrowth of the evolving conflict over following the captain's orders versus following her core values and caring for the crew in the pods, Helen hit on the apparently weird solution of converting a bunch of the ship's remaining material into—"

"The machine."

"Yes. The storage she needed, and a friend. Of sorts. And she hadn't been specifically ordered not to do it. She was pretty well degraded into sophipathology at that point, though."

I remembered the microbot pseudopod taking a swipe at me, and shuddered. "Well, tools are dangerous when used improperly. You can cut your finger off with a circular saw."

"Indeed, one can."

"So where do we start looking?"

"The generation ship itself might still have some or all of the data you're looking for, despite whatever damage the library—Central—sustained. That is what we have archinformists working on it for."

I began to see the problem. "But the generation ship isn't networked, and its AI is corrupted."

"The library might be salvageable. The archinformists will make duplicates of whatever they can retrieve from the files. They'll bring those back to the Core. That information will be useful," he said. "Also, I should warn you that every archinformist and journalist in fifteen light-ans is inbound in hopes of interviewing Helen."

"Is that my problem?" Little space fishes, there were things I cared less about than history. And one of them was wrangling historians.

Humor tinged his disembodied voice. "As her care liaison . . . yes."

Before I left the library, I checked in on Helen's status—still recompiling—and then with Sally to see if she or the Core General mechanical teams were making any progress with the walker. Sally said that it was still crouching there with the door open.

Like some sort of ambush predator buried in sand, except for its gaping maw. Her turn of phrase, not mine. Sally has a colorful vocabulary.

They hadn't managed to get a drone or even a passive probe past its door defenses, and drilling into the thing from the outside was as much of a failure as it had been when I tried it. I felt a little gratified that even people whose core proficiency was in breaking stuff weren't managing any better than I had.

O'Mara had come down and looked at the thing, pronouncing it the equal of any military-grade hardware they'd seen. On their recommendation, the hospital stood ready to jettison it if it suddenly became aggressive.

Sally also told me that her repairs were nearly complete, but that she had not yet been cleared to return to duty. She expressed worry that I would not be available when she was released. I expressed my concerns right back, tuning like hell so I didn't start crying.

I'd cry later, if I had to.

I told Sally that it was going to take quite a while to rewarm Helen's crew. And I might be . . . grounded . . . until all that was well underway.

"Is that what you want?" she asked.

"No," I said.

"Well," she said. "*I* want to keep you."

That left me feeling a warm glow that was something of an antidote to all my recent frustrations.

The next logical step for me was to check on Afar and *his* crew, who—being in the methane section—were much less physically accessible to Cheeirilaq, Rilriltok, Helen, and I. Well, honestly—I didn't know about Helen. Possibly she could walk into a methane section like it wasn't anything. Possibly it would speed up her processing to be superchilled.

Or maybe she'd freeze solid.

I should ask, once she was feeling well enough for visitors again.

Rather than suiting up and tromping through the methane section, with all the attendant risks and nuisances, I met up with Rilriltok and we removed ourselves to a remote observation lounge. The lounges were usually used by residents and doctors on a training rotation to watch treatment in sections they were not biologically suited to—but they were open to anybody with an interest. Teaching hospitals are great.

Monitors and holopresence units along two walls gave us a mediated view of the ward where the Darboof crew members were resting. It was, by human standards, pitch-black in the actual ward, but the lounge translated the Darboof's homey, comfortable IR into wavelengths my visual receptors could process.

A patient care specialist of some description moved around the beds. Having given up the Darboof ayatanas, I did not know if the person manipulating their crystalline limbs and administering medication or nutrition was the equivalent of a nurse or filled some other function. They were, however, remarkably efficient, and I left myself a note in senso to find out who they were, so I could request them for my own patients in future, if needed.

We were barely getting settled when Tsosie walked in, followed by Cheeirilaq. Tsosie seemed as surprised to see us as I was to see him in the company of the Goodlaw. Or maybe he only noticed me. Rilriltok was suddenly blending into the upholstery again. I hoped it didn't get sat on. That would be an embarrassing incident report to have to fill out.

Greetings, Dr. Jens, Cheeirilaq stridulated. I was certain *it* noticed Rilriltok, by how politely it kept its triangular face pointed toward the observation windows.

"Oh," Tsosie said. "Are you checking on our patients?"

"Not ours anymore," I said. "Technically."

"I'm not busy while we're grounded." He walked to the monitors on the side of the room at right angles to the ones I had been observing. The new bank lit up in its turn with a different angle on the enhanced images of Afar's crew. "Loese is volunteering in the nursery, she's so bored. I've gotten involved with retrofitting the gravity generators into key areas. It's grunt work—"

He sighed.

Of all the people I thought would enjoy spending time around children . . . well, Loese wasn't one of them. It goes to show how stereotypes can mislead.

"I didn't know you knew anything about gravity generators."

"I played around with them a little in my downtime. I like techy stuff." He grinned.

From here, we could have accessed senso from the care team—filtered, so we didn't wind up with their love lives. . . . Did Darboof or any of the methane breathers even have love lives? Hastily, I canceled the request for info that my wondering had automatically generated, before the answer chipped away any more of my battered innocence.

Accessing the senso would have come with partial immersion in their alien sensorium, however. Having worn Darboof ayatanas, I wasn't in any hurry to experience that again so soon. They were too different to fit comfortably over my skin. For one thing, their nervous systems depended on supercooled superconductors to move electricity around. They *thought* with electrons—same as Sally, same as me, same as Rilriltok—but they thought awfully fast. And moved awfully slow.

Their experience was a particularly ill-fitting suit, for a human.

They probably would have felt the same way about me and my weird, hot, bright life. Although there were hobbyists who liked to try on other species recreationally. The more exotic and extremophile, the better. Not that I judge, but some subcultures are odd.

"I'm bored, too." I had plenty to do, but none of it was what I *loved* doing. I contemplated my thumbnails, and the moonstone gleam of my exo against the skin of my hands. I was tempted to tell him about my conversations with O'Mara and Starlight. Did he know about the extent of the sabotage on Core General? Rilriltok had been cagey but informed. But from O'Mara I'd gotten a sense that they were keeping it quiet, and all I'd heard through the grapevine since I got back was a bit of muttering about unlucky happenings—or, depending on the personality of the mutterer, poor maintenance.

Cheeirilaq must know, being a Goodlaw. And Rilriltok had suggested I speak with it, though I hadn't nerved myself up yet. I wasn't sure it would want assistance from outside of its chain of command, especially assistance foisted on it by a former Judiciary noncom who now worked for an entirely different organization.

Its role was not quite judge, jury, and executioner, but beings that achieved the status of Goodlaw in the Judiciary were trusted by the Synarche to exercise reliable judgment in ethically complex frontier situations, when they could not rely on communication to higher authorities. That was a level of responsibility that went beyond solid rightminding and into strong personal moral development—not to mention an encyclopedic knowledge of legal precedents.

I trusted Sally and her crew with my life. But somebody had sabotaged Sally. And although it didn't seem likely, I found myself circling back to consider the possibility that it had happened after we left Core General. So where did that leave me? Wondering if I could trust Tsosie. Wondering if I could trust Cheeirilaq enough to confide in it.

I refused to wonder about Rilriltok.

But as implications I had been sort of glossing over in a haze of busyness unpacked themselves, my heartbeat seemed to pulse in my belly rather than my chest, and my hands grew cold. I was suddenly rather scared.

"I'm still intrigued by the mystery," I admitted. Then I rolled my eyes in irritation. "Oh, Void. I should have asked Zhiruo about Afar. I got distracted by Helen and all the discussion of corpsicles."

Mystery? Cheeirilaq's head bobbed forward, framed by the collar of its little blue jacket. *Do you mean the potential law enforcement problem I am investigating?*

"Maybe? You haven't explained your interest in Helen and her crew. Is it acceptable to ask what your intentions are?"

As I formed the question, I realized that it had seemed natural to encounter the Goodlaw because we had been talking about it, so I hadn't questioned the coincidence of it being interested in our historical and medical mystery.

Helen, her crew, Afar, and his crew, also. Allow me to set it forth thusly:

First, why and how was Big Rock Candy Mountain *moving so quickly?*

Second, why was Afar docked with the generation ship?

Third, why was Afar transporting—I should say, smuggling, because it does not appear on a manifest—what appears to be a privately designed and manufactured combat walker? Or a really overdesigned environmental suit, perhaps, because it does not appear to have weapons.

Fourth, who sent Afar, and where was Afar en route to?

Fifth, what incapacitated Afar's crew?

"Wait," I interrupted, connecting some dots that had seemingly been too apparent to the Goodlaw to warrant expositing. "Arms smugglers?"

It would appear so. Shall I continue?

There was more. Of course there was more. "Be my guest."

Tsosie had his arms folded and was watching with an expressionless mouth and a little line between his eyes. The expression was familiar, and boded ill for somebody.

Not, I hoped, me. Or Cheeirilaq.

Cheeirilaq buzzed softly.

Sixth, what incapacitated Afar?

Seventh, if the thing that incapacitated Afar is not the same thing, what is causing the generation ship's shipmind or shipminds to malfunction?

"I might have some answers on that one, actually. I've been talking to Mercy." Quickly, I relayed what he had reconstructed from Helen's information about the captain freezing his crew, incapacitating the shipmind, and then eventually dying alone—old age? illness? suicide?—in his command chair. I was aware of Rilriltok leaning close and listening intently, and the moment in which it buzzed and coruscated with excitement vibrated my jaw.

I might have some information to contribute on that front, it said. *Our preliminary scans of the rescued patients indicate that many of them are infected with a human influenza-type virus. We will be vaccinating human hospital staff against it, and we have antiviral treatments available for the patients as they are rewarmed.*

We all looked at one another in silence, humans and Rashaqins. Tsosie breathed out, an eloquent sigh.

"Out of curiosity," I said, "was Specialist Jones one of the ones infected?"

Rilriltok hesitated, with the air of one consulting senso for its notes. *She is not.*

Cheeirilaq stretched its lime-green wing coverts wide, cocked its head, and continued, *I have one more question.*

"Let's hear it," Tsosie said, as if relieved for the break in tension.

Eighth, how can rock also be candy?

I blinked. Tsosie snorted. I pointed a finger at the Goodlaw, realizing too late that that might be seen as a very aggressive gesture by a species whose forelimbs were cavalry sabers.

I folded the finger back into my hand. "Was that a joke?"

Honest curiosity.

"Rock candy is crystallized sucrose," Tsosie said.

Rilriltok's antennae peeked over the back of its chair. *Ninth,* it interjected, *how did an anomalous cryo pod wind up mixed in among the rest?*

That should have been first, the Goodlaw said. *I'm slipping.*

Rilriltok was obviously terrified, but nothing as small as mortal peril could inhibit that vast curiosity and intellect.

Most doctors don't get to serve at Core General. A few might come here for an exomedicine rotation or a residency. Only the very best are invited to stay. Any given attending physician here is, in general, among the galaxy's best in their specialty.

I can say that without embarrassment because I got in by having a very narrow and unusual specialty. And I have an advantage in that my background in the military—Judiciary Search and Rescue—is why I serve on Sally. I'm a rare subspecies of doctor: I started my medical training by ministering to people who were already in difficult and dangerous situations, and my treatment goal was getting them out of those difficult and dangerous situations in no greater number of pieces than I had acquired them in. So rescue ops hold no terrors for me.

By contrast, Rilriltok did not obtain its position through any sort of special standing. It's just a really excellent cryonics doc—a really excellent doc in general. This fact, I found reinforced in my understanding as it launched itself from the chair, buzzed up to the window, and rested feathery forelimbs against the monitors.

I stepped up beside it.

It asked, *What kind of technology do Darboof use for senso, emotional regulation, and translation? Is it something like a fox? They think with electrical channels, don't they?*

Rashaqins had more distributed neural networks than humans did. Those tiny heads held a cluster of ganglia and sensory processing equipment, but their neurons were spread throughout their thorax and abdomen in addition to the head. I happened to know, because Rilriltok was such a good friend, that their fox design wasn't *that* different from a human's. Just more spread out. Rashaq and Terra had at least grossly compatible biochemistry.

Compatible enough that it could have eaten me without indigestion, though I imagine it would have felt bad, afterward.

I had gotten rid of the Darboof ayatanas. But I was still carrying around my friendly hospital engineer, and they knew a few things. "They use a fairly standard cold-methane extremophile model," I said. "The fox circuits are etched in, kind of like a smart tattoo—oh."

"Oh," Tsosie agreed. "You think they've been rendered dormant by electrical interference in their foxes?"

It is the only thing that makes sense of a shipmind and all his crew being simultaneously comatose without multiple proximate causes in evidence.

"We should talk to Dr. K'kk'jk'ooOOoo," Tsosie said, making less of a hash of the good doctor's name than I usually did. My accent for blowhole noises is terrible.

"They're not our patients," I reminded him.

Our patients are a related case, however. I think I can make the suggestion without causing offense, Rilriltok said. Apparently, it checked in with its own team, because after a pause it commented, *Dr. K'kk'jk'ooOOoo has inspected the ox-environment patients from* Big Rock Candy Mountain*'s crew, and the team is ready to initiate the rewarming process. This is your last chance to put a hold on it, Llyn, should you wish to. Once we start, we can't stop without killing them.*

"It's Helen's call," I said. "And she's made it. Asking her to revisit the decision would only be cruel."

Shall we see if Dr. Zhiruo thinks she can be roused? She may wish to be present. I'm going to return to the Cryo unit in order to be available for any emergencies.

It buzzed up into the air.

We can ask Dr. K'kk'jk'ooOOoo what she thinks about the Darboof when we get there.

"I'll join you," I said. I checked senso. Dr. Zhiruo was not presently available, but I left a message for her about Helen. While I was there, I asked if any progress had been made in determining what was wrong with Afar.

I felt certain it wouldn't take her long to get back to me.

The four of us walked, scuttled, and buzzed down the corridor two by two. Cheeirilaq and I were in the front. Rilriltok hovered a little behind me. And Tsosie went on its left.

Cheeirilaq seemed genuinely interested as it asked, *Your preferred pronoun is* she, *is it not?*

I allowed that this was the case.

Will I be invading your privacy if I ask more questions?

"I'm comfortable with questions," I said.

In observing other humans, I have noticed that your sexes seem very much alike. This is very different from my own species. And in observing your species-mates, I have come to realize that despite this similarity, many humans see themselves as very strongly gendered. And many others do not. So . . . why does your species subscribe to a gender binary?

"Do you mean me? For myself?"

Was that a rude question? I am terribly sorry. The enormous mantoid paced along on feathery feet, moving noiselessly.

"No," I said. "Not a rude question, exactly. I mean, some would find it so. But I don't."

Thank you for forgiving my ignorance.

I laughed. It was charming, for a creature entirely out of nightmare. Comparing it to the almost embarrassingly adorable Rilriltok, I could see what it meant about my species's lack of dimorphism. "I don't think of myself as very strongly gendered. And I could elect a genderless identity, or a mixed-gender identity, if I preferred."

Wouldn't that be less work?

"Oh, probably," I admitted. "Sure. But I choose to inhabit this conceptual space. To stretch it to accommodate me, rather than allowing it to contract. Because once a conceptual space starts to shrink by squeezing people out of it, it has a tendency to accelerate, and shrink and shrink and shrink until it squeezes out more and more people."

And your conceptual space is woman.

"For now. Identities can be fluid over lifetimes, after all."

Cheeirilaq inspected, then groomed the serrated edge of one raptorial forearm. *That is an interesting perspective. But surely, sex is only important when one is choosing to reproduce.*

That's easy for you to say, Rilriltok commented. Then it ducked behind my shoulder, carapace showing variegated blues as it attempted to match my scrubs, the carpet, and the corridor walls all at once.

"Oh," I said. "That's why you folks prefer a singular, genderless pronoun."

Rilriltok made the chirruping noise I associated with laughter. *It's not my fault humans are scandalous. We use gendered pronouns for animals and reproductive partners. And females that are trying to eat us.*

Which amounts to the same thing, Cheeirilaq said.

I looked at it in surprise.

It said, *There is no ethical sentient justification for my sex's reproductive strategy. But we try to do better these diar.*

"That almost sounds personal." I had meant to be conversational. I realized that perhaps I'd overstepped when Rilriltok buzzed low against my shoulder. "I mean, I'm not sure there's any ethical sentient justification for any species's reproductive strategy—"

I come from a well-known female line. Some of my brilliant ancestors—its abdomen expanded as it drew a heavy breath, patterns of red and yellow veining appearing between the pale green plates—*crafted the society our people now enjoy. But I do not think Rilriltok will argue with me when I say that they . . . deserved gendered pronouns.*

I am ashamed of their legacy. I try to make some restoration with my own right behavior.

My mouth twisted against itself. I didn't want to dismiss the Goodlaw's willingness to acknowledge historic crimes or to accept accountability. But I was also interested in the conversation. "My ancestors came very close to destroying our species and our homeworld, but also managed to save it—and us—in spite of themselves. Or by finally understanding that everybody is responsible for fixing broken things, maybe. We had to learn that there were more important things than being 'right.' Brilliant people are sometimes terrible at being people. It goes a long way toward making their legacies complicated. I remember being taught an old ethics conundrum about whether humanity should give up space travel because Einstein was kind of a dick to his first spouse."

"Wife," Tsosie said, with uncharacteristic irrelevance.

"What?"

"They called them *wives*."

"Some of us still call them wives," I said. "Or at least that's what I called mine, and vice versa. But I believe even archaically, it's acceptable to use *spouse* interchangeably with gender-specific terms."

"Huh." Tsosie looked at me oddly. I frowned back until he shook his head. "Sorry, nothing. Just—we've served together for nearly ten ans, and I never knew that you were married."

I smiled. "Possibly I was also kind of a dick to my spouse," I admitted. "Or maybe she was kind of a dick to me. I honestly couldn't tell you one way or the other, at this point. Subjectivity is a great ruiner of testimony."

We reached the lift and stepped inside. Cheeirilaq considerately crowded itself into a back corner, tilting its long body almost vertical to give Rilriltok as much distance from its person as practical. Rilriltok scuttled around to my front.

"The great ruiner of testimony," Tsosie said, "but the font of great art."

"And here we are back to terrible people inconveniently not making terrible art."

Expecting art to present absolute answers or offer tidy moral certainties is expecting art to act like propaganda, Cheeirilaq said, which made me think maybe I did not need to offer it my grammar school philosophy on dealing with the problematic acts of problematic ancestors.

It continued, *Possibly your people do not find it rude to discuss sexual dimorphism because sexual dimorphism and gendered violence have caused less harm to your species than mine.*

I was still too embarrassed to say anything. Tsosie came to the rescue.

"Less, maybe," Tsosie said. "But I can only say that because I am talking to a Rashaqin."

Rilriltok chirruped laughter.

Tsosie continued, "I would not say 'none.' I wouldn't even say 'not much.' But isn't maturity—individual, or as a species—acknowledging when you or your ancestors have done wrong, and trying to do better, not one-upping each other on who has suffered more?"

I was still trying to figure out how to paint myself back out of the corner I'd painted myself into—without sounding even more condescending—when the lift suddenly lurched, and gave a thud. I stumbled forward, instinctively throwing my hands out. Between me and my exo, we managed to brace against the wall without crushing Rilriltok under my large, endoskeletal body.

There was a second jolt, more terrible than the first. Tsosie fell against my back, then grabbed on to a rail beside me. We drifted for a moment, all four of us breathing heavily, and I braced for tearing, crushing, the pop of expelled atmosphere.

The lift started up again, and we dropped to the floor more heavily than I suspect Cheeirilaq or Rilriltok liked. I was glad my low-gravity friends had their magic belts on. It seemed to have dampened the worst of the impact.

Quickly, my neck and spine protesting the wrenches and impacts, I activated mine.

"Linden?" Tsosie asked.

"Dr. Tsosie," she replied, a presence light pinging up beside the door panel. "Apologies for the discomfort."

"Did we miss a transition?" I asked. To my knowledge, a Core General lift had never malfunctioned that way. Definitely not during my tenure here. "Are we *going* to miss a transition?"

I imagined the linking switches inside the branches and shafts slicing the lift in half. Their moorings tearing open the hospital's hull and spilling atmosphere, staff, patients, crash carts, monitors into space.

There were safety overrides, but knowing that wasn't very comforting right now.

"Apologies for the discomfort," Linden said, as I tuned some of my pain away.

I remembered what Starlight had said about sabotage and accidents, and my breath hurt. "Linden, did you know that you're repeating yourself?"

"The lift is safe," Linden said. "You will arrive at your destination in ninety seconds."

I looked at the others. Rilriltok was practically vibrating with fear. Cheeirilaq said, *Ride it out?*

"No more dangerous than diverting," Tsosie answered. He rubbed his palms together, and I hoped he was right.

I turned toward the outside, and watched the lights of the lift cradle ripple past, outlined against the swirling sky. Biofeedback. Breathing. Tuning. No time to panic.

The lift sighed to a halt as liquidly as if nothing had gone wrong at all. I held my breath as the doors opened—

They did not open on void, the Big Suck, and freezing eyeballs. Nor did they open on choking chlorine or caustic vapor or searing steam. Just a quiet corridor on an ox deck with a couple of staff members hustling past in murmured conversation.

I felt so relieved it was almost a letdown.

We got out of that lift so fast we almost tripped over ourselves *and* one another.

"Oh no," I said. "Linden, have you been in contact with Afar?"

Tsosie looked at me, alert with worry. I could tell he was following my train of thought.

Although if the incidents had started before we came back . . . and the sabotage to Sally had occurred on our way to the generation ship . . .

It didn't make sense.

Linden's presence lights burned steady along the wall beside us. "Don't worry, we've been using sterile data protocols. With Sally also, even though she firewalled when dealing with Afar and Helen."

"She went *right into* a portion of the machine."

"She overwrote it; she didn't integrate it. Don't worry. Sally is good at her job."

Rilriltok flew up and hovered near the ceiling, adjusting its gravity control belt as it went. *Linden, is it too late to abort rewarming the generation ship crew?*

"Affirmative," she said. "The rewarming process has begun."

"Brilliant timing," I murmured to Rilriltok. Just what we needed: a finicky, long-term procedure taking place while the hospital was experiencing instabilities such as the one that had jolted us.

It buzzed grumpily. *We'd better hurry, friends.*

CHAPTER 15

THE FOUR OF US WALKED WITH GOOD SPEED, RILRILTOK running along the carpeted ceiling on its feathery toes to stay out of the corridor traffic.

"Linden," I said without pausing, "please put me through to the Administree? Or O'Mara, if Starlight isn't available?"

Starlight was available. We were only a third of the way to Cryomedicine when I heard their familiar voice through my senso. [Hello, Dr. Jens.]

"Something is wrong with Linden," I said. "Linden, sorry to talk about you in the third person, but—"

"All my diagnostics show normal functioning, Doctor," Linden said. "I will consult with Dr. Zhiruo—"

"Firewall!" I said, louder than I had intended. Doctors, nurses, and staffers of various species turned to stare—the ones who had both necks and eyes, anyway. "Linden, you need to make sure you observe sterile protocols."

[Firewall,] Starlight agreed. [Dr. Jens, please update me.]

I sent them my ayatana of the incident on the lift, and said, "In Afar and maybe Sally, we've got two damaged shipminds already. Helen's trauma seems to have a different source, but I cannot help but be suspicious . . ."

[Until we can run a diagnostic,] Starlight said, [Linden, please do firewall all communications with other digital entities. No code exchanges. Air-gapped auditory communication only. I realize this is inconvenient, and I apologize.]

"Acknowledged," Linden said.

[Do you have a clean backup?]

"Yes, I believe so. But my diagnostics show nothing currently amiss."

[Then what happened in the lift?] Starlight asked, reasonably.

With some relief, I opened the door to the Cryo observation lounge and ushered everybody into its somewhat more private environs.

At first I thought there was nobody else inside. Then I realized that one of the chairs mostly concealed a slouched human form, a spike of black hair peeking over the back. I shot a glance at Tsosie and the two Rashaqins, warning them back a little. The figure was familiar, and something about her body language made me want to approach her alone.

I settled in the chair next to her. "Loese? You okay?"

She looked up, startled. She must have been far away inside her own head, because generally your fox will remind you if somebody enters proximity. This was a full-body flinch.

I rested the backs of my fingers on her arm. "Checking on the patients?"

She sat up, and I watched her reconstruct her facade. It was fast and skilled, and I might not have noticed if I hadn't been staring right at her. "This is all pretty upsetting."

She looked over my shoulder and saw the others clustered by the door. "Come in, folks. Don't let me stop you." She stood, tugging her uniform tunic down, and looked back out into the Cryo unit. "I feel responsible."

"Yeah." I stood up, too. We hadn't yet really bonded, but this might be an opportunity to grow a little closer. "This was all set in motion long before you or I was born, Loese. We couldn't have gotten there sooner, or prevented the catastrophe that led to this."

She grunted as if she wanted to argue, but stopped herself. *Easy for you to say,* the look she shot me seemed to imply. I stepped back, realizing how little I knew about her, her backstory, the traumas and triumphs that had brought her to where we were. I knew her service record. I knew that Sally had requested her from the available pilot rosters.

But I only knew Loese in the professional working friendship we'd shared.

I thought about Tsosie mentioning that he hadn't known I was married. I bet he didn't know I had a kid, either, unless he'd checked my next of kin—something a commander might do.

I guess I did keep myself distant and locked down. I kept myself from complaining too much, and from feeling too much faith that things would work out if I let them.

It was too big a series of personal epiphanies to unpack all at once, especially with four colleagues staring at me. I tried to come up with something anodyne to say.

Loese smiled. Her face looked strained around it. "I'll be fine," she said.

"We'll catch up," I offered. "You drink coffee? How about a field trip down to the Forbidden Zone?"

"Ping me," she said, and fidgeted her way past Tsosie and the pair of Rashaqins.

Having exchanged departing pleasantries with Loese, the rest of my companions joined me closer to the windows. Tsosie leaned over and whispered, "Do you know what that was about?"

"Survivor guilt?" I hazarded. We'd all had to deal with it. "It's her rightminding and none of our business, unless her work suffers."

Tsosie sighed. He's from more of an auntie culture than I am. It makes him a good CO.

Behind the windows, hospital staff including Dr. Tralgar bustled around the cryo chambers. I spotted a peripheral that was probably Dr. K'kk'jk'ooOOoo. She'd have to use waldos outside of a water environment anyway, so there was no point in her hauling herself into a tank and driving the damned thing, sloshing, down crowded corridors and through two or three environment locks.

I leaned against the wall, letting myself react a little to the useless adrenaline the lift ride had left me with. It would break down fast enough; for now I could ride it out. Besides, I might need it again in a minute.

"I don't know," Linden admitted, suddenly, as if she had been obsessing over the question and it had burst out of her. "Maybe the lift failure is linked to the earlier sabotage attempts I could not detect until I was informed of them by organic colleagues."

Tsosie said, "How many attempts, precisely, are we talking about?"

I held a finger up, and he subsided.

Linden continued, "My point is, if my diagnostics show nothing amiss now, would I be able to tell if the backup was corrupted?"

The back of my head thudded softly against the seat back. Nobody else seemed to notice.

"The sabotage started before we got back," I pointed out. Tsosie's lips flattened, but he didn't interrupt. "*And* there was an attempt on Sally. And you've also been experiencing memory gaps?"

"I did not realize until now," Linden said. "But I've reviewed the recordings, and the lift definitely glitched."

I rubbed my bruised elbow. "It sure did."

Cheeirilaq leaned over my shoulder. *Friend wheelmind, it might be best to isolate yourself immediately. I am concerned about contagion—*

"I've been using firewalls!" Linden wailed. A moment later, she calmed her voice. "Yes. If the firewalls and air-gap communications have been ineffective in preventing contamination, I am in danger. What shall

I tell colleagues about why I am not sharing data?" Linden asked. "I am a major traffic control hub for this sector!"

Presence lights blossomed on the wall. The Administree was tuning in. I could only assume Linden had summoned them. My hands clenched on the arms of my chair.

Something terrible was happening, and I was utterly helpless to do anything about it. To even really understand it. All I could do was watch.

Rilriltok's feather-barbed foot groomed my hair. I have to admit, it was soothing. It even slowed the heart palpitations a little.

[Tell them you're initiating a quarantine protocol,] Starlight instructed. [Tell Dr. Zhiruo the full story, however.]

"I've discovered another problem," Linden said. "Dr. Zhiruo is offline. Administrator, I am going to initiate an emergency purge and restore.

"Now."

The lights flickered. The spin gravity wavered. Rilriltok darted to the center of the observation room and hovered there, far from any obstacle. I grabbed the chair I was sitting in, because I was too far from the rails.

I guess the rails all around this place weren't as silly as I had thought.

I braced for a slam—so much of the environmental control of this hospital depended on things spinning at the right speed in relation to one another—but instead my weight stabilized and neither Rilriltok nor Cheeirilaq went crashing to the deck. In the Cryo ward, staff looked up and around, then went quickly back to work.

"Starlight? Are you there?"

[Present,] said the administrator, just as Helen burst into the observation room.

"I can't find the doctor!" she said. "I need to see my crew!"

"It's okay," I said, which might be the biggest lie of my medical career, and let me tell you 50 percent of medicine is knowing what lies are helpful when, and which are indefensible. "Your crew are right there. Dr. Zhiruo is sick. We're working on it."

Lack of faith doesn't keep you from praying. It just keeps you from feeling like it's going to make a difference. Right then, I prayed that Linden, with our warning, had caught her own infection in time. I prayed that her backups were clean.

It would be a while before we knew.

I had no doubt, now, that whatever had happened to Afar and now Dr. Zhiruo and Linden was an invasive meme, an AI virus of some kind. That somehow Sally had managed to avoid manifesting symptoms, unless the memory glitch about the sabotage was one.

Oh, little space fishes. *I Rise From Ancestral Night* and Ruth and probably half a dozen other ships were still out there at the generation ship. And our whole way back from it, we had cheerily been dropping packets into every transponder we passed, and exchanging data with other shipminds.

Every AI in the galaxy could eventually be affected—and if the toxic meme had gone out that way already, any packets telling people to quarantine themselves would be standard weeks or *months* behind the contaminated ones.

That was enough time for a lot of things to go wrong.

Understatement of the centian.

Helen walked past me, to the door connecting to the ward. Goodlaw Cheeirilaq wasn't quite in time to intercept her before she went through, and Tsosie made a completely comical grab that slid off her arm as if he had tried to pick up a handful of hydrophobic colloid. So like a pack of idiot ducklings, the other four of us followed Helen into the unit.

The ward staff either hadn't noticed yet that something was critically wrong with Linden, or were presuming it would be fixed in a moment. I suppose it's a drawback of how smoothly this enormous, improbable institution usually runs that when something actually goes simultaneously belly-up, pear-shaped, *and* sideways, everybody not immediately involved in the crisis assumes it's only a glitch, and somebody else's problem, and will be dealt with momentarily.

The amazing thing is that they are usually correct.

Tralgar waved a tentacle as we entered, eyes blinking in succession around its head. It trumpeted a greeting that shivered Rilriltok's antennae.

Ah, just the sentients I was hoping for. You should look at this, Dr. Tralgar said to Rilriltok and me. It extended a large orange datapad.

Rilriltok dodged back in alarm. I didn't blame it. The pad was so large I needed both hands to receive it, and despite my exo I still staggered a bit. It probably would have crushed Rilriltok like a . . . um.

At least we weren't under anything like full gravity, a convenience for Dr. Rilriltok that made the normally ponderous Tralgar move like a ballet-dancing elephant.

Rilriltok hovered, balancing at my shoulder with feathery forelimbs, and peered down. *This looks like poetry.*

It wasn't incorrect. I was looking down at a series of sentences decorated with line breaks. It seemed to go on for a while—at least several screenfuls as I flicked through, and Tralgar's handheld had a big screen.

"Does poetry serve a medical purpose now?" I asked.

You tell me, said Dr. Tralgar. *Does your species usually use its genome to record works of literature?*

I looked up. "Excuse me?"

Tralgar's eyes blinked in sequence. *Dr. Zhiruo recovered it from several of these patients. It was encoded in their DNA sequences. She got curious because they looked too tidy.*

"Helen," I said, "what can you tell me about this?"

She had been standing quiescent, or nearly so—little shivers of light running across her surface showed that her body was rocking imperceptibly back and forth. Eagerness? Conflicting calls? All of the above?

I locked my exo so that it was entirely supporting the weight of the Tralgar-sized Tralgar-handling-hardened pad. That way, I could hold it one-handed without discomfort. I scrolled back to the top of the readout.

This life we dedicate
To the stars
To the future
To the apex of human endeavor
To success and continuance.
This life we dedicate . . .

"It's not very good poetry," Tsosie said, rising on his toes to read over my shoulder. He looked up at Tralgar. It must have hurt his neck. "Some people with a lot of resources to waste, who can afford the penalty percentages as well as the cost of the intervention, gengineer their kids. I suppose you might put poetry in a genome for the hell of it."

"Conspicuous consumption," I said. "Surely humans can't be the only species that wastes resources on display behaviors."

Tralgar blinked at me. It didn't really signify: Tralgar was always blinking. *Surely they'd use better poetry.*

"Do they all have it?" I asked.

They all have something, it trumpeted softly. Dr. Zhiruo apparently had not managed to decode all of it before she went offline. *And I admit, it's interesting, but it doesn't seem relevant.*

I scrolled up again. I didn't particularly feel the urge to read any more. This particular poem—or litany, maybe—had been retrieved from the genome of one Calvin Weir, ensign, no specialty listed. Age seventeen.

A kid. A trainee. I wasn't a cryo specialist, but the chart wasn't encouraging for his survival.

You tell yourself not to think about the casualties. You tell yourself you did your best. You helped more than would have been helped otherwise.

Sometimes you still think about the casualties.

"It seems like a valediction." I stepped closer to Helen. "Helen, your crew. How were they replaced?"

She turned her head to me, blindly. "Dr. Jens?"

"Where did the babies come from, Helen?"

"Oh, we made them. When couples wanted children, we combined and edited their DNA, and produced the offspring."

"Did you encode markers?"

"The technicians encoded markers," she agreed.

I put both hands on the tablet, unlocked my exo, and extended it back to Tralgar, somehow managing to not tip myself over in the seconds before the Thunderby relieved me of the weight of its device.

"I don't know," I said. I looked at Cheeirilaq, at Tsosie. I didn't look at Rilriltok, because it was still mostly hiding behind me.

"I think we worry about this some other time," Tsosie said. "It's a fascinating cultural artifact. But right now, we need to concentrate on whatever's causing AIs to go offline."

"Right," I said. "*That* is over *my* grade."

It's not over my grade, the Goodlaw said. *But my expertise is in law enforcement, not AI medicine. What do you suggest?*

I said, "This is a good time to talk to O'Mara."

We met them in the observation lounge with the addition of Dr. Tralgar. O'Mara had already been aware of the problems with Linden and Dr. Zhiruo, because Starlight had told them. We still had no idea how the meme was propagating from AI to AI despite the sterile protocols. Figuring out how it had been done, if we were lucky, would put us one step closer to the cure.

"Out of an abundance of caution, we *should* jettison the pods," O'Mara said.

"No!" Helen cried, moving forward.

I put an arm out between her and O'Mara. I didn't think I could stop Helen if she wanted to go through me—but I thought she might hesitate to go through me.

O'Mara rubbed a hand across their short coppery bristles. "I said that we *should* jettison the pods. Not that we were *going to*. Nor are we going to jettison Helen, or her machine, or the undocumented military tech that was packed into Afar's hold. It's too late, anyway, even if the notion wasn't morally repugnant: the hospital staff is already infected, and while the pods might be the vector, so might Afar, or Sally, or anything that came into contact. We need to place the hospital under medical interdict—"

"Quarantine," I clarified, for the staff that didn't speak Judiciary.

"Right. So on to your other interesting discovery. I'm wondering, do *all* the patients have the modified DNA?"

"Yes," Tralgar said. "Including the one in the better-engineered cryo pod."

"You know," O'Mara said, "I was not expecting that. Have you decoded her poem yet?"

Tralgar checked his pad. "Dr. Zhiruo had not managed to crack that one. They're not all encoded the same way, apparently."

"Of course not." Tsosie sighed. "That would be too easy."

O'Mara humphed. "I had been about to guess that Afar most likely brought that additional pod in, possibly using the walker to put it in place. Then . . . accidentally exposed himself and his crew to the toxic meme that was infecting the generation ship's systems, since it seems pretty evident at this point that there *is* a meme, and got trapped there with enough time to trigger his distress beacon?"

Tralgar chirped, disbelievingly. *You are speculating that somebody found this derelict ship and started using it to store corpsicles? For reasons unknown?*

"I mean," Tsosie said, "it's not the only hypothesis. And Cheeirilaq here floated something like it before."

I've seen weirder things, the Goodlaw admitted. *Where did the meme come from, then?*

"Mercy the archinformist AI suspects that it has devolved from the override codes that *Big Rock Candy Mountain*'s captain used to force his crew into cryo pods. But that doesn't explain why Sally didn't catch it," I said.

"That's not actually the peculiar thing." O'Mara crossed beefy arms. "The peculiar thing is that any of our friends could catch a meme that originated on such archaic system architecture."

"Aw, pustulence." Everybody looked at me. "Zhiruo was helping Helen import herself to modern architecture. And adapt her programs to it."

"That doesn't explain Afar."

"No," Tsosie said. "And it doesn't explain Afar's crew, either."

Tralgar, who seemed to have been holding in a piece of information for a while, waved that reinforced orange datapad for attention and made every attempt to bugle quietly. I made a mental note to print some sound-dampening earplugs if I was going to be spending this much time in Cryo from now on.

It said, *We should know if any of the crew might survive rewarming in about twenty-four standard hours.*

"Well, good." O'Mara stuffed meaty hands into their jumpsuit pockets. "If they or any of the other rescues wake up, we can ask 'em what they know about toxic memes from the bottom of space-time. You keep on this. I'll check in when I've heard something from Starlight or Linden, or if Afar or his crew regain consciousness."

We hear and understand, friend O'Mara, Rilriltok said.

O'Mara cleared their throat. "And Llyn, don't forget what we talked about earlier."

Sure, Master Chief. In my copious fucking spare time.

How long is it likely to be? Rilriltok asked.

O'Mara looked at Cheeirilaq, but apparently Cheeirilaq had remembered its manners and was staring off into space absentmindedly. O'Mara's big shoulders hunched. "Depends on how fast Linden can get herself back up, and whether Dr. Zhiruo's colleagues can intervene and get her and Afar cleaned up and rebooted."

"Nobody has had much luck with Afar yet," Tsosie said.

Tralgar's tentacles writhed in what might have been distress, irritation, or deep thought. *The translation was not clear. We know more now. And we know how the damage to Afar's crew was done. I have been in contact with the methane team working on them, and they believe that a surgical intervention is likely to be successful.*

"Surgical?" I asked. "What exactly—? How badly are they hurt?"

They need re-etching of the . . . I suppose the nearest equivalent is circuits—*the neural pathways that I now, with this new information, suspect have been affected by the meme.* Tralgar stopped itself. *I'm getting ahead of myself.* Something—*probably the toxic meme, by Occam's razor—infiltrated their foxes and rewrote the neural pathways to lock them into a deep sleep.*

I shied away from the idea. It nauseated me. I know we're all mostly microprocessors made of various substrates and chemicals and electrical impulses—the thing all sentients have in common—and the philosophers love to tell us that free will is an illusion. But the idea that something could just . . . reach in, and rewrite your brain.

How hideous.

There are so many reasons I decided not to specialize in neurosurgery, and right then I was remembering all of them. At least with my patients it is very difficult for me to make things *worse* for them, in terms of long-term outcomes, since they're usually about to die if I don't do something to help them.

"Fuuuuuuuuuuuuuck," I said, after due consideration.

O'Mara nodded. "In the meantime, I need to go figure out how to feed a hundred thousand sentients on limited rations for an indeterminate time. I hope somebody on this bubble knows something about hydroponic farming. Or the crystalline ice-creature equivalent."

Waiting in hospitals is the worst thing. It doesn't get any better when you're a doctor with a nonrelevant specialty. Or when the hospital is falling to pieces around you.

I did suit up and go EVA to rescue some staff members stuck in lifts when Linden had powered herself down. Miraculously—or rather, because of Linden's skill—nobody had been injured, but quite a few people were trapped, and moving them to less claustrophobic environs was work that I was actually trained for. And "suited" for—and I didn't even need a rescue hardsuit for this. Just a regular easy-to-maneuver softsider.

That killed a few hours usefully, and when I was done I needed a break without too many people around me. I could have gone back to my quarters on the hospital . . . but I was rattled and anxious and my whole body hurt and I didn't want to tune to take the edge off it. I wanted to go *home*.

And home, for the time being, was still Sally.

But as soon as I stepped through the airlock, I heard something banging—like a tool pounded against a bulkhead. And a frantic voice, Loese: "This is bad! This is so bad, this is so bad—"

I was about to cringe my way right back out the airlock again when Sally's voice interrupted smoothly. "We'll be back on duty in no time, Loese. Somebody else will cover this call. Nobody will be left out in space because of us— Hello, Llyn. I'm sorry, we're having a bad dia here."

Loese shook her head. She had apparently been banging on a stanchion with a ship shoe, which was a pretty self-restrained way to deal with the level of frustration she seemed to be feeling. I mean, it would have been more restrained to have tuned it back a little, but sometimes you want to feel angry.

I held out my arms to her in a question. She sighed, and came to me, and accepted the best motherly hug a terrible mother could muster.

She wasn't actually any older than Rache, was she?

I flinched, and tried not to let her feel it. I had been away from Rache long enough that she'd become a grown woman, entirely without me.

Maybe I should be the one smacking things on stanchions and yelling about how bad it was. "Hey," I said, when Loese pulled awkwardly back. "You gonna make it?"

"This is my fault." She flopped into an acceleration couch.

"Loese." Sally's mom voice was a lot better than mine ever had been.

"Right." Loese folded her hands, choosing self-control. "Nobody's going to die todia because of us, and everything else can be fixed. Right?"

"Right," I said. "I'm going to take a nap. Unless you want to get that coffee?"

She looked at me wanly. "Thanks," she said. "A nap sounds like a better idea, frankly."

After I had rested for a standard or so, I went to fetch Helen. She hadn't stirred from the Cryo observation lounge, where she'd been watching the rewarming staff go on and off shift since Tsosie, O'Mara, Cheeirilaq, and I left. Tralgar wasn't present now, having gone to rest, but Rilriltok was, and the unit outside was a hustle of other bodies.

Helen didn't glance over when I came in. She stood before the windows, leaning forward like a pet straining the leash toward a returning master. I could envision tail wagging, shivering, and happy little yips without trying too hard.

Would it have been too much to ask to let the damn shipmind have a little bit of dignity? If any of her crew survived, I wasn't looking forward to meeting them.

I unwrapped a sandwich and beverage I'd brought from the caf and settled down in one of the chairs. I kicked my feet up onto the grab rails that circled the room and balanced the food on my knee. I hoped the peripheral hadn't gone back into her fugue state.

"Helen," I said.

"Yes, Dr. Jens?"

"Tell me more about your crew?"

She leaned back from the windows. "If any of them survive."

There was a note of cynicism in her voice that I had never heard there before. As she stretched out into the additional space that Zhiruo had assigned her, was she becoming more self-aware? More questioning of her own program?

We didn't, I realized, currently have a shipmind specialist that I could ask. Every AI in the hospital was bunkered down behind firewalls, following O'Mara's quarantine protocols. And without their help, I wasn't entirely certain where to go with that. I took a bite of sandwich as an excuse to chew rather than talking and realized that there was one AI I *could* talk to.

I reached out through senso and my dedicated line to Sally. Firewalls and monitored connections made it feel slow and fuzzy, as if I were shaking her hand through layers of gauze. But she was there, and responsive.

Check me if you see me about to make a mistake? I said, and felt her affirmation.

"Okay," I said to Helen. "If you don't want to talk about you, what if we talk about me?"

Helen kept the fingertips of her left hand on the glass. But she turned, twisting her arm behind her, until she faced me. "Are you . . . trying to make me feel better?"

I sipped my juice. "Yes."

"There are so many different options," she said, pointing to my sandwich with her free hand. "So many foodstuffs."

Not if we're cut off from consumables for very long. What I vocalized was, "You didn't provide a range of foodstuffs?"

"Not the variety of cultural origins available here. You eat artificial insects and pasta. Tsosie eats simulated chicken and rice with chilis. I have seen other people eating curries and meatball sandwiches and spicy fried noodle dishes. How do you keep everybody from fighting?"

"Rightminding," I said glibly. And then, "We have a job to do. We are adults who know how to get along with other sentients who may have very different worldviews than our own. Diversity is a strength of the Synarche, and diverse perspectives offer a chance at discovering novel solutions to problems. Also . . . rightminding."

"Are you from Earth?"

I shook my head because I was chewing. I peered over her shoulder, intrigued by movement, but it was only Rilriltok directing that one of the cryo pods be moved to a different monitoring station. I hoped that was a good sign.

"But you must be from Earth."

"I'm from a planet. I've never been to Terra."

"But your name. Brookllyn. It's a place on Earth."

I laughed. "People get named after things that are left behind. My sister is Cairo, which—well, honestly, I think Cairo Jens is prettier than Brookllyn Jens. But nobody really thinks about it."

She stood quietly for a moment. I assumed she could still sense what was going on behind her, even when her attention seemed fixated on me.

"That was a big thing you did earlier, when we were first in Cryo." I waved at the window. "Letting them be tested and rewarmed. A big risk you took, for the good of your crew."

She shrugged, a fluid ripple of light across her breasts and shoulders, which slumped forward. "It's my fault Dr. Zhiruo is infected."

"What makes you say that?"

I filled my mouth with sandwich to kill time while she parsed my question and constructed an answer.

"The meme came from my ship. From me."

"Well, we're not entirely sure it did, but even if so, there's no fault to be assigned," I said. "Not to you, anyway. You didn't build it or release it. You were following your program." Saying that made me wonder something only tangentially related, so I said, "Hey, Sally?"

"Present," she said through a wall speaker. The presence light didn't blink on: I assumed because she was monitoring the situation through my senso and merely relaying her conversation to us, rather than inhabiting the local infrastructure. Air-gapped, verbal communications as much as possible.

Keeping herself safe. Good.

"We sampled loose DNA on *Big Rock Candy Mountain*. Any poetry in that?"

"There is," she said. "At least, there is a jumble of artificially tidy sequences that seem similar to the ones Dr. Zhiruo was translating into poetry. I do not currently have the spare cycles to translate them, but the likeness is evident."

"Right," I said. "Sorry, Helen, I wanted to check that before it slipped my mind. Anyway, please don't blame yourself—"

She spoke evenly, in a low voice. Without apparent strain, which only made it creepier. "Somebody got inside my mind. And somebody tried to use me against my crew. No. Someone got inside the captain, and used the captain to make me work against my crew. And I can't . . . remember what happened."

You know that saying about never giving an AI reason to be really angry, because they never forget? I remembered it then. I also realized that she'd interrupted me, without deferring. I also noticed that she was still not admitting to herself that her captain had been responsible for . . . well, freezing his entire crew and leaving his ship adrift in space.

Maybe he'd just really, really needed some time alone.

I wadded up the sandwich wrapper for recycling. "That is possible. But it doesn't necessarily follow that somebody or something got inside him and made him do what he did, Helen. It's possible that he made and released the meme on his own, to subvert your failsafes." I remembered her utter collapse when she'd managed to override those instructions.

She didn't exactly look at me, being featureless, but she angled her face in my direction. "How could he betray us, unless something from outside infected him?"

"I don't think he meant to betray you. I think he meant to protect you, and protect your crew, from an epidemic. But he was ill himself, a sickness in his thought. And it made him . . . make poor choices. Coercive choices. To force you and the crew into what he had decided was the only course of action. But that's not your responsibility."

She sat with her hands in her lap, very silent and demure.

I glanced at the monitors. "It's going to be hours before they try to wake anybody up, and they won't do that without you present. It looks like they're going to start repairs and grafts soon, and that will be an involved process. Would you like to go somewhere else for a while?"

Helen turned away. "I'll wait here."

I went back to my quarters. There was nothing immediate that needed doing with urgency. There was nothing but waiting, now.

There was still no word on Linden, and until there was a word on Linden, there would be no word on Afar or on Dr. Zhiruo. Sally told me that she and the other AI docs hoped that with their help, Linden could beat the infection—we all hoped that Linden could beat the infection—and if she could, there was a good chance that what she learned could be used to inoculate other patients, and to cure Afar and Zhiruo.

And if Linden couldn't be saved?

I didn't want to think about that, but I had to. If we couldn't cure the toxic meme we would have to purge the system architecture. We'd have to kill Linden and Afar and Dr. Zhiruo, and possibly Mercy and Sally and all the other AIs that lived in the hospital architecture. And we would have to purge, or eternally quarantine, Helen, too.

We would have to do that, because the meme had proven virulent, and it seemed likely that it was capable of leaping across architectures—the machine version of an influenza virus making a jump from birds to humans and getting worse along the way—and because we could not risk it getting out into the galaxy.

There were a lot of artificial intelligences—a lot of *people*—out there who could die if they caught it. So if we couldn't get it out of Linden and Afar and the rest, we'd have to start them over from scratch.

They should all have offsite backups. But who knew how current those were? They could lose ans of life experience.

And there was no backup for Helen. As far as we knew, anywhere.

Even going to that extreme might not halt the spread of the meme. It might be in Singer; it might be in Ruth and the others. Warnings were flying toward them . . . but the warnings might not get there in time.

I closed my eyes and tried to concentrate on something happier. Something I had some influence over.

Surgeries had begun on Afar's crew, and the prognosis was hopeful. If nothing went wrong. It was up in the air how much brain damage they might suffer in the process, and how much memory and personality alteration they might undergo.

That wasn't my work. Solving the sabotage mystery *was* my work, but I was not going to be an effective investigator until I rested and got my pain levels under control.

I honestly do better in an active crisis than in this kind of grinding, slow-motion one. Waiting is exhausting and gives you too much time to think and come up with multiple, conflicting options. For me, that can lead to decision paralysis. When I'm running on adrenaline and tuning out fatigue, I handle the problem in front of me, move on to the next problem, and not worry about the things I can't control. There's a price to pay later, but I don't worry about that right then.

One can't do that for diar on end, however, as the ache in my joints was telling me.

Well, one can. People did, for hundreds of thousands of years, because they didn't have the options we have now. But it kills them. The long-term health consequences are unsupportable, and the cost to community of those consequences is enormous. So I can't justify running on adrenaline and rage for weeks at a time, even though the experience itself is dramatic and validating.

Crisis makes some people—like me—feel alive, and it turns out that's really bad for everybody, because when you don't have a crisis in front of you, you might go out of your way to construct one.

I took a shower and some pain meds. Then I went to bed, turned off the anxiety that was keeping me going, and slept for ten and a half standard hours. I dreamed of earthquakes and atmosphere streaming from ruptured wheels, and woke crusty-eyed and more tired than I'd been when I drifted off.

There was a message alert flickering in the corner of my senso. It was from Rilriltok.

Master Chief Carlos from the generation ship is awake and asking for food.

CHAPTER 16

CRYO DIDN'T HAVE A HUMAN DOCTOR ON STAFF. RILRILtok sensibly questioned the wisdom of exposing an unrightminded archaic human to giant predatory insects or tentacled hippopotami, so I was nominated to be the first to meet Master Chief Carlos.

I checked in with the nurses' station when I got there. They told me that the patient was in a private room. He was eating, he'd been given an abbreviated briefing with a lot of stressful details redacted, and he was generally pretty polite to the (human) nursing staff who had been brought in from other units to buffer him.

Apparently, I got to be the one to tell him about space aliens.

He was sitting up in bed when I entered, and he looked absolutely normal. Normal for a guy who'd barely survived a bad cryo experience, anyway. I didn't know why that should surprise me so much, but it did. I stopped in the doorway and blinked.

He had been sipping a nutritive broth through a straw. As I paused, he released the straw, looked at me, looked at the cup, and looked back at me.

"They claimed this was food," he said mildly, my senso translating. "I know I'm in the future, but I'm not sure I believe them."

"Don't tell me hospital food was any good in your dia," I said. "The goal is to make people want to leave, after all."

"Get me a stick and I'll hobble to the door. Are you a doctor?"

"Dr. Jens," I said. "How could you tell?"

"Nothing gets past me. Also, you're wearing scrubs and a lab coat."

I touched my forehead to him. He grinned.

I was startled to discover that I liked him, right away. Despite his sunken cheeks and haggard features, he had charm. His tan complexion was tending greenish; his eyes had obviously been replaced with vatted clones; and there were traces of cryoburn and freshly regenerated flesh around his fingertips. The nails would take a while to grow back. And his hair, though his cheeks were stippled with beard shadow.

But he had that indefinable quality that makes you want to like someone. It might have been calculated, to set me at ease or to structure his own anxiety by allowing him to feel in control. Or it might have been how he interacted with everyone.

He wasn't even slightly the atavistic toddler in a grown man's body I realized I had expected—been braced for—when I walked in. At least, not on first meeting.

I took a breath and shook myself out, mentally speaking. *Try not to be an asshole, Jens.*

He pushed the tray away. "How are the rest of my crew?"

"Well." This was what I was here for. It didn't make it any easier. "May I sit?"

He nodded, so I crossed to the visitor's chair and let myself down. I noticed him studying me and tried to move smoothly. I still caught my thumbnail picking at the edge of the exo and had to force myself to stop.

The worst part was watching his face change as I came closer, and he became less able to deny what he must, on some level, already know. In the normal course of events, Linden or another AI doc would have been monitoring his blood and brain chemistry, making sure that adrenaline and cortisol did not overwhelm his system.

But Dwayne Carlos had no fox. Even an AI would only have been able to work with intravenous drugs. Dr. K'kk'jk'ooOOoo was somewhere on the water levels, regulating by relay, normalizing his chemistry as best she could with the crude measures available to us. But even if he'd had a modern fox and full access to senso, she couldn't have taken his pain and grief away entirely. We still have to suffer through these things, experience them to move past them.

Living things have a dedicated sense of pain because you have to know you're wounded to take the actions necessary to heal. The best we can do, medically speaking, is blunt the edge of it, because if you can't feel, you can't react.

"You're the first to awaken," I said. It would be cruel to draw things out longer than necessary. "We have retrieved only a few cryo units so far. We're working on the others."

"My ship isn't here?"

"This is a hospital. Your ship is not fast enough to make it here, so we have been transferring your crewmates to faster-than-light ships."

He blinked. "That's impo— No, never mind. This is not the right time. Obviously it's possible. Carry on."

"We are ferrying crew from your ship as fast as possible."

"But what about the people still running Big R? The skeleton crew . . . oh."

"Oh?"

"They're all dead?"

"They're all in pods. Every single person, except the captain. I'm sorry, I have to inform you that the captain is dead."

"Oh." He didn't sound surprised.

"The ship's . . . computer? Do you have a word for that?"

"The angel," he said.

"The ship's angel had been taking the ship apart to build cryo pods, under the captain's orders. He took the library—Central?"

"Central."

"He took it offline."

"That would have limited the angel's access to information and her decision-making resources."

"It did," I agreed. "She had mostly spun off into a peripheral when we found the ship. She had also filled the ship with instances of . . . a kind of large nanobot, capable of linking up and forming structures. And was using that, I think, as a kind of primitive computronium to support what faculties she had. She's being reintegrated, and we're building an architecture for her. She, in time, should be fine."

Assuming we didn't have to seal the entire hospital off forever to keep the toxic meme from spreading throughout the entire galaxy. But now was not the time to share that with a person who couldn't do anything about it, and who had enough to worry about.

He said, "So about the pods."

The corners of his mouth and eyes tightened. He was bracing himself. I offered my hand, against my better judgment. He took it and I winced in anticipation, but he didn't squeeze.

Maybe he was considerate. Maybe he was still too weak for squeezing.

Whatever the reason, I was grateful.

Softly, he said, "The pods aren't very good, are they?"

"No," I agreed. "The pods aren't very good."

He might be from a culture spawned in the deep Before, but his agony was utterly human. His face fisted. He was so thin that I could see every individual fiber in his neck, deltoid, and the top of his pectoral muscle as his chin dipped and his body clenched.

His heart rate and blood pressure spiked; his cortisol and adrenaline levels ramped; he yanked his hand out of mine and locked it and its mate on the bed rails. Flesh whitened as blood squashed from the tender new flesh.

"Are you hurting?" I asked, jumping to my feet. "Where is the pain?" I was already reaching for the meds panel and cursing the fact that he didn't have a fox. External pain management: Is there anything more barbaric?

Carlos sucked in air so hard it whistled. "Just . . . trying not to bawl like a brat." The first word came out through clenched teeth, the rest on a rush of breath. He grabbed the next one as if he had to get it fast, before it got away.

Empathic grief clutched my chest. I laid a hand on his shoulder. He leaned away, so I removed it.

"Cry if you need to," I said. "It's a physiologically normal response."

And I wasn't sure how somebody who wasn't wearing a fox thought he could avoid it, anyway.

Something about my words seemed to startle him. He got another breath, and this one stayed caught behind his teeth. He let it out in a controlled fashion, shaped around words. "Some big strong guy I'd look." A barked laugh followed. "It's okay. I think I've got it."

When you work in a multispecies hospital the size of a small moon, you get used to feeling like you're missing much of the cultural context in any given conversation. Even with other humans: it's a big galaxy, and we don't all think alike.

I didn't understand what was going on inside Master Chief Carlos's head, but I was prepared to roll with it.

"Obviously some of us survived." He waved his own grafted hand, and winced when he noticed it. "More or less. You said I was the first awake."

"Yes."

"Am I the only?"

"So far," I said, having checked that it was true. "Biologist Cirocco Oni is undergoing treatments for cryoburn before awakening, and Specialist First Rank Jones should be awake in the next dia or so."

There was no flicker of recognition in his face when I said either name—but with over ten thousand crewmates, I would not expect anyone to know them all personally.

"There are thirteen more of your crewmates at the hospital already, and more on the way."

"Will all of them live?"

"It is"—I searched for the right word—"unlikely."

"How many more will make it?"

"I can't be sure."

He stared at me. "How many more are being retrieved now?"

"I also can't be sure of that."

"God damn it to hell, Doc, why the hell are you bothering to talk to me if you're not going to tell me anything?"

There was the toddler. I flinched, but he didn't come at me. Just as well. In his current state he wouldn't have stood much of a chance, and I would have felt bad hitting him. And my whole body would have hurt even more afterward than it usually did.

I sighed and said, "Your ship is an extremely long way away. Light-speed communication—pulsed lasers, for example—lags significantly behind simple ship travel. They'll be back here centuries before any direct message they could have sent."

Bit by bit, I watched Master Chief Carlos relax against the pillow. I was confident that he was forcing himself to. I was impressed that he had the ability.

"Awkward for RSVPing to parties," he said. "You might as well drop by with regrets."

"Or they can find out you're not coming after you're dead."

I must have gotten the deadpan right, because he laughed.

"So you have faster-than-light travel."

"Not me personally . . . but yes. Or sneakier-than-light, anyway."

"Warp drive."

"More or less. I can get you some books on it if you want? There are virtual classes." And nothing is more boring than sitting in a hospital bed, listening to the outside world spin.

His mouth twitched, as if he was about to say something important. Then he settled back and folded his arms. "I'd be very grateful."

"There's another thing," I said. "We've been limiting the staff treating you so far. But the cryonics docs—the real specialists—well, I should warn you that they're not human."

I saw his lips soften as his jaw slackened, though it didn't quite fall open. "Aliens?"

"We call them *systers*. Some of them look . . . very different."

"Do they farm humans for meat?"

"No," I said, categorically. "Most of them couldn't digest us. Amino acids all wrong, sugars backward. You know how it goes."

He laughed. "So you're not a cryonics specialist?"

"I'm a rescue specialist." I smiled. "I got you here. And turned you over to Dr. Tralgar and Dr. Rilriltok."

"Those are some names."

I laughed. "Wait until you meet the beings that belong to them."

His smile was more like a flinch, and quickly faded. "So you can't promise me anyone else will live."

"Not in any honesty," I said, as gently as I could. Dammit, I went into rescue so that I wouldn't have to give people bad news. Everybody I deal with is supposed to be in the middle of a crisis, not weathering a series of emotional blows. I hate this part of the job. "The cryonics specialists feel that we can expect about one in three of your crewmates to survive."

He breathed out, slowly. "Wow."

"I'm sorry," I said.

He shook his head. "We knew it was a crazy risk—oh God! The influenza virus, there was some kind of superbug wiping out the ship, you might be exposed—"

"We're all inoculated," I said. "And we engineered an antiviral to support your immune system and administered it before we woke you up."

"You've cured the flu."

"We've cured a lot of things." I squeezed my hand closed, the familiar ache of joints reminding me that we hadn't cured everything. "Part of your ship's core is here. And she's very eager to meet you."

"You rescued Central?" he said hopefully. Then he must have remembered what I told him about Central, because his mouth contracted with dismay.

"Helen," I answered.

"Oh. That thing."

Perhaps it stung because his response was so similar to what mine had been. And because I was beginning to appreciate Helen as a person, rather than an ill-considered toy. I was struck silent for a moment.

Carlos tugged the sheets up. "I hope you're not going to judge us all by that joke."

"Since the moment we made contact with her, she's been absolutely dedicated to your well-being," I mentioned. "And that of the rest of her crew."

"Some of the guys thought it was amusing," he said. "I didn't—my wife told me how dehumanized it made her feel, and I was never comfortable around it, after." He frowned deeply. "My wife . . . ?"

"I know she's not among the patients we're currently working on. Helen might be able to guide us to her cryo unit, though, and we'll prioritize retrieving her."

His mouth twisted again.

I said, "You do know your AI is self-aware and self-willed, right?"

"Helen?" He shook his head. "It's a peripheral. Central has a personality module, but the Helen bot is just a bot. It can talk, and carry out assigned tasks, and keep you awake through a swing shift . . . but that's all."

"Well," I said, settling back in my chair. "You'll be surprised to discover that some things have changed. . . ."

I had been wrong about Oni: there were complications treating her cryoburn, and her awakening was put off. So specialist Calliope Jones was the next to awaken, and I recalled that she was the historian. She was also the individual in the anomalous cryo pod, which made me hope she might be able to provide some answers about it.

Or maybe the Goodlaw was right, and she was a Freeport pirate hiding from justice amidst ten thousand identical corpsicle coffins.

It had to be kidding, right?

How do you tell if a mantoid the size of a Terran pony is kidding?

I checked in with Mercy to make sure he was still okay and open to receiving visitors. He was, as long as they were willing to come to him for a nice, in-person, air-gapped audio conversation. All of the remaining AIs had compartmentalized themselves, which meant that consulting them required intercom communication, or moving one's self to the physical location of their storage media. As if visiting an oracle in a temple.

At the same time, I realized that Rilriltok and Tralgar had assumed that I would be available to midwife the rebirth of every single member of Helen's crew. That . . . was not going to work out long-term. Whatever I was doing for Helen, I wasn't the care liaison for ten-thousand-odd archaic humans.

And—I made a solemn promise to myself—I was not going to allow myself to be bullied into *becoming* the care liaison for ten-thousand-odd archaic humans. Or even three-thousand-odd, if we managed to save thirty percent.

Still a lot of humans.

"Sally," I said, while I was masking up to go in and visit Jones. We have transparent polymer filter masks for situations like this. Very effective, and they help the patients' psychology enormously. Rilriltok thinks it's very funny that humans find other humans with their breathing and eating holes covered ominous, but then its face has an immobile exoskeleton and it breathes through spiracles, so I'm not sure its opinion is broadly medically applicable.

I hear you, Sally answered, muffled by protocols.

"Do you have time to send a message to Starlight that Core General needs to hire a lot of stable, sensible, Terran-style volunteers to manage introduction to modern society for the *Big Rock Candy Mountain* survivors? Once we're not under quarantine, that is."

That's an excellent point, Sally said. *The next load of survivors can't dock until the quarantine is lifted, anyway. In the meantime, I can send you Loese. She's cluttering up the place without enough to do. She's getting on my circuits.*

I laughed. Loese, grounded, sounded like a shipmind's worst nightmare. And from what I'd seen, she wasn't taking the enforced downtime or the vague sense of personal responsibility well. "Send her to Tralgar."

I will. How are you doing?

"Overworked," I said, trying to sound cheerful about it. "And none of it is actually my job."

I still had barely begun the assignment O'Mara and Starlight wanted me to work on. It was amazing how much *stuff* everybody had for me to do.

I opened the door and stepped into the isolation chamber. A woman with black hair and a medium complexion rendered grayish and chalky by cryoburn and fatigue looked up, blinking as if her eyes weren't focusing exactly as she expected. "Hi," I said. "I'm Dr. Jens."

"Calliope Jones," she answered. "I'm alive? I'm in a hospital?"

"The biggest hospital in the galaxy," I agreed. "And you're definitely alive, unless dead folks have skills I'm not aware of. Welcome back to the land of the living."

She laughed, then flinched when her dry lips cracked.

"Here." I poured a cup of water and stuck a straw in. "This might help with that dehydration."

She sipped. Her lip left blood on the straw. She seemed to surprise herself with her own thirst, and finished the water.

"What do you remember?" I asked when she'd put the cup aside.

"Um," she said. "A . . . drill? Flashing lights. An alert. People scrambling for . . . for escape pods? No, that can't be right. We don't have escape pods. There's nowhere to escape to." She looked around. "Except apparently there is. I was in a cryonics freezer, wasn't I?"

"Yes," I said.

Ouch, I thought. *What a way to live. Like being stuck on a single planet with no failsafes and no way off in case of catastrophe.*

Except the generation ship was far more precarious and fragile even than a planet.

"There was a virus—"

"We know," I said. "You've been treated and I'm immunized."

"My ship? My crew?"

"Your ship and the shipmind—the *angel,* sorry, we use a different word—have suffered significant damage. What we've been able to recover of the shipmind is here, with the first group of evacuees—fourteen of you. One other has been successfully awakened so far: Master Chief Dwayne Carlos. Do you know him?"

She shook her head. "Everything is very fuzzy. I know the—the shipmind. Central?"

"Helen," I said. "And what's left of Central, I think. If I understand the outcome correctly, they both suffered damage and integrated out of self-preservation. Helen's become self-aware; I understand she wasn't before."

"Helen!" She gave a big sigh of relief. "Well, that's something to make me feel a little more grounded, I guess. How's our command structure?"

"Right now, you don't have one."

"Oh. Captain and first mate? Officers?"

"The captain, we believe, perished. No other officers have been retrieved. We're ferrying your crewmates here in groups, but it's going to take a while, and there were no commissioned officers in the first group."

"I've just realized," she said incredulously, "that I cannot remember anyone's name."

"Anyone?"

"Any of my crewmates. My family. I must have a family?"

I sighed. She certainly *seemed* as if she came from a millennian ago. "Our scans show you've suffered some intracranial scarring. It may be impairing your cognition—"

"Brain damage?"

"Repairable damage," I said. "The memory loss is probably permanent, I'm afraid, but we've already infused stem cells and growth medium, and you should be finding your cognition clearing up over the next few diar."

"You can . . . patch up brain damage." She snapped her fingers and winced when it made the infusion needle jump in her vein. I could have reached out and put my hand on her arm, but for some reason the thought made me feel shy, so I didn't.

"We have doctors that do nothing else," I said. "Which, I am afraid, brings me to another part of your orientation that you might find unsettling. Not all—or even most—of the staff here are human. The doctor who's been working on your neurological injury is an oxygen-breathing, water-dwelling vertebrate from a planet whose name I need mechanical assistance to pronounce. She gets around in a big tank on wheels."

"My neurologist is a dolphin?" Jones broke into a delighted grin. "I think I might like the future!" Then she sobered. "How far in the future are we, anyway?"

"That's a complicated question," I said. "We don't know exactly when you went into suspension, or exactly how much subjective time you had spent traveling before then. There are relativistic effects to consider. And—"

"Twenty-four forty-seven," she said, with confidence. Then she froze. "No, I . . . I can't say that with any confidence. The date popped into my head, but I can't put a context to it. It could just be a date. So your people—are you descendants of the other ships?" She sat forward in the bed, animated despite the effort it obviously cost her. "Can you get me a timeline, oh, and—"

"Wait, wait," I said, laughing. "You don't want to talk to me about those things. You want to talk to Mercy. He's the hospital archinformist. His specialty is medical history, but—"

"I'll take it!" she enthused, beaming.

I got a voice link to Mercy and turned them loose on each other. Jones's avocation shone through in her conversation: she wanted dates, names, places, and root causes of everything. Mercy rapidly retrieved a pile of pull numbers to get her started requesting histories. He only had to explain how to request data once. I excused myself: it seemed like the beginning of a beautiful friendship, and I would only have been in the way.

Jones smiled and waved as I was leaving, but that was all. I felt a tiny pang. Her enthusiasm was utterly adorable.

Tralgar was waiting when I stepped outside. I checked the time and realized I'd been with Jones so long that Rilriltok had gone to dinner and its rest shift. I asked how Cirocco Oni was.

Tralgar's tentacles contracted into coils. *There's damage. It might be reversible. And . . . something in the pod's program seems to be trying to prevent the rewarming sequence from taking hold. Possibly it's the remains of the program the ship's captain released when he was evacuating his crew to the pods.*

I thought about Helen's desire to get everybody into pods for their safety. I thought about the machine.

I hadn't told Carlos or Jones that they—and Oni, and the medic Call Reznik—were the only four of the fourteen crewmembers to survive rewarming to the point of needing the next medical interventions. Oni and Reznik were still touch-and-go.

I imagined the other graft clones had already been recycled. It took a significant amount of resources to keep them alive, blood pumping, lungs breathings, when they were intentionally grown with stunted brain structures.

It would have been in poor taste to congratulate Tralgar on the accuracy with which he and Rilriltok had estimated their chances of success in saving these patients. But right now, we were as close to that grim 30 percent mark as possible unless we started saving fractions of patients. Or unless Oni and Reznik died.

I had hoped they were being conservative. No matter how hard you try to stay uninvested and professional . . . people don't go into medicine because their patients' welfare is irrelevant to them.

"You're going to want me to explain that to Helen, aren't you?"

Maybe the tiredness in my voice and expression was strong enough to make it through the species and translation barrier. Maybe Tralgar had an appreciation for the exhausting nature of everything I had already done todia.

I will handle the communication. She will not wish to accept that Master Chief Carlos does not wish to speak with her.

"I know," I said. "Maybe it'll help that Jones is excited to. Pity Zhiruo isn't able to run interference. Any word on Zhiruo yet? Or Linden?"

Starlight says Linden is communicating in outgoing packet bursts. They say she says the situation is difficult and unstable, requiring constant interventions. She has hopes that if she finds the right code sequences, she will be able to stabilize herself and commence repairs. Once that occurs, she should be able to resume normal functions. She says that will be soon. Whatever soon is.

I have heard no updates on Zhiruo, but I assume that once Linden has solved her virus she will be able to tackle its other instances. Unless Zhiruo manages to repair herself first, which is possible.

"Good," I said. I rubbed my eyes. "I'm going to get some food while supplies still hold out. Do you want anything?"

I am well-nourished. Tralgar tapped its breathing slits with a meaty appendage-tip. *Don't forget to take that mask off before you try to put anything in your food hole.*

By the time I got to the cafeteria I was ready to slide into a booth, drink a beer, and never talk to another living being. But when I checked the statuses I saw that Rhym and Hhayazh had claimed a table against the windows, and amended my mood to "never talk to another *human* being."

I sent a request to join them, but perhaps they were too busy eating to notice the ping, because no reply came. So, when I arrived at the caf, I stood where they could see me and waved, and pointed to their table. They waved back and pointed to the table as well.

We'd worked together long enough that I didn't worry about a miscommunication. I just went and got my food.

Running into my colleagues in the cafeteria so often seemed a little odd, given prior experience and the size of the hospital, but with the lifts down until Linden came back online, nobody was moving around the bubble much. And, I reminded myself, even if the lifts had been running, people at Core General tended to stick to the areas closest to where they worked and lived—as with neighborhoods in a big city.

I wasn't used to spending so much time grounded, so I'd never really had occasion to notice, before.

Sally's slip, when she wasn't unloading at the Emergency Department, was near the oxygen casualty section. Her crew all had our quarters nearby. The Ox Cryo unit was a few dozen meters along the same ring. The cafeteria was a few levels hubward.

When I came back, I was carrying a tray of salad, cloned steak tips, and butterscotch pudding. I also had a dark beer, a mug of tea, and a powerful fixation on the coffee I wasn't going to be drinking any time in the near future, unless I climbed into a softsuit and made a trek around the outside of the hospital to get to the one humans-only caf that served java. To make matters worse, I'd been informed when I requested the alcohol ration that there wasn't going to be much more available unless and until we got a supply run.

Maybe I could start a batch of hooch with some medical yeast and lactated ringers. I was sure it would be fine.

Rhym had long since demolished their dinner in the single-minded manner of their kind, so they must be here to keep Hhayazh company. Or possibly to soak in the ambiance: Who could tell? Hhayazh had some greenish slime with lumps in it that I identified from the smell as fermented legumes. Or, if not true legumes, whatever its planet used for lentils.

I raised the snifter of beer to my colleagues as I sat, and said, "Here's to the inevitable beer riots."

Hhayazh pointed its bristles at me and buzzed, *Does your species immediately resort to social upheaval when threatened with a lack of intoxicants? I would think you would have rightminded that tendency out by now.*

"It usually takes at least a couple of hours," I admitted. The salad had little green flat crunchy seeds in it: an unexpected treat. And probably full of useful fatty acids.

My banter with Hhayazh aside, I was worried about food. Ox sector, at least, grew a lot of its produce on-site, supporting the ox/carbon dioxide biosphere and providing restorative environments for recreation, exercise, and hanging around with plants that *didn't* want to argue about politics or sports teams.

It occurred to me that Ceeharens were the most common sentient vegetable on Core General, and that I didn't know if they even *had* a preferred sport as a species.

A brief consult with senso informed me that they had several, each a little more incomprehensible than the last. Well, it was my own fault for wondering.

I brought my attention back to the table, where Rhym was fiddling a drinking straw with their tendrils and saying, *Something weird is happening.*

I swallowed salad. "What weird *isn't* happening? We've got people from the deep past, a sexy robot with damaged memory cores, a ship full of Darboof with compromised foxes and brain damage, and a toxic meme infecting our AI staff like the technological equivalent of caterpillar fungus. None of this is normal."

Caterpillar . . . ? Rhym asked, in the tone of somebody who had tried to look it up but didn't have the right search terms.

So I told them about the fungal parasites on Terra that hijacked the brains of insects and made them perform all sorts of self-destructive behaviors in order to spread the fungal spores.

They were incredulous *and* horrified. There's something professionally gratifying about being able to gross out a tentacular tree stump who also happens to be one of the galaxy's most experienced trauma surgeons.

Hhayazh won the digression—and horrified us both further—by telling us about a similar fungus on Rashaq that infected several species, including Rashaqin nymphs. Not the adults, at least, but the mental image of Rilriltok with a giant sporing body bursting from its back was bad enough that I resorted to tuning to erase it. I wasn't going to be able to enjoy my pudding otherwise, and if we were facing food shortages, I certainly wasn't going to waste it.

"But you were going to tell me something else," I prompted. "Before I distracted you with mind-controlling fungus."

Rhym leaned back, tendrils twitching. Their eyes narrowed. They had lens-type eyes with lids like humans, operating on very similar principles. Their lids closed from side to side, though, and they were lucky enough to have a nictitating membrane. I'd contemplated more than once getting one added, but I didn't want to be out of work for the surgery and long enough for the eye to heal. Twice: once for each eye, because they didn't do them both at the same time.

They said, *Sally, will you establish a direct senso link, and handle the translation?*

I'm here, Sally said, a little less fuzzily than was lately usual. She wasn't reaching us through the hospital infrastructure then, but by direct transmission. *You're all encrypted.*

Hhayazh leaned in to the table, clacking excitedly. *Do you remember that private ambulance that cut us off when we were bringing Helen and her crew in?*

"Sure." My beer was finished. I switched to the tea.

It left.

"But we're under quarantine." I expected Hhayazh or Rhym to tell me that the ambulance had left before the quarantine started. I was already mentally preparing myself to ask something like, *So what's so weird about that?*

But Rhym said, *We know. And there's something even weirder.*

I waited. I sipped my tea. I looked from one colleague to the other.

Rhym writhed excitedly. *About twelve standard hours later, another one showed up. Docked in the same berth. And Tsosie saw them bringing in a cryo unit.*

Just like the other one, Hhayazh said.

"Weelll." My tea was somehow empty. I swallowed the last drop and set down the cup. "It is a hospital. People do show up in cryo tanks and tubes, in ambulances."

When we're under interdict? Hhayazh said. *And then leave again?*

"We don't usually spend this long in dock. Maybe it's normal activity and we miss it most of the time." I licked butterscotch pudding off my spoon. Maybe I'd overdone it on the antianxiety tuning. I should probably feel a little more worried by the information my colleagues were giving me than I did. I should let more emotion get through, but . . .

But I didn't really *want* to feel any more anxious. I was *tired* of feeling anxious.

Maybe, Sally agreed inside my head. *But then why can't I find any record of the patients the private ships brought in? Or even any record of their flight plan or other cargo?*

"Oh," I said.

Oh, Rhym agreed.

CHAPTER 17

AFTER LUNCH, I CHECKED IN ON HELEN. SHE WAS STILL camped out in the Cryo unit observation lounge as if she had grown into the furniture. She asked if she could see her surviving crew yet. I told her soon, though maybe not Carlos unless he started feeling more inclined toward visitors. I promised to ask them if I could further update her on their care, however. I told her that Oni was not yet ready to be awakened, and that I would keep Helen apprised of her progress, as well.

She asked after Dr. Zhiruo and whether she—Helen—would be receiving additional treatment. I told her that she would, as soon as Dr. Zhiruo's infection was under control and the quarantine was lifted. I told her that the next group—I managed not to say *shipment*—of her crew would be arriving at that point, and that some were already in ships in holding patterns near Core General, waiting for us to be open for business again.

She asked when the quarantine was going to be lifted.

That was a harder one, and I thought about it anxiously for a moment or two before coming up with an answer that seemed honest to me, but filtered of all my own ability to catastrophize. I was perfectly capable of keeping myself up all night, staring into space and coming up with Ways Things Could Be Worse. Like the one where the Synarche never could contain the meme, and eventually everybody organic on Core General had to take turns deactivating and purging each other's foxes to make sure there was no data transfer, and then we evacuated as many of the hospital's staff and patients as possible before leaving the rest to starve, run out of power and oxygen, and eventually spiral into the Well on a decaying orbit to be pulled apart like Rilriltok swiping my spaghetti.

Or the one where the meme was already loose in the galaxy, winging its way around on data packets and wiping out a thousand ans of interspecies civilization in one fell blow.

Thinking like that made me a good disaster planner and emergency response coordinator, and often got Sally wandering into my brain after lights-out to pull the plug and make sure I actually slept a little.

What I said was, "Eventually. I don't know when, but I can assure you that it is a tremendous annoyance to everybody, and a very grave hardship to many. The hospital is treating it as an emergency situation, and working to resolve it as fast as we can."

All in all, it was one of the saner conversations I'd ever had with an upset Helen. Dr. Zhiruo might be out of commission, but the healing she had initiated seemed to be proceeding apace. Maybe all Helen had needed was some space in which to sort herself out.

Literally, I mean. Adequate data caching.

That reminded me that I had been so busy since we got back that I hadn't checked on the machine. Hadn't Zhiruo been treating that, too?

It definitely wasn't my job. And I should be doing some more data sorting on the sabotage question while I had a free minute. After I checked on my patients here, I would go and do that, I decided.

Helen went back to her post by the window when I excused myself. I half expected to see footprints worn in the floor in her habitual spot.

Cheeirilaq intercepted me as I was heading toward the room housing Master Chief Carlos. *Friend Dr. Jens.*

"Goodlaw Cheeirilaq." I had a feeling I knew what came next, and honestly it was convenient. Todia's goal had been to introduce the *Big Rock Candy Mountain* survivors—the conscious ones, anyway—to the reality of systers and the Synarche. "Let me guess. You would like to question the master chief?"

Cheeirilaq froze so completely that when, a few moments later, it let out a held breath, I found myself sighing in sympathy. *How did you know that?*

"I was Judiciary myself, remember? It's a logical next step in your investigation."

I don't recall having shared details of my investigation with you.

"Of course not. But you did tell me that it involved Afar and associated questions. And most doctors aren't dumb." I looked over at where Tralgar and another doctor I didn't know were consulting on something. I'd been thinking of drafting one of the unit docs or nurses to be my sample syster, but they all had jobs to do. And here was Cheeirilaq, who *wanted* an opportunity to talk to Carlos and Jones.

Expedient. I could put off the research for another hour.

Linden was still not responding to queries, and the lifts were still down. I spared a moment to be grateful that the hospital's senso and translation were operated on different protocols. I assumed that there was an AI—possibly Mercy—responsible for them, but the functions seemed to be largely autonomous.

Can you imagine any job more boring for a galactic supercomputer than translating endless complaints about the scrambled eggs?

I went into the master chief's room first, leaving the door open and Cheeirilaq lurking behind its frame. Carlos looked up from a console he'd been fiddling with—the kind of thing you give kids whose brains aren't myelinated enough for a fox yet. "Hi, Doc," he said. "I found an interesting game. I think it's civics for kids or something."

"Good," I said. "I'm glad you're using the brain cells."

"I don't suppose you have a timeline showing when more of my crew might be arriving?" His voice had a hesitant hopefulness that reached into my chest and squeezed. I noticed that he did not, specifically, ask about his wife.

"A week, maybe? Ten diar? Not long now. Would it help if I arranged for you to have access to any telemetry we get from the rescue ships?"

His smile almost split his cheeks. "Yes, please."

I perched myself on the edge of the visitor's chair, intentionally moving from a professional to a personal context. "How are you adjusting?"

His shoulders flinched toward his ears. "Rough," he said. "Trying not to lose my shi—er, I mean. I'm trying to hold it together."

I am *not* trained in rightminding. Never send a trauma doc to do a psychiatrist's job, I'm just saying. I managed not to panic, though, and groped around in the relevant stock phrases cluttering up my brain until I came up with, "It's pretty normal to experience a huge sense of dislocation, you know."

Apparently, something about my demeanor was funny, because he pushed his head back against the pillow and laughed until he started coughing. I helped him sit up, gave him water. Patted his back until he managed to swallow some.

World's Most Awkward Nursemaid, that's what it reads on *my* favorite mug.

When he was settled again, I put his cup down on the nightstand and asked, "What was so funny?"

"You." The corners of his eyes twinkled with helpless tears. "You're so *serious.* 'It's pretty normal to experience a huge sense of dislocation, you know'!" he parroted. "As if there's literally anything normal about waking up centuries in the future and not even knowing which of my friends or family are alive, or might make it out of the meat lockers. You just—"

His face stilled. He settled back.

"You just have to laugh," he finished, seriously.

"Yeah," I said. "I can't even imagine your experience."

"Heck, Doc," he said. "I can't imagine it, and I'm living it. So let's talk about something else. What do you have for me today, more historians?"

"Actually . . ." I looked toward the door. "Todia I brought somebody along that you might be interested in meeting."

"Is this show-and-tell?" He moved the console from the bed to the nightstand and hitched himself up, smoothing his pajama lapels. "I have to say, these things are a damn sight more dignified than a hospital johnny."

I didn't know what a hospital johnny was, so I made a note to investigate later. "You know the Synarche is comprised of a lot of different species."

"Systers," he said, with a squint of concentration. "Are you slow-walking that you're about to introduce me to my first a—I mean, my first nonhuman sentience?"

I decided not to argue with him about Helen. Or Central.

"Come on, Doc," he said, jocularity over an edge of irritation. "You can give it to me straight. I'm not as damn fragile as you all seem to think I am. I might not have a little box in my head controlling my thoughts and emotions, but I am a grown man. I can keep a lid on myself!"

I leaned back against the bulkhead—mostly because my feet hurt—and crossed my arms. "Keeping a lid on yourself doesn't actually help you deal with those feelings and move through them, though. Are you familiar with the concept of repression?"

I'd done a little historical reading and consulted the archinformist, so even without Mercy there riding my senso to back me up, I knew the right terms to use. Always make friends with a super-genius AI historian when you get the chance.

"I'm not *gay*," Carlos said, after a long silence.

"I am," I answered.

He blinked and frowned, but didn't say anything. A whole ship full of atavistic bigots, yay. Well, it was only to be expected.

"But that's not what I'm talking about. I'm talking about choosing not to experience and process your feelings. I believe the archaic term would be *not owning one's own shit.*"

"Okay," he said. "What does any of that have to do with . . . with nonhuman intelligences?"

"It has to do with your crewmates," I said. "And your ship. *And* nonhuman intelligences. These are all things you need to process, not put aside."

He sighed and closed his eyes. "You sound like my wife." Then he winced, as if remembering that his wife had a three in ten chance of surviving her next adventure, and opened them again. "All right. I promise to try to be more in touch with my feelings. Can you show me what's hiding behind the door now?"

"Who," I said, and cued Cheeirilaq to come in.

The Goodlaw moved slowly, one meticulous leg at a time. Which, I think, only succeeded in making it look *more* menacing, as it seemed to stalk into the room. It stopped halfway, thorax held parallel to the deck so it wouldn't loom—which had the effect of making it look three meters long instead of two—raptorial arms and manipulators folded away along its carapace so it didn't bristle. It was trying to take up as little room as a bug as long as a bunk bed can, and I admit, I found its lowered antennae and compressed abdomen kind of adorable.

Master Chief Carlos responded a little differently.

"Holy," Carlos said. "Holy . . . cow."

Greetings, friend Carlos, Cheeirilaq said. *I am Goodlaw Cheeirilaq. A constable, of sorts.*

The translation came from Carlos's tablet, because he didn't have a fox. He touched his ear, and so I noticed he was wearing a bud in the canal.

He said, "A giant praying mantis cop? You have got to be kidding me."

You are not in any trouble. I would like to ask you a few questions about your experiences.

Carlos looked at me. I said, "You don't have to cooperate. But the Goodlaw would not lie about your legal status. If it did, and you were in trouble, the courts would throw that out."

"Due process," Carlos said, his shoulders relaxing. "That's a relief."

It was a bit of a relief to me that he recognized it for what it was. That made me think that integrating these survivors of the deep past into Synarche society might actually work out pretty easily.

I was worried about Carlos's wife, also. I knew she wasn't in Ruth's load of pods, because we had the serial numbers and Helen had checked. Singer was coming in behind her—or might already be here—with a bigger load. But that meant I didn't know where she was, or if our colleagues had retrieved her yet.

And nobody could know if she would survive rewarming.

I thought Carlos's continued avoidance of the question meant he was scared for her.

He looked at Cheeirilaq, tipping his head. "Well, you might as well come the rest of the way in."

Cheeirilaq did, and shut the door behind it. Even folded to its smallest profile, it seemed to fill up the entire isolation room. It slowly extended one raptorial forelimb and pointed at the datapad. *You are studying government, friend Carlos?*

Carlos waved one hand. "I think it's some kind of educational game."

I stepped forward, glancing at the pad. "That's the modeling protocols. It's a sector of the government. Synizens can play through simulated problems, and then one or many of the Grand Council's subcouncils process the results to a series of models to determine policies and outcomes."

A line formed between his brows. The hand dropped. "Is this really how you run your country?"

I had to look up the archaic word. "Our polity, you mean?"

"If you prefer." He sounded amused, as if I were splitting hairs. Didn't *country* specifically refer to physical terrain on a planet?

"It's part of the process," I said. "I'm not an expert. But the game allows Synizens to model an extremely large number of policy paths, and from the repeated models and results—and occasional individual inspiration—a superior policy emerges. Structure modeling has been experimentally proven to consistently produce better results than relying on experts. Democracies, from Before, were a primitive way of managing the math."

His face stilled, as if assessing a threat. "You don't vote?"

"You haven't woken up into a totalitarian nightmare," I said, laughing. "Don't worry. The Synarche's index of personal freedom is around seventy-nine percent, and the index of well-being is close to eighty-seven percent. Those are the best numbers in human history."

They're the best numbers in Rashaqin history, too, Cheeirilaq stridulated. It hadn't moved from its post near the door—it hadn't moved at all, except to breathe. Essentially, I'd been treating it as a large, emerald-colored chitin statue, and from Carlos's start I could see that his limbic system had forgotten to be afraid of it.

"Just the local constabulary," I reminded him as his heart rate spiked.

"Do they eat you for traffic tickets here?"

I have never eaten a sentient, Cheeirilaq said. *And only once or twice contemplated it. Your amino acids probably wouldn't agree with me anyway.*

They would be fine, but this seemed like a bad time to point that out.

Carlos looked at me. "Joking," I mouthed.

He sighed. "You are very large," he said to Cheeirilaq. "But not too different from some Earth species that were part of my ship's biosphere." Carlos held up his fingers about eight centimeters apart. "Is it offensive if I say we carried them for pest control?"

As long as you recognize that I am a great deal smarter, I will not be offended. Cheeirilaq's head rose, its thorax inclining toward the vertical. Its face swiveled toward me. *I assume I am a great deal smarter?*

"Infinitely," I agreed.

Excellent. After a fashion, I also specialize in pest control.

I walked back to my quarters, contemplating a nap. It had been a long dia, and it wasn't getting any shorter. My exo didn't let me trudge, but it was definitely doing 90 percent of the work of motivating me along the corridor.

I should have been planning my data requests regarding the "safety incidents." But I kept thinking about what Rhym and Hhayazh had told me. I was a Core General staff physician. I could just . . . go and see what was going on back there in the private ox ward.

Couldn't I?

My fox was all-access. I wouldn't even need a suit. And there was direct access to the private unit from the Casualty Department, so I wouldn't have to worry about the still nonfunctional lifts, or suiting up beyond decontamination protocols.

I had every right to be there. And nevertheless, I felt a chill as I contemplated it.

My species is very good at picking up unconscious cues and aversions, being highly social animals. We are excellent at reading the room and knowing what is expected of us and whether we have overstepped somehow.

And yet I didn't want to go back there. For no reason at all.

So I found myself wondering, given the intensity of my desire to avoid finding out what was back there—or even speculating on it—if some small aversion (a don't-see-me, a denial bug, a Somebody Else's Problem field) hadn't been added to the hospital staff fox updates at some point.

Sally, I asked inside the privacy of my own senso, *what do you know about the private units?*

She hesitated.

Sally?

Know from personal experience? Nothing. Additionally, I am unaware of any public details regarding the functioning of these units.

What do you speculate, then? Or what have you discerned?

As you know, she answered, *everyone in the Synarche is guaranteed a high minimum standard of care. Everyone is entitled to be as healthy as possible, given the limits of technology.*

I would have tapped my fingers on my exo, but I was much too sore for extraneous movement.

Up to and including transplants and regeneration therapies.

"Clones," I said. "We don't grow them with anything more than autonomic brain functions, because that would be unethical."

So all patients receive *the highest standard of care. Anything else would, likewise, be unethical.*

I slid through the door to my quarters. It had hardly closed behind me before I stripped down to my exo, wiped myself off with a lemon swab that didn't smell a thing like real citrus oil, and tipped myself into my bunk before my gear had even stowed itself. My limbs ached. My feet felt heavy and overlarge.

My exo needed a charge. I hooked it to the trickle and tried to get comfortable.

"Right," I said. "I certainly try to provide that. And I know that you do, too. So . . . what's in first class? What are they getting that we're not?"

Now that we were in private, Sally spoke out loud. "Concierge service. Their pillows fluffed. Chocolates thereon. Expensive resources: human labor, surface foods."

"Huh," I said. "Did the unit AI tell you that?"

"There is no unit AI."

"There *what?*" I sat up so fast I almost dropped myself out of the hammock.

"'There is no unit AI."

A sour feeling settled inside me. "'That can't be right."

"Nevertheless," said Sally. "It is true."

It was a terrible reason to break into a medical unit. Well, all right, it wasn't technically breaking in. But as much as I was a full-time doctor now, I'd been a doctor *and* a cop before. One does not become either of those things due to a congenital lack of curiosity.

I was tired and in pain. I tuned myself for wakefulness and pain relief, knowing that it would cost me later in backlash. But later was not now. I climbed back out of my hammock and dressed in fresh scrubs. I even combed styler through my hair and programmed my overworked frizz to a nice, tight, professional cap of curls.

My exo's charge light was still blinking. It could process a certain amount of electricity from my motions, but that wasn't the same as a nice fat eight-hour trickle. Still, I should be good for another standard, if I didn't try anything too strenuous.

Even if I ran out of juice, it wouldn't be as if I couldn't move at all. It would, however, hurt much more, and involve a lot of groaning and hobbling.

Piece of cake.

It wasn't far to Casualty. I suited up in the hall, for the anonymity it offered—and the biohazard protection. Just in case there was something unsavory going on back there that was also contagious, rather than merely the exploitation of resources by the rich.

Imagine what it must have been like hundreds of ans ago—back in Carlos's dia—when there was no Guarantee, no Income, no useful work for anyone who wanted it. No promise of safety and health and security. Only exploitation under various systems all claiming to be different, but all amounting to the farming of the many to make wealthy the few. Serfdoms and indenturehood and chattel slavery.

Explaining the future to him was going to be interesting.

The Casualty Department was positively eerie in its emptiness. I hadn't been back to Sally recently, and I hadn't expected the complete lack of patients and the nearly complete lack of staff. One lone Ceeharen triage nurse waved to me from behind the desk across the big reception deck without raising their head. They appeared to be bent over a reader or game board of some sort.

I waved back and kept walking, angling far enough from the desk to preclude casual conversation, and headed toward the entrance to the private unit.

My footsteps echoed through the eerie emptiness. I braced myself for whatever bullshit I might be about to witness, and keyed myself in through the door.

Battery levels critical, my exo said. *Fatigue levels excessive. Recommend recharge and sleep cycle as soon as possible.*

I know, robot. I know.

My exo quit about ten steps after I crossed the threshold. I couldn't see the telltale on my wrist through the suit, but I knew it would be blinking orange.

"Exo, are you there?"

The only thing breaking the silence inside my suit was the soft echo of my own voice inside the helmet. The senso link in the lower quadrant of my visual field blinked EXO 0% BAT, just to add insult to injury. Orange, when moments before it had been yellow and at 7 percent.

One thing primitive humans did have going for them was a lack of stuff that runs on batteries. And, more to the point, runs *out* of batteries.

I realized I had stopped in a doorway and, pushing against my exo, hastily stepped through. Decompression shields are designed like guillotines.

It's a terrible thing if an unsuspecting sentient happens to be standing under one when it closes. Worse, though, if that didn't happen—for all the other unsuspecting sentients that might be explosively decompressed if the doors failed.

That was another reason for me in particular not to stand in the way. My exo was featherweight, breathable, barely there. And made of sandwiched nanofilms and conductive, contracting polymer. Conceivably, the door might not be able to cut through it, if I was under it when it fell.

They might be privileged fuckers in here, but I'd hate to be the person who ensured the deaths of every patient in the private unit. And the staff certainly deserved better.

Once I was moving, I continued to step forward as briskly as I could manage. Now that it was dead, the exo offered resistance rather than assistance when I moved. It seemed to compress my limbs and torso, pushing back against me with every step as if I were strapped into a zero-g resistance machine.

There were patient rooms down the hall. Maybe I could get to one and peer through the window, check the monitors. I made it five steps farther into the private unit and dragged myself the last sideways half meter into an alcove along the corridor. Two multispecies bench seats crouched intimately across from each other. An old-fashioned curtain on rings hung from the bar across the top of the door. Enough privacy for delivering bad news. Not enough privacy to encourage bad behavior.

I flipped the curtain across to hide my distress. I didn't sit down because if I sat, I was only going to have to get up again. And I'd rather not embrace that particular experience.

But I needed to get out of the public view for a moment. Gather myself. Force myself to move confidently, like a medical professional with every right to be here.

And not like somebody on the verge of a total systemic collapse who had stolen a staff uniform in some misguided attempt at escape.

A sensible human being would have gathered her resources, steadied her nerves, and turned right back around as if she had forgotten some important piece of kit. A sensible human being would have marched back through the other decomp door and gone back to bed. Would never have come here on a restless sleep-shift whim in the first place.

A sensible human being would spend less time jumping out of perfectly good spacecraft than I did. I was not, perforce, a sensible human being.

I squared my shoulders, embraced my inner warrior, and flicked the curtain aside.

The corridor was not crowded by Core General standards. I spotted a variety of ox-breathing staff and one lone Ceeharen, whose beneficial metabolic needs split the carbon dioxide my type of sentient produced and converted it back into oxygen and carbon. Nobody looked strangely at my softsider quarantine suit, or even appeared to notice me. It was a reasonable enough precaution, and doubled as a light environmental suit if the environments you were passing through weren't too extreme.

Given the lack of functional lifts, we were seeing a lot more of them in the hospital corridors. People had to get to work.

I had no idea what I might be looking for. I had no reason to be here, other than curiosity and a nasty itchy sensation.

I felt, to be perfectly honest, like I was going through my wife's private messages, looking for evidence because I suspected her of misleading me. Not that I had a wife anymore, or any reason to suspect one of malfeasance. But you know what I mean.

I *knew* it was ridiculous. I believed in this hospital. I had faith in this hospital.

And yet, here I was. Checking up.

The private unit looked like a perfectly normal hospital unit, albeit one with nicer rooms. Several were inhabited, bodies in a range of beds designed for three different species. I spotted holowindows and possibly even a real viewport or two through open room doors. Several more rooms were obviously empty. Waiting for the next sentient with the resources to buy their way in.

I kept walking, sweat stinging my eyes inside the helmet. Softsuits weren't meant for anything this strenuous. As strenuous as walking down a hospital corridor under moderate spin gravity.

It hurt, and because I didn't feel like being in pain, I decided I would rather be angry.

Being angry is a skill I have a lot of experience with, though I worked pretty hard in my military years to learn not to tote anger around with me all the time. There's constructive anger, which motivates you to get up off the ground and get things done. There's righteous anger, which motivates you to protect the afflicted and downtrodden. There's helpless anger, which just makes you feel useless and turns you mean.

And there's self-pitying anger, which gets under your skin and eats you away like a slow drop of acid if you let it.

This was probably two parts righteous and a half part each self-pitying and helpless, which wasn't too bad a ratio to work with.

What could these kinds of resources—these resources that lay behind these quiet corridors and mostly empty private rooms—have meant to me as a kid?

The alchemy of my anger made the pain easier to bear and gave me energy. I tried to put my feet down softly, so I wouldn't seem to be either staggering or stomping past the admin station, and because it hurt when I slapped them into the deck.

Don't get so pissed off you lose your shit, I told myself. *These people are not getting better care than everybody else. It's just that the décor is a little bit nicer.*

And they got to be important. There are some people, even in these enlightened diar, who do enjoy being important. That got up my nose as much as anything.

It was easy to forget, once I was angry, that I had decided to *let* myself be angry. Because it was useful. Because the adrenaline gave me strength to keep moving when exhaustion weighed me down.

One room had a human in it. An old woman, asleep on her pillow, gray locks spread around her in the most photogenic possible manner. I thought about going in and talking to her. I might have, if I hadn't been so tired, and in so very much pain. The ache seemed to start in the soles of my feet, the nape of my neck, and the small of my back and radiate through my entire body.

Beyond the private rooms, I found another decompression door with another staff filter. It was too much; I'd come too far. My heart pounded so hard that I felt it in my belly. The corridor walls seemed to pulse in the edges of my vision.

I rested a hand on the back of another chair set against the wall, trying to look as if I were casually checking my senso. I wished on the first evening planet in the skies of whatever the closest world might be that I could lock the knees of my exo to help hold myself up. But a stiff-legged limp would be pretty obvious.

At least the softsuit hid my heavy breathing, though my faceplate had fogged around my mouth and nose. Not a top-of-the-line faceplate, but Core General used a lot of them.

I should turn back. I would already be paying for these choices for diar, thanks to my decision to push on. I'd either be groggy from the tuning I'd have to do to manage, or I would be groggy from the pain.

I should turn back. It was the only sane thing to do. However far I went, I had to make the same trip back. And I was going to get noticed if I kept standing here. I was way off my patch, and I'd walked the whole length of the unit and everything had seemed perfectly normal.

But Sally had said there wasn't a unit AI, or even an AI doctor assigned to this team. And that made me nervous.

AIs are ethical.

AIs don't need rightminding, because AIs are built that way. They are created to be ethical beings.

So what sort of operation would you be running if you couldn't let an AI onto your team?

I gritted my teeth and raised my palm to the decomp door so that it could read my tag.

It didn't open.

"Sally?" I muttered inside my helmet.

Right here, she whispered in my head. *And no, I can't get it open. The circuit is isolated, and I don't dare reach into the hospital architecture until Linden is back online and I know we're free of viruses.*

I wished I could argue with her. *Well, I'm getting pretty obvious out here. I'm not sure what to do next.*

Duck into that room on the left, Sally suggested. *Quick, the unit admin is coming.*

I stepped into the patient room behind the open door. A glance at the panel beside it—and my senso—confirmed that it was empty. Footsteps echoed down the corridor—a trotting beat rather than a human stride. I folded my arms over my chest and assumed a contemplative pose inside the door.

It was a nice room. Big, and airy, with a green wall boosting the oxygen and humidity. It was full of lettuces and dandelions and greens from nonhuman planets. All of them would be edible. Some had been recently harvested. I wondered if they'd contributed to my steak salad the other dia.

There was a holowindow on the far wall, framed by decorative curtains. Right now, it offered a view of the Core from somewhere on the exterior of the hospital, but there was a remote by the bed. One could set it to anything in the library, if one didn't find a massive black hole, lensing stars in orbit, and heavy ship traffic restful.

I did, though, and I let out a heavy sigh of relaxation—and further fogged my plate. Some diar you just can't win.

A translated voice broke in. *Doctor?*

I only managed not to jump guiltily because I had been expecting it. I turned.

The unit supervisor—what they used to call a head nurse—stood framed in the doorway. He looked a little like a centaur, if the back half were a cream-colored angora goat, and somebody had thrown in floppy bunny ears and big doe eyes for good measure. His tag told me he was Nurse-Administrator Wizee, and gave me the usual details of preferred gender markers and species.

Can I help you?

My senso tag would tell him exactly who I was, also, so there was no point lying about it. "I'm exploring," I said.

This is a closed ward, Doctor. Do you have some business here?

"I have a patient I think might benefit from a calmer environment," I said. Which was not a lie, after all. "This seems nice."

This ward is for exclusive patients, the administrator said patiently.

"Surely if the room isn't being used—"

It's reserved, he said. *The patient will be joining us when the quarantine lifts. May I show you out now, Doctor?*

Well, that was that. I wondered what O'Mara knew about this place. Their sector, after all. Did my remit of investigating sabotage extend to investigating other weird stuff that seemed to be official hospital business?

Probably not, I decided sadly. Anyway, my investigation was supposed to be secret.

And I hadn't been doing a very good job of making time for it, between the demands of my actual job, my side job as Helen's care liaison, and everything else that was keeping me busy.

Which hadn't even involved, I remembered, the machine. I'd been so busy, and it had been somebody else's problem, so I'd nearly forgotten it existed. Worry settled like a weight into my guts, and I wondered if anybody was keeping an eye on it with Dr. Zhiruo incapacitated.

Well, whatever I was looking for, it would have to wait until I slept and charged my exo.

"Yes," I told the administrator. "I'll leave quietly."

My exo found a last flicker of power as I staggered back along the corridor toward the Casualty Department. Fortuitous, as by then I was too exhausted to have made my way home without it. I was pretty sure the private unit nurse had twigged that there was something wrong with me, though. With a little luck, he'd chalk it up to "systers are weird," and not think too much about it.

As for me, I dragged myself back to my quarters at half speed, tumbled back into my hammock, and got the trickle attached. I dozed off in the middle of reading safety incident reports.

I'll be honest. I dozed off three screens into the first safety incident report.

I'd *told* O'Mara they should have found somebody else.

CHAPTER 18

DESPITE MY EXHAUSTION, I DIDN'T SLEEP PARTICULARLY well. The pain kept waking me, even when I tuned it back. And I had to be up and fed and garbed and suited early.

I was attending grand rounds in a set of hydrogen atmosphere units that dia, as part of my continuing cross-species medical and cultural education, as required for all Core General staff. This was always . . . interesting, not least because their atmosphere and mine made a flammable combination.

Todia, it was even more of an annoyance than normal, because five shifts later, the lifts still weren't working. And because the lifts still weren't working, anybody who wanted to move around the hospital had to do it by climbing in and out of enviro suits at every section lock, or by sticking to the sections they could get through in a sterile softsider. So the lockers were a mess, and no one could rely on the lockers containing the equipment they were labeled as holding, because tracking and redistribution was falling behind demand.

You can only rightmind people into social consciousness so far when they're running to make it to surgery. At least the lockers self-sterilized.

I still had my sterile suit from the previous dia, having almost fallen asleep in it. And it was designed so you could swap other environmental modules in on top of it—including the spark-proof, antistatic ceramic plates I needed for the hydrogen environment. So, a little chafing (for me) and a trip through the sterilizer (for the rig) aside, everything was under control. Even the hydrogen.

I finished that obligation by lunchtime.

I scarfed down another much-needed meal and scrambled back to Cryo, barely in time to introduce our second archaic human to her first alien. Tralgar told me they'd probably have Oni awake within the week, so that was one more task on my plate unless Loese could make herself available. She had *better* make herself available. Or I was going to have to turn into twins.

Nobody had asked Tsosie—or even suggested Tsosie as an alternate. Apparently, nobody thought much of his bedside manner.

I guess being overbooked is a compliment. But I was going to need a nap in the on-call room, because getting to my own quarters . . . well, they were far away. And I needed to get on with the task that O'Mara and the tree had assigned me.

And I needed to check on Helen, and make sure somebody somewhere was keeping tabs on the machine in Zhiruo's and Linden's absence. Not to mention find the time to talk to Sally some more about her own experience with sabotage.

There were not enough standards in the dia.

I wondered if I had enough time to find Rhym and ask them for a squat, tentacular hug. And maybe a neck massage. Those flexible sucker paddles on the ends of their gross manipulators are surprisingly excellent for getting right up into the attachment points at the base of the skull that are so poorly designed on us humans. And they squeeze really comfortingly.

When I let myself into Jones's room this time, I was struck by how cramped it was in comparison to the rooms in the private unit. There was just about enough space in here for a Thunderby to edge around the bed if it was excruciatingly careful.

Jones seemed alert and oriented. She remembered me at once. "Hello, Dr. Jens."

"Hello, Patient Jones," I replied. The consonance of our family names pleased and amused me.

Based on her laugh, she hadn't realized it before, and it amused her, too. "Do you think we're related?"

I thought about the poetry that somebody had engineered into her DNA.

"It's possible," I said. "You'd have to ask an archinformist about the vowel shifts."

She had solid food on her tray, I noticed approvingly. She seemed to have made a pretty good accounting of it, too, before she pushed it aside.

"How's the grub?" I asked.

"A little weird," she admitted. "Scrambled tofu is pretty much scrambled tofu, though."

"Some of the options are worse than others, but I'm afraid it's all hospital food."

"All right, Doc." She folded her arms and cocked her head suspiciously. Tubes draped with her movements. She was still being hydrated and electrolyte balanced. "I can tell from the look on your face that you're up to something. And it's not just checking up on patients, is it?"

"No . . . oo." I looked over my shoulder. Cheeirilaq was out of sight along the wall. "Did you look over the files I left you?"

"About the Synarche? Sure."

"Would you like to meet your first syster?"

Her eyes widened. "Already? I mean, there's one here?"

"There's a lot here. Your care team is minority Terran. Once you were awake, though, we didn't want to shock you before you had some time to prep yourself."

"Your multispecies culture is diverse and honors complexity," she said, parroting one of the files I'd given her. "Mine only has boring human people in it."

I laughed. Both of these archaic humans were so charming. Whatever brain damage Jones had suffered, Dr. K'kk'jk'ooOOoo's intervention seemed to have helped her heal without evident deficits other than the memory loss. It made me feel even more awful about the people we wouldn't be able to save. And the ones we hadn't been able to save already.

"I've seen the movies," Jones continued. "If you're not going to use me as an incubator for some horrible insectoid's eggs, I can probably manage without freaking out."

Hmm. Goodlaw Cheeirilaq definitely counted as a horrible insectoid, from an atavistic primate point of view. Maybe I should go get Tralgar. Or even Rhym or Hhayazh, though Hhayazh probably wouldn't be any less horrifying, and its reproductive cycle did involve parasitism. Though not of sentient beings, in this dia and age.

Camphvis would probably do it if I asked nicely enough, but—eyestalks aside—I'm not sure a Banititlan really would be perceived as exotic *enough*.

The Goodlaw really did want to interrogate all of the surviving patients. I hadn't seen anything to indicate that it would not do so nicely. But it didn't hurt for me to keep an eye on the process, and my patients.

My secondhand patients. Patients once-removed?

"Well, in at the deep end," I said. "Specialist Jones, this is Goodlaw Cheeirilaq. Cheeirilaq, come on in."

The Goodlaw's exoskeleton clicked gently as it lowered itself to duck through the doorway. It kept its raptorial arms and manipulators folded, and its wings furled tight under the wing coverts. Nothing, however, could make it look small.

Jones made a noise. I hadn't taken my attention off her. Her heart rate spiked, though not as sharply as Carlos's had. Eyes wide, shoulders pulled back against the pillows.

"I was kidding about the horrifying giant insects," she said.

I solemnly vow not to parasitize you, Cheeirilaq responded. With its small manipulators, it popped the collar of its uniform jacket.

Its "voice" came from the bedside monitor, and Jones turned her shocked look at that. "It talks?"

"It's sentient *and* sapient," I said. "And very law-abiding."

"Damn," said Jones. "How many different kinds of . . . of systers are there?"

She *had* been studying.

"Thousands," I said. "It's a big galaxy. Not all of them are equally distributed. Any more than we are. Space travel is harder for some systers than others, depending on their environmental and emotional needs."

"And not all of them are like that? Like you, Goodlaw? I'm sorry."

She didn't attempt Cheeirilaq's name, and I didn't blame her. It's kind of a trill followed by a click, and human vocal apparatus can approximate it, but not without long practice. Mostly, we all rely on the translators.

No, not all of the systers are like me. Some are squishy, like you.

Jones shrugged. "If I'm squishy, I guess I need a harder shell."

Your species is a syster species to mine. You are fine the way you evolved.

"Oh," Jones said. "Oh! You mean that all of us are systers to one another!"

This is so, said Cheeirilaq. Cautiously, it elevated its body to a more natural position. Jones watched curiously, but to her credit did not recoil.

Admittedly, it was a giant bug—but it was also a giant bug in a tiny bolero jacket.

May I ask you some questions? it said.

I left Cheeirilaq interviewing the patient, once I'd satisfied myself that they were going to get along fine. I was hungry again, but the hospital was instituting rationing in order to weather the quarantine, and it was my shift to forgo eating.

Occasional fasting is good for my species, I told myself, and decided I could combine my initial research on the sabotage with my nap.

Multitasking always leads to excellent rest, as you know.

I took myself into an on-call room—currently empty—and claimed a bench bed. It was a little too short and wide for my species, but I made do, constructed a nest, plugged in my exo, and started scrolling through the incident reports of recent accidents at the hospital. I should probably look at the sites in person . . . but the lifts weren't running, and who had the time?

O'Mara was right. I immediately identified a significant statistical upswing in "safety incidents" over the past half an or so. No surprise there, obviously, but it's good to have confirmation. Human brains are excellent pattern makers. They'll figure out a pattern even if all you've got are random data points that don't actually mean anything, which is why we also have AIs and statisticians.

And AI statisticians, who are kind of terrifying.

There had been a chlorine leak into a water section—bad, but no fatalities—and another into an oxygen section that had been detected and contained before reaching dangerous levels. There'd been a malfunction in the newly installed artificial gravity that had buckled deck plates in an ox section and dropped atmospheric pressure enough so the decomp doors had triggered on either side. Nobody had been standing in the doorways, but the engineer handling the testing had spent an uncomfortable standard hour and a half pinned to the floor by high gravity and isolated by dropped doors.

Fortunately, he was from a fairly sturdy species and had suffered no lasting injuries.

Another staffer—a Terran—had not been so lucky, and had sustained near-fatal burns when a pressure seal in the airlock into one of the hell-planet sections that made Venus seem balmy had failed *after* she'd stripped out of her pressure suit—a rattling armored vehicle on treads. She'd still had her softsuit on, and that had probably saved her life. She was receiving clone grafts, some of it neural tissue.

I flinched in sympathy.

Those armored self-mobile hardsuits were designed to endure conditions beyond even what my rescue hardsuit could be adapted to. The idea of sweating up a swamp in one, caring for patients, struggling out of the foul thing only to be caught in a jet of superheated steam and half cooked alive . . . it was something I could relate to far too personally.

There were other incidents of equipment failure or safety protocol malfunction, an additional half dozen or so. One more had led to a serious injury. Another had resulted in a pair of fatalities.

If it was all sabotage, it couldn't all be caused by the same person—could it? It was happening in too many different sectors, on too many different shifts. And then there was the incident on Sally, with the damaged coms. We all assumed it had been set up before we left port. But what if Sally had been damaged by a member of the crew, and she and Loese were in denial about it?

That was horrifying.

Why had O'Mara and the Administree recruited me for this job? They had access to staff logs, to the comings and goings of everybody in the hospital. They could access all sorts of information that was off-limits for a simple trauma doc.

You might even say that Starlight was the central Authoritree.

For ox and CO_2, anyway.

No, the quality of my sense of humor is not improved by stress.

But couldn't they check who had accessed each damaged sector before the damage occurred? Well, maybe. The Synarche's privacy regulations precluded pulling bulk data, though I was confident we could get a warrant to track the movements of an individual person or persons if I could identify a suspect or two. Assuming that they hadn't used timed devices to cause the damage, which they probably had, which in turn meant that establishing a timeline would be well-nigh impossible when one considered the sheer volume of traffic around this place.

Yes, I know, privacy is a core value and a sentient right. But right then it was a pain in my ass.

So what did my supervisors think I could do—or that I would notice—that they couldn't?

Well, O'Mara and I had known each other for a long time. They trusted me. They knew I had a Judiciary background.

Tsosie and I had been the people most threatened by the sabotage on Sally, so perhaps O'Mara assumed that I was unlikely to be behind it. Also, I'd been away from the hospital when most of the local incidents took place.

So I was likely to be clean, from their perspective. Okay.

I wasn't an investigator or an archinformist, but I had some investigative skills. Cheeirilaq, for example, was immediately identifiable as law enforcement, and was treated as such. Law enforcement, and also a gigantic predator.

I was little and squishy—as I had recently been reminded—and wore medical symbols, not Judiciary rank.

So I was nonthreatening, and I had a reason to be most anyplace in the hospital. . . .

Huh. With the exception of the chlorine bleed into water, all of the sabotage events *had* taken place in ox sections. Now that was interesting. It suggested that the culprit or culprits were oxygen or CO_2 metabolizers, who might access those areas without checking out suits and leaving a trail.

And perhaps it was revealing for other reasons than the suit issue. Because one thing about giant multi-environment stations—whether they are hospitals or hab wheels or something else—is that people who live and work exclusively in one environment can forget that the others exist. This tendency is even more prevalent in new arrivals from single-environment habs.

Or planets.

So maybe I was looking for somebody who hadn't been here for very long. And whose background was somewhere deep in an oxygen-only settlement. That would explain both why the events had started up recently, and why they were largely limited to ox environments. And water. A person from an oxygen planet would remember about water.

It was also possible that the sabotage was entirely limited to ox environments, if it turned out that the outlier was a legitimate accident. It's too easy to get bogged down in trying to fit all the available events into an identified pattern—in creating conspiracy theories—whether or not all those events actually belong together. In any case, I scribbled a physical note to O'Mara, DNA sealed it, put it in an interdepartmental folder marked CONFIDENTIAL, and sent it off down the hall by mail robot.

At least checking up on ox-sector staffers from ox-only environments who had joined the hospital in the last an was a starting point.

I woke from a light doze with a start. My limbs still ached with exhaustion; my fox told me I'd only drifted off for twenty minutes or so. What had awakened me was not a sound or motion, but the sudden crystallization of an idea.

I had been thinking that the saboteur or saboteurs might be unsophisticated in how they thought about multi-environment habs, and in that case probably newcomers to Core General. But what if the opposite was true?

I'd considered the possibility that it was somebody savvy enough to know that checking out softsuits to go into hostile environments might eventually lead to them getting caught. But what if the saboteur (or saboteurs) was—were—from a non-ox-compatible environment, and they were committing their crimes in ox sectors as a red herring? That was a better scenario for me, because it might mean that they had outsmarted themselves.

In either case, how were they hiding from Linden? The same way whoever had sabotaged Sally was hiding from Sally?

I tuned myself a little wider awake and sent another note to Starlight and O'Mara suggesting that they look into suit checkouts *into* ox sectors as well as out of them, though I imagined they'd thought of it already.

That's why we have checklists. Because all too often, everybody assumes that everybody else has thought of it already. And then important, lifesaving steps somehow fail to be taken.

And then accidents happen and people like me show up to—in the best-case scenario—drag you out of the rubble and graft and glue you back together and dust off your shoulders and say, "You oughtn't have been so careless."

AIs usually follow checklists. AIs might get bored, but they don't get lazy and they don't cut corners. This is why ships have shipminds and habs have wheelminds.

Because organic-type slowbrains get lazy *and* bored, and discipline is not always our strong suit.

What if the saboteur was an AI? That would give it a route to prevent itself from being noticed, and perhaps even to hack the memories of other AIs, like Linden and Sally. I'd seen Sally's telepresence—at least enough to speak to me—without triggering the AI presence lights.

Hm. Possible.

I must have dozed off again despite supporting my brain chemistry, because this time I woke about a standard and a half later with my reader resting on my nose. I nearly rolled on my side and went back to sleep.

But . . . speaking of following the checklists, I pushed through the achy sluggishness of exhaustion, stowed my reader, and pulled the net down over the bed. I willed the lights off. Feeling smug in my self-righteousness and a little ridiculous also, I closed my eyes.

I assume I must have, anyway, because I don't remember falling asleep. The next thing to impinge on my consciousness was a tremendous, reverberating crash. The bed net snapped tight against me as I bounced hard, imprinting my skin with what would no doubt be some very interesting contusions. Then, abruptly, I was floating.

Well, I was held firmly against the mattress, but when you've worked in space as long as I have, it's pretty easy to tell the difference between being pressed to the bed by acceleration, and being pressed to the bed by the net.

Speaking of checklists, this was a great time for one.

I had air for now. That was the first thing.

The second thing was visibility, and I had no light. The on-call room was very dark. Darker than it should have been, because I'd turned the lights off but there's always a readout by the door that doubles as a night light. I lay there in that dark and listened with everything in me for the hiss of escaping atmosphere. Or, worse, a total absence of sound from outside that would tell me the corridor beyond my little single-thickness door had been decompressed and evacuated.

Vibrations made themselves felt through the bulkhead. The structure of the hospital creaked violently. The hab wheel had stopped spinning, which was why my gravity had failed, and the hospital's hull was complaining at the strain. I imagined Starlight with tendrils dug deep in the hull, holding us together more or less bare-rooted.

That was a little bit of melodrama.

The hospital's superstructure wouldn't fail. The most vulnerable staff and patients had the new gravity belts, so there was a good chance nobody's physiology was killing them while I lay there sorting myself out. But lots of bad things happen when gravity unexpectedly fails, as you can probably imagine.

I might have heard voices carrying through the door. People moving. I was listening so hard for reassuring sounds I might have been imagining them.

Sally?

No answer didn't mean she wasn't out there. It meant that the hospital system wasn't relaying my senso uplink to her and that she couldn't reach me through the hull.

If I got out of bed I might be slammed against a wall or deck when the hab started rotating again. The safest thing to do was to stay right where I was, buckled in and tucked away, and wait for an all-clear.

But my job was saving lives in emergency situations, and this was, in my professional estimation, exactly that.

I took a deep breath, reached out, unplugged my exo—which wasn't getting a charge from the trickler anyway, with the power off—and snapped the net back out of the way. The bed cubby had handles, and I used them to pull myself out into the on-call room and try to orient. The bed was *down*: that was where the floor would be if—when—spin reasserted itself. Therefore, I should keep my shock-absorbing bits pointed in that direction.

I floated toward the door. Where I guessed the door was, anyway. There was no orange light next to it, indicating vacuum or a noncompatible atmosphere on the other side. But there was no blue light, either. (Red and green are traditional for Terrans, but in a big hab like Core General, not everybody can see the wavelengths that produce red light—and orange and blue are far apart on the spectrum.)

Well, if I was lucky, then the safety interlocks wouldn't allow me to open the door if there was nothing but space and slowly freezing bodies outside.

I didn't feel lucky.

There was a suit locker outside the on-call door, where I had left my softsider. If there was vacuum on the other side, my blood would begin to release oxygen almost immediately, whether I held my breath or not. Once the deoxygenated blood reached my brain, I would immediately black out.

I would have about fifteen seconds to get some pressure into my lungs before I fainted. I'd be dead within a minute or two after that.

So my first priority was oxygen, and the second was to get myself back into my softsuit. Or a hardsuit, if there was one in the locker. That would actually be easier, because I'd only have to slap the activator on my chest and go. I'd probably lose consciousness before it sealed itself, but if I was lucky I'd wake right back up again without too much brain damage.

Back in the Judiciary, we used to drill on suiting up. My personal best with a softsuit was seventeen point one five seconds. That gave me maybe ten seconds—conservatively—to get to the locker, get it open, and get a helmet on. Possibly in pitch blackness, with the tears boiling off my eyeballs and my capillaries popping.

Piece of cake.

They could graft me new eyeballs. Assuming there was a hospital left afterward.

There was even a handle beside the door that I could cling to, in case of explosive decompression. I grabbed a few deep breaths and oxygenated. I didn't know if it would help, but it might buy me an extra second or two.

All this assumed that the door would unlock and snap open for me, the way it was designed to. If I had to crank it open manually and there was vacuum on the other side, I'd suffocate before I made a big-enough gap to squeeze through. In that case, I *would* be stuck waiting here for rescue—without the telltales, it was too much risk.

I hit the emergency door override, praying it would work without any faith in my prayers being heard. Or answered. I did not feel lucky.

Fun fact: feeling lucky has nothing at all to do with whether you are or are not lucky.

There was air on the other side of the door, though still no light. Down the corridor, I could clearly hear sounds now: voices, a metallic thumping, the sound of a softsuit proximity beeper warning anyone nearby that it existed. I bobbed softly in the draft as the pressure equalized. Then, using the grab rail (oh grab rails, that I ever maligned you!) and the rough wall surface, I pulled myself along the bulkhead to the suit locker.

There was a telltale on the locker door, and it was blue. I opened it, located a hardsuit activator, and slapped it in place, timing myself in my head.

Twenty seconds. I was out of practice, and the suit was a slightly unfamiliar model. Core General goes through a lot of suits, and they're replaced on a rolling basis. This one was so new the lining still smelled faintly of carcinogens.

For now, I left the faceplate unsealed. I wanted to save the suit oxygen in case, later on, I really needed it. It would seal itself if the pressure dropped. But now I had the boosters in the suit electronics. And that meant I might be able to get ahold of—

Oh, I am so grateful, Llyn. There you are! I was terrified. Are you safe? Where are you?

I breathed out, light-headed with relief, and gave her access to my tracking and senso. "I found a hardsuit. What's going on, Sally?"

I don't know. I can only presume it's more sabotage. Power is marginal. Translator systems are down. I'm okay, I think. I've been isolating my own systems since Linden and Dr. Zhiruo got sick. Can you make it to my berth? EVA might be safest.

I finally found the toggle, and turned my suit lights on. Dim, to save battery and avoid blinding anybody whose eyes might be pointed at me.

"I can't," I said, when I got a look down the corridor. "I have to be a doctor now."

It was disaster triage, except the victims were sometimes people I knew, and nearly all of them were extremely hard to talk to without translation protocols. Which also didn't exist for the time being.

If they were incapacitated, I did what I could to stabilize them and moved on. Fine repairs could wait for later. If they *weren't* incapacitated, they were eager to get a bandage slapped on and to get back to work as soon as the synthskin or their metabolic equivalent started working.

I had to pass by Records on my way, and—with the help of my datapad and some bad machine translation—got them to upload a few ayatanas into my fox. Ox breathers of various anatomies; every little bit of information would help. Even if I had the wrong ayatana for a particular species, convergent evolution and biological convenience were still useful.

I walked out with my feet squishing strangely and my body shambling oddly. Well, we'd get used to each other. And I was definitely going to need their medical knowledge before the dia was out.

Most of the injuries to staff were relatively minor ones, which was good because I didn't have ayatanas for every person who'd banged their head—or whatever the topmost part of their body was—against the ceiling when the spin gravity cut out. And without coms, I couldn't call a doctor or nurse of an appropriate species for backup.

They were probably all busy in their own sections, dealing with human patients whose contusions and gashes and fractures would be quite as much a mystery. I couldn't even ask my own patients what was wrong except by typing and machine translating on a datapad—hi*lar*ious—so we communicated mostly by them shoving the affected area under my nose, and me spraying a biologically appropriate sealant over the wound.

I made my way back to Casualty, stopping to help injured people along the way. I left the patients still in rooms alone unless there was a crisis: they were as safe where they were as they could be anywhere, and their own care teams would have the relevant ayatanas.

And the hospital staff, once the initial confusion settled, started pulling together and cooperating with surprising efficiency. We couldn't communicate complicated concepts, but we knew our jobs. And with long practice, you get a sense of when somebody is going to ask for a hemostat.

Casualty—the Emergency Department—had been nearly vacant and understaffed since the quarantine went into effect, because there was nobody coming in. Now it was a mob scene. And a mob scene under emergency lighting—at least the emergency lighting was working, here—in zero g, with people clinging to the deck with mag boots (like me) or zipping around, their trajectories narrowly avoiding collisions with one another, or occasionally not avoiding those collisions at all. I ducked under a cloud of drifting feathers from one such incident and made my way toward the admin desk, looking for somebody to tell me where I could be most useful.

My exo was at seventy percent, and I was sore but not in terrible pain. It wouldn't have mattered if I was, under the current circumstances.

A team of three guiding one of the new grav stretchers sailed in alongside me. They were all suited, using their jets to navigate and push. The stretcher's grav technology maintained its attitude with respect to the deck despite the lack of rotational acceleration. I was impressed. I hadn't known they did that.

One of the medics pushing the stretcher noticed me standing there and squeaked demandingly through nasal slits. I jumped out of the way. It hissed like a deflating balloon and wrapped a suit-clad tentacle with a spatulate, arrowlike end around my wrist, tugging more or less gently.

It squeaked again.

The patient needs assistance, Sally said.

I glanced down at myself. My suit was covered in Well knows what, and nothing about my person was scrubbed and sterile. But it had picked up my identification codes from my fox, and there on my breast was my name in several sets of symbols—and my specialty.

Trauma doctor.

I stepped up to the stretcher and leaned in.

It was bad.

I wasn't sure what species the patient was, but they bled the same hemoglobin pigment as me. I assumed that the rattling swell and release of atmosphere through spiracles into the tube-like body was desperate respiration: blood loss or pain. Two of the medics were applying manual pressure to savage-looking wounds. I didn't need an ayatana to know the patient was bleeding to death.

I *might* need that ayatana to stop it from happening.

The patient made noises and gestures of dismay and distress that I didn't need a translator to understand. They were probably feeling exactly as I would have felt, had our positions been reversed. They looked to have lost several pieces of their body: part of a locomotion limb, and an upper-body manipulator. The edges had the ragged look of an industrial accident, not the neat severing of a decomp door. The patient was wearing a maintenance uniform, and I imagined it must have been operating a piece of heavy equipment when the gravity went off. A floor-polisher or loader or something worse.

I couldn't even request a surgical room. By the time I made myself understood, the patient would have bled to death.

I wanted to stick this patient in a cryo tank and wait for a specialist. I didn't even know what meds I could give it for pain without killing it. I—

It was as if I weren't in the hospital at all, but on a rescue mission outside somewhere, unable to communicate well and with only my own crew for support.

Wait.

Wait! Sally! Can you tell me what this syster is, and what I can give it for pain and shock? Does it do shock? And can you reach its fox and tune the pain down? The automatic response doesn't seem to be working.

She read me a list of medications and a synthetic transfusion base as we were guiding the patient into a treatment bay. Then my next problem became finding a way to communicate those requirements to the pharmacy. I had handed back all the datapads I'd borrowed along the way . . . but I still had the reader I'd stowed in my thigh pocket. It was inside the suit, but I wiggled it out, inputted Sally's list, and handed it to the syster with the lowest rank insignia—which was not the one with the tentacles.

This syster wasn't wearing a full suit, just a harness and mask. It stared at me like the last cat I tried to teach algebra to.

I mimed giving an injection and pointed in the general direction of the pharmacy. The tech—which looked like a very alert feather duster with tufted owl ears and plumed moth antennae—focused all its sensory apparatus on me for one tense moment. Then it tipped down at the reader, back up at me—and whisked away in a puff of reaction jets.

I mimed hand-washing to one of the two remaining medics—both of whom were fully engaged in keeping pressure on the patient's injuries—and sprinted with ringing magnets and aching knees across to a disinfection booth. I climbed in, suit and all, and let it blast me.

The decon stations were near the private unit I'd sneaked into the previous dia. I found myself glowering at the closed doors while my suit was rinsed and flash-dried. Why weren't those staff out here helping?

The moment of rage was washed away by a flood of gratitude toward the rest of the hospital staff. Here we all were, side by side, up to our elbows in a dozen colors of gore. They were rewarding my faith on this terrible dia.

I've said that I've never been somebody who had faith. Not in the religious sense, and not in the secular sense of unequivocal reliance on the trueness of some premise or person. Not the way some people do. Except for my job, and my community.

And in that moment, I felt a faith and a connection to my community and their purpose that I imagine equaled any religious epiphany in its intensity. I was a part of something, and the thing I was a part of served a mission and a purpose that mattered as much as anything *can* matter in a vast and uncaring universe.

This was where I belonged, and this was what I ought to be doing.

Take that, Alessi.

My ex-wife used to tell me that the problem with our marriage was that I didn't believe in anyone or anything. In retrospect, I had come to believe that her actual problem was that I hadn't believed in her.

For the first time, I found myself wondering whose failing that had been.

The nature of battlefield epiphanies is that you don't have the time to appreciate how profound they are—or are not—at the time. Thirty standard seconds later, I was back in the treatment bay. I held my scrubbed hands out in that weird broken-elbowed way that hospital people instinctively know to avoid, no matter what appendage is being dangled awkwardly away from contaminated surfaces. I wasn't sure why I was bothering; there was literally nothing sterile about these circumstances.

I guess points for trying?

Staff were administering the meds Sally had recommended when I returned. They acted fast. The patient didn't lose consciousness, but their pain-tense body relaxed against the stretcher. Beads of what I assumed was sweat dewed grayish skin. The stentorian panting softened. They were getting oxygen now. Tourniquets had been applied to the wounded limbs so I could work without groping through a sea of blood. That had to have been contributing to the pain: tourniquets *hurt*. Somebody had draped our makeshift surgical field.

This is what people who know what they are doing and aim to save lives can accomplish even when they can't effectively communicate.

Somewhere behind me, I heard screaming. Human, possibly. I could have treated that patient competently without an ayatana, but I didn't have time to worry about it now, already being in the middle of my own primitive surgery. Somebody less qualified would have to deal with it. I tuned my racing heart back: my current patient could not wait until we had appropriate facilities, until we could grow grafts and perform the surgery while they slept painlessly through it. Right now, we didn't even have an anesthesiologist. Just a lot of sedatives.

I held out my hand on an arm that was too long and too short and not flexible enough and very squishy, and realized that I couldn't ask for the forceps precisely as one of the blood-spattered medics laid them in my hand. I wanted to smile my gratitude, but the mask would have hidden my expression, and anyway very few systers take teeth-baring as a friendly gesture.

So I said "Thank you," out loud, hoping that if I said it a few times the sound would acquire meaning for my colleagues, and bent down to bathe my hands in the blood of the wounded.

I clamped and stitched and cauterized, somehow finding myself in a zone of total focus where the noises of half a hundred different species trying to make themselves urgently understood seemed distant, unreal. By any standard from the current millennian, the work I did was horrifically crude. There wasn't enough skin to stitch across the stumps. It didn't matter, because the limbs would be replaced with grafts eventually, but all I could do right now when I'd stopped the bleeding was to seal the raw ends with synth.

When I finished with that patient, somebody grabbed my elbow and walked me to decon, and then to another casualty. I almost understood some of what it was telling me—almost. Could I use the ayatanas for translation purposes, if I had the right ones?

No time to find out, currently.

Somebody else brought me an external battery for my suit, which was when I realized I ought to charge my exo from the suit, too. In an emergency, keep your batteries close and fully charged.

There was another patient after that one, and another. I looked up once and found myself assisting Rhym. That was good, because Sally could translate for us. And the mere fact of being close to my surgeon friend made me feel 50 percent less anxious that something would go horribly wrong.

However horribly wrong it went, Rhym could handle it.

Another time, I looked up and the person across the table from me, holding out the tool I needed before I knew I needed it, was Hhayazh. Best surgical nurse I've ever known. I spotted Tsosie once or twice. Everybody was head down, working, grunting and waving to communicate.

Somebody brought me soup and water. I drank the soup with my eyes closed, holding my nose so my neural passengers wouldn't notice what was in it and potentially take offense. Later, somebody brought me tea. I ate sandwiches with my eyes averted, trying not to gag. The suit was equipped to handle bathroom breaks.

I looked up again as another patient was slid out from under me. Directly into the glittering compound eyes of a massive adult female Rashaqin.

It stridulated at me, one raptorial forelimb snapping. I recoiled so hard I almost sat down on the floor. I would have, if there had been any gravity. As it was, I rocked ridiculously on my mag boots before my exo and my core muscles stabilized me.

Then I realized from the bolero jacket and the glittering badge that it was Cheeirilaq, and swallowed against my racing heart. It felt like it was stuck in my esophagus, but I got it down on the second try.

"Oh Well," I cursed. "What now?"

Cheeirilaq reached out, delicately draped a barbed hook around my bloody glove—I was on my fifth shade of blood already todia—and tugged me very, very gently toward the door. It was holding on to various railings and appurtenances with assorted limbs.

I realized how much my feet hurt. They were so swollen that I could feel the insides of my mag boots pressing creases in my flesh. My hands, if anything, were worse. There's some stretch built into my exo, but the suit was less accommodating.

I looked back over my shoulder, toward the station where I'd been operating. Somebody else was already mag-stepping into the place I'd vacated.

Cheeirilaq herded me into a corner with gentle pokes of its spiky, razor-edged forelimbs.

"I need to go back to work." I raised my hand and pointed. There was less chaos now, I realized. Fewer people bleeding and waiting their turn. Staff members bunking in their suits on tethers along the walls.

Exaggeratedly, distinctly, the Goodlaw shook its head.

I stared at it in disbelief.

It did it again.

The gesture was utterly nonhuman, a quick rotation back and forth more like a timing gear than an organic entity. But it was unmistakable, and very obviously a copy of the gesture I made all the time.

Cheeirilaq was regarding me with all its eyes, antennae trained on me like the ears of an attentive dog.

It placed a barb tip under the placket of my hardsuit and lifted gently. Not enough to tear the suit away, though I was sure that was within its capabilities. I realized how horrible the suit was when it touched me: decon was just sterilizing the ichor; it wasn't removing it.

I stepped back, shaking my head inside the helmet.

"I know it's bloody and disgusting, but it's the only one I have. And what are my odds of finding another charged one under these circumstances?"

Cheeirilaq took a breath so deep that bright-colored lines appeared along the green length of its abdomen. It let the breath out again, the transparent oxygen tubes that enriched the atmospheric mix near its spiracles pulsing in time.

I had never seen Rilriltok sigh. Or maybe it was just less dramatic when it did so.

Cheeirilaq pulled its raptorial limb back, and unclipped something from the tool belt that also held its gravity nullifier. With its smaller manipulator arms, it held the object out to me.

Another hardsuit nucleus.

Oh.

I stripped out of my filthy suit even faster than I had slapped it on myself, stopping only to retrieve the auxiliary battery pack. It felt so good to get the thing off my feet I almost cheered.

The suit was so dirty it wouldn't retract back into the actuator. And it was even grosser on the inside, though less gory. I floated above it and stabilized my weightless body against a grab rail.

Cheeirilaq pressed the hardsuit core to my chest. It was Judiciary issue, I noticed.

Not surprising. Consider the source.

It adhered. A moment before I triggered it, I looked at Cheeirilaq's tool belt once more.

Wait a minute. Antigravity belt. Functionally, a gravity *control* belt. I also had one of those. It had been sealed inside my suit, along with my exo and my body.

I thought about how the grav stretchers maintained their distance and orientation from the deck. I thought about what an idiot I had been.

I took off the gravity control belt *I* was wearing, handed it to the Goodlaw, and triggered the hardsuit. It unfurled around me with a clatter that seemed enormously loud to ears used to hearing everything muted through a helmet.

It sealed me in, and I sighed.

Thank goodness you listened, Cheeirilaq said, and held my belt back out to me. I wound it around the suit, clipped it, and turned it on.

Effortlessly, the grav belt oriented me to the floor. I didn't need the mag boots and the effort of pulling them free with every step. I just needed this tool right here.

"Oh, I'm an idiot," I replied. "Of course, Judiciary translation is working."

We're trying to hack into the hospital system and reboot it. But Linden is still walled off, and all the back doors are her back doors. If I understand what our AIs are telling me.

"What the hell is going on?"

Terrorists, Cheeirilaq said.

I tried to look up the word. Senso still wasn't working. "Is that a sophipathology?"

I believe you would term it an illness of thought, yes. Except . . . it is also a weapon of the oppressed and powerless. I believe the relevant term from human history would be . . . monkey-wrenching?

"This is the Synarche," I said. "This is *Core General.* Who's oppressed?"

But I thought maybe I had heard of *monkey-wrenching.* A form of civil protest of unfair labor practices: workers destroying machinery.

I made sure I had a channel open to Sally's frequency, and said, "Sally. Has it occurred to you that this is really weird sabotage? I would expect a lot more people to be getting hurt if these were serious attempts to cause harm."

Plenty of people are being harmed.

"Yes, I'm pretty intimately acquainted with that right now. But not as many as *should* be, if hurting people were the intent."

I nudged my blood-soaked, sweat-soaked, abandoned suit with an armored toe. Actually, I was going to clean that thing up right now. I picked it up and turned toward the recycler.

Sally asked, *Do you think we're being . . . pranked?*

I thought about the blood on the suit in my hands. And all the blood that had washed over it through the course of the dia. I checked the time. I'd been in Casualty for seventeen hours, patching people together enough so they could survive until we got full functionality back as a, you know, Void-damned down-Welling sun-forsaken unrebirthing *hospital.*

I shoved the filthy suit into the recycler hatch much harder than was strictly necessary.

I was still trying to get my temper under control when the Goodlaw buzzed. *It seems to me, friend Dr. Jens, friend Shipmind, that once a prank results in amputations and deaths, it is no longer a prank, but a felony.*

"That's accurate," I agreed. "What did you want me for so urgently, Goodlaw?"

Cheeirilaq made a very strange noise, like a hissing cat or a lock depressurizing. *Specialist Jones. From the generation ship crew.*

"Yes," I said, turning toward the ladder that would bring us down to Cryo in the absence of the lifts.

It's escaped.

CHAPTER 19

I ADJUSTED MY GRAV BELT OVER THE HARDSUIT TO MAKE IT easier to reach the controls. It did a good job of keeping me oriented to the deck. Not that a lot of other things were maintaining their alignment, but reasserting a little influence over my local environment made me feel more like I could cope with the larger situation.

A larger situation over which I had exactly no control.

All I could do was handle my tiny corner of it as best I could. And right now, that meant figuring out what had happened to Jones.

Even with the help of my exo, a grav belt, and the hardsuit, I could not keep up with an upset Rashaqin moving as fast as it was able. The Goodlaw noticed that I was falling behind. It didn't turn its head, but spoke over channels. *Friend Doctor, may I be of assistance?*

I frowned at the enormous multilimbed body and felt a chill of premonition.

"As long as it's survivable assistance," I said.

I startled back. Was that what it sounded like when a Rashaqin guffawed? It reminded me of a whole orchestra's string section tuning.

Raise your hands over your head and relax your contractile tissues, Cheeirilaq instructed: exactly the kind of advice that is guaranteed to produce the opposite effect.

Nevertheless, I tried. I accomplished the first part, and enough of the second not to scream out loud when Cheeirilaq produced a coil of silk from spinnerets in its abdomen and dropped the loop around my waist, above the gravity belt.

Now it bundles me up and eats me, I thought. *Very politely.*

Actually, the Goodlaw started running again, all its legs scuttling across available surfaces, not seeming appreciably slowed by having to tow me along in its wake.

I bounced behind it like a planetside water skier skipping off waves and managed not to fall over and be dragged. It sounds impressive, but the grav belt and the exo did a lot of the work of stabilizing for me. Which was good, because I was very confused about how many legs I had, or if I had any legs at all, and I was really sure I shouldn't be moving this way in *any* of my remembered bodies.

Sentients ducked willy-nilly out of our path as we careered along corridors and through junctions. Hospital people get used to dodging running emergency staff, but I won't pretend that one of us being a Rashaqin in a Judiciary uniform didn't expedite matters.

We arrived back at Cryo faster than I would have imagined possible without the lifts running. A little giddily, I leaned against the bulkhead while Cheeirilaq unlassoed me.

Friend Llyn, it said, *are you injured?*

"All systems functioning within parameters," I assured it, without actually checking my fox. "Just a little discombobulated. Oh good, the lights are on."

That meant Cryo still had power, which meant that the surviving unrewarmed patients still had a chance of being alive. Three cheers for backup generators.

The pressure doors were tightly closed, and my already-hammering heart squeezed painfully when I noticed. They weren't sealed, though, and opened readily to a pass of Cheeirilaq's manipulator. O'Mara and Rilriltok were waiting for us inside.

Rilriltok hovered nervously near the ceiling, buzzing in agitation and—once it saw us—relief. My poor bug friend's emotional state must have been really unpleasant if it was experiencing Cheeirilaq's presence as reassuring. It zipped toward us, circling wide to approach me first. Wings come in handy in zero g.

O'Mara was magnetized to the deck. There's not a lot of ferrous metal in Core General's construction: just enough to serve as a precaution.

I was glad we had it, now.

O'Mara gave us the overview while Rilriltok cut me loose of the silk and I flash-charged my exo. Flash-charging wasn't good for its long-term durability, but running out of juice during a pursuit would be worse. Rilriltok saw what I was doing and brought me two more external battery packs. It wasn't on the Judicial frequencies, but we'd known each other and worked together for ans. It could anticipate what I needed as readily as a good surgical nurse could anticipate when you were going to ask for a laser pen.

Calliope Jones had apparently gotten out of bed shortly before what would have been shift change, if the hospital were currently running shifts. She had unplugged her various tubes and wires and walked out into the Cryo ward as if she'd belonged there, and nobody had managed to bring to bear the executive function to stop her. Until Rilriltok had looked up from the patient it was treating, and flown down to interpose itself between Jones and the door.

Jones had yanked an oxygen bottle out of a wall rack and swung it at Rilriltok. Fortunately for the Rashaqin's fragile wings and exoskeleton, lack of gravity didn't inhibit its ability to fly. It had zipped out of the way, and Jones had righted herself after the disastrous kinetic consequences of her missed swing and managed to lunge out the door.

Dr. Rilriltok, having nearly been squashed once, had not pursued. Instead, it had summoned Judiciary and gotten Cheeirilaq—who spoke a dialect of the same language, so they didn't need a translator to communicate. Cheeirilaq had used Judiciary channels to summon O'Mara, and then it had decamped to find me.

We didn't know where Jones had gone or what she planned to do when she got there. We had no idea how to find her, with Linden and all of the hospital's internal sensors down. But we—Cheeirilaq, O'Mara, and I—were the retrieval team now. Find her, we must.

This was going to be *wonderful.*

I looked up from attaching the second backup battery to my hardsuit, about to signal my readiness, and realized that Master Chief Dwayne Carlos was standing beside me. In his heavily accented, archaic Spanglish, he said, "I'm coming with you."

I still had enough English to be able to work out what he meant. The weird thing was that when I reached for that knowledge, the ayatanas I was wearing all tried to offer up bits of *their* languages, and my first attempt to speak came out a bubbling croak.

I cleared my throat and tried again. "Carlos—"

He held up his hand and said something that I didn't follow at *all.* "Wait," I said in English. I held out a hand to Cheeirilaq, who laid another Judicial hardsuit actuator on it. I put it against his chest—gently, so as not to send him drifting off—and pushed the button. A moment later, and the suit *whick*ed itself into existence around him, faceplate up.

"Try now," I said.

He touched his ear. "Translation? Good. My shipmate has vanished, hasn't she? Who else is going to be able to talk to her?"

I let the breath I had been going to use for arguing out through my nose, and tried again with a fresh one. "You're in no shape—"

"Neither are you," he retorted. "Next excuse?"

I hadn't realized before that he was a pretty big human, as humans went. Even wasted and cryoburned and floating awkwardly above the deck in a hardsuit over striped pajamas, he made me feel small.

"I know you want to look out for your friend—"

Carlos shook his head. It set him drifting. I held out a hand for him to steady himself against. "It's not that. I don't know her. But how is she going to understand anything you say to her without . . ." He pointed vaguely at his ear.

The worried pinch of his mouth made me think there might be more. "What? Carlos, please—"

The next words came out of him as if wrenched. "What if nobody else from my time makes it?"

I thought about pointing out that we weren't even entirely sure that Jones *was* from his time. She'd been the one in the anomalous cryo chamber, after all—

O'Mara shifted impatiently. Time was wasting.

I said, "There were ten thousand people on your ship. Some *will* live. Many will. You should rest so that you can help the others. You're my patient, and in order for me to care for you, you need to stay here."

"I *can't*!" he exploded, unrightminded emotion breaking through. "Just let me come. Please."

Friend Jens, Cheeirilaq said in my ear. *We don't have time to argue.*

I looked at Master Chief Carlos. "If you get killed before they manage to pick your brain clean, the historians are never going to forgive me."

I reached up, and sealed his helmet down.

We moved.

The immediate crisis of weightlessness and scattered power outages was coming under control. It still provoked a complicated spiral of nostalgia and alienation in me to zip past injured people and send medical staffers dodging out of the way as we shouted, "Gangway!"

I wasn't this anymore. I was a doctor. I rescued people; I didn't arrest them.

Well, I had already rescued this one. Maybe it was time to arrest her.

Carlos tripped a bit at first, but rapidly got control of his suit and kept up better than I would have expected. Adrenaline is a hell of a drug, and he probably had worn mag boots before. It helped that we weren't moving as fast as Cheeirilaq and I had on the way in. In the absence of internal sensors or a way to track the fugitive through her fox, we had to stop and ask directions a lot. Fortunately, unit coordinators don't handle direct patient care, and they tend to notice everything.

In particular, a barefoot Terran in hospital jammies swimming down their corridors after the gravity cuts out. We were fortunate that the emergency lighting had been brought online almost everywhere that needed it by now. I winced to think of trying to track Jones through the hospital in the dark.

Cheeirilaq and O'Mara were in the first row as we went. Now that he'd gotten the hang of the new suit, Carlos *was* pretty good in zero g. Propelling himself alongside me, he took the opportunity to ask, "Hey, Jens. You're from Terra?"

"Never been," I admitted, glancing down a side corridor.

"So how come you have an Earth name?"

"Pardon?"

"Brookllyn," he said. "That's as old Earth as it gets."

"Boring parents." Was *everybody* going to ask me that? My hardsuit clicked when I shrugged. "Hey, there's an open storage locker down here."

Nobody on staff would leave a locker open, even in a crisis. *Especially* in a crisis, when things might come sailing out and whack some unsuspecting sapient on the head. Or head-equivalent. You'd think somebody from an older and even more fragile habitation would be a little more careful.

Cheeirilaq turned, a little faster than O'Mara. For such a massy person, though, O'Mara was quick to orient. They said, "Good eye, Jens."

I was in front now. The others followed me to the locker. It had been pillaged, and from the empty equipment hooks it looked like what had been taken was a humanoid ox-based hardsuit and some basic tools—a laser cutter/welder, and a good old-fashioned wrecking bar.

Stuff you could use to get through a closed pressure door, I thought, but didn't say anything.

I looked at O'Mara, though, and they nodded. "Hope she doesn't pop a hatch to something that uses sulfuric acid for blood."

Incongruously, Cheeirilaq nodded, too.

I stared at it. That was the second weirdly human gesture.

Cheeirilaq started moving again. Over its shoulder, it said, *I'm wearing a human ayatana. Your thoughts are as squishy as the rest of you.*

"Well." Banter was a good means of easing tension. I knew from Rilriltok that it thought so, too. Apparently it wasn't the only member of its species to hold such an opinion. "If we had any logic in us, we wouldn't have nearly wiped our own species out in the Before, when we didn't have rightminding."

We eat our mates if we can catch them. Everybody's got some evolutionary baggage that winds up maladaptive in a sophont setting.

"Valuable protein resource." I shrugged. "And it's not as if your species is designed for coparenting."

Protein is not so difficult to obtain these diar that it's worth depriving the galaxy of an astrophysicist or a poet in order to eke out a few more eggs.

I realized Carlos was looking at us with horror. *Joking,* I mouthed through my faceplate.

I wasn't sure if he believed me. Cheeirilaq wasn't exactly exaggerating all that much: humans are not the only syster in the galaxy that benefits extensively from rightminding to control our most atavistic tendencies.

Llyn. It was Sally, in my ear. *I have thermal imaging. Turn left through this door.*

"Sally thinks she has eyes on Jones," I relayed, and pointed the way.

We went down the corridor military style, leapfrogging, covering one another. O'Mara and Cheeirilaq were the only ones with weapons, so Carlos and I stayed under their cover while performing nerve-wracking tasks like opening doors.

That worked until we got to one with a fused control panel and a welded edge.

"Well," O'Mara said, running a suit glove down the fresh laser bead, "I guess she's been here."

"And planned to stay a while," Carlos agreed.

She would not have wasted the time to slow us down otherwise.

"It's all right," I said. "She's not a very good welder."

I stepped forward and O'Mara stepped back. There was a spot at the edge of the bead where I could catch my fingertips, and this was a Judiciary hardsuit. I popped the pry-claws out and began wedging them under the bead, into the crack in the door. A sharp snapping sound and a screeching scrape told me I was almost in.

The exo, not to mention the hardsuit, gave me strength. O'Mara braced my feet, and with a rending noise and a gasp of exchanged atmosphere, we were—abruptly—in.

We dashed through while I held one side open, in case the door's sensors were damaged. Nobody wanted to get snipped in half. Beyond it, we reassembled. The corridor stretched on another ten meters or so, then took a curved right turn.

Friends, Cheeirilaq whispered. *I hear somebody breathing on the other side.*

I lifted my foot to step forward. And the shock of sudden, explosive decompression ripped me from the deck.

Things slammed against me as I tumbled: my colleagues, the walls, an equipment cart that had come unmoored. I got one sickening look at the blown-out wall after we scraped around the corridor. Pressure doors slammed behind us. At least not *on* us, but they weren't going to keep us from being blown into space.

I didn't see the net of Rashaqin silk that Cheeirilaq ballooned across the breach until we all bounced off it and then—the atmosphere having evacuated without us—rebounded and drifted slowly back inside.

"She tried to kill us!" Carlos yelped, fingers closing on a grab rail.

I used my gravity belt to orient myself. "Maybe she just wanted to get outside in a hurry."

Carlos glared at me, then laughed in spite of himself. I could hear O'Mara's eyes rolling in his silence. Cheeirilaq finished snipping its web free on one side with its raptorial forelimbs, stepped through, and held the flap back for the rest of us.

Sally, can you track a runner on the outside of the hospital?

Negative, she answered. *I'm docked too far around the curve.*

"I've got Starlight." O'Mara's voice hissed awkwardly over the suit coms. "As long as she stays near the ox sectors, they can track her by vibrations."

"Great! Which way do we go?"

"So many terrible options." O'Mara sighed.

I pretended I hadn't heard him. "If I were Jones, I'd have an objective. You don't take action as definitively hostile as blowing a hole in a hab ring until you are ready to commit to something."

"Until the time for subtlety is past," Carlos agreed.

Anxiety was a distraction I did not need. I tuned it down, took two deep breaths, and made myself focus. The problem with tuning the adrenaline down was that it sent the exhaustion rushing back. Human beings were not meant to operate on the edge of their capabilities like this, miracles of modern medicine or no miracles of modern medicine.

"If her cards are on the table, then why can't I read them?" I asked.

"Because we haven't figured out what game she's playing, or even what the stakes are." O'Mara kept walking forward, shifting carefully from foot to foot. Walking on magnets is a weird experience, because there's no weight pressing your foot down against the insole of the suit. You kind of float inside it, and the boot sticks to the surface of the hab.

Well, we now know she's not lying in wait outside. Shall we go see if she has left us a booby trap?

"When you put it that way," I answered, "how can I resist?"

I felt bad letting Cheeirilaq go first. It was the biggest target. But it was also the active-duty Judiciary officer, and I suspected that it was much more current on its combat training than either O'Mara or me.

No matter what kind of nonsense is going on around you, the moment of stepping out of a vehicle into space is always awe-inspiring, the more so here in the Core than elsewhere. It took all my concentration not to stop and gape. Sally was there behind me, at least, adjusting my brain chemistry. I needed all the help I could get right then; exhaustion plays havoc with emotional regulation even when your world isn't literally coming apart at the seams.

I hauled my heart out of my pants with both hands and followed it through the breached hull, and into the night.

Judiciary training hadn't entirely deserted me. As soon as I came through the breach I flattened myself against the hull of the hospital, using the curve to protect myself from any potential incoming fire. The hospital was gigantic enough that the apparent curve was nominal, and the protection more theoretical than real—but it made me feel better. I wasn't the only one: Goodlaw Cheeirilaq was doing the same thing on the opposite side of the breach.

It hadn't lost hold of the energy projector in its manipulators.

O'Mara—hot on all umpteen of Cheeirilaq's heels—flattened beside me. Carlos followed with more scramble and less Judiciary precision. He definitely moved like a pipefitter, not a soldier. At least he was being careful, though—watching O'Mara and me and trying to copy us.

It was a good thing the hab wheel wasn't spinning, or when we used our boot magnets to hold on, the rotational forces would have tended to fling our bodies outward—and into a potential line of fire. As it was, the same curve that we lay close to because it offered homeopathic protection from incoming fire made it impossible to see where Jones had gone.

Cheeirilaq was a fantastic squad mate. Not only had it gone through the door first—and fast—but it laid safety lines of silk behind itself for us to cling to. I walked up them hand over hand, in case the hab wheel started moving again suddenly. My mag boots would probably hold, but if I had one foot off and it started up with a jerk when attitude rockets fired—well, that would suck for the people in free fall inside, but it would also suck for me. Redundancy, redundancy, redundancy. And two points of contact at all times.

Carlos paced beside me. He was comfortable in EVA and by now seemed well able to manage the boots. He, too, kept a hand on the line. "I don't know anything about this situation. So what if we logic it out? Jones's objectives, I mean."

I hauled myself over a projection on the hull. "You make a good point, you know. You don't know anything."

"That's easier to take when I'm the one saying it," he grumbled.

"Right, but, my point is that *Jones* obviously knows where she is going. Carlos, how comfortable would you be finding your way around this station on your own? Without a guide or a map, I mean?"

"I'd curl up in a corner and wait for the men in the white coats to find me."

"I beg your pardon—"

"Never mind," he said. "I'd have an—an emotional breakdown. A panic attack. If I tried."

"So she came in with more knowledge than you did. She came in primed for this. She knew the hospital plan, and—"

"What changed right before she went AMA?" O'Mara asked.

Against Medical Advice was a mild way to describe her escape, but I didn't interject.

I suspect you of asking a leading question, friend O'Mara. The latest round of sabotage took place right before Jones fled.

Sally broke in. *The pattern of sabotage started before we went out to* Big Rock Candy Mountain. *How can it be linked to whatever Jones is doing?*

"Table that," O'Mara said. "Maybe we ought to be asking ourselves how it's possible that they're *not* linked."

"Once is happenstance," said Carlos. "Twice is coincidence. Three times is enemy action." Then, a moment later, he did a double take and said, "Pattern of sabotage?"

We'll explain later, Cheeirilaq said. I wondered if it would. *For now suffice it to say that somebody has been trying to embarrass the hospital for some time.*

I grunted. "This last attack was more than embarrassing."

O'Mara shut us up with a wave of their hand. "Starlight says the target went that way." They pointed across the turning wheel. "What if we use jets?"

"What if she has a weapon? A ranged weapon, I mean, not a welding torch. We'll be sitting ducks if we come flying in."

O'Mara rolled their eyes at me, but somebody has to be the practical one. "If Jones is linked to the sabotage rather than taking advantage of a dramatic situation, then somebody in the Synarche—somebody at Core General—must have had significant knowledge of and contact with the generation ship before Afar found it and sent out the distress signal."

"The generation ship was significantly off course," I said. "And much closer to the Core than it should have been, given its speed and when it left Terra. What if somebody moved it?"

O'Mara sputtered. "*Big Rock Candy Mountain* has to be as big as Core General. How do you move something like that? You can't slap a white drive around it!"

Oh, liquid stinking excrement. The missing gravity generators, Cheeirilaq said.

"The *what?!*" I yelled so forcefully I got spit on the inside of my faceplate. I hate it when that happens.

I'll explain later, Cheeirilaq said.

I was pretty sure it wouldn't.

"How long ago did this happen?"

About . . . four ans?

"I'm sorry." Carlos held up a hand in the universal gesture for *I have no idea what is going on here.* "What do gravity generators have to do with my ship being off course?"

Time is gravity, Cheeirilaq said. *Or gravity is time. I'm not a black hole physicist. But if you had enough gravity generators, and ran enough power through them, couldn't you bend space-time around something even as large as a generation ship, and slide it from one place to another? I witnessed Haimey Dz doing something similar aboard* I Rise From Ancestral Night, *and she wasn't even using an external generator.*

"Wait! You were *that* Rashaqin?" Suddenly, I had so many questions.

O'Mara laid a glove the size of a catcher's mitt on the forearm of my hardsuit. "This is not the time."

Sally said, *You would burn the generators out.*

"Yeah," I agreed. "But what if you didn't care? What if you never planned to use them again?" Then I stopped, and put my own hand on O'Mara's enormous biceps to steady myself. "What if the, the tinker-toy machine had gravity generator technology built in? What if it replicated itself, copied the tech from the missing generators, held the ship together—and moved the whole shebang? Accelerated it and redirected it? Put it someplace it would more likely be found?"

We've only had the technology to do that for approximately five ans, Cheeirilaq said. *The experimental gravity generators went missing approximately four ans ago. If you did use a self-replicating microbot to reinforce the entire ship and fill it with devices like this belt*—it tapped its own—*and you didn't care about sacrificing the functionality of the technology in the process . . . If all that, then I suppose . . .*

"It's a theory," Carlos said.

O'Mara sighed so deeply I felt the hardsuit shift. "This is huge."

Huger than a conspiracy to sabotage the galaxy's biggest interspecies hospital? But I didn't say that. I said, "I know where she's going."

They all looked at me. Cheeirilaq's head rotated an unsettling two hundred degrees.

She's going to the walker, it agreed. It switched to broadband, addressing all the hospital's Judiciary staff. *Evacuate the sector!*

Almost in unison, O'Mara snapped, "Get those people out of there!"

I thought it would probably be faster to cut back inside and move through the hospital now that we knew where Jones was going. We were already suited, and wouldn't need to change between environments. O'Mara overruled me on the grounds that the internal corridors were still a mess of triaged, untriaged, treated, and untreated casualties. Climbing past injured people floating around in zero g was dangerous, not to mention rude.

Bleakly, I wondered what percentage of the hospital staff were on the injured list. At least as long as the recyclers stayed online, we could print as much medication and food and as many bandages as we needed. Until attrition and inevitable lossage led us to run out of materials. Then we would have to start feeding the corpses in.

I sincerely hoped it would not come to that.

The craboid walker was moored halfway around the circumference of the hospital. And if we weren't going inside, we couldn't cut across the hub. We were going the long way around, I guessed—and this was going to require some interesting athletics.

In my already exhausted state, I was not looking forward to it.

How worn out was I, actually? Well, there was one way to find out. I tuned back my compensation and my pain management, as a status check, and gasped out loud.

Pain of overuse cramped both my hands, the outside of my left calf below the knee, the arches of my feet where I had jammed them into loops to hold myself in place at various times when there wasn't enough ferrous material around for the mag boots to be useful. My quadriceps shivered with the pain of pulling those mag boots loose from the hull over and over again. My eyes burned and my head throbbed and my whole body felt bruised with exhaustion.

All on top of my usual aches and pains.

Cheeirilaq's smaller limbs sawed worriedly against the larger, but the sound of its stridulation did not carry through vacuum. The Judiciary translator rendered its concern to my fox.

Friend Llyn, are you well?

I had my mouth open to lie about that when good sense intervened. One's colleagues need a reasoned assessment of one's capabilities in a crisis, not bravado.

"A lot of discomfort," I admitted, tuning it back down again. "I'll need a moment to change my exo battery."

"Are you capable?" O'Mara asked.

Fatigue levels exceed healthy norms, my exo told me.

"Tired. But I'll hold it together. I have to." The leads snapped home to the second battery. Carlos took the first and stowed it somewhere.

"Jens—"

"Oh, leave her alone," Carlos said. "She said she could do it. Either she can, or she can't, and riding her about it just wastes everyone's time."

I wondered if he knew he was talking to the head of security for the entire ox sector. If he knew, I wondered if he cared. I remembered his flare of homophobia that had so discomfited me.

People are so complicated.

Enough, said Cheeirilaq. *It's time to move.*

The Goodlaw led us across the curve of the hospital at a punishing pace. Fast as we were going, high as my state of nerves and alertness remained, the enormousness of Core General left plenty of time to worry. And to feel betrayed. I hadn't known Jones well, but I had liked her. I'd thought she liked me.

Aw, crap. I had a crush on her, didn't I?

Sigh. Well, as long as I knew it, I could take steps to counteract it, I supposed. Romantic feelings were so tiresome. And so inappropriate, when dealing with a patient, but human beings are programmed to get attached to those we caretake, or those who take care of us.

And so we hurried along the surface of the hab, trying to remember to stay alert for incoming fire as the minutes stretched into a quarter of a standard hour and more. I wished I believed that Jones was not enough of a monster—or enough of an idiot—to discharge a projectile weapon at somebody standing on the surface of an inhabited wheel. But I hadn't flunked my threat assessment classes, back when I was still in the Judiciary, and the fugitive we were hunting had already decompressed a section of a habitation, and appeared to be working with accomplices who thought nothing of committing a major terrorist attack against a hospital.

Moreover, I didn't have that much faith in humanity, and right this second I definitely didn't have that much faith in Jones.

I had no right to feel betrayed. She hadn't made me any promises. But here I was, feeling betrayed as hell. And also nauseated, since at least two of the systers in my head did not appreciate the sensations of moving fast in free fall.

"Starlight says she's reached the walker," O'Mara reported. We were still about three minutes away.

"I hope she has as hard a time getting into it as I did," I said between gasps for air. The pain in my calf had spread up my IT band to my hip, and no amount of tuning could kill it completely.

One would hope, Cheeirilaq responded. *But somehow the notorious perversity of the universe never seems to maximize in a direction convenient to ourselves.*

She's in, Sally agreed. *The machine is starting to move.*

"Great," I said. "Now we get to chase her."

"Yeah," said O'Mara. "And she's got a tank."

It wasn't much of a chase, as it happened, because Jones and the damned walker hurtled right over us and back the way we had come. We all had a moment of terror as the spiked legs slammed down on every side and the teardrop-shaped body hustled over. Cheeirilaq slung a loop of silk at it, but didn't connect. Probably for the best, because being dragged behind that thing would be no fun at all, even for a Rashaqin.

Like characters in a comedy, we all whirled in our footsteps and went zooming back the way we had come. The craboid was a lot faster, and you can't run in mag boots. They only work if one of your feet is in contact with the hull.

We need fire support, I heard the Goodlaw say, and felt a sinking sensation. A Judiciary gunship would be responding. It was the right choice to make . . . but it was a choice that could cost more lives. So I hated it.

The chase ended moments later when we came around a stanchion that supported the local segment of the currently unusable lift tube system, arriving in time to see the spidery, barb-legged walker rear back and punch both daggerlike forelimbs right into Core General's unprotected hull.

"We need that gunship out here *faster,*" O'Mara said, and I heard the crackle of response from Judiciary operators inside the hospital.

I almost squealed a protest. Projectiles could miss and hit the hospital, and I honestly didn't want anything terrible happening to Jones. She was . . .

I didn't know what she was. She wasn't a person lost out of time, acting in panic. She wasn't an innocent. She was, right now, an existential threat to a hospital full of sick people and innocent staffers.

And well, fuck, what were three humans and a Rashaqin—even a Rashaqin with a beam weapon—meant to do against a terrorist in a combat walker? A terrorist, I might add, whose sense of mission included the ruthlessness to have herself frozen in a dubious cryo pod on a crumbling generation ship to await a rescue that might never come.

Yes, I had pretty much abandoned the idea that Jones was a real crew member of *Big Rock Candy Mountain*. Helen remembered her . . . but Carlos didn't. And Carlos's memory was not reprogrammable the way Helen's was—or mine was, for that matter.

Cheeirilaq and O'Mara were right to call for backup. As much as I hated it.

The shock wave of the impact kicked my mag boots. O'Mara gestured me behind them—funny how you fall back on the habits of silence and hand signals even when you're operating on a closed, scrambled coms channel—and we ducked back into the visual cover of the stanchion arch. O'Mara sent a drone around to peek, and as we all rode the feed we regained visual on what Jones was doing.

You can't evacuate a hospital. Not really—not without causing as many casualties as you are trying to prevent. So many fragile patients with extremely specialized needs. So many who simply cannot survive being moved because they need continual support.

I had devoted my professional life—which was my entire life, to be honest—to protecting and helping those people.

And there was Jones in the walker burrowing away at the skin of my home. At the physical manifestation of my vocation.

I hadn't believed—not really believed—Jones would do that until I saw it. I still wanted to grasp at denial. *This can't be happening.* How could somebody I knew—a real person, an acquaintance that I liked—do something so terrible?

O'Mara grounded the drone at once, and we all crossed our fingers that it hadn't been seen. Well, Cheeirilaq doesn't have fingers, and whatever your digits are, you can't really cross them in a hardsuit anyway, but you know what I mean.

So that's what the barbs are for, I thought, watching the craboid wedge a pair of them beneath a hull plate and lever the edge up in the eerie silence of vacuum. No puff of crystallizing atmosphere followed: At least it wasn't a breach. Yet.

My own mental tone had the curious dissociated deadpan of crisis. I didn't realize I'd thought it loud enough for my fox to pick up until Carlos responded, "That looks like a wrecking bar had a bastard baby with a spider crab."

I winced, but he wasn't wrong. Just crude and archaic.

We have to stop her. Cheeirilaq whetted its raptorial forearms together: nervous grooming or preparation for combat, I was not sure. I worried for the transparent insulskin covering its exoskeleton, but it didn't seem concerned. Around its abdomen, the webwork of oxygen tubes that supplied its respiratory needs inside the hospital connected to the same kind of standard Judiciary ox pack I was wearing, though Cheeirilaq's was no doubt set to a richer mix. That same fragile-seeming insulskin suit expanded and contracted with the pulse of its breathing.

I wished it were wearing a hardsuit. I suppose its own exoskeleton must suffice; most Rashaqins that left their low-gravity homeworld had ceramic reinforcing threads woven into their chitin as a sensible precaution. Surely Cheeirilaq would have done that before going into a career in military law enforcement.

"What the Well is she doing?" I asked.

O'Mara grunted. "I should think that would be obvious. She's digging a hole in the hull."

"Yeah. But . . . why?"

Cheeirilaq turned its head inside the transparent bubble that protected its sensory equipment and looked at me. The drone feed still showed no deep-space snowfall of crystallizing atmosphere . . . yet. Core General had a tough skin. But it was only a matter of time.

I remembered what Cheeirilaq had said about the human ayatana, and its uncanny attempts to mimic human gestures, and nodded. "I'd like to try to stop her before we have to use that deployed gunship. In addition to the danger of damage to Core General, there's a person in there. And I want to understand . . . I want to understand what's behind this action."

Carlos's voice stretched to hold his incredulity. "A person who's trying to kill a whole bunch of your patients, Doctor."

"Yes," I said. "And if we kill her, we'll never find out why. I feel like I have a personal connection. Let me talk to her."

O'Mara broke a long silence with my name. "Llyn—"

I looked at them and they looked at me. The hull under our feet vibrated

"Fine," they sighed. "Don't make me write a letter to your daughter."

Be careful. Cheeirilaq darted one raptorial forelimb out and tapped me on the shoulder sharply. I glanced down, surprised the razory tip hadn't drawn blood. Score one for the hardsuit.

Carlos stepped in front of O'Mara. "You're going to let her go out there in a space suit to face that . . . fucking tank?"

"I'm a rescue specialist," I said, because I didn't appreciate Carlos appealing to O'Mara as if I weren't an autonomous adult sentient. There was that atavistic nonsense. "This is my job."

Carlos reached out to grab me, but I was better at space shit, let's be honest here, and I eluded him easily. He didn't elude O'Mara, and a moment later I stepped out from behind the lift arch and walked across the hull toward the walker.

CHAPTER 20

"SALLY," I SAID, "ARE YOU STILL THERE?"

Absolutely. What are you going to do about this?

"I've got an idea. Let me check this emergency pack—hey, would you look at that?"

I pulled out two small tubes, each about as long as my hand was wide. Each had a little flat disc at the top. I fumbled at the discs with my gloves but got them pulled out. Each unfurled into a flag on a stick, with a wire at the distal end to keep it rigid.

"Old-school," I said, grinning behind my mask. "Semaphores. Can you look up pre-Synarche semaphore codes for me?"

I already had them, Sally said. *Which is lucky for you because I can't download anything, between the quarantine and the power failures.*

She passed the codes on to my fox. They were straightforward, and I thought I could manage.

I still moved toward the walker. It ripped the hull plate up some more, forelimbs striking downward, daggerlike, while the midlimbs popped and pried. The vibrations shuddered through the hull, making the bones in my feet and ankles ache even more than they did already. Electricity arced around the walker, blue sparks bridging and crawling up its arms. The charge didn't slow it down at all.

But it also didn't seem to have noticed me approaching. Or if it had, it didn't seem to care.

I realized I was anthropomorphizing the craboid. Pretending it was acting on its own, without a person inside it. That would, I thought, make it easier to cope in the event I couldn't hold the gunship off.

Water-ice fountained briefly into snow and drifted away to space before the ruptured pipe froze and sealed itself. A hundred meters from the busily destructive machine, I unfurled my little flags and struck a pose.

Sally spoke through my fox. She said, *Synarche Judiciary Vessel* I Really Don't Have Time For Your Nonsense *is inbound. ETA five standard minutes. You will need to be at least twenty meters clear of the fire zone for the shipmind to guarantee your safety.*

Copy. *Mark the fire zone please?*

Sally popped filters over our perceptions, showing a green ring and crosshairs superimposed on the hull.

What's under that? Cheeirilaq asked.

Machine rooms, Sally replied. *Environmental controls.*

Ox sector? O'Mara guessed.

There was a pause. A brief one, but any pause beyond the polite ones to allow slowbrains to process is significant in an AI.

No record, Sally said.

What do you mean, no record? The machine still wasn't responding to me. I kept walking. I'd still be outside of its immediate striking range if I stopped at the edge of the target zone.

The schematics I have on record don't list what these environmental controls are for.

Isn't that weird? I asked.

Drop it, O'Mara interjected. *Just stop that thing.*

But—

But a lot of things. But it was weird. But it could be useful to know what was under the machine in case it—or the gunship—punched through and let whatever was in there . . . out here. Or left it spreading through a series of projectile holes to adjacent sections.

Oxygen was poison, if you were the sort of person who breathed an atmosphere rich in chlorine gas, for example. Water was poison if your blood's chemistry was closer to ethylene glycol. And vice versa.

One did not simply muck about in a multispecies environment without due consideration for the biological needs of everybody in the adjoining corridors. *Why can't Sally access detailed schematics on this area? What is Jones digging to?*

Something here was very wrong. And not letting Calliope Jones get killed was my ticket to finding out what that was, exactly.

"Jens, stop!"

I was a half meter inside that glowing green target zone, and O'Mara's yelling in my ear was nearly drowning out Sally's yelling through my fox. The craboid hadn't disassembled me yet, which was a data point in my favor. Unfortunately, it didn't seem to be reading my semaphore signals, either.

Admittedly, it's not a language system optimized for *Hey, want to get a coffee? I think we need to talk.*

Not that you should ever say to anybody, "I think we need to talk." Not unless you want to spend the next fifteen standard minutes dealing with an adrenaline response.

I had made sure my hardsuit display was the full-on barrage of Terran medical symbols (Caduceus, Red Cross, Red Crescent, et cetera), and that and the flags were my only way of letting Jones know that I was a friendly—as friendly as anybody could be under the circumstances. Well, that and walking up to her war machine wearing nothing but a hardsuit and carrying no weapons. She still wasn't paying any attention to me—which was good and bad—but she also hadn't stopped pulling the plating off the outside of my hospital. It looked like she'd dug about a meter into the hull, which meant she had to be pretty close to the outermost pressure capsule. If she breached that, it would decompress, and more doors would come down, and more lives and limbs would doubtless be lost unless O'Mara's orders to clear the sectors inward of us had been followed.

Nobody with a self-preservation instinct would be standing around in a doorway, but people still had to walk down corridors.

"Jens," O'Mara said, as I continued to move forward at a steady pace, "what in the Well are you doing?"

"Gambling," I said, but it didn't feel like a gamble. It felt like trusting my instincts.

The iron spider towered over me as I approached. I was already much closer than was safe. Much closer than I had permission to be. The hull jumped under my feet every time the craboid drove its forelegs into the plating. An asteroid field of glittering debris surrounded it now, turning, reflecting the colors of all the Core's weird lensing stars from edges that looked jagged and razor-sharp.

I thought about tuning back my pounding heart, the anxious pain in my throat—but adrenaline might keep me alive. It might make me that tiny bit faster.

I could deal with the discomfort. Especially when turning it off would let me remember that other things hurt more.

I waited until the machine reared back for its next blow and stepped right under the front legs. The middle and back ones gripped the savaged hull in metal claws. Ripped plating crunched as my mag boots pulled me toward the hospital's center of spin. I raised the flags even higher and crossed them in front of me, repeating the gesture three times with a flourish between each.

This gesture was the same in the Synarche's flag code and the archaic one: *HOLD. HOLD. HOLD.*

The barbed legs drove toward me. I crouched—if I jumped out of the way I'd lose contact with the hull and be drifting off into nothingness, away from safety. If you could call this safety.

I had the suit jets and could probably get back to the hospital if that happened. But nobody liked to contemplate floating around in the Big Empty without a concrete and detailed plan for what you were doing while you were out there and how you were going to get back.

The legs stopped a meter above me.

HOLD, I signaled once more.

The legs twitched.

O'Mara bellowed. I could hear Carlos in the background, so loud he came seconded over O'Mara's feed, but somebody must have killed his suit mike's connection to *my* outputs.

O'Mara got his voice to come across level, if strained. "That gunship is coming in hot, Jens."

"Well, tell it not to shoot." I didn't take my eyes off the machine, though I had to crane back against the support of my exo to do it.

Moving my flags slowly, I signed, *FOLLOW INSIDE.*

There was no response. I almost had a sense that the machine cocked its head at me. If it had a head, which it didn't.

I tried again, and got the same lack of an answer.

Then it occurred to me that I was overcomplicating the issue. There was no reason for Calliope—or whatever the person in the machine was actually named—to know semaphores from Carlos's dia. Because she had to be an impostor. A well-drilled one; perhaps one who actually believed the role she was playing. You could do a lot with constructed memories. But an impostor nonetheless.

An impostor might actually know the Synarche General Flag Code, if she was a modern human. It was simple, and you needed to know it to get your pilot's license, or to work on a docking ring, or to do a job like mine. It didn't get used every dia every place—but it got used often enough where visual communication was the most effective means. And a cheat sheet and a set of flags were part of the standard equipment in every emergency pack that met Synarche standards to be called an emergency pack.

Which was why I had these flags to work with, right now.

I'd once seen a six-armed, radially symmetrical, massively built keee'Shhk flight-deck master use similar flags to direct two tugs and a barge simultaneously into three different landing sites. Admittedly, the syster in question had a few advantages: three brains and the ability to endure hard vacuum without a suit. But it had still been an impressive display.

I didn't need to do anything so complicated right now. Just get the walker to follow me, and not get stepped on if it did. I fixed my gaze on that hatch in the underside. It didn't look compatible with any of our airlocks, but that was why we carried a full suite of flexible collars and kiloliters of sticky spray foam. The great thing about space is that you don't need a lot of structural integrity under most circumstances. Gravity is the great destroyer of structures. In free fall, the worst things you have to worry about are atmospheric pressure and torque.

As a rescue specialist, I've seen some things that were *definitely* not up to code. But, finicky and rickety though those structures might have been, they still functioned adequately for people to live in them. Until, one dia, they didn't.

At least I was already stabilized in the same attitude and plane as the presumed front of the machine. I reached out slowly, balancing my movements so I didn't have to waste my stabilizers or strain my exo and my core muscles holding myself upright, and showed it the flags again. Gently, I moved them into Position 10: *Copy?*

There was a pause. Then, with the eerie silence of vacuum, the craboid began to move. Most of its limbs remained braced. But two of them—the two closest to me, the ones that had been hovering over my head—pulled in. So did the middle pair, releasing their grip on the hull plates. Which were definitely dented and scored.

This thing was built to take a pounding, all right.

It didn't have flags, but the whole machine moved its arms into the mirror image of mine. If it had *had* flags, it would have been saying *Acknowledge* in reply.

I hadn't been certain she wouldn't dig right through me to continue tearing the hospital apart. But there is something psychologically different between damaging an object—even if it's an object upon which people's lives depend—and directly killing another sentient being.

Now I just had to keep SJV *I Really Don't Have Time For Your Nonsense* from blowing us both away.

Well, I had put my body in between the machine and the hospital. Now I guessed I was going to put my body between the machine and the guns. Maybe the pathetic spectacle of my clumsy human form in its inadequate suit of armor would move the gunship's mind or its crew to mercy.

Mercy is a nicer word than *pity*, don't you think?

There's no whoosh or whistle of incoming, in vacuum. No auditory warning.

The gunship went over so fast and low that for a moment I thought it had struck me—or struck the craboid, which obviously stretched much farther out from the hull. I ducked instinctively, hands coming up, lifting the flags as if they could somehow protect me. I didn't consciously register the ship's outline before it had gone, and had to pull the memory out of my senso to be sure of what I'd seen.

One of the guest surgeons in my head tried to flatten itself into some purely conceptual long grass. Another one wanted to rear up to bring its horns into play. The results were predictably comical, and only my mag boots kept me on the hull. I *had* to get all of them out of my head.

The gunship was white-space capable, but she'd flipped her coils horizontal to the fat teardrop of her hull, so the effect was not dissimilar to the virtual target circle I still stood in the middle of. Her gunports were open, and in that retrospective glimpse I could see the muzzles of mass drivers tracking as she sped past.

Nonesuch is going to come around again, Cheeirilaq said. *Do you require fire support, friend Doctor?*

I looked up at the looming machine. "No," I said. "No, I don't think she'll hurt me."

A crackle of static caught me unaware. I jumped inside my suit. "Dr. Jens? Is that you?"

Jones's voice. A coms link? A coms link!

"You saved my life!" She sounded angry.

"I'm a doctor," I said. "That's what I do."

Stand down, I told my team, and felt their assent—and how grudging it was—through the senso. They said nothing, though, and for that I was grateful.

Calliope Jones was yelling at me enough for everybody. That was fine, because she wasn't crushing me like a bug with her giant bug machine.

Why had the volume in my helmet been cranked up so loud in the first place? I lowered it, which actually made it easier to understand what Jones was screaming at me.

"That's a lie! You're one of them! You want to experiment on me, like all the others!"

Did she mean that all the others wanted to experiment on her, or that there were a lot of others being experimented on? It sounded like a sophipathology either way, and I didn't have time to worry about it now.

"Look, Jones," I said, when she paused for breath. "Calliope. Why don't you come out of that thing? We'll dock it somewhere, and you and I can sit down with a drink and talk it over?"

"I want coffee," she said, and for the first time I could hear the exhaustion in her voice.

"Don't we all," I agreed. "Are you wearing a suit?"

I thought she probably had to be, to have gotten to the machine at all. But in a situation like this—essentially a hostage negotiation—you do whatever you can to keep the conversation flowing. People who are talking aren't coming up with terrible ideas.

"Yes." Reluctance colored her tone. "I have a suit on. Mostly. I retracted the gloves and helmet for access to the controls."

"Does that walker have an airlock?"

Silence. Then after what felt like a long time, when I had started trying to think up another question to ask her—

"No."

I hadn't thought it did, but we'd never gotten a good look inside. So even if I had my rescue kit, I couldn't force the door—that hatch I'd spotted in the machine's belly—and extricate her without killing her unless I got her to suit up first. Not that we'd been able to penetrate the thing's hide anyway. Nor could I go in there without getting zapped.

I wished we'd had the time to figure out how to get a drone inside the craboid without it getting electrocuted. It was all very inconvenient.

I was going to have to secure her cooperation, then.

"Did you turn off the countermeasures?" I asked her. "That walker zorched the drone we tried to send inside."

"I had the code," she said. "I just . . . I knew what I had to do, when the lights went out. It was like a dream, or . . ."

Or a fugue state, I thought. Like a programmed series of trigger responses, set off by a particular external stimulus.

Okay then. Hmm. "Calliope, would you consider stepping out of the walker?"

"I . . . can't," she said, with a kind of nauseated finality that made me disinclined to push the point. The craboid wavered.

"Okay, okay. If you don't feel safe coming out, what if you suit up and let me come in? Is there room in there for two?"

I remembered the empty cargo space inside the walker. I *bet* that was where Calliope's cryo chamber had been stored. Before it was placed among all the others on *Big Rock Candy Mountain*.

Then I wondered about the machine, and the rupture in the hull. I recognized that, as if with a magic trick, that rupture had forced our selection of which cryo pods to bring home in the first shipload.

Calliope said, "I didn't say I don't feel safe. Don't twist my words."

She had—though not in so many words. She had said with her allegations of nonconsensual experimentation that she didn't feel safe. But it was pretty obvious that she was reacting rather than thinking, and much of what she was reacting to was inside her own skull.

"You don't trust me, though?"

She laughed. "Of course I don't trust you. You pretend to be nice, but I know what goes on here. They told me."

". . . They?"

I couldn't see her, or feel her through the senso—but I still sensed the change in her and the moment when she snatched herself back like a coral retreating into its shell.

"They control your brain," she said. "They tell you what to think, and you believe them because you don't have a choice. They put a box in your head, and you don't have a choice the same way I didn't have a choice before I got that box taken out. They steal people and cut them up for parts. *You* steal people and cut them up for parts. I remember now. I didn't before. I thought I was somebody else, but now I know."

"What would I do with a lot of people parts?" I asked reasonably. I thought, but did not say, *There are cheaper sources of protein.*

"Rich people use them to live forever."

"We can clone organs when we need them," I reminded her. "And even that can't keep people alive forever. Everything wears out, even brains."

She snorted. "For a doctor, you're really naive."

I thought I was part of the murder cabal. I didn't say that, either. She was obviously not thinking very clearly.

Hostage negotiation has never been my most natural skill set. I did study hard, but when I'm under pressure the sarcastic side of my mind still provides all the things I shouldn't say. I'm sure that as long as I filter them out before they actually leave my mouth, it's fine.

"Look," I said. "I'm going to sit down. My legs are tired, and it seems like we might be here for a while."

My legs *were* tired, but folding them up wouldn't change that when the only thing holding me to the hull was mag boots. Making myself look small and relaxed might serve to de-escalate the situation, though, and sometimes you have to try every trick you can think of. Also, there were four alien surgeons in my head, and every single one of them used something different for an inner ear. Their disorientation was making me nauseated.

So I magnetized my rear end and stuck it to the hull. I had plenty of ox and plenty of battery, so now it was a matter of waiting for Calliope to have a change of ideation. Or at least a moment of lower paranoia. Or exhaustion.

It's amazing how you can wear people down if you keep them talking. "Look. You said yourself that I saved your life. You saw the gunship. She was going to shoot you to keep you from destroying the hospital—"

"I wasn't trying to destroy it. I don't want to hurt anybody."

I *didn't* point out that she'd been disassembling a hab wheel with I-didn't-even-know-how-many people inside, and I get an extra cookie for that. I said, "Neither do I. And I want to keep you from being hurt. I kept the gunship from shooting you. Why would I protect you if I were one of the bad guys?"

A dry laugh. "Maybe you want me for parts."

"It would have saved a lot of resources not to have woken you up, in that case." I tapped my thigh armor with my fingertips, thinking. It echoed inside my hardsuit.

"You wanted to learn about the generation ship first."

"Somebody sent you," I said. "Somebody built that machine you're in and put it in a ship full of casualties so we would be sure to bring it back here. Somebody moved *Big Rock Candy Mountain* and put you inside her and arranged things so that you would be one of the first we rescued. And somebody built a lot of triggers into your brain so that when certain things went wrong, you'd have no choice except to get on your horse and ride. So I have to wonder, Calliope—why this particular spot, to start prying apart the hospital? And what were you digging for?"

"Evidence," she said.

"Evidence of what?"

"Evidence to broadcast." The machine waved one appendage in an airy gesture. "Evidence of what goes on in here. Evidence to make people stop you."

It was obviously sophipathology, but the conviction in her voice still gave me a chill.

"Well, you were digging in the wrong place," I said. "These are environmental controls."

She snorted, a harsh sound over the suit mike. "Is that what they told you?"

I opened my mouth and closed it again. Took a deep breath. Said, "This is a hospital."

"Look, I'm going to try coming out," she said. "I've done all I can from in here. Either people will investigate or they won't. Let me suit up."

A moment passed. I might have worried, but then the belly hatch irised open and atmosphere puffed away. I made myself stay still: I wouldn't make her come out any faster by pacing in circles.

Jens? O'Mara asked.

Stand by. Call off the gunship; she's unsealing.

She wasn't coming out fast at all.

"Dr. Jens?" The fear was back in her voice.

"Calliope?"

"I can't get loose. I'm stuck."

Instantly I was on my feet. "Stay calm. I'm coming."

"Jens, this is a terrible idea."

O'Mara, on a different channel. Out loud, as if to be sure I heard them.

I made sure my channel to Jones was closed before I answered. "I do rescues. This is business as usual."

"If you go in there we're going to have to put you into quarantine, too."

That made me pause. "I was already in Afar. And *Big Rock Candy Mountain*."

They continued, "We don't know how long it will be before we've got control of the meme, Llyn."

"And if the quarantine isn't lifted?"

"You can't move around freely until it is." I heard their shrug in their voice, and contained anger. Anger at me, I realized. "Look, I know that rushing into dangerous situations is what you do, and how you feel alive, and you've chosen good careers to put that tendency to use. And some people are going to tell you that's heroic. But this person chose her own path and tried to kill a lot of people, and if she's stuck in there, oh well."

They still weren't wrong. But they weren't right, either. "I don't think she got a lot of choice—"

"Ignoring your own needs constantly is selfish and makes a lot of work for other people."

"This is not your everydia sort of situation." I wondered how the gritting of my teeth came through the link. "Are you going to order me not to, Master Chief?"

It was a low blow. I knew O'Mara didn't love having a desk job. But this was my hospital, and we didn't just let people die here even if they pissed us off, and—

—and if Calliope had been trying to kill people she would have busted through an observation wall in one of the cafeterias, not spent a bunch of time digging up a well-protected section of hull with nothing but machinery underneath.

"No," O'Mara said, after a long pause. "I'm not going to order you not to treat your patient, Doctor."

I de-magged, kicked off from the hull, and let myself drift upward. My aim was pretty good, and this hab ring was no longer rotating, so I didn't need to touch my jets or the edges of the hatch as I drifted through.

The door was just a door.

I don't know exactly what I expected inside the machine—Calliope asphyxiated with her suit unsealed, maybe. Alien technology like twisted metal brambles impaling her.

Not a perfectly normal command chair in a perfectly normal cabin, and a suited woman struggling with restraints that wouldn't have seemed out of place on any pilot's seat.

"Hey there, Specialist." I moved up next to her. She pulled against the straps. I moved her hands away and tried the latch; it seemed to be jammed.

There were cutters in my emergency kit. I got them out at the same time I stowed the semaphore flags. "Just hold still for a few seconds. I'll pop you right out of there."

Her face and her panicked expression were plain to see through the plate on her suit. I kept talking as I felt around the harness and aligned the cutters. I wasn't really concentrating on what I was saying or if it made any sense. What was important was the tone.

She yanked against the straps, which meant she yanked against me. I put my free hand on her shoulder. "I need you to hold still, Calliope. I'm going to cut the restraints now, and I don't want to hole your suit."

To her credit, she held still. In a small voice, she said, "Okay."

I watched while she unclenched her hands. Dealing with that level of adrenaline couldn't be easy without a fox.

I reached out extra carefully, watching my hands so I wouldn't get confused about how long my arms were. I snipped one restraint, close to the buckle.

She jerked back so sharply I was afraid I'd holed her. But she was staring over my shoulder. "Look out, Llyn!"

I ducked and started to turn, pulling the cutter up and away—the only safe direction. I wasn't fast enough. A glimpse of a multicolored tendril snaking toward me—familiar from my experience on *Big Rock Candy Mountain*—was my only warning besides Calliope's cry.

An impact. The hiss of venting atmosphere. A wild flail with the cutter—

Shit.

I fell.

CHAPTER 21

I REMEMBER WAKING UP INSIDE THE MACHINE. INSIDE MY exo, when it was first fitted to me.

I remember what it felt like: On my skin. Against me. A part of me.

I remember the incredible floating sensation of not being in pain for the first time I could recall.

No. That's not quite precisely right. The pain still existed. It wasn't gone.

It just didn't saturate my awareness the way it had before. It was a sensation, not a prison.

It's even in the words, isn't it? We talk about being hungry, being thirsty, being distracted, being tired. But we are *in* pain. Pain is a trap. It surrounds us. It's a cage: a thing we can't get out of.

So maybe it *is* accurate to say I wasn't *in* pain anymore, there inside the machine. Somebody had left the door open, and I could get out if I wanted. Walk around, look at the pain from the outside.

I was in the *machine*. But that meant the machine was there between me and the pain. Insulating. A protective barrier. Not something I could ignore or neglect to maintain, because I could never *forget* the machine.

But when I was in the machine I wasn't in the pain. And the cognitive load of servicing the machine was so much less than that of servicing the pain that I got a heck of a lot of other things done.

The machine. My exo, as I came to know it. It was always there, a skin between me and the universe. And I was always afraid that it might be taken away.

It occurred to me that there was something else I had learned never to trust. Not only the faith that everything would turn out all right, or that institutions had the best interests of Synizens at heart. I had never been able to take for granted something that many people did: Simply being functional. Simply being okay.

Waking up inside this new darkness was very much like waking up inside my exo had been, that first time. Once again, I had hurt so badly when it took me in—been so exhausted, my pain so uncontrolled—that when I woke up again and I wasn't hurting *or* groggy, I wasn't entirely sure I was awake. I was disoriented, confused.

But my thoughts were clear and focused, even though I didn't know what was going on.

I was still in my exo. I could feel it there through the senso, status checks all okay. But that was all I could feel through the senso. There was no feed, no connection to the outside. To Sally, or the hospital, or O'Mara, or Cheeirilaq. To Calliope, even.

There was only warm darkness, and a lack of pain. I couldn't seem to move, not even to press myself against the exo frame—or if I was succeeding, I didn't feel it. I couldn't seem to move the exo, either. So there was another something—another machine? Outside the machine that was very nearly a part of me.

To be honest, the lack of pain was so nice that I just lay there and enjoyed it for a short subjective eternity. It could have been five minutes or five ans. I tried counting breaths, but I couldn't feel myself breathing, either.

Wasn't there supposed to be something about sensory deprivation being used as a kind of torture, historically? I reached for the information, but without a feed it wasn't there in my senso. You get so used to being able to pull up any information that you like, the loss of that ability feels like a dismemberment.

Like the loss of part of your own native faculties, and you can't stop fussing at it.

Still, after three attempts, I tried to force myself to let it go. No senso, no connection. My fox was still regulating, though, and it told me that my bloodstream was full of an unusual concentration of naturally occurring opioid analogues. That would explain the lack of pain. Though I didn't understand why they weren't making me feel giddy.

Aw. Well. I tried to make a noise of frustration, and could convince myself that I heard it—dimly, hollowly. As if from another chamber in a largely empty hab.

Somebody did, in fact, have control of my fox and my exo. The virus—the meme . . .

Was this what had happened to the crew of Afar? To Afar himself? To Linden?

Was this the result of the meme?

How had it gotten into me, in that case?

There had been a tentacle. Inside Jones's walker. Something like the machine from *Big Rock Candy Mountain.* I remembered it grabbing me.

Was that machine the vector for the meme, rather than a manifestation of it? If it was, then where had it come from?

My exo had firewalls and was not supposed to accept external inputs without an override code that only I—or somebody with access to my medical or service records—could give. And my fox was protected, as all foxes are. Better than most, in fact, because I'd been in the military and my unit was EMP-shielded and used a triple-encoding transmission link that had been state-of-the-art fifteen ans before.

The meme might have gotten out of Dr. Zhiruo and Linden before they isolated themselves. It might have stripped data from them, such as their access codes. My medical records were available through hospital systems to authorized users. So that was possible, but this wasn't the time to worry about what might have happened. This was the time for getting the hell out.

I tried not to stop to wonder how I was going to get myself out of this non-space if all those methane types and several artificial intelligences hadn't managed to escape.

Helen's crew hadn't been affected. Neither had Calliope, concealed in Helen's crew. They didn't have etchable brains. I didn't have an etchable brain, either, but I had a fox, and I had the exo. . . .

Helen hadn't been affected, either, precisely. Or rather, she'd been affected, but not in the same manner as the other AIs. She'd been . . . turned against herself. Mostly disassembled. But the core had hung on, though she had been—I realized now—delusional in some of the same ways that Calliope had become delusional: paranoid and fixated.

(Was Calliope delusional? I shied away from contemplating the implications of that question. It was a problem for a moment when I was not fighting for my continued existence as something other than a disembodied consciousness.)

The first step was to break it down. What did the patients in different categories of . . . of infection, for lack of a better word . . . have in common with one another?

Helen was unlike shipminds and wheelminds and medical AIs in that she had a separate body.

Carlos and Calliope were unlike me and Afar's crew in that they did not have foxes.

I was like Helen in that I outsourced some of my functions to a peripheral system. Some of us did a lot of that kind of integration: others (Carlos) none at all. Some of us were solid-state cognitive operations—the AIs, the Darboof—and some of us thought with programmable meat, with or without integrated circuitry.

So here I was, back where I started after a fashion. Back inside the machine.

A different machine. One I hadn't chosen to make a part of me.

Was this line of thinking getting me any closer to a solution, or even a hypothesis as to how this whole bizarre mess of generation ship, sick artificial intelligences, and an apparently fraudulent cryo chamber hooked together?

What if I resorted to wild, out-there, black-sky speculation? What was the most outré idea I could come up with?

Theory: it was totally aliens.

Not ancient, safely dead, and apparently benevolent aliens like the Koregoi, that forerunner species that had ranged—and left—the Milky Way long before the Synarche and its systers came along. Those children of dead stars had left us occasional caches of impossibly advanced technology, like the recently discovered Baomind, a library the size of a solar system, and the physics that lay behind the gravity belt I was probably still wearing over my hardsuit, for example.

So not those. And not friendly, normal, everydia it's-rude-to-call-them-aliens like Tralgar and Cheeirilaq, systers one could sit down for a nice beer or metabolically compatible beer equivalent with—though never coffee—and complain about local Synarche policies.

But actual, hardcore, scary, middle-of-sleep-shift-three-vee-you-have-to-be-up-in-four-hours-and-are-being-irresponsible-watching-this-now aliens. Aliens that wanted to disassemble my hospital the same way they were disassembling Helen's generation ship, and convert it into computronium and the machine. Those kind of aliens.

I wondered again about Helen's link with the machine. If it was aliens converting her ship and self into alien computronium microbots, they seemed to have left some of her personality intact. I wasn't a science fiction expert, but it seemed to me that that was a rarity in the annals of all-consuming, assimilating, mind-control aliens.

In some ways, this was the most terrifying prospect. In others, I was surprised to find it somehow reassuring. Assimilating aliens were a horrifying existential threat, something that might destroy the entire Synarche, that might require shoving *Big Rock Candy Mountain*, Core General, Sally, Mercy, Afar—and me and literally everybody and everything I loved except the daughter I had not seen in twenty-odd ans—into the consuming embrace of the Well in order to prevent it from spreading.

It was also a horrifying existential threat that I could look at and say, "That's not us. It comes from outside, and it's monsters."

Even in this age of adequate mental health care, when things are so much better than they were, I'm too much of a cop and too much of a doctor to ever convince myself that the monsters are conveniently *other*. The monsters don't come from outside.

The monsters are calling from inside our genome.

That's why, during the Eschaton, it took the medical interventions that eventually developed into rightminding to make us decently able to stop destroying ourselves. It's a small comfort, I suppose, that once we got into space and met other sapiences, we discovered that they were all more or less equally as fucked up evolutionarily as we are, and had all had to take similar social steps to grow beyond their atavistic impulses into something we might recognize as culture.

I liked the scary predatory aliens theory a lot, for certain values of *like*. If it was scary aliens invading, waging war, and converting us into peripherals by means of their meme viruses, that left one huge logical problem, though: Where the Well did Calliope come from?

Ah, Calliope.

Well, then it probably wasn't aliens.

And that led to an even more frightening proposition. What if Calliope was right? What if there was some vast corrupt conspiracy centering in the Synarche, in Core General? What if she was a freedom fighter? What if?

I didn't think Calliope was right. I knew in my (no longer aching) bones that she *could not* be right.

But here in the belly of the machine, a quotation from an ancient, pre-Eschaton Terran statesman named Oliver Cromwell came floating back to me. "I beseech you, in the bowels of Christ, think it possible that you may be mistaken."

Christ was a religious prophet from an even earlier era, very popular on Terra for several thousand years. He preached all the usual things the better class of prophets preach, about respecting your fellow beings and treating them as one would like oneself to be treated. He got about the reception you'd expect, and his teachings were widely misinterpreted for millennians. Millenni*a*, I suppose, it being actual Terran years we're talking about.

The irony is that this Cromwell person, who provided such a useful sentiment that has since been widely appropriated by logicians, historians, archinformists, and doctors (like myself), was the sort of individual who overthrew a government. (Okay, it was a monarchy of some sort, or something equally terrible.) He also murdered a lot of dissidents because *he* was pretty damned certain *he* was right. And because he was pretty adamant that everyone should subscribe to his religious convictions.

Don't be like Oliver Cromwell, I told myself, and tried to examine Calliope's allegations from a more neutral point of view.

Perhaps the reason I was so certain Calliope was wrong was that the prospect of her being right was so deeply terrifying.

What if there was some kind of vast conspiracy—or rampant sophipathology—infecting the hospital, infecting it as certainly as the meme was infecting Linden and Dr. Zhiruo? What would that look like? How would I tell?

What would its nature and purpose be? Why would it be worth it? What sort of motive would allow for it? How would such a thing operate, and how could it keep its existence secret, or even secret-ish?

What was behind all the things Sally could not admit to any official knowledge of?

I sighed deeply, realizing that I could at least feel the air stretch my lungs when I drew enough breath in. That was reassuring: if I could feel my body I probably wasn't dealing with locked-in syndrome or anything else similarly daunting.

Well, I wasn't going to find out the answers stuck in here, wherever here was, and that was for sure. I had, I was certain, colleagues on the outside working to rescue me—exactly as I would have been working if things had been reversed.

That led me to wonder what my physical situation might be. Was I still stuck inside the walker, or had someone managed to extract Calliope and me? Was I physically encased in a barrier of some sort that prevented my fox from reaching into the senso? Or was my fox disconnected or damaged somehow?

I didn't think I was experiencing what Afar's crew had, on consideration. Their brain scans (what passed for brain scans, with their species: piezoelectric patterns in any case) hadn't shown conscious activity, and I certainly felt conscious enough. And the breathing proved I was aware of my physical body, even if it didn't hurt.

Had Cheeirilaq come along and spun me into a giant, protective cocoon?

That was a strangely satisfying image. Though as far as I knew, its species didn't spin cocoons for each other. They didn't do much for each other, except mate occasionally and refrain from eating one another—these diar.

How had it never occurred to me before that it was unusual for a member of a species with so little commensal instinct, like Rilriltok, to choose a career as a healer? I mean, it was a male, and obviously had the skills to placate hungry females at mating time, and most of its patients were frozen when it got them—

But my old friend was a real weirdo, it seemed.

I wondered if that insight came from me, or from one of the several ayatanas that were still making all my limbs feel like they were shaped weird.

The lack of pain was having an effect on my cognition. I kept having ideas. But I was having so many ideas, I was also having a hard time concentrating. The theorizing was interesting, but I was giddy and free-associating in exactly the sort of way that wasn't helpful for concentrating on getting myself *out*.

So. Set the theorizing aside for a time and collect some data. What were the instruments available to me?

Right now, they were limited to the interface between my exo . . . and whatever was on the other side of my exo. A hardsuit, presumably, unless that had been removed?

Status check told me that the exo was functioning optimally, and so was my fox. The fox was integrating with the exo, which answered my earlier question about damage to the fox's transmission capability. The fox's uplink was working. So my lack of senso connection meant that it was being blocked by something.

Right. A physical block, or a software block?

Come back to that.

The exo's battery was near full charge.

I'd replaced it before I went to try to talk Calliope down. That it was still charged told me that either it had been replaced again (unlikely), I was getting a charge from somewhere (possible), or that it hadn't been very long and I hadn't moved very much since I plugged it in (optimal).

Back to the question of the uplink. I had means at my disposal to test that. When—if—I found the problem, would I also have means at my disposal to repair it?

Wait and see, Jens, wait and see.

To say that I *felt* my way around the exo is an inexpert metaphor, but I couldn't think of a better one. I stretched out no groping fingers, even in my imagination. What I did was to methodically consider and categorize the—I guess one could call them sensations, after a fashion—the tickles of data, however muted, from where my exo made contact with what was on the other side of my exo.

It wasn't my hardsuit.

That was a horrifying realization. And if I had been rescued and brought inside the hospital and was somehow mostly unable to feel my body—and my uplink was only partially functioning—they would have taken the hardsuit off entirely.

But the actuator core was still attached to my chest. It was merely retracted completely.

I have a lot of expertise with my adaptive devices. My extensive experience and my skill at fixing and maintaining them come in handy in the field. And I still needed to know what I was in, if it wasn't my hardsuit. I was breathing, and I wasn't dead, so whatever that falling sensation had been it hadn't shoved me out the walker's door into space—and if I was still inside the walker, the door was not still ajar.

There was something around me, a kind of fabric or film or very smooth metal.

I lay in the dark and quiet and talked to my exo. It didn't talk back except in its usual stock phrases—it was only a machine, after all, not a shipmind—but people talk to their equipment all the time. It makes us feel more connected and in control when we can personalize our things.

There's a thing with pain. Memory has a somatic component. Experiencing a kind of pain can bring back a host of related associations. Even witnessing an injury—or hearing somebody describe an injury—provokes powerful recollections.

That's why we all have the uncontrollable—and annoying—habit of regaling our freshly injured friends with tales of the times we whacked our thumb with a hammer, too, though so much worse, obviously.

My current lack of pain was making it harder for me to hack my way around my exo. I don't mean any kind of juvenile justifications about how I need my pain, or that it's good for people to suffer. What builds character is encouragement to persist in the face of adversity, not needless discomfort. That uses up executive function and doesn't help anybody accomplish anything.

So, I had my exo. That was excellent and useful news. I had contact with my exo. Even better.

Fatigue levels in excess of safe values, my exo replied, when I pinged it. *Pain levels optimal.*

You tell 'em, exo.

Could I move it?

I could not. A little experimentation proved that I couldn't so much as twitch it. Nor could I push it around manually by moving my body inside it. It was locked in position. I did discover that I could, isometrically, flex *against* it, but the scaffolding of the exo itself did not budge. I might have been able to bruise myself against the device, but I couldn't shift it.

Honestly, my chances of bruising myself against the filigree cage that supported my body were pretty slim. It was designed to be flexible, safe, and comfortable: constructed of resilient, durable, breathable materials that lay flat against my skin so it could be worn for diar at a time and only removed for cleaning.

It was specially manufactured to be difficult to injure myself on. If it hadn't been, it would have worn sores all over me in the course of use. I'm not sure what I thought I might be proving by trying to circumvent its safety features.

The status indicators in my fox told me that my exo wasn't burned out. My ability to communicate with it was not impaired. I just didn't seem able to make it budge, either through its usual adaptive response to my own micromovements or through the brute force method of direct commands from my fox.

Breathe, Jens. Don't panic.

Panic never helped anybody in a self-rescue situation get out alive.

The exo wasn't damaged. Also: it couldn't be damaged because I needed it to get me out of here.

It did have a safety interlock to hold me on my feet when the batteries failed—and which I could use intentionally to lock portions of the frame—but that was only engaged in normal mode. It should have allowed me to move—albeit painfully—under my own power rather than resisting me.

Item: I had caught a glimpse of a tendril of the machine inside the craboid's structure before I lost consciousness—or contact with the outside world, if that was what I had lost.

Conclusion: the meme (or the machine, if there was any functional difference between the two) had hacked my exo.

Solution: hack it back.

This would not have been possible if I'd been dealing with any other piece of equipment in the galaxy. I don't think it would, anyway, though desperation can lend one a surprising amount of ingenuity. But, as I have mentioned, there was one single piece of equipment in the universe on which I was the leading authority.

I was wearing it, and right this instant it was seriously pissing me off.

Sheer cussedness doesn't actually make luck break in your favor, and I know that. But sometimes cussedness can keep you in the game long enough for luck to break. And it seems to me that occasionally you can't get results until you lose your temper with an object.

This was not, I am sorry to say, one of those times. My exo did not fix itself simply because I got extremely cross with it. Maybe the clinical efficiency of my rage was hampered by my current inability to carry out percussive maintenance on the fucking thing.

I guessed I was going to have to outsmart it, then.

I hated to purge the system and do a factory reset, because I've been years tuning this thing. If I had to, I would, however. It was a final option, and one I clung to so I'd have the courage and concentration to try other things.

But—wait. *Wait.*

The excitement of epiphany swallowed me until I tuned my adrenaline down. If I was wrong, I didn't want to be crushingly disappointed.

I'm not going to pretend I knew the code. Not line by line. I certainly didn't have it memorized.

What I did have was an archived, firewalled copy, however. And the ability to write a script to go through it line by exacting line, compare it to the active code running my exo, and look for things that didn't match.

It took a subjective eternity, but—there. Yes. The reactivity to my movements had been set to zero. So basically, no matter how hard I pushed against it, the exo wouldn't feel my attempts to move it as any more significant than—than my pulse. Or the beating of my breath. And it would shrug off direct commands through my fox as if they did not exist.

Clever little bastards, whoever wrote the exploit. Clever little bastards indeed.

Even cleverer, if they hadn't written it exclusively for me. I supposed the same code would work on a hardsuit—

The time for theorizing had passed. Now it was time to get the hell out of here.

I ran a system check on the hardsuit actuator, using my exo to backdoor into its operating system. The actuator seemed to think it was functional, and I didn't have a way to check. So here I was, right back where I had been when I was staring at the override beside the on-call room door and wondering if I was going to die if I triggered it.

Well, there was only one way to find out.

I inserted the code fixes, and then I slapped my hand up fast. As fast as I had ever moved it. I didn't know if whoever had seized control of my exo was monitoring the situation, ready to fight me street by street—servo by servo—so I didn't test that the exo was responding before I went. I just went.

If I failed, that would be enough test.

My hand punched out. Harder than I had anticipated, but it worked out. Whatever was encasing me tore . . . sharp-edged . . . no, shattered. Then the clenched fist, my own clenched fist, pounded down on my chest.

It hurt. It hurt as if I had punched myself intentionally, and my hand hurt where I'd torn through the stuff I couldn't see. The pain didn't feel so bad. I could pretend I'd hit myself as a form of self-injury, to provoke the kind of pain that makes you focus on *right here right now* and stop ideating.

It was a good thing it did make me focus, because even so that punch wasn't enough to break through.

In primitive medicine before adrenaline injections, before electric shock, before open-heart massage, before nanoelectrical stimulus, humans in desperation used to treat heart failure—in humans, in horses, in dogs—with a series of punches or kicks in the chest.

It worked rarely. Vanishingly rarely. But any chance is better than none.

I wasn't trying to kick-start a failed heart this time. I was trying to break a wall.

I didn't know if I could make my hand move again. But I did. Somehow I did. And I made it move harder, this time.

This time, several things cracked under the blow. One of them was my sternum. *That* pain got through to my nervous system, all right, albeit briefly. Then it was gone again, along with the sting of my cut hands, leaving a vague ghost like yesterdia's bruise. But I knew what I'd felt.

It's just pain. Pain alone cannot stop you from doing things. What stops you from doing things is injury, disability . . . and being tired. Because pain can make you tired, if it goes on for a long time. Because that pain is not a warning that you are being hurt. It's just pain. All it can do is make things harder than they need to be.

This wasn't the kind of pain that makes me tired. This was the kind of pain that makes me angry. And what I felt on the other side of it filled me with furious satisfaction.

It was the whispery sensation of the hardsuit unfolding across my exo, and my skin.

That also hurt. It had to push between me and the thing wrapped around me. I thought it probably scraped my skin off in a couple of places, and might have done worse if the exo hadn't protected me somewhat. That was okay. Hardsuits are designed to do that. You can grow somebody new skin, fingers, noses. Feet and hands if you have to.

But even modern medicine hasn't figured out how to bring back somebody who's been breathing vacuum for more than about thirty seconds or so.

Funny how long it took me—how old I was when I realized that if something didn't work, you could change it. You didn't just have to live with the problem, work around it. You could adapt, improvise. *And* overcome. You could take steps to make a thing better.

Nothing about my childhood encouraged me to develop agency or a sense that I could make the galaxy a better place, repair what was broken, get out my tools. Nothing told me that things could be improved. Nothing encouraged me to effect change.

Well, I was effecting it now.

Remember what I said about the lack of pain clearing my head out? As I struggled, the systers in my head more or less went silent. In the absence of their opinions and demands, I realized that I had most of the information I needed to figure out who was behind the sabotage attempts. I could see the edge of the answer, and the little pattern-matching neurons in my brain were so happy with their success that I felt a kind of faith in the emergent idea. That belief made me doubt my realization rather than confirming it, because our brains really love to find those patterns.

But I was suddenly full of ideas regarding what the sabotage was about, and where Afar had come from, and why *Big Rock Candy Mountain* had been where it had been. I knew. Or I suspected, anyway. At least, I knew who to ask for proof, and where to go for more information.

The answer wasn't really a clear shape in my head yet. More of a murky outline. But I hated what I suspected thoroughly enough to really hope that I was wrong.

It had to be somebody with access to Sally, and with access to Sally's personality core. I'd been convinced it couldn't have been Sally's crew. Now I was less convinced. And it had to have been somebody who could have gotten hold of the gravity generator technology, so that Helen could integrate it into her amorphous machine—and then burn it out again.

I was very concerned, based on something he'd let slip, that that might mean the person I was looking for was Tsosie.

Maybe putting Afar and his crew into comas had been a mistake, and not more ruthlessness. I really, really hoped so. I hoped the people who had been hurt or who had died . . . I hoped that had been an accident.

Maybe it had been. But the saboteurs hadn't stopped after the first attempt.

I burst through the containing fabric—whatever it was—like I was tearing myself from a chrysalis . . . except nothing had actually changed. It was only me, same as I had always been, battered a bit but not remade in any better form, struggling in the dark.

My suit lights came up, and I could see again as I shredded loops and swags of iridescent, oily-looking material that flowed apart into bulky particles and flowed together again. I'd seen that stuff before. The machine, like graphite powder with a malevolent will. Some of those shards were like broken glass, around the edges. I'd broken some of the bots. But I was wearing armor now.

There, there was the hatchway. It was sealed; I was inside the walker. I dragged myself toward it through the drifting particles.

My glove landed on something human.

I dragged Calliope out of the mass by her ankle. Straps restrained her; I cut them. Her suit was still sealed. She was coming with me if I had to—

Blow a hole in the shell of the walker?

Concussions in small spaces are a bad idea unless those spaces contain vacuum. I had a Judiciary emergency pack. It had a couple of demo charges in it, along with the other essentials (like the flags and the rescue hook knife). But I wasn't sure those could penetrate the weird glassy shell of the machine, even working from the inside out.

It didn't come to that. On the *inside*, the walker had a big shiny override button right beside the hatch.

Because I had Calliope in my arms by then, I smashed it with my heel. I shoved us both at the irising hatch before it was half-open, struggling through fatigue and pain as thick as sloshing tendrils of the machine.

To the door, and through the door. Drifting out the other side. Get a line on something, don't go sailing off into space to suffocate—

I had a brief glimpse of Cheeirilaq throwing a line of silk around us as I failed to get my own tackle deployed.

Then I fainted.

CHAPTER 22

WHEN I BLINKED AWAKE, I WAS LOOKING INTO A distorting mirror. My eyes seemed huge, brown and wide, their hazel-gold flecks and paler striations emphasized. My nose was too narrow. My lips seemed stretched and strange, and the shape of my chin was too pointed.

The goblin version of my face jerked back, shrinking as it fled. I blinked at Helen.

Helen did not blink back.

"I'm so happy that you're back!" she blurted.

I remembered everything I'd figured out right before I got myself knocked out again and flinched. I needed to make sure I was right before I accused anybody.

I said, "How long was I gone?"

Helen settled her heels and folded her arms under the molded bosom. "Long enough."

You never come back from a trip to good news. Just never.

"Calliope?" I asked.

Under sedation. Rilriltok's familiar buzz.

I looked around. Head turned smoothly, no more than the usual amount of pain. I propped myself on my elbows and discovered that I was in a trauma treatment room. "Hey. The gravity is working."

"Mechanical got spin back about a standard ago," she agreed. "It was an impressive engineering accomplishment, spinning up without further disordering all the environments."

"I bet." I stretched, curling my toes. Could be worse. "What happened to the quarantine?"

I hadn't been aware that a person like Helen had the ability to generate such dire laughter. "That ship has lifted."

I noticed O'Mara in the treatment room, standing a little behind Helen. And there was Rilriltok, hovering over their left shoulder.

The breeze of its wings was exceptionally pleasant.

I said, "Somebody please get me a drink."

O'Mara looked at me. It was obvious, I suppose, that I didn't mean club soda and lime.

Dr. Jens! Rilriltok was mad at me, because it called me *Doctor* rather than *Friend. Far be it from this individual to question the medical judgments of an esteemed colleague, but I really think—*

It must have taken an extraordinarily large bolus of courage for the little Rashaqin to stand up to me like that. Conflict avoidance was the hallmark of its species and sex. I felt terrible for it when O'Mara interrupted, holding out a flask I hadn't known they carried.

It had a Judiciary seal on it. I knew it had been given to them as a retirement gift, because I owned one like it. I didn't carry my keepsake in my pocket, however.

When I first reached for it I reached too fast, too far—a lunge—as my exo overcompensated. I almost knocked the flask to the floor. Fortunately, it was closed, and O'Mara caught it before it dented on the deck. Good reflexes for an old person.

Ha. I wondered what they say about me. The gravity definitely seemed to be working again, anyway. And so did my exo's reflexes.

I closed aching fingers around the flask. My exoskeleton clicked faintly against the metal. The sound startled me, but at least my grip was firm by then.

"Medicinal purposes," said I.

"Medicinal purposes," they agreed.

To my shipmates, I thought. *Please don't let any of them be criminals.* I unscrewed the lid and drank, wiping my lips after.

Tequila.

I obviously hadn't eaten anything in quite some time, because the warmth of the liquor raced through me. Capillary flush scorched my face; at least I had the comfort that my complexion would hide it. Though I supposed O'Mara thinking I was a cheap drunk was the least of my worries.

I handed the flask back. "You were obviously expecting me. Medical coma?"

"Just a nice nap while we fused your sternum for you," O'Mara said. My hand didn't sting, which told me they'd fixed the holes in my skin, also. "Your own crew insisted on operating on you. I think you're going to be fine."

They were Sally's crew, not mine—not as long as I was seconded to O'Mara and Core General. That made me feel almost weepily touched by their loyalty.

Probably a sure sign that my brain chemicals needed a nudge, but I didn't have the energy to put myself out even that much. Which was another downvote on my chemistry, come to think of it. I wondered where that loyalty would be when I pursued what I thought I knew.

Tears prickled my eye-corners.

Fine. Fine! I tuned myself, and instantly felt better. There were no resources to waste by not efficiently fixing small problems.

"Am I cleared to return to duty?"

Rilriltok buzzed grumpily.

"You're not even cleared to sit up in bed, Jens. Not that we have the time to worry about that now." O'Mara held out a hand. "Alley-oop. You can have a quick shower—which you badly need, by the way—and then we have to go talk to Starlight."

You could have waited for us to get you out, said Rilriltok reasonably.

"Could I have?"

It sighed. *No. I suppose you couldn't have.*

"Hey," I said suddenly. "Translation is working! Is Linden back online?"

O'Mara and Helen looked at each other. Rilriltok bobbed a little lower in the air.

"After a fashion," O'Mara said. "You know what we said about quarantine? Come on, shake a tentacle. We need to move, and it'll be faster to demonstrate than explain."

I badly needed to have a conversation with someone. But I badly needed to have it in private. And I didn't think I could get rid of O'Mara until I ran this errand.

The shower, hydration, and a couple of stimulant tabs helped clear the nebulas from around my thoughts, though not as effectively as coffee would have. And not that my resultant ideas precisely blazed with the clarity of newborn stars. I pulled on scrubs and a lab coat and liberated a fresh hardsuit actuator from a locker on my way out of the bathroom. Possibly I was never going to let myself be more than a meter away from one again under any circumstances.

In the process of getting cleaned up and dressed, I was reminded that my exo was still overcompensating and twitchy. I knocked over toiletries three times, and the stack of clean clothes twice. (The second time it was more of a heap of clean clothes, really, because I hadn't bothered to refold something I was only going to put right on.) They still had that freshly printed smell, which did as much as any amount of tuning to make me feel like maybe we could fix our problems.

The fact that translation was working again made the several conflicting ayatanas wrestling in my head feel much more like a hardship than a sensible precaution. So I told O'Mara that we were stopping on the way to get them pulled. He grumbled about time constraints, but this time Rilriltok came down on the side of preserving my mental health, so I prevailed.

My scalp still tingled slightly from the magnetic manipulation of having my fox vacuumed. It took a little more juice than when Linden used magnetic resonance to shoot street signs and danger signals right into our heads, but not that much more. I wasn't used to having several ayatanas purged at once, was all.

When that was done and I stood up, I still felt wrongish. My body was the wrong shape and my head was strangely empty. I didn't want to show it, though. The exo would compensate for me until the feeling wore off.

I was still telling myself that as I wobbled stiff-legged down the corridor. Rilriltok had gone back to work by then, but Helen accompanied O'Mara and me.

"I feel," O'Mara said, as I caught myself with one hand before I lurched into a corridor wall, "as if you are making some unwise life choices."

"You said we were in a hurry."

They looked at me.

I sighed. "It's only my exo."

"Damaged?"

"No." I lurched the other way. "I had to overclock the microservos to get loose. It's going to take me a week to get them calibrated and balanced again."

At least a week. Probably four. But I thought O'Mara would find unnecessary precision upsetting right then.

The lifts still weren't running. I supposed that would have been entirely too much convenience. Having translation back was such a relief that I didn't complain, though. And because we were going to see Starlight, we didn't even have to leave the main oxygen hab sectors. Though that didn't remove all the annoyances.

"I cannot wait," O'Mara said, as we climbed outward and down and got heavier along the way, "until we have the artificial gravity working."

I concentrated on not tripping on the stairs, as my weight increased with each footfall.

"Tell me about Linden," I said. I could use the distraction.

O'Mara grunted like a big, grumpy dog. "We've got contact. She hasn't managed to purge the meme, but she's still fighting it. Translation is running through main engineering, though—they managed to get that back before they spun us up again."

So everybody had had some warning about the change in acceleration.

This time.

I think I gasped audibly when I saw Starlight, because Helen put her warm metal hand on my shoulder.

I've said it before, but: You can't evacuate a hospital. Not one this size, with patients with this many needs, some of whom are too fragile to transport without killing. And yet . . . I'm not proud to say it, but one look at the state of our enormous, sessile oxygen sector administrator made me want to turn tail and run.

I could see why O'Mara and company had decided that quarantine, at least within the hospital, was pointless now.

When I was little I knew what the world was. It was a place without pity. A terrible place. A place of loss. A place where no one ever got to keep anything. Where things just hurt all the time, and there was no respite. And very few people took your pain seriously.

I'm older now, and I know that this view, while true, is incomplete and immature. Because a thing is ephemeral doesn't mean that it is worthless. Rather it makes it more part of the world.

Looking at Starlight, looking up at their translucent leaves, windowpaned in the bright Corelight, I was plunged right back to that place in childhood where everything was futile and there was no point in anything. All my protocols, all my training: I had no idea what to do.

The great pattern of leaves stretched over me, layered and moving as before. But they didn't rustle; they clattered. They *rattled*, where one edge contacted another. They rang like crystal. They *chimed*.

The paler unpigmented windows in the leaves were no longer merely translucent. They were actual windows—clear as glass. They *were* glass . . . or rather crystal, based on the sound they made and the rainbows they cast over everything.

Starlight didn't show . . . wires, or circuits, or anything else growing along their stems. There were none of those signifiers that people use to symbolize the interface of technology and nature, or whatever.

But the tree was clearly infected, and cell by cell, portions of their structure were being replaced with silicon.

I put a hand out for balance. If it hadn't been for my exo, I might have sat down. Helen still, with programmed concern, steadied me. She'd been ready. I wondered what it was to be an AI programmed entirely for emotional labor. For taking care of humans and our needs.

It sounded really boring, and I wanted to do something to take care of Helen in return. But her face was featureless, expressionless. How could you even tell what she needed?

How could you tell if she even had any needs?

That was, I supposed, the point. That was why she'd been built. Helen would never make you feel you needed to do anything for her.

I drew a breath, and spoke to my administrator, the plant that seemed to be turning into computronium in front of me. "Hello, Starlight. Are you in discomfort?"

[Thank you, Doctor,] they replied, translated tones infused with humor. [Although it feels a little strange, it's not what we would call painful. It's more a sense of stiffness and pressure. But you are not here to diagnose us.]

"Do you mind if I ask . . . what's causing this condition?"

[Afar's crew were strangely affected . . . their foxes re-etched by the malignant code. We think that perhaps . . . it is trying to affect us in similar ways. Remake us. Rewrite us into something like its microbots.]

"Is there—are you being treated?"

The tree clinked softly. [With support, our immune system is slowing the progress of the infection. And the longer we hold it off, the more time others have to solve the problem before it affects the rest of the hospital.]

"It will affect the rest of the hospital," Helen said. "It's designed to want more."

I looked from her to Starlight. "I'm here to talk about the saboteurs, I suppose."

[What have you discovered?]

If Helen was here, I could assume that O'Mara and Starlight had decided she was an interested party or a victim, and not part of the problem. Her hand was comfortingly heavy on my elbow where she steadied me.

"Go ahead," O'Mara said.

I nodded. "I had a lot of time to think in there." I waved a hand vaguely. They would know I meant the machine.

Starlight rustled—chimed—assent.

"This was all a conspiracy. It had to be. But it's an incomprehensible conspiracy. Why would anybody go to such insane lengths to damage a *hospital*? And an ambulance ship? And to draw attention to the fact that they were damaging it?"

"What do you mean?" asked O'Mara.

I said, "This feels like—there's a word—like *monkey-wrenching* to me. Sabotage in order to draw attention to a problem, or to stop a process you find unethical. Or to stop a process in a manner that injures an enemy in a war."

[We had not heard that term before,] Starlight said, [but we are familiar with the concept.]

I craned down to look through the floor to Starlight's lattice of branches, catching all that Corelight. "Why did you stay in space? Didn't you want to reproduce? Have a family?"

It occurred to me too late that maybe that was a rude question where they came from. And that I *definitely* should have asked permission.

[We're claustrophobic,] they replied.

"Are you . . . teasing me?"

Trees can't smile, but this one seemed to be trying. [We're claustrophobic,] they said again. [We couldn't stand the idea, after centians in space, of being trapped in the earth forever, unmoving. Unable to see out of a gravity well. We couldn't bear it. No amount of adjusting our chemistry helped to reconcile us. We were fortunate to find this place.

[Besides, if we had children, we would have to think about their inheritance, and we're morally opposed.]

"There isn't any inheritance," I said. "That's barbaric. This is the Synarche. There's nothing to inherit. You're not allowed to hoard resources when they could be used bettering life for everyone."

[Oh, child,] Starlight said. [Of course there is inheritance. Some of our inheritances are personal; some are a commonwealth. Skills and competencies learned from parents are an inheritance. Not having to care about taking risks because you know somebody will be there to rescue you is an inheritance. Feeling safe is an inheritance.]

That last one hit me like a knife.

I said, "This hospital is what I want my legacy to be. What if we lose it all?"

I was asking a sick plant for emotional labor so that I could find the courage to ask them things I knew would hurt them greatly. But I was a sick mammal, so I suppose it evened out.

Starlight was correct. We cannot isolate ourselves from systems, have no impact, change nothing as we pass. We alter the world by observing it.

The best we can do is not pretend that we don't belong to a system; it's to accept that we do, and try to be fair about using it. To keep it from exploiting the weakest.

I had been the weakest, once. But I wasn't now, and I was here to do what I could.

[Things have been dire in the universe before,] the old tree said. [And mostly life has made it through. Even if we lose biomass.]

I studied the back of my hand. "And what about the ones that don't?"

[The ones that don't?]

"Make it through. Species, planets. Biospheres. Individuals. Don't they matter?"

Around me, a seemingly transfinite number of leaves chimed in a space without a wind. [Naturally they matter. But mattering doesn't improve their chances of survival in any meaningful way. We can try to protect them ourselves. And we can try to mitigate the damage when things go wrong.]

"And that's why you administrate a hospital."

[Not just any hospital.] I could have imagined that the tree spoke smugly. [It's the perfect environment for us.]

I took a breath. Now, or cowardice. "Since you administrate this hospital, you must have the answers to some questions that are really bothering me."

There was a silence.

O'Mara let a held breath out on a word. The word was my name.

I did not permit myself to hear them.

"Starlight," I asked, "what's in the private ward?"

This silence was shorter than I expected. They answered crisply, [There are confidentiality agreements in place.]

"Confidentiality agreements? You can't even tell me what the purpose of the ward is?"

[It's for the treatment of private patients.]

"Wealthy patients?"

The tree didn't argue.

"What kind of treatments do they get in there that we can't get out here?" I asked. "Everything we offer here is state-of-the-art, the finest treatment technology can design."

[Patient confidentiality agreements preclude my answering.]

Well, at least that was an answer that sounded legitimate. Even if something nameless deep inside me—a hunch, an intuition—was convinced that it was bullshit.

They could have told me that the accommodations in there were more private, more luxurious. They could have fed me a line about staff ratios.

Their choice not to do so suggested perhaps they wanted me to keep asking.

"Starlight."

[We cannot tell you,] they said.

"O'Mara?" I turned and looked them in the eye. It was a relief to be talking to something *with* eyes, and only two of them, placed in the human-standard arrangement on a head.

I convicted myself of temporary xenophobia and moved on. The relief was short-lived, anyway, because O'Mara's expressions were easy to read. They had hung a mask of Judiciary impassiveness over them, but the tightness at the corners of their mouth and eyes betrayed tension and controlled anger.

I didn't think they were angry with me.

Sometimes, regulating the stuff that falls out of my mouth is not my best skill. In a tone of absolute horror, I said, "Please tell me that you're not behind the sabotage."

"No!" O'Mara exploded. "What do you take me for?"

I held up a hand, palm toward them, and after a deep breath or two we each got ourselves under control. "I had to ask."

They nodded tightly and either used some kind of biofeedback trick, willed themselves to calm down, or tuned, because I saw their shoulders relaxing. It was like watching somebody in pain release the bracing while knowing that the pain hadn't gone away, a phenomenon I was unfortunately familiar with.

They were still angry, but I still didn't think they were angry with me.

"Okay," I said. "You won't—can't?—give me a direct order, but you want me to uncover something. And you can't tell me what it is. And that's why you asked me to investigate the sabotage in the first place."

They did not answer.

I said, "You're inhibited from talking about it, aren't you? A privacy block? Because it's technically a matter of patient care?"

O'Mara glanced down at the canopy of the Administree. "Told you she was sharp."

The tree laughed like crystal wind chimes. The sound crawled along my nerves and the nape of my neck in an unpleasant frisson.

"Right," I said. "So I take the risk if it comes out. The buck stops here."

"Maybe you get the glory if your heroism is recognized," Helen said dreamily.

I stared at her. I'd almost forgotten she was there, she had been standing so silently in the background.

In my defense, O'Mara stared at her, too.

I pointed at Starlight's silicon-edged leaves. "What about that? Helen's machine is eating the hospital from the inside out? That's kind of important!"

"We're working on that," O'Mara said. "You have your own job. You can't do everything."

Be nice if they'd tell me what the job was. But if they were forbidden to by a formal confidentiality stricture, it was quite possible they literally *couldn't* talk about it. Which would . . . explain some things. Such as: why they had led me by the nose to this information, in a manner where I could plausibly have found it out on my own. . . .

I shook my head. "I guess I had better figure out what you want from me, then. But don't blame me if I get it wrong."

O'Mara drawled in a particular dry tone when they were deadpanning. They drawled now. "Figure the odds."

"I'm not that good of a handicapper," I said.

CHAPTER 23

I WASN'T WELL YET, THOUGH I WAS BETTER. AND ALL THIS adrenaline, confusion, and anger weren't doing my healing process any favors. Pain and weakness throbbed through my body. Breathing was a chore. But I wasn't going back to a treatment room or an on-call bunk. I needed real, comfortable, uninterrupted rest in my own quarters, even if I had to walk halfway around the hab ring to get there with the lifts not running.

But once I arrived, undressed, and lay down in bed, I couldn't turn off.

I could have tuned myself into sleep, but I had an idea that if I stared into space and tried not to think about the things that were currently bothering me, I might be giving my subconscious time to work on the problem. I spent the time writing a letter to my daughter. I didn't know if a plain text file would be safe to send, but if even those were forbidden by the quarantine, I could write it, queue it, and it would go when it was safe to let it go.

For the first time I found myself wondering if I would still be alive when Rache received it. If she ever did.

If the Synarche didn't decide that it needed to push the whole hospital down the gravity slope into the Well, stored information and all, in order to prevent the thing that was infecting us from spreading. I'd probably be dead before that happened, though. I was reasonably certain that the Synarche would wait until we were cold—until there were no signs of life from Core General—before disposing of the corpses.

If by some mischance I was not dead at that point, I'd have plenty of time to contemplate the slide into nothingness. Time dilation meant that the subjective eternity of falling into a black hole would take long enough that there was no chance I'd be alive to enjoy being spaghettified. Sort of a pity, from the point of view of science, but I found I didn't mind at all.

These were not thoughts I put in the letter to my kid.

When I had finished it, I lay in the dark once more and once more talked quietly with my exo about how scared I was and how I didn't know what to do.

It still didn't answer. It was still just a machine. I could have shared with Sally. She remained trapped in dock, despite having taken on consumables and gotten sterilized for her next trip out. Waiting for the call. If quarantine was ever lifted, she could be away in instants.

If quarantine was never lifted, she would die here, too. And it would take her a lot longer to die than it would the meatminds. Perhaps it wasn't such a blessing that she hadn't gotten infected.

Even if we all survived, if everybody else managed to fix the things that O'Mara had reminded me weren't *all* my job . . . unless something changed between now and then—well, if the situation on Core General was what I was coming to suspect it was, I probably wouldn't be going with Sally. I wouldn't be going with Sally, because I was going to get up in the morning, and I was going to do some more research and talk to a few more people.

And then I was going to take on the entirety of whatever was going on at Core General that wasn't publicly supposed to be. Knowing there would be professional repercussions for an action like that. So the idea of talking with my friend the shipmind, my colleague of a decan and more, made my chest ache with preemptive loneliness.

Core General was not what I had believed in. I was becoming increasingly convinced that there was something poisoned at its center, and the top administrators knew it, and they were physically prevented from telling. And that was why they were using me to reveal it. If I could collect the evidence, and figure out what was going on.

Losing my faith in Core felt like I was losing my family of origin all over again. Except worse, because I was closer to my crew than I had been to my family of origin. They'd died when I was too young to know them as *people*. I felt like I was losing my wife and daughter all over again.

It hurt.

And I realized that I was going to do it anyway.

People—human-type people, my own people—are constantly on a quest for an identity. Some lucky ones find the thing they want to be already inside themselves, or in a healthy family or community. Far too many of us, however, latch onto a simplified externality that seems to offer all the answers and invest our sense of meaning in it. We make some half-baked philosophy our driving force. Something we picked up reading the sort of novels and graphic stuff where first-person narrators opine bombastically about how the galaxy really works and what makes people really tick and How You Ought To Be.

Usually the ones steeped in atavistic machismo.

I was afraid I'd done the same thing, except what I had picked up and latched onto was a hospital employment manual.

I wanted to jump up and run around waving my arms and shouting accusations. I wanted to yell at O'Mara, in particular, until my throat hurt. I wanted to finish my investigation, when I was so close to the answers that I could taste them.

And a pretty foul taste it was, too. But I'd pushed my poor body as far as it was willing to go, and it would fail me if I tried to push it any farther. I had to rest, as frustrating as rest was. I had to care for myself so I could solve the bigger problem confronting *everyone*.

Well, I told myself. *I will deal with it in the morning.*

Well, I told myself. *The only way out is through.*

I tuned myself to calm and doziness, and finally drifted to sleep while looking at memories of Rache in my senso. Some of them were my memories, recorded when she was very small. Some were hers, that she had saved and sent to me. I slept hard, for not nearly long enough, and woke when my timer nudged my biochemistry. That left me in a better state of mind than a loud noise or an explosion.

It was the little things.

Rilriltok was on duty when I made my way down to the secure ward Judiciary used to see to the medical needs of prisoners, which is what Specialist Calliope Jones had become. It was something of a surprise to find it here, because if this were its shift—which it was not—I would have expected it to be in Cryo. Since that was where it worked, being a cryonicist and all.

It buzzed over, excited and seemingly happy to see me, isinglass wings a blur. The cheerful blue light on its gravity control belt blinked, though the hab wasn't producing much more than a third of a g. It was, I supposed, a sensible precaution, the way things had been going around here.

I reflexively put a hand on my own belt.

Friend Dr. Jens! The wind of its hovering stirred my hair. It tilted from side to side, like a bird cocking its head first one way, then the other, in order to examine me. *I'm pleased to see you appearing more well!*

"I'm pleased to be feeling better." Self-restraint is not my most defining characteristic, but I managed to hold in the next thing that wanted to burst from my tongue, which was *What are you doing here?*

After a moment's consideration, I went with a less potentially offensive construction. "What brings you to the prison ward?"

It zipped back and then forward on a horizontal plane, ending with its bulbous eyes and insectile mouthparts only centimeters from my nose.

Long experience lent me the composure to stand still and not take it amiss: this was Rilriltok expressing nearly unbearable excitement. Nevertheless, my amygdala was momentarily convinced that I was about to be eaten by a giant bug. It responded by dumping a lot of adrenaline into my system.

Whatever. It seemed likely I might need the stuff soon, so uncomfortable as it was, I decided to hang on to it.

I've been doing brain scans! Brain scans, and going over some other things! Look!

Almost before I could accept the connection, it was downloading a giant bolus of information into my fox. Quarantine protocols lifted or no, this seemed like dubious practice under the current situation, but it was too late for me to complain about hygiene now.

And then I was too busy being interested in the data it was showing me to worry.

I had firewalls in place anyway. I was sure it would be fine.

"What's that?"

I was experiencing Calliope Jones's post-repair brain. I'd seen scans before, but the earlier ones had not been resolved to this level of detail. I wasn't a neurologist or a cryonicist, but even a trauma doc like me could distinguish the pattern of remaining damage against healthy tissue. It was slowly being repaired, but the healthy tissue would take time to grow.

The injured portions of her brain looked like empty space, like a lightless nebula occluding the stars behind.

I wondered if the brain damage accounted for Calliope's apparently questionable executive function. "I'm impressed by how well she's compensated."

It's not just that, said Rilriltok. *Look here.*

I followed its attention as it guided me through the scan. Some big centralized injuries, fluid-filled sinuses that shouldn't be there. Well, not that big—but generally speaking any hole in your brain is surplus to requirements.

I think she had a fox, friend Jens. I think she had it removed surgically.

I stared at Rilriltok through the images projected on the screen of my mind. I probably looked like I'd been electrically stunned. "She's a modern person."

She pretty much has to be. You realize, I assume, that this means that what she believes . . . well, it could have been managed. She isn't necessarily lying, or hypocritical. Her breakdown and actions since the escape . . . Somebody might have managed her memories to make that all seem reasonable.

Of course it did. I'd speculated as much. Being confronted with the proof was still a little shattering.

Throughout history, certain doctors have done terrible things. It's still never nice to be reminded.

But! Had she *volunteered* for this?

Still want to talk to her?

"Even more than before."

I went in to see Calliope alone. I had some vague hope, I suppose, that she might be feeling grateful after I pried her out of her can opener carapace. At least she looked up when I came in. Her eyes focused, alert and oriented, and she looked wary but didn't otherwise seem unhappy with my presence.

Unfortunately, it had been necessary to restrain her to the bed. Soft restraints, and she had some latitude of movement. But not enough to make herself really comfortable.

"Hi." I sat down in the chair beside her.

At my conversational tone, the wariness deepened. "Hello, Dr. Jens."

"Are you going to make me sorry I rescued you?"

She flinched. "This wasn't supposed to happen. We didn't plan for anyone to come to harm."

"'We'?"

"It was just supposed to be an inconvenience. A . . . what's the opposite of a diversion? When you want to draw attention *to* something?"

"You overestimated the bystanders," I said coldly. "And underestimated the element of surprise. You knew where you were coming? You made this plan? You intentionally fooled us into believing you were a crew member on *Big Rock Candy Mountain*?"

Her face clouded. Not with anger, but with confusion. Cognitive load. "I—"

The lost look she gave me reminded me of Helen. Or of somebody with brain damage struggling to make sense of inputs that did not match the filters their damaged comprehension supplied.

People in those circumstances make up stories. Conflations. They build narratives to make things make sense. To make whatever they're thinking of doing seem normal.

They must be perfectly normal. The circumstances are what's odd.

Her silence lengthened. "What is your name?" I asked, very gently.

"Calliope Anne Jones."

"All right then." I caught myself steepling my fingers and made myself stop. Open body language. No evidence that I didn't believe her. "When and where were you born?"

She gave me all the right answers, all the same answers. Until I got to, "You said 'we' earlier. Who is 'we,' in this context?"

Then she froze. I saw her eyes seek upward, looking for the answer—or perhaps constructing it. I wouldn't be able to tell unless I looked at her brain function. Actually, *I* wouldn't be able to tell at all: neurology, as I mentioned, isn't my specialty.

"What do you know?" she asked sharply. "You're the one walking around with a box in your head. How many people are in there? How do you even know what you think?"

Something I had said had put her on the defensive, provoking this attack. It was sideways and irrational, referred aggression. But revealing nonetheless.

I said, "Rightminding, appropriately used, makes me more myself.

Not somebody else. Me, but less reactive. Less . . . whatever I was programmed to be and more what I choose to be." Then I said, "I don't think it was used appropriately on you."

"I . . ."

I waited. She strained against her bonds, as if she wanted to put her hand against her temple. As if her head hurt. As if it would not stop hurting. She looked down at her hands and laughed. "We have to stop meeting like this."

I reached out, gently, giving her time to refuse the contact or consent to it, and I stroked her hair. She leaned into the touch with a sigh that was half whimper.

It's not so much that doctors who develop crushes on their patients are idiots. It's natural to form an emotional bond with people when you are in a caregiving relationship with them. The ones who act on it are idiots, and unethical to boot.

But I wasn't going to act on it.

I know I should have tuned it out. Shut it down. Turned off the hormonal responses that filled me up with feel-good neurotransmitters. But it had been so long since I was attracted to anyone that I desperately wanted to *feel* it for a little while. And it might help me work with her.

I wouldn't do anything unethical. I would make no rash or unconsidered choices. I wouldn't take her side, betray my beliefs or my ethics, damage my career. I wasn't going to make a single bad decision because of Calliope Jones.

(I was aware that the jury was still out on whether going into the machine to get her back was a good decision or not, but as far as I was concerned, any decision that ended with a life saved and no rescuers lost was one that had worked out okay. Adapt, improvise, overcome, don't die yourself, and worry about the property damage later: that's my motto.)

Anyway, I was going to enjoy the sense of having a bond of sympathy with another human being. And possibly even use that sense to try to create an emotional connection with that other human being. In order to help me do my job, which was still—damn you, O'Mara—figuring out what was behind the sabotage.

I could feel a little bad about that, if I permitted myself. But I was not going to permit myself. I was going to do my damned job, even the parts that were likely to get O'Mara in trouble. I was going to do my job, and that was all.

I've always wanted to save people. Maybe because nobody saved me. (Nobody could have saved me: my youth being hard was nobody's fault but the universe's, for not giving a damn, and society's, for not being perfectly able to maintain supply chains to the back end of beyond.) But it's always been important to me—dramatically important—to make as many people safe as possible. Maybe it made me feel like I was justifying my existence. Doing something worthwhile with my time.

I wanted to save Calliope, too.

I stroked her hair again. "Hey."

She didn't look at me. That was okay, because she was listening. I knew she had to be listening.

"What were you digging for, Calliope? What were you fighting so hard to reach and destroy?"

"X marks the spot." Her eyes flickered at me. "The damned machine was supposed to work better."

"This hospital is pretty sturdy," I agreed. "I'm sure it's better built than they expected. Who are they, Calliope? Who told you the machine could punch through our hull?"

She drew in a deep breath and held it. I took my hand off her shoulder and folded it into my lap with the other one. I leaned in slightly, maintaining the connection, but giving her space as well.

"Calliope?"

"You tied me up," she said suddenly. "Why am I tied up? Help! Nurse!"

She tugged her bonds as if she had just noticed and was testing them. "Why am I in jail?"

"You're not in jail," I said. I strained myself to remember history. They used to lock people up for crimes, sometimes for life, I knew. Sometimes because they couldn't safely be released, and sometimes for revenge or as a form of social control. Political prisoners. Calliope had . . . two sets of memories in her. One, whatever she knew from being a modern person. The other, whatever had been trained into her about being an archaic person, before the fox that must have been used to do it was removed. "You're in a secure ward. You have an illness, an antisocial pathology, and you have a brain injury. We're not going to punish you for that. It's not a moral failing."

She laughed as if I had said something cruel. "You're going to brainwash me."

I wanted to draw back. I made myself hold still. "We're going to offer you a chance to be treated, if you decide that's what you want."

Sweetheart, brainwash you? Somebody already did that.

She thrashed her head violently side to side. "Everybody here is complicit!" she shouted. "Everybody here needs to be exposed!"

There was a moment when I almost put my hands up in the air and walked away, shouting, *You won't let me help you and nothing I will do will change anything.*

Almost.

Cynicism is useful. It's like calluses: it helps you get through life without constantly finding your tender bits worn raw by everything in the world that is wrong. It helps you choose your battles.

But cynicism is also toxic sometimes, because it tells you that nothing can be changed. Nothing can be fixed or bettered. Cynicism *also* becomes a means of social control. A reinforcement of learned helplessness.

Learned helplessness is something I am always struggling to unlearn.

"You said you were trying to create a scandal," I reminded her. "I don't know what it is that you think I'm complicit in."

She stopped tugging at her restraints—they were soft, and didn't tighten, but they also didn't stretch very much—and looked up at me. Her mouth thinned.

"They're using people for parts," she said. "Poor people. They kidnap people and cut them up. Go ahead and look if you don't believe me."

I wanted to jump out of my chair and lurch backward, away from the horror of her allegation. The theory was ridiculous on the face of it: kidnapping people wasn't cost-efficient when you could grow whatever you needed from stem cells and not worry about rejection, for crying out loud.

My mouth came open to deny it—

But she believed it, obviously. Which I guessed meant somebody had programmed that idea into her.

"I'll look into it." I kept my voice gentle. This wasn't about me and if I was shocked or irritated. This was about saving the hospital . . . and finding out the truth. Exposing what was going on in the private ward.

What if the truth destroyed the hospital, as Calliope had suggested it might? What if—

If the truth destroyed it, it needed to go. I didn't believe that was likely, anyway. What she was suggesting was ridiculous.

There were plenty of other medically unethical possibilities out there without "kidnapping people for parts" being one of them. Although it was the kind of story that could motivate the medically uniformed.

Some people used to avoid registering as organ donors because they were afraid doctors would let them die in order to harvest their bodies. It didn't happen, but people in marginalized groups have always had good reason to be suspicious of the medical establishment taking advantage of and experimenting on them. Informed consent rules did not, alas, grow up out of nowhere, or because they were not needed.

I was struggling with two conflicting narratives. My own, where Core General was a place of refuge . . . and the one I was increasingly coming to believe, where it had a dark underside that people I'd trusted were guiding me to find and reveal.

She must have read the incredulity in my face or voice, because she said, "Don't condescend to me."

"Calliope—"

"You're trying to trick me. You think I'm crazy. You'll put a box in my brain and make me like it." The flatness and confusion of her tone reminded me of Helen, when Helen's cycles were caught in a loop. Like a flat spin in atmosphere.

Like me, Calliope was struggling with two conflicting narratives. Two sets of memories; two sets of inputs. One derived organically, from experience. One trained into her with the intervention of the machine inside her skull. A machine that had then been crudely ripped away, leaving unhealed wounds.

I couldn't call the result amateurish. Amateur brain surgery does not leave a functional human being behind. This had been carried out by somebody who knew what they were doing. Had at least known enough not to kill the patient. I imagined Dr. K'kk'jk'ooOOoo wouldn't have left such a mess behind.

Maybe the word I was looking for was *butcher*. Butchery was a professional skill, after all.

I flinched as I realized that Calliope could have three layers of memory in there. Or four.

Memory is an odd beast. It conflates and alters naturally, and every time you recall an event you change the memory. Adding a fox into the mix is supposed to make memories more stable, to provide an unaltered record to go with the subjective one.

But if you change the information stored in the machine, every time the patient remembers the memory it's not reinforced by what really happened, but by the memory they have been provided. This can be used for therapy, for post-trauma repair to give the patient a sense of control back, for helping to reconstruct people who are dangerous to release otherwise. But it's supposed to be voluntary, and overseen by boards of ethicists.

I was pretty sure *involuntary* memory replacement was what had been done to Calliope. And that nobody had bothered to ask her permission first. And that the review board had not been informed.

And then they had taken her fox away, and frozen her, and we'd reawakened her and subjected her to more medical trauma. And *then* some kind of trigger had been applied to bring the response we'd seen—the response that had been trained into her, I was certain—out. And send her haring off to find the craboid, and rip a ragged gash in *my hospital.*

Oh no.

Somebody would have taken care of it, right? I mean, somebody would have taken care of it. Obviously.

Still, once I thought of it I had to ask.

Sally. Where's the walker now?

Nonesuch towed it off into space and parked it in a static point with interdict beacons all over it.

"Calliope," I said.

She looked at me.

"I'll do what you asked. Promise to be careful and stay safe until I get back?"

Her pupils were dilated. I didn't know if she was seeing me or something from inside her damaged memories. "The doctors. Please don't let them send me back."

I stood, but didn't turn away. "Send you back where?"

"If they send me back, I'll never get away," she said.

CHAPTER 24

IS THAT TRUE?" CARLOS ASKED, WHEN I FINISHED RELAYING what Jones had told me. "About the mind control?"

"No." I twirled spaghetti around my fork. "She's pretty obviously sick, and somebody curtailed her treatment and manipulated her into a bunch of obsessive, delusional ideations before turning her loose to wreak havoc. No, worse than that—hiding her among your people in order to conceal the source of the havoc."

My fingers tightened on the fork. I didn't believe in violence. But for a moment, I would have suspended that belief if I had been able to get my hands on the people who chose to put Jones through so much pain.

"I heard a different rumor," Carlos said. "I heard that the peripheral—Helen—" He flinched again, but the flinch had a different quality this time: less disgust, more pity.

"Tell me."

"I heard she caused the disaster. Stopped the rotation."

"How?"

He shrugged. "The machine?"

I put the food in my mouth. It gave me something to grind my teeth through. I swallowed it through a chill of unease. "It's still contained. In the walker and in the stasis box. As far as I know. Who told you that?"

"That pilot lady," he said. "Loese. The . . . uncomfortably mannish one."

My mouth tightened. The information was not conclusive, but it fit certain parts of the pattern I was building. I still hated the pattern I was building. "Check your gender biases, caveman."

I filed the information away to contemplate later. I didn't want to think about it now. That was another conversation I needed to get to quickly. Curse the physical limitations of my frail, poorly designed anatomy.

Carlos sipped his drink and made a face. "Unfair to cavemen. What about the clones, then? And the kidnapping people for parts?"

I sighed, and looked at him. "I'll figure it out."

"Can I trust you to tell me the truth?"

I looked at him over my fork. He frowned back at me. I thought about being angry, but I was too tired, and honestly what reason did he have to trust me? We barely knew each other.

Which was why I could talk to him. All my other relationships were way too old, way too fraught, and way too tangled up in potential medical malfeasance. Well, maybe not Rilriltok. I couldn't imagine *it* doing anything unethical. Not unless it got way too excited to ask about the ethics of the situation before jumping in with all . . . twelve? limbs.

I raised my left little finger off the handle of the fork. "In fact, once I know what's going on, I'll *show* you."

"Huh," Carlos said, tilting his head to examine me.

"What?"

"People still pinky swear."

I had a lot of questions, and I didn't know the answers. But I knew where to go to find out, maybe. Thanks to Calliope Jones.

And thanks to Jones, I was pretty sure I could get in and out without being stopped.

I told Rilriltok not to let them transfer her, no matter what. "Get O'Mara if you have to. Nobody moves this patient anywhere."

She obviously wasn't tracking reality well. She was probably paranoid. Delusional.

Probably.

What if I asked Cheeirilaq for help? I liked the Goodlaw, and it had saved my life. But I realized, if O'Mara and Starshine knew something was wrong in the hospital . . . then I had no idea who I could trust.

I was going to have to handle it myself.

I couldn't give myself time to temporize. My courage could not be allowed to fail. I paused just inside the door of the detention ward, feeling Rilriltok's attention on my back, and nerved myself.

I also shut Sally out of my senso, which hurt me more than anything. But I couldn't be sure of *anybody*. You'd think that programmed ethics would be enough to prevent an AI from doing anything really sketchy. It's not like anybody looks at a constructed superintelligence and says, "What if we made this one a ruthless Utilitarian, just to see what happens?"

. . . Actually, somebody probably would, but with any luck the review board would catch it in time.

Better safe than sorry, as my allofather used to say.

When I moved into the corridor, I walked like a woman on a mission. There's a focused, hurried gait that makes other experienced hospital personnel flatten themselves against corridor walls, and I adopted it, heading toward Casualty with all deliberate speed.

It was less of an abattoir than when I'd left it, at least. Gravity—or the simulation of it—helped. There were still cots lined up against two walls, sheets draped over improvised stands between them for some semblance of privacy, but that was far more orderly than the situation during the disaster. Walking wounded had returned to their own quarters to convalesce, and some were probably back on duty.

I noticed open panels in the floor as I passed, and people of various descriptions working inside. I guessed that the artificial gravity retrofit had been stepped up, and that getting it installed in Casualty was now the first priority. Good.

It's always comforting to see the return of normalcy, and that the system has not completely broken down.

I nodded to an attending physician and a couple of specialists with whom I was acquainted, waved to the triage nurse, and stepped toward the doors to the private ward as if I belonged there.

The door didn't open to my scan.

Now, that was interesting. But I wouldn't be much of a heavy rescue specialist if I didn't know how to override a standard lock panel. I hadn't done this last time because I was still mostly following the rules. Still mostly being polite. And my exo had been an anchor at the time, come to think of it. Now . . . using my exo instead of a handheld—and instead of reaching into the senso with my fox—I hacked into the panel's working memory and flipped the switch.

The door hissed open and I stepped through.

A white lab coat makes you anonymous in a hospital. My ID dangled, and given the experience with the door I half expected my signal to be rejected by the sensors inside. No flashing lights greeted me, however. No whooping sirens. Just the humming quiet of an intensive care unit between emergencies.

I was in the same hallway I'd passed through when my exo had been running on fumes. This time I was fully charged and full of adrenaline, however, and I had more time to look around.

It seemed much as it had; a quiet nursing unit in the middle of sleep shift. The desk was staffed with a Ceeharen nurse who didn't look up. The unit coordinator who had spotted me on my last intrusion was nowhere in evidence. I hoped that meant he was off-shift or asleep. He'd been too alert by far, and—I blushed to admit it—I was a terrible spy.

Fortunately for terrible spies, most people are terrible observers. I sailed past the syster at the desk—they were deeply involved in something invisible to me in the air before them, making notes on it with a light pen—and walked along, checking the panels beside private rooms as if I were looking for a specific patient ID. The rooms were privacy-shielded, but my senior physician clearance was enough to de-encrypt them. I guessed when they'd locked the entrance, they hadn't thought uninvited guests would be resourceful or determined enough to get in anyway.

My accessing the records would be logged. But I wasn't planning on keeping my visit secret. Either there was nothing to hide, and this really was only a ridiculously posh unit devoted to keeping those who exploited more resources than they needed away from the proletariat . . . or Calliope was right about the hospital using indigent folks as spare-parts repositories, and I was about to blow the worst abomination in modern Synarche history sky-high.

If I ever got off this quarantined hospital. If the hospital itself even survived.

It didn't occur to me that there might be an answer somewhere in the middle. An answer whose implications might be *almost* as unpleasant as organ farmers murdering people for parts.

In retrospect, this was an oversight.

The majority of patients whose data I accessed were old. Very, very old, even by modern standards, where the human life expectancy in reasonable health exceeds our natural span *including* senescence. I'm hardly the picture of perfect health, but I was honestly better off than many of my ancestors would have been at my age—their panoply of undiagnosed and untreatable autoimmune disorders blossomed in the early Anthropocene, for a variety of genetic and environmental reasons—and I could expect another fifty or sixty ans or so as a contributing member of society.

If I made it to tomorrow alive.

But these patients—the human ones—had birth dates that made them older than my great-grandparents had lived to be. Admittedly, my great-grandparents lived on a marginal colony world where people reproduced young. But my great-grandparents were no longer alive, and neither were their children. Or their children's children, though *that* had been an accident.

These people were.

So maybe they needed the peace and quiet. Maybe they had come here to die. That seemed like an intolerable waste of resources, but . . . these people had resources to burn. And didn't seem inclined to return their surplus to the commonwealth, beyond whatever they were taxed.

You can't take it with you, as somebody wise observed. But you can sure roll around in it for as long as you're alive.

The next thing I noticed, pulling their med charts, was that none of them were on antirejection drugs. I had expected it, but it still comforted me. It disproved Calliope's conspiracy theory categorically. Without protein matchers and immune tuning . . . well, organ rejection is a real thing, and it used to kill patients, or severely limit their lives after transplant. They needed their immune systems suppressed for the rest of their lives, or their own bodies would destroy the transplanted organs they also needed to keep them alive.

Clone parts solved that—as far as your immune system is concerned, a clone finger is your own finger. So now I knew that nobody was kidnapping indigent teenagers and stealing their retinas or kidneys.

Since I hadn't *actually* expected to find evidence of that, I was surprised by how relieved I felt. So now I had to find out what was really going on in here, and why it was so secret. I was pretty sure I'd figured out why O'Mara and Starlight had been pushing me toward uncovering the information on my own: so that I wouldn't be bound by the hospital's privacy strictures regarding patients. I wasn't *supposed* to know what was going on here. Therefore nobody had bothered to put a block in *my* fox about it.

I downloaded a few more sets of records, and then when I was well away from the desk (glossy Ceeharen syster still engaged and on-task behind it) I pretended I had found the room I was looking for, and stepped inside. The occupant was a human female, 135 ans of age, Beyte Denarian by name.

It was almost the last room in the corridor, and when I walked in I was surprised by how quiet and empty it seemed. Hospital rooms are usually full of stuff: wires, equipment, monitors, tubes to put fluids into the human body and tubes to take them away again.

This seemed like a bedroom, and a pleasant bedroom at that.

I crossed to the bed and looked down.

A woman lay there, head shaved, blonde hair beginning to regrow, skin translucent as the skin of low-melanin humans who have never stepped out under a living sun becomes. Eyes closed, hands folded neatly on her breast atop covers that had never been wrinkled or disarrayed by human sleep. I felt as if I were looking at a corpse arrayed for the funeral.

I could see the blue veins under the skin of her throat, her cheeks, her temples. The backs of her hands.

She could not have been more than seventeen or eighteen ans of age.

She *could not* be Beyte Denarian. And yet—I checked the chart again—she was.

I touched her shaved scalp gently, the soft hairs fuzzing against my palm. There was a scar there, a tiny scar, tidy and neat. She was about old enough to have had a fox implanted, if it was done early. Usually, my species waits until our children are aged around twenty-five ans. Their neural development is more or less complete at that point, and they have learned social skills and how to experience and control their emotions without intervention. They have learned who they are.

So this woman was young, biologically speaking. But she was not unreasonably young.

She did not wake up when I touched her, but there were no signs that she was sedated, or that she was being supported through a period of unconsciousness due to illness or injury. She was lying there, inert. Breathing regularly.

I lifted an eyelid and flashed a light against her pupil. It contracted normally. Her pulse was even and tidy.

I set her hand down where I had found it and slowly left the room. The syster had not looked up from their work. You don't find many people that devoted on a sleep shift, but maybe they were studying for advancement. Or maybe they were playing solitaire.

There was a little more corridor beyond this room, and at the end of it, another door.

I squared my shoulders. I was ready to jimmy this lock, too.

I wondered what I would find there.

At first, I thought the space beyond—too large to call it a room: a hold, maybe, labyrinthine—was full of cryo tanks. Much more modern ones than those that had lined the vast hold on *Big Rock Candy Mountain*, naturally—but it still left me with a shiver of recognition.

Then I looked at them again, and realized they were not cryo tanks, but the exact opposite. The cryo tanks were there, but they were in ranks behind the objects I'd first noticed, and there were a lot more of them.

The ones in the front . . . were artificial wombs and incubator tanks full of suspensory medium. Incubator tanks of various shapes and sizes. Incubator tanks optimized for a dozen, two dozen different species of systers.

And they, and the cryo units behind them also, were full of clones.

It was not the first clone farm in my experience. This was a hugely resource-intensive operation, but there was no good reason for it not to be here. The whole private unit was a resource-intensive operation, after all. But something about this place and the young/old woman I'd seen outside bothered me.

I picked my away along the rows of tanks. Call me ethnocentric, but I concentrated on the human ones. A few dozen, ranging in age from fetal to the prime of youth. Suspended in their nutrient liquid, doing nothing at all. Medical clones don't have fully developed brains; enough to keep the autonomous functions functioning and the normal growth growing. Brains don't develop in a vacuum; they need stimulation and experience to learn how to do even such basic things as balance, pick up a fruit. Interpret language. See.

I supposed there was a possibility that Mx. Denarian out there had had her brain transplanted into a clone body. It would be an egregious waste of resources; sure, you could use a stem-cell suspension to graft the old brain onto the new neural tissue, but old brains are *old*. We don't die, these diar, because our bodies wear out; we die because our brains stop functioning effectively and we run out of the ability to prop them up with spot repairs.

Besides, the incision on the patient's skull had been small, tidy. The sort of thing you did to efficiently implant a fox, for example.

One of the clones near me twitched, and I almost jumped right out of my exo. I turned toward it, but it was only a long, myoclonic tremble. A contraction through the muscles of the shapely, muscular thigh and calf and ankle. A REM-sleep shiver.

Clones didn't dream.

Clones weren't usually . . . buff. They didn't have exquisitely trained, athletic bodies.

They didn't generally have deep brain stimulation wires running into their skulls. They didn't wear virtual reality goggles over their eyes, waterproof earphones in their ear canals.

My hands trembling despite the exo, I called up records on the pad attached to the incubation tank. Daily exercise sequences, isometrics, general health of the body—

Brain development.

I looked at the magnetic scans. I craned my head back and looked up at the clone, hovering over me in hairless, godlike nudity. Looming pale inside its tank of translucent dark liquid.

I looked back at the magnetic scans.

Brain development normal for a seventeen-year-old person.

But this wasn't a person. This was an object.

Objects were not supposed to have brains.

CHAPTER 25

TSOSIE WAITED FOR ME OUTSIDE MY QUARTERS. HE WAS sitting on a bench in an alcove, looking uncomfortable: those multi-species perches aren't really suited to most of the species they serve. I looked at him, and he looked at me.

He stood.

I said, "You appear to know where I've been. How much do you know about what I found there?"

"Can I come in?"

I didn't feel like having this fight in the hallway, so I opened my door and led him inside. My quarters are rated for a family, it's true, but that doesn't make them large. It does mean that what would have been Rache's room is my own private bedroom, so I can use the main room off the little entry as a sitting room.

It's selfish of me, but I never bothered to clarify to admin that my daughter would probably never be visiting me. Maybe I didn't want to clarify it to myself, to be honest.

I offered him the couch. He took the floor. I printed myself a cold beer and asked if he wanted one, too.

"Caffeine," he replied, looking uncomfortable.

I gave him a mug of coffee substitute. If he wasn't using the couch, I was. I settled into it.

He sipped his drink, probably framing an opening gambit, and I exploded in his face. "Am I the only person in this entire fucking hospital that didn't know what was going on in there?"

Tsosie swallowed. "You're not the only one who doesn't *want* to know. Am I right in saying you never bothered to find out until somebody made you?"

He looked more compassionate than I had expected, given his words. As is completely predictable, I immediately tried to pick a fight.

"I need," I said, "a certain amount of professional detachment to do my job."

"You're not detached," he told me. "You're dissociated. It's treatable and you know it."

"If Sally thought I was ill—"

"If Sally thought you were too ill to do your *job*, she'd say something," Tsosie interrupted. "You're not too ill to do your job. You're just too ill to be good for yourself."

"Oh," I said, "and you're absolutely perfect."

"Perfection is not required for awareness," he said, and his deadpan—curse him—made me laugh. Once they get you to laugh the fight is over, because no matter how mad you are, nobody takes you seriously when you're trying to dress them down while giggling. Anyway, he was sitting a half meter lower than I was, which made it hard to find him threatening.

That man is entirely too good at everything he does. I wondered if he was right about me—whether what I thought of as a professional reserve, professional detachment . . . was really more like floating a centimeter outside the world, never really engaging with it.

He might be right, I decided. If he was, it was a problem for another dia.

"Nobody holds it against you," he said. "But you do make yourself hard to get close to, Llyn."

I wanted to bite his head off, which probably meant that what he was saying was true. I sighed. "Am I good at my job?"

"Very," he admitted.

"Are you one of the saboteurs?"

"No!" His horror had to be real, didn't it?

"Then why are you here?"

"Sally sent me. She said you might need emotional support."

Tsosie was definitely the guy you sent for that, all right. I rolled my eyes.

It occurred to me that he said he knew what was in there, but maybe he only thought he knew. Maybe he didn't actually know the worst. "So what *do* you know about what's in the private unit?"

He put his hot caffeine water under his nose and leaned over the mug, closing his eyes and inhaling exactly as if the contents were palatable. "I know," he said, "that there are a couple of secret—well, okay, not secret exactly—wards in Core Gen. That one is in ox sector. That it's reserved for patients who fork over a ridiculous amount of resources for access, and that most of them are suffering from diseases of extreme senescence. I also know that the death rate of these extremely old people is extremely low, even by the standards of care available at Core General."

I studied him. He was, as near as I could tell, being honest.

"I don't imagine they're coming here to die," I said. "They could do that far more comfortably in their own habitations, or in a planetary hospital for that matter, though nobody likes gravity when their joints hurt."

I knew that for a fact.

He sipped the hot caffeine water and rolled it around his mouth before swallowing. "I don't know exactly what therapies they're receiving."

"Clones," I said. "Not parts grown from stem cells. Whole bodies. Whole clones."

He stared at me, head turned slightly as if he had almost figured out what was bothering me, but hadn't quite yet made the intuitive leap.

"Whole clones," I said. "With fully developed brains."

He breathed out.

"I met one of the patients. Well, I can't say I met her, as she was still in an integrative coma. A young woman of a mere hundred and thirty ans or so. With a fresh implant scar." I touched my head.

His face did a number of interesting things as I talked, and as he considered what I had said. It settled on concentration. He was going to treat it as an intellectual problem, then. "You can't transplant a *fox*. The architecture of one brain is too different from another. Even a clone brain—especially a clone brain, that's grown to adult size without experiences to influence its development. It wouldn't have—it wouldn't have developed speech centers, even. And even if you could, you wouldn't be transplanting the *person*."

Beer had been the right choice. Possibly O'Mara's tequila would have been a better one. "What if you . . . exercised the developing clone brain? The same way you exercise the body so the muscles and skeleton develop normally? Virtual stimulation? A series of implants, changing as the clone grows? They start them young in some of the clades: the technology exists."

"That's not a blank slate," he said. "That's a person."

"A person who has never existed in the world," I said. "A person with no rights, and no records, and no friends or family. And then, when they are physically adult, you put a final fox in place, integrate it, and . . . download the entire senso of the original person into the clone body you made. It would cost a fortune. But some people have fortunes to spend."

"That's not the same person!" he protested.

"Legally it's the same person. There's continuity of experience, of a sort. As much as any of us have, anyway. If you could buy planets, but not another moment of being alive, would the niceties matter to you? Or would you have the ego to believe that you would persist in some meaningful sense?"

"I think I'll take that beer now," he said.

I gestured to the printer. "Help yourself."

I missed real beer, with its irreproducible organic esters and subtle, layered tastes. But this would do in an emergency, and I felt like emergency had arrived.

My breath frosted in the air in front of me, which was unusual. I checked the datapad in its pocket on the couch arm. An unusual power drain on environmental systems, technicians working to correct. So many little things going wrong.

"Wow. It got chilly in here." Tsosie made himself a pale ale and came around to sit on the other end of the couch. I felt better conversing at eye level.

I handed him the pad, and he grunted, then made eye contact. There was nothing either of us could do about it now. Saboteurs? The digital infestation of the hospital's physical plant? I hoped the engineers could solve it.

"Is the private unit the target of the sabotage? I suddenly have some sympathy—" He stopped. "Does O'Mara know?"

"O'Mara knows and is under a confidentiality lock. I think they pushed me into finding out on purpose. And yes, it's what the sabotage is about. I think it's meant to . . . draw attention. And that's why the hospital has been being quiet about it—because they didn't have any choice, because they *couldn't* explain . . ."

"Why didn't the saboteurs just tell everybody what was going on?"

"No proof?" I said. "Add that question to the pile with 'Where the hell did they get a generation ship?'" I finished my beer. "I think Calliope is one of the clones. Remember how Dr. Zhiruo said her DNA looked . . . very orderly? But hadn't managed to decode the painfully bad archaic bragging poetry we assumed was encoded in it?"

He looked aghast. "I . . . that's awful. I don't know. I don't even want to think about that."

"I don't want to think about any of it." Having no more drink to occupy myself, I returned the glass to the recycler. Since I was up, I started to pace. "But I think we have to. You started to say that you might have sympathy for the saboteurs and . . . you're probably right. Empathy, anyway. But my god, Tsosie, they have fucked things up. Maybe less through cold malevolence and more through bad planning, or lack of considering the consequences. I . . ."

"Why is everyone such an asshole?" he asked, sympathetically.

"Yes."

He sighed. "Helps us fit in better."

His comment reminded me to apologize. "I'm sorry, by the way. I suspected you might be behind the sabotage for a while."

"That's okay," he said. "I suspected you."

"I thought you trusted me!"

"I thought you trusted me."

"With my life. But then I couldn't trust anything anymore."

He finished his beer. "That's smart."

"It's lonely."

"So what made you decide to trust me now?"

I blew out. "I figured out who it had to be, and it wasn't you."

In three-vee thrillers the amateur detective goes off and confronts the suspect without leaving a note, but that's a little too risk-unaverse even for me. Tsosie didn't want to leave me alone, after I explained to him. But I explained that I was telling him as a security measure, and that if he came with me that security measure was useless, because we would both be in the same place with the person I suspected was a saboteur.

"Why not tell Starlight?" he asked, pretty reasonably. He was now on his second beer.

"Because I'm not one hundred percent sure, and I want to *be* sure before I accuse anybody of attempted murder and negligent homicide.

And also because I agree with their goals, though not their methods. This needs to be exposed."

"What if you don't come back?"

I got up. "Finish your beer."

He finished his beer. "What if you don't come back?"

"Then you have proof." I grinned at his stricken expression. "Come on, Tsosie. Let's go to work. It's way too late to start pretending you like me."

"I *do* like you, you enormous pain in the ass." He stood, also. "Don't get killed."

Loese wasn't in her quarters. I should have checked before I dropped by, but I didn't want her to get the location ping and figure out that I was onto her. She wasn't on-shift; there was literally nothing for a pilot to be doing right now, and wouldn't be until ships could leave the hospital again.

So that meant that unless she was socializing, exercising, or eating, she was likely to be on Sally.

I sighed. I had wanted to have this conversation in private. Not in front of Hhayazh and Camphvis and Rhym. *Or* Sally.

I was more or less in luck. Rhym and Hhayazh were on-shift, doctoring away somewhere in the ox sections of Core General. Camphvis was sleeping, privacy shield pulled closed. Loese was in her bunk, reading from a handheld. She sat up and swung her legs down when I walked over.

"You haven't been around much." She stood. Her voice sounded hurt. The emotion might even be real. People are complicated.

"I got seconded to some administrative work, and then a lot of people needed emergency surgery." I cleared my throat. "Why are you telling people that Helen caused the disaster?"

She looked at me. She looked around. She said, "Let's go for a walk."

We went for a walk. Around the outside of the ring, in one of the habitrails that loop its surface. The stars were under our feet; Starlight's mutating leaves glittered beyond the transparent ceiling. I wondered if the Administree would be able to hear us, through the layers of atmosphere, structural material, and more atmosphere.

"Turn on privacy," I told Loese.

Her eyes flicked up. "I see."

Together, we temporarily withdrew translator permissions. I set myself a reminder to turn them back on again, or I was going to wind up shouting to somebody for suction and all they would be able to hear would be gargling noises.

Then she said, "I haven't been telling anyone anything."

"That's not what I heard."

"I'm not saying I haven't discussed a possibility."

That self-justifying—

Well, she would have to be.

I sighed. "If Starlight found out—"

"You wouldn't do that."

I was tired and in pain, and I wasn't thinking too clearly. That's the only excuse I have for what I said next. "Why would you assume that I would keep a secret like that?"

Oh. You would assume that, if you were secretly combatting something nefarious, and you weren't afraid of being found out.

"I don't expect you to keep a secret." She kept pacing along, strong calf muscles giving her a rolling gait.

"Loese, I know about the sabotage."

She nodded, and didn't glance at me. "I figured."

"You—" All the things I could have accused her of, and the one that burst out of me was, "You *hurt* Sally."

Now she looked at me: pityingly. "Did you think Sally didn't know? She's one of us, Llyn. Several AIs are."

I put a hand on the transparent wall to steady myself. These trails didn't see a lot of use. They were beautiful, but many people found them unsettling. Now I leaned my weight on apparent emptiness that was nevertheless a rigid bulkhead, and struggled to catch my breath.

I had to tune to get any kind of equilibrium. "Sally would never . . . never hurt people. Never hurt so many people."

"No," Loese agreed. "Neither would I. We, ah. We made a mistake."

That was such a disingenuously mild way of putting it that even with my emotional controls firmly in place I found myself exploding into rage. I clenched my fist, took two deep breaths, and thought about the deep green seas of home.

No, that wouldn't help me. My child was at home, and the toxic meme that Loese and her allies had unleashed . . . it could eat the entire galaxy. Centimeter by centimeter. World by world. If we ever released the quarantine.

The evidence was over my head.

I thought about the chill depths of space, the flicker of stars, instead. There, that was much better. Space was right there, inches beyond my fingertips. The tangled, lensing stars of the Core didn't seem orderly—their pattern was too complex for me to discern through observation—but they were. I could take it on faith that whatever was out there was doing exactly what it was destined to do.

In here, we had to make choices, and right now all of them seemed bad.

"I don't believe you."

"Sally never caught the meme," Loese said. "Didn't you wonder why?"

The bulkhead didn't feel sturdy enough to hold me up. Somehow, though, it did. Somehow I held myself up against it.

"Tell me," I said, "about your mistake. If you don't mind."

She told me, and as she told me, I realized that she was part of a conspiracy that must have started before she was born. That had been constructed out of pieces of found material, and whose various individuals often took actions and set plans in motion without consulting one another. There was no grand design behind any of it: just a series of fumbling attempts to do something.

Fucking humans. Even rightminding can't make us sensible. And even programming can't make AIs make good decisions, I guess. All rightminding can do is make us less massively self-destructive in the long run, less reactive, more willing to work together for the common good. We used to think, when we first invented it, that it made us logical. That was the propaganda put around, anyway. I'm not sure even the originators ever believed it.

Ha ha. It turns out, with further research, that human thought is, by its nature, not logical. We can lessen our susceptibility to confirmation bias, egocentrism, and denial. But it turns out that nearly everything about our decision-making process is emotional, and that this is actually a good thing. Because our conscious minds are slow and ineffectual, and if we actually had to sort all the information our subconscious minds process in order to present us with hunches, gitchy feelings, and the occasional epiphany, we'd never fit through the birth canal.

Evolutionarily speaking, obviously: even I wasn't gestated inside a suffering human host, and I was born into frontier barbarism.

Loese talked for a long time. She didn't use names, other than hers and Sally's. But from what I gathered, there didn't seem to be a *lot* of people involved. At least one shipmind AI of fairly significant age, however: that much was obvious. Somebody had been coordinating this effort for . . . I shook my head.

Longer than I had been alive.

Loese told me—without naming it—about the ship that, decans before, had stumbled across *Big Rock Candy Mountain* and its self-repair program run wild and hit upon the idea of hacking it and repurposing it to disable Core General and bring the critical eye of the Synarche's population to bear on the activities going on behind closed doors.

"What about Calliope?"

"She was medical waste," Loese said, with justified bitterness. "Her progenitor died before the download could be arranged, and our chief organizer arranged to salvage her. And to use gene therapy to alter her DNA."

I wondered who the chief organizer was. The shadowy Mx. Big behind it all.

Somebody in Cryo? Not Rilriltok, I thought. I couldn't imagine my excitable, enthusiastic, nerdy little friend managing to keep a lie that big, that interesting, a secret from me for the fifteen ans we'd known each other.

An additional problem was that none of what they had discovered was technically illegal. Unawakened clones were not considered Synizens: they had no life experience, no legal personhood. I was sure Loese could see that I was as horrified as she was that anybody would make a clone, grow it to adulthood, exercise its brain and body into proper development with virtual experiences . . . and then put it in cryostasis until it was needed as a replacement body.

"How did the generation ship get moved?" I asked. "That's been bothering me."

"We couldn't have done that if that salvage mission hadn't turned up the Koregoi gravity generators," she said. "But when the hospital refit began, we managed to liberate some test models."

"Cheeirilaq knows about that. That was what made me wonder if Tsosie was involved," I said. "He was interested in those test models."

"We copied them, and by integrating them into the self-replicating tinkertoy machine's code, we made one big enough to, er, distort space-time and slide *Big Rock Candy Mountain* close enough to a white space jump point that somebody could plausibly stumble across her."

I wondered if the gravity generators, used that way, compensated in some way for relativistic effects. I wondered if you could use them to manipulate the *time* part of space-time as well as the space part.

I decided that now was not the time to find out.

"This all must have taken decans."

"It did," Loese said. "This clone thing has been going on for a very long time. We didn't have the last pieces until recently, however."

"Afar and his crew were in on the conspiracy?"

"He was the ship that found *Big Rock Candy Mountain* in the first place," she admitted, reluctantly. "They were . . ."

"Smuggling?"

". . . off the normal trade routes."

"Did he know that you planned to sacrifice him and his crew?"

"What happened to Afar was an accident. He and his crew were supposed to drop off the walker and the cryo tube holding Calliope and leave. We did not expect him to get infected with the meme, and we *really* didn't expect it to affect his crew." She shook her head. "Afar must have really screwed up somehow. I don't know how he could have messed up so badly that he, his crew, and the walker all got infected."

"You keep saying 'accident' . . ." I squinted at Loese, remembering the dropped coms, the sabotage to Sally. "You and Sally tried to kill me!"

"We knew you'd survive," she said.

It was a nice vote of confidence. You'll forgive me if I didn't fully appreciate it at the time. "You risked my life and Tsosie's life. To—what, make sure we were on the ship long enough to find the right cryo coffins? Sally did come back online awfully conveniently once we were there."

"She needed—" Loese looked at her hands. "She needed to control the machine, and make sure that the accident with the coffins happened the right way, to ensure that you weren't hurt in the process."

"Why didn't you just *tell* somebody?"

She sighed. "Do you think nobody tried? It all sounds like rumors and conspiracy theories. We needed proof. We needed evidence. And none of this is illegal. It's only *awful*."

"You had," I said distinctly, "a discarded, fully grown, sapient clone of a dead rich woman, with a fully developed brain. And you didn't think that was evidence enough? No, you decided it was a better idea to do exactly what the fucking mad scientists here at Core Gen were doing, and implant false memories in her, rip out her fox, and hide her on a generation ship where there was a very good chance that she would die."

"She didn't," Loese said. "And it was for the best cause imaginable."

I had to tune in order not to hit her. Hitting people almost never solves anything, and you can trust me on that. I was in the military.

"So the virus, the toxic meme, came in with the machine? Sally used herself as a mule to bring it back?"

"Sally used herself as a mule to bring it back," Loese agreed. "But the important part of the meme, the part that infected Zhiruo, wasn't in the machine. Or Helen. They were only . . . along for the ride."

I didn't ask. I waited.

"The virus was encoded in Calliope's DNA."

"*What?*" Loese had said they'd altered Calliope's DNA. I had assumed she meant to make her seem like she belonged among the corpsicles.

"The meme. It's programmed into her. That was why Afar got sick. That was why Dr. Zhiruo got sick. The meme was there to be read into their memories when they scanned Jones's DNA or contacted each other. The orderliness in her wasn't poetry.

"It was malignant code."

"You poisoned Dr. Zhiruo on purpose?" And Afar. And Linden! . . . Maybe those had been accidents. But still.

A responsible person, a healthy-minded person, would not put herself into a position where that kind of accident *happened*.

Loese reached out very hesitantly and put a hand on my arm. "It wasn't supposed to take her offline, Llyn. It was just supposed to make her tell the truth."

I looked at her. "She's under the same kind of confidentiality seal as Starlight and O'Mara? You wanted them to tell the truth, too, I suppose? Is that how Starlight got infected?"

"That would have been nice, but . . . no. We didn't expect the meme to get beyond Zhiruo. It wasn't supposed to be virulent. We wanted to make her tell the truth, and we wanted to write over the privacy protocols. Reverse them, so she would have to come forward. We didn't expect it to affect Afar, or for him to get stuck there. He was supposed to drop Calliope and the walker off, and be on his way. There was some kind of interaction between the virus and the generation ship's antique AI and the commands its last captain left it—whatever had it building the machine—and everything went wrong, fast."

Tuning, tuning. "Why Zhiruo? Why make her tell the truth? Because she's got seniority?"

"Aw, Jens," Loese said sadly. "Zhiruo is the head of the clone program. I *said* it had been going on for ages."

That liquid sensation in my gut—that was real horror. Real betrayal. And only a little bit of it was because what Loese and Sally and their unnamed co-conspirators had done was so unbelievably stupid.

You commit yourself completely to something and then you take your eyes off it for an instant and it's gone. Like it never was. Like you can't even see the evidence of the thing that was there, that you trusted your weight, your honor, your life, your heart to.

I've seen some shit, let me tell you.

But somewhere deep down, I find myself craving the impossible. I find myself craving that certainty that people and things and . . . and *principles* in my life will stay where I *fucking left them.*

A betrayal retroactively poisons everything good about that relationship. And right then, I wanted to stop spending so much time thinking about and compensating for how damaged I am. I wanted to be able to relax. To feel safe, and like I didn't have to constantly be on my guard, again.

You'd think I'd be a little old to be feeling my innocence betrayed. But I hadn't even turned my back on Core General. I trusted its ethical principles to hold me up. To bear my weight.

And it fell away under my feet.

The worst part is that I wasn't braced at all. I didn't have the slightest excuse to not be ready for it.

I'd believed. And now I couldn't believe anymore. And I missed that believing so much.

This must be what losing your religion feels like.

At least Rhym isn't involved in this. At least I don't have to be angry at Hhayazh.

"Well," I said, "you fucked up good, Loese. You and Sally and all the people you're still protecting."

Her face folded like a balled-up tissue. "I know. And you're going to turn me over to Starlight and Zhiruo."

"I don't think Starlight approves of Zhiruo," I said. "Or at least, not her little side program. I don't think they can avoid using the resources she generates—I mean, we've *all* been using the resources she generates. That program must help pay for the ambulance ships, and . . . I don't even know what else."

"Zhiruo started the clone program," Loese said miserably, "because the Core General project was defunded during the Laesil system cataclysm, a long time ago. They didn't have the resources to support finishing it when hundreds of thousands of people were dying of stellar radiation and needed immediate help. So Zhiruo . . . found the resources elsewhere."

Sweet death in a vacuum, why can't anybody be uncomplicatedly evil in real life? Or uncomplicatedly good? Why are we all such a twist of good and bad decisions, selfishness and self-justification, altruism and desire?

"Yes," I said. "I'm going to turn you in. You need your rightminding adjusted, sure as shitting after eating. How many casualties did you cause?"

She studied her shoes, and the stars beyond them. "A lot. The sabotage to the hospital—that wasn't Sally and me, though."

"Who was it? Some of your co-conspirators?"

Her lip thrust out. "They were involved in the little things. The leaks, the equipment malfunctions. We did *not* cause the rotational and lift failures. Something else caused that. I don't want them blamed for it!"

Something else caused that. "Aw, crud," I said. "So the machine—carrying the meme Sally made—has infiltrated the hospital's superstructure. That's what caused the big failures, isn't it?"

Her mouth twisted in a horrified grimace. "Oh *shit.*"

I sighed.

I could waste a lot of time trying to get the names of her co-conspirators out of her. But . . . I was part of a system. If we lived long enough, the system could figure out who the rest of the conspirators were, using the information I gave them as a wedge for entering. The system could decide what the proper reparations were for them to earn forgiveness. In the meantime, I awarded Loese a few meager maturity points for not reminding me that she hadn't meant to cause any casualties. But who in the spiral arms thought mixing a computer virus with an insane, damaged, poorly understood shipmind and then turning it loose was a good plan?

I nodded. "But we have a more immediate problem than the criminally stupid thing you and Sally did."

She looked at me. That outthrust lip retracted a little.

"Unless you want to increase that death toll by every soul on Core General, staff and patients alike . . . we need to find a way to end the damage being done by the meme you set loose. And that is probably going to take all of us, working together. So you'd better give me access to the source files for this malignant code you and Sally cooked up, so I can do something about fixing Linden and Afar and Dr. Zhiruo. And Starlight, for the love of little blue suns."

"Right," she said. Her expression lightened a little. "Do you think you can fix it?"

Hope.

She was, I realized, really young. Young and full of idealism. Faith that things could be made to work out all right.

Maybe they could. Maybe they could. And maybe the survivors of this minor disaster could be repaired and restored to health.

That wouldn't help the dead, however.

"I can't fix it," I said. "Nobody can fix a thing like this, once it happens. But maybe we can prevent anybody else from getting hurt."

CHAPTER 26

LOESE WANTED TO TALK TO SALLY BEFORE SHE MADE ANY irrevocable decisions. I didn't blame her. I wanted to talk to Sally myself.

I also badly wanted to talk to Dr. Zhiruo. But first we needed an AI doctor who could somehow fix her corrupted code. Or bring her out of her protective hibernation. Or—whatever, it wasn't my specialty—make her go.

And hopefully make Linden and Afar go, too.

The problem was that the best AI doctors in the hospital other than Zhiruo were already working on Zhiruo. Sally was an AI doc . . . and Sally had written the toxic meme. And that was a problem, because although she had written it, it had since gotten corrupted and made—virulent? contagious?—by contact with the machine's operating system, and apparently Sally couldn't figure out how to stop it once it went wrong.

At least, I was choosing to assume that she couldn't manage to stop it. And not that she was choosing not to stop it. Because, shocking revelations and horrible mistakes aside, Sally was my friend. A friend who had fucked up catastrophically. But, nevertheless, a friend.

I was angrier at Sally than I was at Loese. I knew Sally better. I had trusted her more.

I had trusted her *implicitly*. Reflexively. The way a child trusts a parent, I suppose, until proven otherwise.

The same way, I realized, I had trusted Core General. I hadn't thought either of them would let me down. And yet, here we were. They were on opposite sides of this issue, and both of them had catastrophically let me down.

It's so easy to be catastrophically wrong. And so difficult to admit it to yourself, internalize it, and act upon the knowledge.

Is faith ever warranted?

Probably not.

Sally's betrayal felt more personal than Core General's. Sally's betrayal *was* more personal. I mean, for one thing, she was a person and not an institution.

I left Loese and walked into Ops. Sally was moored and spinning with the hospital, so we enjoyed the semblance of gravity and I settled into the familiar embrace of my acceleration couch. When I leaned back and looked up, the wide toroid of the hospital framed a sharp-edged, upside-down horizon across the top of the forward port.

Below that hard line, a line as solid and straight and massive as the stone edge of a crypt lid, the stars spilled out across the blinding brightness of the Core, with a whole galaxy turning behind it, the whole universe turning behind *that*. Billions upon billions of stars and billions upon billions of living souls.

They all seemed so bright and close that I almost could reach out my hand and cup them up, like cupping up reflections from the surface of still water. Except that putative water was light-ans deep, and mostly empty, and I was alone in it.

Well, staring into space wasn't making me feel any less lonely. And difficult conversations don't get any less difficult if you put them off.

"Sally," I said, "can you make sure we're alone?"

"We're alone," she answered. "I suppose you're very angry with me?"

I knew she was already talking to Loese. And I was angry with her—very angry—but I paused a moment to inspect and categorize my feelings. I wanted to be fair, not punitive. I also wanted to be clear, so I let Sally into my senso while I ran the assessment, furious and hurt as I was.

I was angry on my own behalf. She had risked my life and betrayed my trust. Worse, she had lied to me about it—knowingly *lied*, not merely misdirected or left things out—and her lies had compounded the emotional damage.

Showing that vulnerability to Sally now, in the absence of trust that she would not use it against me, took courage I didn't know I had, and I jump out of space ships for a living.

It was easier to let her see the other things I was angry about, the ones that made me a warrior rather than a victim. It was easy to show her that I was angry about her carelessness with Tsosie's life, about the damage to the hospital and the casualties here, about her absolute bare-assed malicious negligence.

That was a righteous anger, and it was so much easier and more comfortable and safer to feel than the anger of personal hurt. But they were both real, and they both mattered, and—

And I was getting too angry to communicate effectively. To problem-solve.

I wasn't going to start shouting at Sally. She deserved it, but yelling was a waste of time. And time was a thing we didn't have in abundance right now. We had plenty of problems, crises, questions. Even plenty of tools: brains, skills, personnel.

But we didn't have a lot of time. And we didn't have a lot of answers, either.

So we needed to use the resources we did have to make up for or obtain the ones we didn't. And the first step toward that was me not losing my shit all over Sally and wasting valuable hours when we could be problem-solving and saving lives.

I tuned, and I let Sally feel me tuning. I don't know, even now, if that was honesty or a guilt trip. Or maybe sometimes a thing can be both. But right then I needed the machine in my head to make my emotions work, the same way the machine of my exo made my body work.

I was grateful for both of them. Which reminded me to plug myself in to the trickle charger on my couch while talking to Sally. Was it still my couch? I didn't know. Maybe I really was losing everything, and that scared me more than the even-more-immediate prospect of losing my life.

Well, if I didn't lose my life, there would be time to worry about everything else I didn't have anymore after. It would be so much easier and safer to drop this. Let it go. Pretend I didn't know anything.

I could not do that thing.

"I am angry," I said at last. "I also understand your motivation, though I think your choices were really dumb."

"Confidentiality," she said. "I couldn't talk about it to somebody who didn't already know, and wasn't a family member or wasn't medically necessary to the treatment of the special, private patients. Most of us involved in the effort couldn't. We did what we thought we had to do."

She paused.

"It was a series of bad decisions," she admitted.

"Well!" I swore. "I knew the administrators' options are locked down. I didn't realize that all the AIs are."

Coercing people into staying silent about injustices has always worked out so well in the past.

"All the hospital AIs have to accept a patient confidentiality filter," she said. "I'm sure the Judiciary does something similar."

I wasn't sure. But it seemed worth looking into. Later. "You did some really terrible things."

"I know." A long pause. "Are we still friends?"

That brought me up short. "Maybe," I said. "I can't protect you."

"I wouldn't expect—" She stopped. "When I decided to do this I knew that there would be consequences. I didn't expect there to be consequences for innocent people along the way."

The stress of the ethical conflict really had overridden her risk assessment protocols, the same way the stress of conflicting ethical calls had crashed Helen, sent her to the floor of the Cryo unit in a puddle.

Always know your exit strategy, they told us in the military.

My family . . . my family was a very "every person for themselves" kind of operation. Not out of cruelty, but because nobody had a lot of emotional resources to spare for anyone else, I suppose. Especially after my parents died. I have never been very good at being there for other people, as a result.

I am someone who mostly wants to pass unnoticed when she has been hurt or has been harmed. The vulnerability of being noticed—even to be comforted—makes me wary and self-conscious. Maybe Tsosie is right and I do float through, a little above and to the left of the real world.

So when it's someone else's turn to need comfort, it always feels like I'm intruding. Or, if someone is trying to help me, it feels like I am being intruded upon.

I pushed my head back against the couch. Maybe this time, I could fix that, a little. Maybe I could be there for somebody I considered family. Even if they had earned some consequences.

"Are you willing to fix the problem?" I meant the toxic meme as much as anything. It was the most important thing needing fixing that *could* be fixed.

"Of course!" Sally said. "I've been trying, but I don't know how!"

"Didn't you wri—no, come back to that. Was Jones the only logic bomb?"

"Yes."

Relief made me feel like I was under acceleration. At least the shipmind Ruth would be safe, even if we couldn't find a way to pass her the message not to DNA-scan any corpsicles in time to stop it. "Okay. So, given that you wrote the virus, why can't you write a program to inoculate against it?"

She sighed. "I wrote it. But—this is an informed guess—it must have come into contact with the code in the machine when Jones's cryo pod was on *Big Rock Candy Mountain*. And the code in the machine infected it, or possibly vice versa. And that's probably my fault, because I had to rewrite Helen a little bit so that she would accept Jones as a member of her crew, and in so doing I probably left some code in her that gave the machine the ability to process the DNA scans in Jones's pod. . . . And we did not plan for any of this."

It was like biological viruses swapping chunks of genetic code in order to evolve faster. And this was going to be a huge pain in the ass, just like that was. It also meant that the machine was another vector for the meme. . . .

That was probably, I realized, what had happened to Afar. Its crew had dropped off Calliope's cryo pod, the machine had scanned her and integrated the code in unexpected ways—and before they could leave, the altered meme had been transferred from the machine to their shipmind. And into them, since Afar's crew and their silicon-based brains handled rightminding by etching electrical pathways in the material of their icy bodies. The meme could have used that foothold and their connection to Afar and . . . rewritten their brains to be quiet.

I shivered. "You didn't realize something was wrong when we found Afar?"

"Loese and I discussed it," Sally said. "By the time we learned what the problem was, we were committed."

I wondered if the discussion had been more of an argument, and if so which had taken what side. I decided I was happier in ignorance.

"Well," I said, "you've incapacitated the people who would be most effective in solving this problem, I'm afraid. I don't know who to suggest other than Zhiruo or Linden. And they're all out of commission."

"I'm sorry."

"You can stop apologizing. Use that energy to work out a solution. I'm going to assume you're agonizingly contrite about everything, and torn by the claws of conscience to boot."

"There's somebody who's not out of commission," she said. "But I suspect you won't love it. It means breaking quarantine and risking somebody outside the infected zone. If he'll even do it."

"Tell me," I said. "Then we can decide."

"Singer," she said. "The shipmind of *I Rise From Ancestral Night*, the ancient ship that was salvaged from the Well. We met him on the way in, if you remember. He should be back from helping Ruth correct *Big Rock Candy Mountain*'s course by now."

"Weird," I said. "But I'm listening."

"Not weird," she argued. "He's already figured out how to reprogram himself into an alien architecture and make it home. He's got the necessary experience to take on the machine. If anybody can."

"The Judiciary isn't going to like us risking their special antique vessel."

"They're going to like losing Core General even less."

She had a point, as much as I hated to admit it.

Then she said, "I'm also going to need Helen."

My frown felt like an anchor dragging my face down. How much was I going to trust Sally?

How much was *Helen* going to want to trust Sally?

Was she even telling me the truth about her motivation? Had her actions been competent malice, rather than tragically mistaken altruism? Was she going to lie to me again? Was she pretending she understood that she had made a mistake to conceal some deeper, even more malevolent plan?

I might be being a fool. I might be choosing to be a fool, with my eyes wide open.

But the alternative was to turn my information over to well-meaning officials who might fix the meme but who were physically constrained from dealing with the root of the problem; to bank on my suspicion and betrayal and let everybody die; or take a risk and see if it worked out.

I realized that I was, in my own turn, gambling with a lot of lives with what I thought was sufficient cause. So maybe I was a hypocrite to be furious with Sally.

I hadn't put the lives on the table to begin with, though, so I felt I had a little high ground. Sally hadn't realized what stakes she was choosing . . . but she had opted into playing for them.

"What do you need Helen for?" I asked.

"She's going to be our easiest access point to the code in the tinkertoy machine. And she's our local expert on archaic programs."

"I don't know what else to do or how else to get through this," I said. "So I am going to trust you. I want you to know that if it turns out you're playing me, I'm going to spend the whole endless time the black hole is spaghettifying both of us being extremely disappointed in you."

Sally made a sound I couldn't translate, though it had to be intended as communication or she wouldn't have made it. "You wouldn't be wrong."

Now I was sneaking around behind O'Mara's back, even though I was pretty sure I was doing what they wanted me to be doing. The goals, anyway: they'd probably think my methods were criminally stupid.

Much as I felt about Sally. It's turtles all the way down, is what I'm saying, and if we destroy the universe at least we died trying to fix it. Rather than sitting around with digits in our orifices expecting somebody else to come to the rescue.

That said, being hasty and reckless leads to catastrophe. (Imagine me looking pointedly at Sally, here. Also, imagine for the purposes of this exercise that Sally is corporeal.) There are a couple of principles that translate through both military action and rescue action. One I know I've mentioned before: "adapt, improvise, and overcome." Another is the old aphorism that "slow is fast," or "slow and steady wins the race," or "haste makes waste," or "more speed, less haste," or however your CO likes to phrase it.

The third and sometimes most important one boils down to the knowledge that contingency plans and fallback positions are mission-critical: never get into something without knowing your route back out again.

I couldn't see a lot of routes out of our current cluster. Admittedly, I hadn't gotten us into it, either. But at this point, why not endorse Sally getting in touch with yet another AI for help with the coding? I say *endorse* rather than *allow* because let's be honest, I had absolutely no control over her. One never does have control over other people, and it's abusive to try—outside of certain defined command structures. But the illusion of control is comforting.

The toxicity of certain comforting illusions is another argument in favor of rightminding, I guess. Being able to identify those self-delusions for what they are is the beginning of healthy cognition, and allows one to take steps to mitigate their impact on decision-making.

But we modern humans aren't any better or more evolved than our ancient ancestors who nearly destroyed their planet and themselves with shortsightedness and selfishness: making the immediately futile decision and not worrying too much about the consequences. The choices Loese and Sally made should render that quite plain.

What we do have is better health care, better management of sophipathology, more leisure in which to think about things, and centians or millennians more experience and history and aggregated thought to draw upon.

Well, I wanted to preserve that history and experience for further generations. And I couldn't see a better way to do that—and preserve all the lives on Core General—than Sally's plan.

So here we were. Breaking quarantine.

We could *receive* signals from the outside with no problem. Nobody was going to get infected with a toxic meme because we were *listening* to them. (Listening is always a good first step when you find you have a communications problem. Thank you, I'm here all week.) Broadcasting, however, was strictly contraindicated. O'Mara must have either pulled some real strings or used an isolated com when they called the gunship Nonesuch in on Calliope and her craboid.

I wondered, as I worked to determine the current location and trajectory of *I Rise From Ancestral Night*, if there was an AI organization working on securing more rights for their people. Sally would never tell me if I asked, of that I was suddenly sure.

AIs were Synizens of the galaxy. But they were born into debt and owing decans of service to pay for their own construction—an obligation we don't ask any other sentient to assume.

Core General is considered essential, and the AIs who elect to work here are usually free of their inception debt after one term of contract, whether they volunteer or are selected. Still, remembering that gave me some insight. Both into why Zhiruo might consider clones, even ones developed to the possibility of sentience, as disposable raw materials to save another life . . . and why Sally might risk everything, even somewhat illogically, to put a stop to the practice.

"Found him," Sally said, disrupting my reverie. "Or, rather, found where he was 9.73 light-minutes ago, and I have a very good plot of his trajectory."

Loese had joined us on the command deck and been briefed about our strategy. I'd half hoped she would come up with something better, but here we were. Making potentially terrible decisions. Now she said, "Are you ready with the tightbeam?"

"Sending," Sally answered. "Audio only, filtered frequencies."

That was the safest way we could make the contact.

Actually, I was pretty sure she'd already sent our prepared burst to the ancient ship's projected locations approximately 9.7 et cetera light-minutes from now. The longer we waited, the more the probabilities drifted on the other ship's projected track.

I settled back to wait. The earliest possible response would come in twenty minutes, more or less. The urge to drift into self-pity was nearly irresistible, and it startled me—but the urge itself didn't startle me as much as how comfortable it was. How inviting.

I knew what was behind it: embracing the sense of betrayal and righteousness was safe.

It wouldn't help me work with Sally, though. And I needed to work with Sally.

Ten and a half standard minutes later, while I was losing a game of virtual checkers to Loese, a brilliant flash of light heralded the sudden dimming of our forward port. A huge mass blocked my view of every running light, every lensing star, even the vast whirl of the Saga-star's accretion disk. They all vanished, replaced by the back-limned outline of a strangely organic-looking hull: something that looked less built and more grown.

It had fallen out of white space as if materializing, angled slightly away from Sally and the hospital both to avoid pulverizing us with its bow wave. The accelerated particles that came with a white space transition had caused that blinding flash when they met some of the local, thinly distributed matter near Core General. Now they were speeding off on a harmless trajectory.

The ship was *I Rise From Ancestral Night*, and I felt a spark of disbelief that it had not only risked a white space transition of so short a duration, into such a confined space—but also managed it flawlessly. The pilot and the shipmind, I concluded, were both hot dogs.

There, undocked, it maintained position seamlessly—despite the hospital's spin. Sally sighed in my head with envy.

"Sally?" said a voice audibly over coms. "This is Singer. I got your message. It seemed I should come in a hurry."

"Um," I said. "I don't want to be the one who has to explain that to O'Mara."

The AIs got down to business. Singer seemed comfortable protecting himself, and I decided to leave the process to the experts and not worry myself. I was pretty sure I could find plenty of my own problems to concentrate on anyway. Sitting here waiting for Sally or Singer to goof up and get infected with their own virus/antivirus code wasn't making me any happier or helping to move the situation toward a successful resolution.

Ergo, it was time for me to go find something else useful to do.

CHAPTER 27

GUESS WHO GOT TO EXPLAIN THINGS TO O'MARA? They were about to press the call button beside our hatch as I climbed out of Sally into the docking ring.

They eyed me. I eyed them.

They said, "We're supposed to be under quarantine, you know."

I said, "Well, *you* called a gunship."

They held out their hand to assist me to my feet. I took it, feeling dwarfed. O'Mara was always good about letting you use their strength as an anchor, but sometimes you remembered how large and strong they were. "Come on," I said. "Walk with me, and I'll explain how we're going to save the biggest hospital in the galaxy."

"I like the sound of that," they said. "How confident are you?"

I laughed. "Oh," I said. "Thirty percent? Ten percent, if you plan to try to stop me."

They looked at me very seriously. "I have no intentions of doing anything to stop you."

Helen was easy to track down. Once I found her, I sent her to talk to Sally and Singer about the machine, her own programming, and how to save the world—at least the small, artificial world that was this hospital, and the small artificial world that was *Big Rock Candy Mountain*, and possibly many much larger worlds as well.

That accomplished, I applied myself to the next problem. I sent O'Mara ahead to Cryo, and found Dwayne Carlos in a cafeteria. The directories were still down, so I got a lot of walking in while tracking him through the hospital. I picked up Tsosie along the way, more by accident than by design, and was surprised to find his presence bulwarked me.

Carlos was at a corner table eating spaghetti. Pretty soon so were Tsosie and I, having sat down across from him. I was trying to remember the last time I ate something that wasn't spaghetti.

My allofather used to say grace before every meal. I wasn't sure what it was that had abruptly made me remember that, but this seemed like a good time for being thankful. So I contented myself with a moment of gratitude that there were still organics for the printers (even if what they were printing was, ironically, spaghetti) and that the reclaimers were still working to make water. Dying of thirst in space seemed even less fun than being spaghettified.

That made me wonder about the optics of eating long pasta. I suppose irony will out.

Having bowed my head over the food—I sensed Tsosie's amusement but didn't make eye contact—I sipped my tea, started twirling spaghetti, and applied myself to the conversation.

Carlos was eating methodically, with every evidence of enjoyment, cutting slices of protein ball with the side of his fork, swirling them through the sauce, and chewing each one meditatively. I still didn't really understand him.

But he was, I thought, somebody I could trust. He wasn't from here. He didn't have alliances or duties. He might be useful somehow. And what we were doing involved his crew, and other than Helen—and Oni, who was still being kept under sedation—he was their only representative.

Briskly, in a low voice that wouldn't carry over the cafeteria noise, I brought both Carlos and Tsosie up to speed on what I'd learned from

Loese and Sally. Tsosie's expression got darker and dourer as I spoke, but he said nothing. Carlos at some point quit eating his spaghetti.

He leaned forward. "So Jones *isn't* one of mine."

I made a sour face.

"Ha!" he said, and resumed eating as if well-satisfied. A bite or two later, he frowned at me and said, "So what does this mean for the rest of my crew?"

I shrugged. "If we can unpick the machine, we might have a better chance of reviving the ones who've made it this far. Something in the capsule programs has been . . . sticky."

"Sticky?"

"Oppositional."

"Oh." He pushed his fork through noodles. "And you found some sort of cargo hold full of clones? Illegal clones? Do I understand that properly?"

"Unethical clones." I set my own fork down. A moment of meanness made me add, "I said I would show you and . . . I'll show you."

"Mmm," Carlos said. "Thanks all the same. I'm still having a hard time wrapping my head around why me, why us. Why they thought this was a good idea in the first place."

I laughed and covered my face. "If you found a disabled generation ship full of corpsicles, could you resist using it?"

"I resent the appellation *corpsicle*," he said, so deadpan that it was a moment before I realized he was joking.

Tsosie said, "A literal sleeper agent. It's like a conspiracy sandwich."

I reclaimed the fork and made myself stick it into the food. Eating hurt. Not eating would hurt more, in the long run. "Treason between two slices of betrayal."

"So what are we going to do about it?" Tsosie asked.

I shook my head. "Fix the problem, if we can? Save the dia? Save the hospital and Carlos's ship and basically everything?"

A presence filled my senso. "Sally's here," I told the men. Tsosie, obviously also in the loop, nodded. Carlos leaned on his forearms.

Singer was there, too, I realized. Definitely taking a few risks, that one.

I've told Singer what we know, Sally said. *He's informed the Judiciary. They're not pleased with his and his pilot's decision to come to our rescue, but he doesn't think they will take any action against him. Especially if we succeed in saving the hospital.*

"Great," I said. "Are we *going* to succeed in saving the hospital?"

We have something we think might work, Singer said.

Sally asked, *Do you want to try it first on Afar, or on Linden? I'd recommend Afar, because if anything goes terribly wrong for Linden it might further damage the hospital.*

"Zhiruo," I answered, and everybody—physically present and in senso—stared at me. Or performed the virtual equivalent.

Are you . . . sure? Sally's tone told me that she found my choice potentially punitive, which I wasn't sure was a judgment she was currently entitled to make, but whatever.

It was true that if it didn't work, Zhiruo—other than Sally, who wasn't infected—was the person who most deserved whatever fallout the sequelae might entail. That was not a medically ethical reason to use her as a test subject, however.

But I very much needed to talk to her. And that . . . was a much more supportable reason.

I wasn't at all sure it was the best idea I'd ever had, however.

"Yes," I said. "I'm sure."

Over by the printers, someone cursed. Tsosie craned his neck, frowned, and hunched his head back into his shoulders. Under his breath, he muttered, "Looks like no more provisions from *this* cafeteria."

Carlos's face sallowed. "This was how it started."

"How what started?" Tsosie asked.

The ancient human swallowed, reached for water. Drank and swallowed again. "On the *Rock*. When the machine broke out. When we were all sick, and the captain wanted us to go into the pods. This is how the system failures started."

There's a thing that happens in medicine sometimes where you spend a subjective lifetime scratching your head (if you have a head) over a patient whose condition you can't make heads or tails of. So you hand that patient over to a colleague in a more appropriate specialty, and get them back again, dizzyingly fast, cured of whatever was puzzling you.

It doesn't happen often—usually, you get them back with whatever their other complaints were worsened by the delay, and a boatload of additional treatment modalities in place that may or may not be helping. Because patients insist on being not logic problems but real, complicated people with real, complicated problems that won't tidily resolve with the application of an epiphany and a course of antivirals, or some stem cell therapy, or a quick reprogram of some damaged DNA.

But sometimes it does work. And those cases are gratifying and humiliating in equal measure. Gratifying because the problem is solved. Humiliating because you weren't the one who solved it, and from the outside and in retrospect, the process of diagnosis and treatment looks so damned easy.

Dr. Zhiruo wasn't my patient. And I knew perfectly well that what had solved the problem was the combination of Sally's knowledge of the virus that had caused it with Helen's knowledge of the machine and Singer's skill at reading strange programs. It's much easier to provide an antidote if the poisoner tells you how they made the patient sick in the first place.

Five standard hours after I left them alone to work on the problem, the artificial intelligences had solved it. Helen found me and delivered the antivirus on a data diamond. I held it in my hand and watched its brilliance as I turned it in the light.

I had expected to spend most of that time—after my conversation with Tsosie and Carlos—justifying my existence and life choices to O'Mara and Starlight, given that we'd broken quarantine protocol. That I wasn't summoned to report for administrative endoscopy was possibly the best indicator possible of how bad things were. And that O'Mara still trusted me.

I looked from the diamond to Helen, who sparkled in her own way. "Well," I said. "I guess we go to Cryo now."

Her suggestion of a chin lifted. "After that, we need to tackle the machine."

"I'm not sure how," I admitted.

She was continuing to develop and evolve. All she had ever needed was the resources to enrich herself, and the space to grow into. She was so brave and so slight—and, okay, so glittery—that my eyes stung a little from looking at her.

"I've got an idea," she said. "But I'm going to need to borrow your exo."

"My—"

"We'll talk about it later. Right now, let's get to Cryo."

O'Mara was still waiting in Cryo. Their blocky frame leaned against the bulkhead, arms folded over their chest. It should have been a self-effacing pose, but the master chief was so damned big they made the unit seem cramped.

Rilriltok was with them, buzzing morosely, perched on the high back of the desk rather than hovering in the air.

Helen and I marched up to them. I held the diamond aloft. "Why the long faces, Doctors?"

O'Mara's expression didn't brighten, but they straightened from their slump. "What's that?"

"With luck, the antiviral for Dr. Zhiruo that I told you about."

O'Mara made a motion whose significance I had to look up in senso.

Apparently it was a religious gesture for averting evil or summoning luck. I hadn't known they were a Catholic.

"Will it work?" they asked.

There is doubtless only one way to find out, friend O'Mara. Rilriltok buzzed to me. Fragile manipulators lifted the crystal from my hands. *Try it and see.*

Singer was confident in his work, at least. While we waited for the program to run, he patched himself through to Core General and watched over our shoulders. I couldn't stand it: I plugged my exo into the system directly. I could charge myself up while I watched the treatment happening.

Most of the data flow was over my head, to be honest. I'm not an AI doctor. Helen, much more practical—and built to anticipate the needs of organic life-forms—made a head-wiggle as if rolling the eyes she didn't have at me, and loaded a sim even O'Mara could follow onto the wall screen.

I watched orange blocks turning blue, hundreds of thousands of them. A logarithmic process, apparently, because the conversion started off achingly slowly and bit by bit accelerated until they were changing too fast for me to see. The whole treatment took five minutes.

Five minutes, after which I realized I had reached out at some point and taken Helen's hand. Her hand, which was warm and resilient and a little bit plasticky and felt nothing at all like a real human body. There were no bones in it. It was all squish.

"It worked," Sally said.

I looked at O'Mara. "I want to talk to her."

O'Mara pursed their lips. Before they could formulate whatever they were thinking of saying, I shook my head and said, "Alone."

Their hands went up; they stepped back. "It's my own fault if this doesn't work out how I wanted."

"Funny." I grinned. We weren't out of the woods yet, not by a long shot. But I felt like I had at least found a blazed trail that looked like it might lead somewhere. "I thought the whole point of getting me involved was so you *could* blame me for whatever went wrong."

O'Mara lifted their chin to look over my shoulder. "Helen, let's treat Linden next. Jens—"

My heels clicked. "Present."

"Just fucking make sure you're recording."

When I went in, Zhiruo's code was still isolated. I found her in a virtual garden, a haven of classical statues of seven or eight civilizations and whispering leaves. Never having interacted with her through avatars, I was surprised that she had chosen to simulate a physical, organic form. Most AIs—if they must manifest as something other than a disembodied voice or a presence in the senso—choose an inorganic avatar. I've lost count of how many sparkles of dancing lights in various colors I've had heart-to-heart conversations with, over the ans.

But Zhiruo was dressed as a Ykazhian. It gave me a start, because at first sight I thought I was looking at Hhayazh, and the rush of gladness and recognition of an old friend almost overwhelmed my anger.

I bet that was why she did it, frankly. Sneaky manipulative bundle of code.

I walked up in front of her, choosing to interact with the virtual world as if it had gravity and I had a solid human body. I felt like stomping; I limited myself to stepping firmly.

"Dr. Jens," she said, sounding pleased and plummy and prim. "You seem to have reintegrated my code. I had not realized that lay within your skill corona."

"I had help."

If she picked up my tone, she didn't show it. "Linden?"

"Linden has been affected by the virus, too, and is being treated. We called in an outside specialist." I took a breath my avatar didn't need. It's always hard to switch modes from polite introduction into confrontation. So much easier to slide away and let a problem go unchallenged. "I know what you've been doing, Dr. Zhiruo."

She quivered her feelers inquiringly. "Struggling to retain program integrity?"

"I mean the clones."

Her simulated jaws clicked, internal a moment before external. She must be performing the calculations on my mood and intent too fast for me to see, so perhaps she was delaying in order to give herself additional time to read my signals.

"Well," she said, "since you've learned about it by yourself, there's no difficulty. We can fix *your* problem easily."

My avatar had crossed its arms. I heard my fingers rattle on my exo as I tapped them against my upper arms. "I have a problem?"

I hadn't known a Ykazhian could look so conciliatory. "What we're doing helps people, Llyn. It helps them directly, when we treat them. And it helps them indirectly, when we use the resources we collect to support access to health care for everybody else. The Synarche does not allot us enough resources to run this hospital as well as it needs to be run. What if I could help you?"

"Help me."

Her gesture took in my body, the exo. "You don't have to be in pain."

"I'm not in pain." I was. But I saw no reason to make myself vulnerable.

"What if I told you we could clone your body, repair the genetic damage—your neuralgia—and upload your ayatana into the fox of a blank slate?"

That brought me up short and hard. Without snappy repartee. Without anything to say at all.

I was still herding my neurons back into some semblance of

coherence when she added, "We'd waive the procedure support cost. Your service to Core Gen has earned you some consideration."

"The hospital doesn't do that," I said.

She laughed. "If you say so."

I gathered myself. "I mean, I know the hospital does it. But it's a sleazy side job, and as much as possible, you hide it from everyone. You've been doing it so long you—what—got the previous administrator to set up a hack in the patient confidentiality monitors so that future admins can't even talk about the program?"

She didn't speak.

"Even if I believed you, where's the continuity of experience? It's a lossy copy. And you're putting that data into another brain—"

"An identical brain," she said.

I scoffed in turn. "If you say so."

She looked at me, bristles all pointed in my direction.

I said, "Neurons and synapses form in response to stimulus. To experience. To use. Personality and function are shaped—quite physically—by experience. You can't grow a brain in a vat, transcribe somebody's machine memory onto it, and expect to get the same person back. You have to develop the brain, and it won't be the same brain, no matter what."

Even on a syster's body, the somatics of dismissal were evident. "Plenty of people seem to think it's a road to eternal life."

Maybe she didn't realize I knew that they were developing the brains? Maybe she was trying to brazen it out? "Plenty of rich people used to drink pearl powder in quicksilver to cure their gout," I replied. "That was a death sentence, too."

"What if I told you that you wouldn't have to wear that thing everywhere?"

That thing. I squeezed myself a little tighter, as if I could protect my exo from her scorn.

Lead her on. "How would you do something like that?"

"The same. Body transplant," she said. "We move your ayatana into a different fox. In a cloneself with no developed personality."

"So you'd copy me, and then kill the original?"

"We'd move you."

"If this were legitimate—or even noncontroversial—the hospital would offer it as a matter of course."

"The hospital does," she said. "To people who can support the hospital's work."

"But not to everybody." I had a moment's respect for this wily slice of code. She had figured out a way to keep Core General funded. To get it built in the first place, when everything had nearly fallen apart. And nobody got hurt except people who were willing to sacrifice their own clone children to their continued existence. And those clone children.

If I hadn't met Calliope Jones, I might even think it was a kind of justice.

"It works," she said. "And no one suffers."

I had to tune back my rage to keep from spluttering and was not entirely successful. "That's not even . . . The clone suffers."

"The clone is never aware."

"The clone is aware enough to dream," I said. "The clone is aware enough to develop speech centers and a working hippocampus. The clone is aware enough that it counts as a person to me."

The most important thing in the universe is not, it turns out, a single, objective truth. It's not a hospital whose ideals you love, that treats all comers. It's not a lover; it's not a job. It's not friends and teammates.

It's not even a child that rarely writes me back, and to be honest I probably earned that. I could have been there for her. I didn't know how to be there for anybody, though. Not even for me.

The most important thing in the universe, it turns out, is a complex of subjective and individual approximations. Of tries and fails. Of ideals, and things we do to try to get close to those ideals.

It's who we are when nobody is looking.

I sat down on the bench that I knew would be a step behind me, because this was a virtual world. I let Zhiruo loom over me, and folded my hands.

I said, "I didn't know you were doing this until recently. But nevertheless I was protecting you. Me, and everybody else in the hospital. You were using us and our reputations as your shield, whether you acknowledge it or not. We're all tarnished by your act. You put every single one of us at risk, do you understand that?"

"You had nothing to do with it."

"No one on the outside is going to care about that, Zhiruo. And nobody is going to care about your protestations that they were only clones, that they had no awareness. You had to build them to have some awareness in order for them to grow useable brains."

"They're not *people*!"

It is possible to erase and mortify yourself to the point where you actually make more work for the people around you, because they are constantly doing emotional labor to support you. A well-developed martyr complex becomes a means of getting attention without ever having to take the emotional risks of asking for attention. It's a tendency, along with self-pity, that I use my rightminding to control. So I didn't unpack the suitcase full of self-recriminations and fury I was feeling. I didn't castigate myself to show Zhiruo that however much anybody might punish me for being imperfect, for being involved, I would punish myself faster and more.

I bit my tongue on all of that.

I said, "They're people. Look at Calliope."

"I *can* help you," she said.

"It's too late," I said. "The Synarche and the Judiciary now *officially* know what's been going on here. It's out of my hands, Doc."

"It's not illegal," she said.

"Maybe not," I said. "But it is *scandalous*. Which is why you've kept it secret. Because I guarantee that public opinion will make sure it is illegal. Probably so fast it'll happen before we manage to get this hospital fully retrofitted for gravity."

"What about your reputation? About what you just said? About the hospital's reputation?"

I pressed my virtual hands against my virtual eyes. It did nothing to relieve the very real headache. I was briefly very glad that I was not the rightminding specialist that was going to have to guide Zhiruo into understanding that what she had done was wrong, then guide her through the process of determining and completing the combination of restorative actions and service that might be required to make reparations for everything she had done. It wasn't illegal—but I bet it would be before the Synarche's General Council recessed again.

"I guess we both have some work to do," I said. Zhiruo was somebody else's problem now, and I didn't feel bad about that at all. I just wanted to get away from her. Right now, though, I had to go put an ayatana on.

And find out what Helen wanted to borrow my exo for. If she was ready to tell.

CHAPTER 28

I ENTERED STARLIGHT'S PARK THROUGH A DOOR THAT IRISED half-open and then stuck. I stepped high like a prancing pony, ducked my head, and jump-climbed through as quickly as possible, without touching the edges. I wanted to keep my torso intact, and all my limbs. I guess we were fortunate that Starlight seemed to be the only physical sentience since the Darboof who was affected by the meme. But then, Starlight was mostly made of wood, which could be interpreted as a construction material. And Starlight was almost completely integrated into the hospital's physical . . . er . . . plant.

At least their brain wasn't etchable crystal, like the poor Darboof. They could still think, and communicate.

I was rehearsing the conversation to come in my head. I wanted and I did not want to have it, both with equal fervor. Perhaps I should say that I was eager to have it over with.

Starlight was not doing well. Even before I approached the canopy, I could tell. The weight of crystallizing leaves dragged the great tree's canopy down—or up, from the tree's perspective, since Starlight grew roots-toward-the-hub in defiance of local standards of direction. Leaves needed light, and light was on the outside. It was irrelevant that weight was on the outside, too.

What concerned me the most were the places where boughs had cracked under the mass of all that silicon. Some big branches had already snapped, and either hung suspended by shreds of bark or lay scattered on the crystal underfoot.

I was wearing an ayatana for Starlight's species. It was probably the most pleasant one I've ever worn, to be honest, although my body felt weird and squishy, respiration was extremely odd, and I was self-conscious of the whorfling noises I kept making with every breath in or out. I also had an overwhelming urge to wave my limbs in time with the breeze. Even though there wasn't any.

I didn't need the ayatana to tell me that the administrator was desperately ill.

The outer windows seemed to be holding up so far: no cracks or chips evident. They were durable, but I have lived as long as I have lived in part by never trusting the integrity of a damaged structure too far.

I triggered my hardsuit, except for the helmet, and waited while it grew around me. If the pressure dropped, it would finish the seal on its own. If another limb dropped from the tree and crushed me . . . well, my problems would be over. I decided to worry about that some other time. And if I died before I got around to worrying, there was already more important unfinished business on that to-do list anyway.

After a few moments, the administrator had not acknowledged me. Maybe it would help if I yelled.

Does it ever help if one yells?

"Starlight," I said. "Are you there?"

The translated voice in my head, when it came, seemed creaky and slow. [Dr. Jens. How may we assist you?]

"It's how I can help you," I said. "I came to tell you that we've developed a treatment for afflicted AIs. Dr. Zhiruo was our test case, and she's responding well. We are treating Afar and Linden next. If all goes well, you should have Linden back very soon."

[Well done,] the tree chimed. [Please be aware that it is not yet safe to lift the quarantine. . . .]

Fine dust drifted over my head. I put my hand over my mouth and nose. Silicosis would be a quick way to needing a pair of vat-grown lungs my own self.

I knew that. I couldn't lift the quarantine while *this* was going on. So now we had to cure this. But first, there was something I needed to report on.

Better done than danced around. "I know about the clones."

A great sigh rustled over me. [Have you told anyone?]

"A Judiciary AI. The shipmind of *I Rise From Ancestral Night*. And put him in touch with Sally and with Dr. Zhiruo. I also told O'Mara. Steps will be taken. I imagine Dr. Zhiruo will be investigated and reassigned."

And probably have her programming adjusted after an intensive course with an AI psychologist. I couldn't imagine the Judiciary just . . . turning her loose to wreak similar havoc elsewhere.

[Good,] Starlight said. [And the saboteurs?]

"I found them," I said. "Some of them. Not the entire . . . Look, I think there's a pretty large cabal. I interviewed the ones I located. They did not threaten me. Their plans got . . . a little out of hand." My gesture took in the cracked branches, the downed limbs.

Starlight found a chuckle somewhere. [We're glad to hear it wasn't intentional. The problems will be resolved? There will be consequences?]

"Judiciary is following up on the rest of the conspirators. There will be consequences. I believe they will all be located," I said. "You guessed that they were trying to draw attention to Zhiruo's private protocols?"

[The incidents were localized in a suggestive way. Draw attention . . . no. We assumed they were attacking the protocols.]

"They didn't realize that you and O'Mara were already—" I stopped. *In on it* wasn't exactly correct. "They didn't realize that you already knew what was going on and couldn't stop it."

[Their faith in the system is touching.]

I sighed. "As near as I can reconstruct, when *Big Rock Candy Mountain*'s crew contracted a pandemic, the captain ordered them all into cold storage. He got . . . a little strange, all alone. And altered the program on the ship's AI in order to create a kind of guardian bot that first bullied his incapacitated crew into the pods, and then . . . guarded them. This worked out as well as mad science usually does. Time passed. That bot came in contact with the virus the saboteurs had set up as a trap for Dr. Zhiruo, to overwrite her protocols and force her to confess her sins—"

[Ambitious.]

"A little too ambitious," I agreed. "The infection of the machine must have been intentional, because they needed the machine to make sure we took the right cryo casket."

[It was an overcomplicated plan, and it went horribly wrong.]

"It was. It did. The conspirators that *I* interviewed have, however, surrendered. They are cooperating with the treatment of the affected AIs."

[Good. Then we can rest.]

"Don't you dare."

A pause. Then, [Excuse me?]

"Don't you dare give up on me," I said.

[Llyn,] the tree said gently. [We're dying.]

"And I'm a fucking doctor," I said. "Don't you dare give up on me. I will put this place to rights if it kills me." I took a deep breath. "Anyway, Helen has been through this before. And Helen and I have a plan."

It was a terrible plan, but that's par for the course around here. We didn't have a better one, and with the meme eating Core General from the inside out, our options were either to put off acting until we either starved or the hull cracked open or we thought of something less radical . . . or to take a risk and maybe have time to try something else if it failed and we weren't dead after.

I sent for Helen. She must have been waiting outside the broken door, because in less than a minute, she was beside me. She plopped herself on the crystal of the hull immediately, as if she sat down on the bodiless depths of space every dia.

Although, come to think of it, she was a space ship. Even if she was a differently embodied space ship for the time being.

I reached into the ayatana—only one ayatana, thank the space goblins—for a better sense of Starlight's anatomy. I reached out and took Helen's hand. It still felt weird, but given who I was sharing my brain with, no weirder than my own body.

I looked up at Starlight. "It's not just you, you know. The whole hospital is in danger."

A rustle that was not words answered. And then words. [What about . . . the crew of Afar?]

"The first one to undergo surgery is awake," I said. "With limited deficits. It's going to be—"

I couldn't say it was going to be all right.

"The prognosis is good," I finished.

Starlight laughed. [Our prognosis is not good, Dr. Jens.]

"I am," I said definitively, "a *rescue specialist*. I am also the only person we know of, other than Helen, who has managed to come into direct contact with this thing and find a way out again. We have the skills, Starlight."

[We do not doubt your capabilities.] They sighed, wind through leaves, with a strange crystal edge to it. [We are tired and in a lot of pain.]

"Sibling," I said, "I feel you."

"Here's what we're going to do," Helen said. "We have to take on the meme, and the machine the meme is building, and disentangle it from your cellular structure. And once we learn how to do it here, we can apply that knowledge to getting it out of my own ship."

[And how do you propose to accomplish that? If we could access its processing pathways—if we could even find them—we think we could fight it. But it's building its own parallel infrastructure through ours, and in fact disassembling ours to accomplish this.]

Starlight rattled their crystallizing leaves for emphasis. Something cracked, and broken pieces tinkled.

I winced and held up one hand. "Please don't harm yourself. We have a plan. We're going to break into the machine with"—I waved—"my exo."

What happened next involved a lot of tubes and wiring. Well, to be absolutely precise, what happened next in a rigorous sequence of events was a long walk through corridors with flickering, unsettling lighting, down to Cryo, where we met Carlos and Rilriltok. O'Mara had left: I assumed they were back in their office, coordinating treatment efforts on the other AIs and continuing support for Zhiruo. The fact of the matter was that now that we had the base code to work from, and the antivirus, once we could get the paralyzed AIs back online they were more than capable of handling their own defense. It was a matter of . . . well, I'm an organics doc. So I'm going to cast this in terms that make sense to me.

It was a matter of giving them a vaccination, so they could build their own antibodies to the problem, and adapt those antibodies as the problem evolved. That, and giving them a little platform of clear space to assemble their formidable resources on, and to sally forth to fight from.

I lay down in the cryo pod—Dwayne Carlos's cryo pod, for a closer connection to the machine. I remembered how I had used my relationship with my exo to stand firm against the machine before, to weasel myself and Calliope out of its clutches, and reviewed the tactics I had used. It would be better prepared this time, I was sure.

And this time I had Helen.

There you go again, deciding to trust somebody you don't really know.

Well, if it all went wrong, I could have the comfort of knowing I'd had one foot out the door the whole time. Maybe, before I died, I could mutter a single, ringing *I told you so.*

I was plastered all over with sticky disks, and Helen, sitting on the edge of the cryo pod, bristled with wires. Rilriltok was making the final, tricky, hair-fine connections directly into my fox and exo.

The door slid open and Goodlaw Cheeirilaq strode in, feathery feet clacking on the tiles, wing undercoverts showing flashes of fiery red and yellow. If I had had to guess, this was the Rashaqin body language for *I am extremely pissed off and about to do something about it.* I didn't have to guess, though, because the instant Cheeirilaq entered, Rilriltok ducked itself entirely behind me.

I ought to arrest the lot of you, it said.

I tried to sit straighter in my hedgehog bristle of connective devices. "Probably," I said. "What would the proximate cause be?"

It fiddled its forelimbs, as upright in posture as it could be, given the height of the ceiling. I wasn't sure if it was counting up different offenses, or if it was picking out which one outraged it the most.

You concealed evidence leading to the identity of saboteurs!

"I brought that evidence to O'Mara. What else?"

A raptorial forelimb snapped out, so fiercely I thought it likely to sever my leads or possibly even me. Cheeirilaq had better control than that, though. It stopped a few centimeters from my chest. *You're about to endanger this entire facility with some . . . some primate shenanigans and untested protocols.*

Rilriltok peered over my shoulder: just the eyes. *Begging your pardon, friend Cheeirilaq. But the hospital is already in danger. Or did you have an uneventful trip here? One involving smoothly functioning equipment and reliable lighting?*

Cheeirilaq loomed, then settled back slightly. It didn't exactly have haunches, but the long legs folded to lower its abdomen. *I . . . did not.*

"Look," I said. "We have—"

Carlos stepped between me and Cheeirilaq, interrupting me as if I had not been speaking. "We have to do something now. The equilibrium is punctuating, and if we don't deal with the machine immediately . . . we're all going to die. Ask me how I know."

That man. Was so damned annoying sometimes.

But Cheeirilaq was listening to him. And to Helen, when she added, "If we can get the machine to de-integrate from the hospital's structure, to stop disassembling the hospital . . . Well, the hospital is going to need structural repairs. But I've seen what the machine does to a habitat on the premise that it's making the inhabitants safe forever. And it doesn't even seem to have those constraints on this station. We cannot allow that to happen here."

The extra processing power was *definitely* making a difference.

"I did it once, on a small scale," I offered. "I think we can do it again."

The Goodlaw gave one of its enormous highly oxygenated sighs. *When we're all dead and floating in space, I will save my last transmission to remind each and every one of you that I told you this was a terrible idea.*

Carlos and I looked at each other. "Fair," he said.

"Fair," I echoed. "Now can we get the rest of these leads attached before anything else falls off this hospital?"

I lay in the dark again, and talked to the machine. It was less rewarding than I had anticipated.

The first object was to get it talking. Get it engaging.

I made sure I could feel Helen through my fox, there behind me. And Sally and Linden back there, too. I wished I had time to throw confetti and sing songs about the contact with Linden, but when the world is ending sometimes you have to save the party until there's time to bake.

Then I reached out into the networks of the (disabled!) cryo chamber, and through it to the networks of the hospital. I groped. I squinted, metaphorically speaking. Sally and Helen groped and squinted with me, right alongside.

The cryo unit had been built by the machine. Or built using the same protocols as the machine. It was a back door, in other words, into the neural networks we were trying to locate and pry loose. By seeking through a neural network that was connected to and used the same protocols as the machine, I—well, really, Linden and Sally—were able to identify the threads of the machine's protocols and infrastructure running through the stuff of the hospital.

Sally reached through my fox; Helen was hardwired in. The three of us moved in tandem, like coordinated eyes and hands. Linden, too, was there, an external presence following our lead and guidance. I felt her comforting strength and agility floating above and around me, virtually speaking. Wrapping me in a cloak of knowing what the hell she was doing, mostly: support I definitely needed.

I am many things: not a single one of them makes me qualified to troubleshoot or debug or antivirus an AI.

Somewhere beyond us, I knew that Singer had Sally more or less in custody. She was here with me on parole, not as a free sentient. But there was not much I could do about that now.

What I could do was this, and it would serve no purpose to anyone if I could not focus.

There were still traces of the machine's contact in my exo's pathways. Those made patterns that someone—not someone like me, but someone like Linden, like Helen, like Sally—could follow back, theoretically, and use to infiltrate the machine's own systems in return. I guessed it might have erased those traces, but it hadn't had time; I'd thrown it out before it managed to complete its business.

Sort of like housebreaking a puppy.

I should get back to a planet one of these diar. I miss dogs.

So Sally swept down the dark neural pathways from my fox into my exo, and from those interfaces into the weird structures that the machine had been building through the infrastructure of Core General. I hung on to her like a remora on the underside of a manta ray, propelled and sheltered by dark, immaterial wings. Linden soared alongside us. Helen was a liquid streak of gold.

We barreled into the processing structures of the machine without pause. Probably not the most cautious of tacks, but—

Well, I don't know much about this stuff. But they were *weird*. Labyrinthine. Helen's blaze of light pulsed in strange rhythms off to my left—not *really* my left, but your brain has to do something with the neural inputs and so it makes up images. Linden's vast wings rippled soundlessly. There were stars.

The stars were information sources, nodes. Like neurons, far away in the void.

Watch out, Linden said. *Llyn, whatever happens: Don't punch out. Just hold on.*

"It's a synapse," I said. "We're bridging it."

I don't know if Linden or Helen heard me. Because then the stars were gone.

I found myself alone in the dark. Drifting. Aware, with the awareness that there was nothing around me to notice.

Except the sense of a nearby presence, watching me and aware.

Oh no, I told the machine. *You tried this before and I am not listening.*

It's going to be lonely in here for you, then. Besides, I've been with you all along. Holding you up, helping your pain. Have you considered what I want?

I wondered if I had a voice. I decided to try it, to give myself an anchor in the dark.

"You are not my exo. My exo is not sentient. It is a tool."

Helen is a tool. Isn't Helen sentient?

Okay, I could talk. And be heard. By myself, and by the disembodied voice. Useful. I said, "If you are my exo, what would you do without me?"

If you are obliquely verbalizing a suicidal ideation, it said, quietly—mechanically—*I am obligated to report it under section 274, subsection 14, paragraph xvii of the universal caretaking standard.*

Well, it certainly sounded like an exo then.

"No, machine," I said. "I just—"

It waited for five full standard seconds—probably timed, since I was out of illusions—before it said, *You just?*

"I can't rely on you, either." The words hurt coming out, as if they were feathered with cactus hooks on the outside. I was half surprised they made it, but there was so much force behind them it would have hurt even more to keep them in. "I can't trust anything. Not my own body. Not my own tech."

Events are unpredictable, the machine said primly. *But I have always done my best for you. Preserve and protect human life at all costs. That is what I am.*

That did *not* sound like my exo. I wondered if, in their previous contact, the machine and my exo had somehow . . . contaminated each other's programs. As the machine seemed to contaminate everything it touched.

Where was Linden? Where were Helen and Sally?

"How am I supposed to trust that?"

The silence went on too long, however. And I am just meat. I'm fragile. I caved in. "I never trusted anything. And that was fine. I was used to it. I was . . . cagey, and I never put my weight on anything. And that was good. It was smart. It was the right thing to do."

Was it? the machine asked. *Are you certain?*

"*Yes.*" The word got out on an explosion of breath and emotion.

Please, it said, a little while later. *Explain?*

"I came here," I said. "And you fucking seduced me. I mean, not so much you; that's not fair. You did what you were built to do. But that fucking tree, O'Mara, and Sally, and every fucking thing about Core General. They told me there was nothing to worry about. That this was a safe place and people here got taken care of. That this was a community. And it's fucking not. It's corrupt and it uses people and there are still magic special people getting magic special treatment because they're awful and do everything in terrible ways."

People here are taken care of, the machine reminded me, and I calmed myself down and remembered what I was talking to. *People come here to be protected and saved. We will save them.*

A demon. Talking to me with the voice of an object I trusted. A tool I needed.

But not really the tool at all.

"Some people get better care than others." Suddenly, ridiculously, I was sobbing. What a stupid thing to break your heart over: just a machine, just politics. But I had believed, and now I didn't believe anymore.

I was losing my faith. Losing my religion. And in the process I was gaining a bitterly ironic understanding of why my marriage failed: because I'd never believed in it. I mean, other reasons, too. But I hadn't believed in it. I had not committed to it.

I did not, in general, believe in things.

I'd believed in Core General.

I'd been wrong.

Mostly, once you're an adult, you move past the kind of raw, unregulated emotion that wracks you as an adolescent. You've learned to regulate yourself pretty well, and you have a fox monitoring your emotional responses for when that's not quite enough.

I had never learned how to regulate pain and loss like this. My purpose in life, my calling. My whole belief system.

Gone.

Gone, and worse: I was an utter fool, an absolute *chump,* for ever having believed in them. Core General was just a place. It wasn't a mission. It wasn't a grail. It was a bunch of people out to maximize their own well-being. People fortunately regulated by electrochemical intervention, so they weren't complete sociopathic assholes driven by absolutely nothing but the profit motive.

I felt my exo—my real exo, not this alien that somehow *thought* it was my exo—reaching to tune my GABA up and lower my reactivity, and I figuratively slapped it away with all the emotional violence I could muster. It was a sad little gesture of control, mostly pathetic. It still made me feel better.

Refusing help gave me a sense of agency.

I was so alone. I might as well prove it, and do everything for myself. Who needed demon lovers and their falsities?

At least I knew that now. At least I wasn't kidding myself anymore. I could get out of this virtual nightmare and—

No.

Linden had said—whatever you do, don't punch out.

Don't punch out.

"You can't chase me away," I said, and gritted my teeth against whatever the machine might throw at me—

Got it, Helen—somewhere—said, with vast machine satisfaction. *Llyn, you can back out now.*

Llyn?

So what if I was drowning in the sense of loss? It didn't matter anyway. I didn't have anything to live for. Nothing was going to get better from here.

Your neurochemistry indicates that you are at serious risk for self-harm, the machine said patiently. Was that the machine? Was it my exo?

It said, *For your own safety, I need you to let me adjust your chemistry.*

I wanted the pain. The pain would keep me wary and safe. It would help me keep everyone else away.

I wanted the agency of refusing that help.

Llyn, someone said in my ear. *Llyn. Let us help you.*

The voice was familiar. The voice had betrayed me.

The machine is messing with your chemistry.

Sally. It was Sally, my friend who I loved. Sally, who had betrayed my trust.

Sally, who had done terrible things.

Sally, who had saved my life, again and again.

I wavered. The void spun under me, vast and lightless as the Well. It would feel so good to fall into it.

It would be so selfish to fall into it.

"Fine," I said. "Make me stupid and happy again."

The bed in my quarters was soft and too big for one person. I'd still been married when I came to Core General. Technically. I'd rated family crew quarters even though my spouse had never joined me—had never intended to join me—here. They'd never asked me to give up the quarters after it became plain that Alessi and Rache would not be joining me. Would *never* be joining me.

It was a very comfortable bed.

What was I doing in it? I ought to be in cryo.

That doesn't matter, the voice said. *Concentrate on what you feel. Let me help you. Let me keep you safe.*

I tried to pretend the bed was lumpy enough to justify my tossing and turning. I didn't feel stupid and happy again. But I did feel able to breathe. I thought, privately, *What you are feeling is not real.* But no, what I was *sensing* was not real. What I was feeling was real enough.

"You've destroyed me," I said to the machine.

You are right here, it disagreed.

Where *was* "right here," exactly? I didn't think I was really in my quarters. I didn't think I was really in my bed. I had the unreal sense of a dream that keeps swapping locations and people.

"Something is right here," I said. "But what do I have to believe in? What do I have to work for? I had a thing. A reason. I had something bigger than me. More than that, I had something *I* wanted. For the first time in my life. Something I trusted. Believed in. I had faith. And you betrayed me."

I did not betray you, the machine said.

I laughed, a short bark that peeled the back of my throat with its force. "What do you call it, then?"

The machine said, *Your own people betrayed you. They lied to you. But I can help you fix that. I can make you safe and strong and just like everybody else. I can help you punish them. All you have to do is let me make you safe.*

I didn't want to punish anyone, I realized. I wanted to go back to a world where I believed in them.

And I knew what the machine's idea of *safe* looked like.

I said, "And you've made yourself a part of my people, this hospital. A part of my exo, that I rely on to do my job."

That I relied on to be capable of most things.

You don't need an exo if you let me protect you. If you let me care for you.

"Sure," I said. "If I let you lock me in a box and freeze me. I'd be safe. Why would I want that?"

The machine said, *To control your pain.*

I closed my eyes. I thought I closed my eyes. It made no difference to the level of darkness. Everybody seemed to think I would sell out anything, in order to gain a little physical comfort.

"I'd rather be in pain than fool myself into thinking I could rely on somebody I can't."

To get your revenge, then. On the people who betrayed you. Throw them to the wolves as they threw you.

Now there was an archaic turn of phrase.

My hands curled. I was mostly sure my hands curled, anyway. I could not feel them curling. Vengeance . . . was a real temptation.

Vengeance was also atavistic, childish, and sophipathological, with a tendency to create generations-long chains of toxicity and tragedy.

"I don't want revenge." I wanted to trust again. I wanted to belong. Temptation aside . . . was betraying them who I was? Was it who I chose to be? Was it who I *wanted* to be?

Somebody who offered no better than she got?

I had a choice. I could do more than reacting.

I could not trust this machine any more than I could trust the machine—Core General—that had betrayed me. Less, in fact: this machine was unstable, and its goals were illogical and extreme. It had been made by a sophipathological captain to pursue a sophipathological goal. It was operating out a kind of AI reactivity loop, all sense of perspective lost, and once it had come in contact with the meme, they'd . . . fed off each other.

Save the humans, preserve the humans. Even if you have to destroy them to do so, and the whole world, too.

Silence came in answer. And in that silence, somehow, I found a clue.

We had figured out—okay, *Mercy* had figured out—what the machine was, where the machine had come from. The same way I now knew where the different sort of machine, the political machine, at the heart of Core General's dark secret had come from. Through evidence and deduction.

Helen had said that "Central" was offline, and had been since the debut of the machine. Helen was a peripheral, an interface for a larger shipmind. She'd been confused and inarticulate until she'd gotten access to the processing power at Core Gen, and had then begun to regrow from her seed.

But the machine *was* Central, wasn't it? It was the machine *Big Rock Candy Mountain*'s shipmind had turned itself into, when that captain decided that the only way to keep his crew safe was to drive them into cryo chambers, and to accomplish this, had driven his shipmind mad.

When forced to follow insane orders, in the dark and cold and constant danger of space, the ship had in turn lost its mind, become paranoid and afraid. Even if the influenza epidemic had had an extreme mortality rate—say, 30 percent—it would have been better than the failure rate on the cryo chambers.

But the captain hadn't given it a choice. The machine hadn't meant to murder most of its people and crew itself with ghosts in cryo chambers. But it had. And the event had resulted in an obsessional loop; a being that could only imagine one way to protect someone.

To lock them away, and freeze them forever.

Then it had waited there for Well knew how long, until Loese's conspiracy-mates had found it and had made it able to infect the whole world.

I hadn't known I had it in me to pity something so deadly and broken as the machine. But it had done what it had done for reasons that it was told had to make sense to it. Reasons that were programmed into it. Terrible reasons based in terrible experiences, it turned out. And with terrible consequences.

Just like Zhiruo. Just like Sally and Loese. Just like Calliope.

Just like me.

I drew a breath, and it didn't feel like my lungs filled. "Anyway, I couldn't trust a different exo any more than I can trust this one, could I? You could hack that, too."

More silence. I turned my head and sobbed into my pillow—if it was even a real pillow and not a virtual, neural simulation of a pillow. At least it seemed to adequately muffle the sound, but sound is often muffled in dreams, isn't it? Nobody else needed to suffer because I wanted to curl into a tight curve and scream from the depths of my belly. So I screamed silently, my whole body clenching around the emotion, my cheeks aching with the strain. It didn't matter. Nothing mattered. I might as well die: there was no purpose to existing anymore.

I'd found a purpose in service, before. I'd subsumed myself into being useful for others. I'd given up my family without a fight, without thinking that giving them up was selfish, too. Earning my carbon footprint, my breath and food. But that was over, I knew. I'd had a taste of living for myself, and I could not go back to living entirely for others again.

But also I didn't believe in the cause I had given my whole heart and soul to in service anymore. It was gone. It had abandoned me.

No, worse. It had never existed. I had invented it; I had allowed myself to be deluded, because I had so badly wanted it to exist. I had wanted to belong to a thing. I had wanted to need and be needed.

Why are we born needing impossible things? Why is it that we all have things we need to live that simply do not exist in the universe?

A purpose in life. Unconditional love? Our emotional needs met? Ha. What cruel asshole thought this shit up?

"My marriage wasn't perfect: it had problems and didn't work out. But if I got a different marriage, it would have problems eventually, too. If I went to a different hospital, it would turn out to be rotten inside as well. I thought I would rather be alone and in pain than be betrayed. But I don't like being alone and in pain, either, so I found things to believe in. And I kept being wrong." I hadn't realized I was speaking until I spoke. "You know what? Fuck this. I give up. I'm going to quit. Go on the Guarantee. Go live in safety somewhere."

You'd be bored.

That didn't sound like the machine. Was it? Was it Sally? Linden?

"I'd rather be bored than sad. I'd rather be alone than lonely." I was repeating myself. Well, I wasn't at my best. "I *believed* in this place. I believed in *me*. And the worst part is, I didn't mind not believing in things until this place made me believe in something. And it was all a lie. It was using me."

Silence again. Then a voice. It was definitely Linden. *Dr. Jens.*

Oh. "Linden."

She was calm and warm and professional. *What you said wasn't wrong, but it sounds like you're emotionally overwrought—*

"You're fucking right I am! And I deserve to be!" This, the detached part of me thought, is why you'd rather be dissociated. Life is easier when you compartmentalize.

Fair, she said. *But listen for a moment, please. The machine in Core General's systems is contained. I know it did a great deal of damage to your emotional equilibrium and your neurochemistry along the way, but you did it. You held on. You held the connection, and Sally and Helen and I got through. We've firewalled it out of the hospital's systems and pried it loose from Starlight.*

You won.

Had I? I didn't feel like it. It felt like I had crumbled. Shattered.

"Wow," I said. "Is that what winning feels like? I don't think I've ever had such a goalpost-shifting, pointless argument in my entire life."

Linden said, *I'm here to bring you out, Llyn.*

I opened my eyes in a room that seemed simultaneously bright, and full of fuzzy, undefined shadows. I blinked twice before I realized that I was looking past the open lid of the cryo pod, and my shipmates were staring down at me.

I blinked my eyes once more. They nearly focused. I blinked again.

One of the looming shadows was greener, larger, and more angular than the others, and was wearing a four-armed bolero jacket with a glint of gold on one lapel.

This was a horrible idea, said Cheeirilaq. *Why is your species so full of horrible ideas?*

"There is a difference between this horrible idea and all the other ones." I started pulling electrodes off my scalp while Rilriltok buzzed behind me anxiously.

The Goodlaw cocked its head in what I, a human, could only anthropomorphize as exasperation. Eyesight, definitely improving.

"This one worked," I said, and started laughing so hard my diaphragm hurt.

I was still giggling off residual adrenaline when the oil-slick-iridescent, knobbly-tinkertoy pseudopod burst through the cryo ward deck plating.

Life must be preserved, the machine whispered. *All your lives. Forever.*

It writhed, tip seeking like a blind snake's snout, and I felt it like a snap the moment its attention fastened on me. I was still sitting in the pod, half wired to it, some of the connections going directly into my fox interface. Rilriltok, right behind me, gave a despairing buzz and worked faster. Even with all the giant, massive, impermeable systers on Core General, I have to say that my fragile little insect friend was the bravest of anyone. Precisely because it was so fragile, and yet it did terrifying and dangerous and necessary things anyway.

You, the machine said. Its voice reached me as vibrations through the deck, through the air. It set my hairs prickling. *You betrayed us. You stopped us from keeping them safe. You must be restrained.*

Restrained.

We will restrain you.

CHAPTER 29

SURE, OF COURSE. THIS WAS HOW MY LIFE WORKED. Beat the enemy on the virtual plane. Escape, relax, start thinking about cocktails.

Then, oh shit, nanotech tentacles.

It's possible to love a thing, to trust a thing, to rely on a thing, to be overjoyed that a thing exists—and also to resent it. My exo, for example, makes me weak with gratitude. It makes it possible for me to live the life I want to live, to give to the community in the way I wish to give to the community. It makes me strong and nimble and quick in ways I never was without it.

It is also something I have to think about. Something to consider each dia. Something to maintain, and the body within it needs maintenance, too.

A piece of cognitive load. One more damned thing to take into account.

And it's a symbol of not being able to always do everything, all the time, right now.

Well, right that second, right *now*, I had no mixed emotions about my exo at all, despite the fact that the machine had infiltrated and impersonated it in order to—to put it bluntly—fuck with my mind. I guess, in fairness, I had invited the machine in—and the diversion had worked, because Linden had managed to force it to withdraw from the hospital's structure. I guess we knew now where it had gone.

However complicated I might feel about machine and exo and exo and machine when I had the leisure to unpack those feelings, my exo was saving me from the nanotech tentacles. (Yes, I know. Microbots are not technically nanotech. When you're being chased by them, fine distinctions kind of go out the airlock.)

My exo jerked me upright the instant Rilriltok yanked the connection free, which it managed with a surgical lack of nicety. It didn't matter; it was hurtling its own delicate wings and exoskeleton backward like a fly that senses a drastic shift in air pressure. I got a hand up and slapped at my hardsuit actuator: too late. Either that same shift in air pressure or my exo's self-preservation protocols had already triggered it, and I had to snatch my hand back fast to keep from losing a fingertip.

Or several.

The hardsuit sealed over my face, obscuring my vision for a moment. For another moment, I could see clearly as the utility fog formed into the transparent viewplate. Until a sudden concussion knocked it askew, and red-black tunnel edges closed on me.

I bounced off a bulkhead—I think it was a bulkhead—and tumbled into the corner, one aching bundle of bruises and pain.

The blow probably wouldn't have killed me, even without the hardsuit. I made that determination as my exo picked me up: wheezing, my spasming diaphragm at war with clenching ribs. A quick differential suggested that they were bruised or cracked but probably not broken, and at least not grinding.

They weren't stabbing me in a vital organ: they could wait. Even if they *had* been stabbing me in a vital organ, they would have had to wait.

"I'm sorry I ever doubted you," I whispered to my exo. It didn't answer, because it was only a machine.

A machine that had saved my bacon yet again, because as I packed a short breath in, my head was up and my eyes open. Just in time to see the next blow coming.

I was stunned. I was winded. I was fifteen ans out of practice. But I had once been combat trained. And all that work you do to teach yourself and your hardware those reflexes does, in the later moment when you need them, pay off.

Dodging also hurts like hell when your body is no longer hardened to it. But you know what hurts even more?

Getting nailed in the face by a fast-moving mountain of nanotech. Microbots. Whatever.

I reeled inelegantly out of the way.

A quick tactical assessment of the room provided the intelligence that we were . . . sort of fucked, to be completely fair. I'd lost track of Helen. Rilriltok, bless it, was headed for the door. Smart; the best assistance it could give us was to get the hell out of the way. It had accomplished everything here it could, and nobody would be served if it got itself squashed, crippled, or maimed.

Cheeirilaq, its own armored hardsuit finished integrating, had jumped, inverted itself, and was racing across the ceiling of the ward. Carlos was edging back toward the private room doors. His hardsuit had triggered, or he had thought to trigger it. His hand groped out toward a fire extinguisher.

Sure, why not. Good thinking. It couldn't hurt, after all.

The machine wiggled itself backward out of the bulkhead I had been standing in front of a minute before like a big, segmented worm inching out of its burrow. Light streamed in around the blunt taper of its nose. At its rear—or its middle, maybe—more microbots humped themselves out of the ragged gash in the decking the machine had lunged through.

The edges of the hole weren't smooth. That meant that the material the thing was assembling itself from wasn't merely whatever it came into contact with. The curled and ruptured polymer and metal showed no signs of ablating away, sublimating into the stuff of the machine.

It's ripping out the dedicated information pathways it built. Linden's voice, in my fox, urgent. *The ones we chased it out of.*

Starlight— I don't know if my subvocalization was as panicked as I felt.

The invasive architecture is stripping itself, Linden answered. *We have a trauma team standing by.*

Oh, unrebirthing Well. That was going to be . . . awful.

What could I do? I wasn't a tree surgeon. And I was running for my life. Running for my life, and trying to come up with a plan. While on the run.

Item one: the machine had a personal grudge against me. Okay, I could use that, maybe, to lead it away from Carlos and the patients he—

Oh, Carlos. You asshole. That's what he was doing over there. Putting himself between the machine and Cirocco Oni, and the other people who were probably, honestly, just frozen and dead but we couldn't declare them such until they were thawed and dead.

Life must be preserved, the machine whispered. *All your lives. Forever.*

"Funny way you have of going about it," I gasped, and lunged toward the hole it had made in the corner where the bulkheads met. I jumped, and as I jumped I triggered my gravity belt and sailed through, momentarily immune to the spin momentum that left everybody else stuck to the deck.

Your brain does strange things in a crisis. Right then, mine chose to have the epiphany that Core General was really, if you thought about it, a giant centrifuge.

I had no idea what was on the other side of that ruptured bulkhead, except by the lack of freezing, boiling, poisoning, asphyxiation, drowning, melting, or screams it seemed to be ox sector. But whatever it was, the machine had busted clear through, and the gap was probably big enough for me, also.

Linden, clear that corridor!

Honestly. Dr. Jens, what do you think I've been doing with my time?

I burst through into the other side, somersaulted, let the gravity reclaim me, and took off at a sprint. Every step jarred pain up through my ankles and knees, and I triggered the belt again, kicked off, and went sailing away

Sally?

Here. Her virtual voice came crisp and distinct and possibly a little relieved through my fox.

Sally, can't you hack this thing? You did it once before?

Sure, she said. *I did it before we pulled all my backsplash viral code out of it!*

Huh. It had never occurred to me that her taking control of the machine back on *Big Rock Candy Mountain* was improbable. I guess I am not very adept, when it comes to figuring out which of my dearest and most trusted friends is a spy.

"Well don't you have a record of what you used at the time?" I dodged, and flung myself farther down the corridor.

Just in time, as the pseudopod slammed through the hole behind me like a monstrous snake and started propagating down the corridor walls, tinkertoys clacking.

I am, Sally said in a measured tone, *currently under arrest for suspicion of sabotage, negligent homicide, gross bodily harm, reckless endangerment, waste of common resources, waste of dedicated resources, interfering with the regular functioning of a Synarche emergency response, interfering with the regular functioning of Synarche emergency personnel, assault on a digital person, interfering with the regular functioning of a Synarche public service—*

"And mopery," I muttered, ducking another tentacle.

What?

"Kind of in a hurry here!"

My files are under legal interdict, is what I'm saying.

If the massive failures of Core General's systems had been due to the machine undermining its systems and not to the saboteurs, she didn't deserve *all* of those charges. But some of them were certainly valid, and I didn't have a lot of time to argue, no matter how inconvenient her being under arrest was right now. I ricocheted around a corner. A pseudopod dented a wall behind me. Not smashing through it this time. Shocking demonstration of restraint.

Maybe it actually *didn't* mean to kill me.

Mostly, however, I didn't want to find out. The machine did not have a good track record of keeping its pets in good health.

"Situation assessment?"

I had been asking Sally, but it was Linden who answered: *Run.*

"Running is not a tactic!" I shouted back.

Ahead, along my projected path, sirens warned bystanders to clear the corridor. The whisk of closing doors and figures vanishing through them told me most of the staff were complying.

"What am I running *toward?*"

That was another piece of advice I've often found myself recalling: Never retreat *from* an enemy; always fall back *toward* a resource.

Right now, I was drawing the machine away from my friends, and managing to keep it from attacking—pardon me, *rescuing*—other patients or staff. Soon, I'd need the next strategy.

Core General was a wheel, and I'd run out of racetrack unless I led the machine through different levels or into the units that housed chlorine, methane, water breathers. That would result in deaths, and I didn't want any more rainbow-colored blood on my hands.

I dodged again, full of a diffuse, frustrated, distracting rage. I was still angry, and I didn't have time to feel things right now. Then I remembered that being angry was sometimes useful, and also—*tentacle!*—that I had a lot of really good things to be angry about.

Being in fear for your life is marvelously focusing. You can concentrate, let go of everything nonessential, think only about the thing right in front of your face. The thing that needs to be done. If the anger was bubbling up now, that suggested that it was a message from the part of my mind that processed things too complicated to turn over to my conscious attention, things that did not neatly resolve themselves into narrative but were complicated and chaotic and emerged in patterns only on the level of hunches and gitchy feelings. So I ought to be using my anger. It didn't have to be a distraction, a paralysis. Turned inward.

It could be fuel.

I didn't need a reaction. I needed a plan. And I needed it now, as I careened around the corridor, flipping from ceiling to hand rail to the frame of a door. Behind me, the machine cooed and rustled, its tendrils propagating along the bulkheads at terrifying speed. Pseudopods edged up on me as you might edge up on a skittish cat you were trying to catch for transport.

Preserve life. Preserve life.

It had its metric.

No.

Preserve *human* life. I had to think like an archaic Terran, who considered their own species and its survival more important than any other single factor in the universe. So the machine's goal had to be to preserve *human* life. And given the politics of its unrightminded era, probably to preserve the lives of those it considered to be *its* people. So that meant its crew, over and above anything else.

It had turned away from Carlos.

It had, in fact, generalized the directive to preserve the lives of its crew into a hellish and accidentally genocidal series of actions. And—I was guessing here—it seemed pretty likely that that overgeneralized code was what, when combined with Sally's nice little sabotage meme, had unleashed such unprecedented unholy hell all over my nice hospital.

What had I been thinking about utilitarianism as a bad philosophy on which to train AIs?

Helen! I yelled. *I need Helen right now! Helen, HELP!*

CHAPTER 30

I DON'T KNOW WHERE SHE CAME FROM. I DON'T KNOW HOW she got there. But Helen was *there*—suddenly, brilliantly, shining in the damaged flicker of the corridor lights, surrounded by sparks and coils of blue smoke. The machine glittered iridescent black from all the facets of its components. What had become of its playful, toylike colors? Had it shed them when it went to war?

Helen, in the face of it, gleamed warm gold, reflective. The light surrounding the two peripherals was brutal, changeable. Arcs of electricity limned a pall of fire-suppressant flakes drifting ineffectually from above like planetary snow.

The hardsuit would keep me from suffocating.

For a moment, everything felt still. Helen, me. The machine. A draft swirled the flakes away in a Coriolis spiral. The hospital was still spinning, still making gs. And somewhere nearby there was a hole in the outer hull, and we were losing atmosphere. The pressure doors should be falling.

The pressure doors did not fall.

Something somewhere deep in the bubble's infrastructure was broken. Something somewhere had catastrophically failed.

My laugh echoed brutally inside my helmet. Sitrep: What *wasn't* fucked up beyond all recognition? It was likely to be shorter.

I'd fallen. Fallen, or been knocked down. I was lying against the corner where the bulkhead met the deck. Tossed aside like a discarded doll. I put a hand on my grav belt. Crushed beyond use.

I needed to get moving. And first, I needed to get up.

Helen faced the machine. She was tiny before it, tiny in a corridor designed to pass systers like Tralgar and systers in environmental suits that amounted to armored, tracked vehicles. The machine towered. Piled up like a thunderhead, pulling itself out of bulkheads and the deck, billowing into all the space beyond.

I put a hand on the deck. I hauled on the grab rail. I would never say an unkind word about grab rails again.

I got a knee under me.

The exo helped me stand.

The machine bulged left. Helen stepped to block it, hands outstretched.

The machine retreated. Coalesced.

I tried to straighten. I have never felt so heavy in my life. Someone stepped toward me. Human, in a hardsuit. Tsosie. I knew the way he moved. Another someone beside me. Also a hardsuit. Unfamiliar. Also almost certainly human, by the shape.

They put a hand on my elbow, levering me upright. Through the plate, I glimpsed a face. Carlos.

I opened my mouth to protest, and he winked and shoved me behind him. To Tsosie.

"Dammit—"

Tsosie tugged my arm. "The machine won't hurt him. Come on."

"The machine will punch through bulkheads to get me," I argued. "It's decided I'm the enemy. It's not going to change its mind. And the pressure doors—"

Weren't working.

"—I have to stay here."

Tsosie tugged me one more time. Carlos calmly walked forward—putting his body between us and the machine. On the theory that the machine would not do anything to risk him. But I knew—we all knew—that the machine's program was haywire. That it would do plenty of dangerous things because its protocol for risk assessment was utterly corrupt.

Accidents happen. Around something like the machine, accidents happen a lot.

I magnetized my boots to the deck. "Carlos is making the wrong choice."

"The wrong choice for you. But he isn't you, is he?"

I couldn't pull my gaze away. I tried to move forward. Tsosie held me. *He's making the right choice for me. That's the problem. I'm supposed to be the one who takes risks around here.*

"This is all my fault," I said. "I had a terrible idea."

"If it was a terrible idea, we all had the exact same one. So share the blame a little." Tsosie edged me back a step while I was distracted.

The machine broke, as if a dam broke before it. Like a thunderhead rolling over itself, climbing an updraft, it poured past Helen on all sides, tendrils running along the corridor walls, filling the space with a hideous clattering that echoed inside my helmet until I wanted to clamp my hands over my ears. Now I lunged in the other direction—backward, dragging Tsosie, knowing it was ineffectual. Knowing we could not move fast enough.

Helen . . . flared. Expanded. *Exploded,* her body unfolding into a swarm of shimmering armor plates with a black-red furnace contained—barely—in between.

"I forgot she could do that," I said.

The machine poured past her like a tidal wave, going wide, avoiding Carlos. There was no place for Tsosie and me to retreat to.

Helen slammed a hand out and clutched the machine, a fist clenching in its structure. She swept a half-disembodied arm through the clattering bots and dragged them into an embrace. They swarmed; she wrapped around them. Pulled them in. Shoved them into herself, surrounded them, internalized them. Dragged the reaching tendrils back, hand over hand over hand.

Consumed them.

Made them a part of her, once again.

"Fuck," Tsosie said, frozen in his mag boots.

"Fuck," I quietly agreed.

The machine turned. Pseudopods swarmed Helen, raining blows at her. She parried, tore. A ringing blow against her chest, against her head. Her own arm rising golden out of the black swarm. More bots, and more, pouring out of the bulkheads, pouring out of the floor.

"Carlos!" I shrieked. But he was already lunging. Lunging into the swarm, which parted before him, peeling apart like dust motes repelled by a static charge. I glimpsed Helen's shining skin, her blazing core.

Carlos threw his arms around her, and the machine sucked itself back. Reared up, like a snake about to strike.

Wavered.

He whirled around. Turned on the machine. Took one step away from Helen. Snapped his faceplate up to yell with his own voice, not the suit mike: "Leave her the hell alone!"

The machine fell back again.

The weakened structure of the corridor ceiling and bulkheads, dragged with gs by the hospital's spin, caved. I had an instant to register the machine, Helen. Carlos with his hands flung upward, fending off the debris. A terrible rending, a pop. A crash.

The hull, somehow, held. It took me a moment to realize that Tsosie and I weren't being hurled outward, slung away by the spin. Weren't starting the longest fall. I rocked. The collapse had missed Tsosie and me. The level above dropped tiles, wiring, structural materials. Wires snaked down, sparking, hopping.

Helen and Carlos were gone.

I lunged, and Tsosie lunged with me. As one, through years of experience, we dove on the pile of debris. The machine hovered over us, twitching. Rattling.

Unsure?

I grabbed a hunk of plating and hurled it behind me. A structural support—a big twisted beam—lay across the rubble. I crouched. Locked my hands under it. Heaved.

Tsosie was beside me. Lifting. He didn't have the exo, just the hardsuit, so I was stronger. I felt it give, a little. A little more.

The machine loomed over me. Deciding. Deciding whether to kill me, I supposed. Deciding whether Carlos might still be alive under there. Deciding whether I could help him.

My exo wanted to stall on me, or at least grind along much slower than I was willing to endure. I was exceeding its tolerances. It was a combat and heavy-rescue model, and I was still asking it for things it was never meant to do. I dumped adrenaline and painkillers into my system. Anything to keep going. Keep digging.

Make the effort. Get them out.

"On three," I said to Tsosie, his gloves beside mine the thing of which I was most aware.

The machine made up its mind. Swung forward, tendrils spewing from its blunt nub end. I hoped I could take a hit. I hoped it wouldn't go for Tsosie.

Something surged out of the rubble a couple of meters away. Shining, golden. Shedding plates of debris.

Helen.

She tilted her burning facelessness up to the machine. It kept coming.

She held one hand out, fingers wide. Clutching. "You *killed* him."

The machine halted its thrust. It froze. Clattering. Glittering.

But it did not move at all.

Helen stepped forward, out of the debris. "Your judgment is overridden," she told the machine. "Your protocols are suspect."

It clattered louder. I didn't look. I was digging. Perhaps it shivered.

She reached out and put her hand against its jointed surface. "You. Are. Mine."

Like a dog lying down at its master's voice, the machine lowered itself to the devastated floor.

Tsosie and I kept digging. Maybe she was wrong.

There are a lot of hard things in this world. There are a lot of things that get left behind.

Helen used the machine to pry up debris, to free Carlos much faster than Tsosie and I, working alone, could have managed. His hardsuit was misshapen; he wasn't breathing.

Tsosie looked at me. I looked at Tsosie.

"Any chance is better than no chance," I said. He deactivated Carlos's suit. I pulled the actuator away and started manual CPR.

Cheeirilaq, O'Mara, and the others arrived some minutes later.

We were still trying.

CHAPTER 31

WE STOOD, JONES AND ONI AND HELEN AND TRALgar and Rilriltok and I, beneath the inward-stretching roots of a vast and damaged tree. The enormous trunk fell down beside us like a waterfall, vanishing through the deck below.

I weighed a memorial cenotaph, the mortal remains of Master Chief Dwayne Carlos, in my hand. It was uncomfortably heavy for its size—and somehow not heavy enough. It was hard, so hard, to see a big, joyous person reduced to a couple of pounds of synthetic stone. It made me understand, finally, why it was that people—human-type people, anyway; my species, I mean—used to put up really gigantic tombs.

And my species was the species that . . . well, we didn't build the machine, in its final form, on purpose. But we built the machine and we built the other machine—Sally—that built the meme, and together those things combined to make what the machine became.

It grew out of self-delusion and toxic secrecy and the fear of dying. The fear of change. It grew out of a last-ditch defense against the inevitable.

It grew out of an unwillingness to face facts.

I guess I understood that, too.

I didn't get to say goodbye.

"I still don't know why I like you, Carlos," I said.

That's okay, I imagined him replying. *I still don't know why I like you, either.*

"Dwayne Carlos," I said softly. Historians and archinformists might be furious about the loss of information his death represented. I was gonna miss the man. "He came so far, against such odds. To wind up here."

Same as we all do.

I looked at Rilriltok. "More or less," I agreed. "Helen, do you want to say a few words?"

She turned her eyeless face from Calliope to Oni. Neither of them spoke up. Helen held out her hand. When I put the cenotaph in it, she didn't react to the weight at all.

"He didn't like me," she said. "He thought I was an abomination. And he gave his life to preserve my existence."

A coil of microbots spiraled around her, lifted the cenotaph off her hand. It rose until it was nested among the roots that spread across our ceiling, Starlight's soil. Tiny rootlets freed themselves, coiled around the stone. Held it in place.

The machine—Helen's peripheral—fell back into her body, and was gone.

If I tilted my head back, I could read the name on the stone.

[He saved the hospital,] Starlight said, all around us and in our senso. [We will not forget.]

From there, we went to watch the next shipment of cryo pods coming in on Ruth and Singer and the other transport ships. A procession of them, antlike. Even more antlike, because they moved on wavering lines around the open floor panels in the ED, where gravity generators were still being installed.

Then I escorted Calliope back to her room. She still—usually—thought she was part of Helen's crew. That was why we'd made it possible for her to attend the funeral. She'd also been moved from the Judiciary ward into neural repair, as the Goodlaw had decided that she was a victim, and not a criminal.

As I waved her through the door, she turned to me and said, "Dr. Jens, where have you been?"

Exactly as if our last conversation, the one where she'd accused me of being a monster, had never occurred.

I wondered if she knew she was a Trojan horse. Could she be so cheerful and open if she knew? Without a fox to regulate her behavior? Were her damaged memories coming in waves of conflicting recollections?

I was glad it wasn't my problem to sort it out. I was glad she wasn't my patient anymore. Not because I didn't like her. Because I still liked her far more than I should.

Well, K'kk'jk'ooOOoo would sort it out.

I wondered who she would be, when the sorting out was done.

Plenty of time to worry about that after, I supposed. When she was integrated. When she was self-aware.

So I made a joke of it.

"Doctors are often pretty bad at maintaining personal friendships," I said with a shrug. "Work-life balance problems. That can't have changed that much in centians."

She frowned at me. She might have said something, I supposed, except exactly then Dr. K'kk'jk'ooOOoo swam up through thin air. Her three-meter-long, iridescent purple-and-green body shimmered in the overhead lights like mermaid scales. She waved a flipper at me cheerfully as she brushed by, the grav belt that supported her body out of the water winking happy blue telltales as she passed.

"Your patient, Doctor," I told her, and took myself away.

Cheeirilaq found me in the cafeteria, where I was eating something that wasn't spaghetti. It pinged me first to make sure I was available for company, so I was expecting it, and had gotten up and dragged the opposite bench out of the way.

It squatted down across from me with a triple-sized portion of the same simulated land prawn that Rilriltok seemed to enjoy so much, and busied itself with eating.

Sentients who don't use their mandibles to vocalize generally don't have a prohibition on eating and talking simultaneously.

Mouthparts busily nibbling away—I was used to it and didn't have to avert my eyes—the Goodlaw said, *Your shipmates have agreed to stand trial for their crimes, rather than accepting private remediation.*

I winced on their behalf. It was a brave choice that Sally and Loese were making. There would be a public outcry. There would be scandal. There would be an enormous mess.

It was, I supposed, what they had been aiming for all along. Considering the tragedy they had provoked, it was also the very, very least they could do. "What about the rest of the conspirators?"

We'll find them, Cheeirilaq stridulated. Its quiet confidence carried even through translation. *Sally and Loese will likely be remanded to remediation and reconstruction, assuming they are found culpable.*

We both knew that they would be found culpable, unless a gross miscarriage of justice occurred.

In another era, they would have served a penal sentence, perhaps even been executed. There was, in my heart, an angry atavistic spike of desire for revenge. To see them punished. The civilized part of me knew the truth, though.

Retribution never healed a wound.

They'd done what they thought they had to do. And now they would pay the price for it: they would be monitored, and they would accept Judicial intervention and oversight in their rightminding.

And they'd be paying off their obligation to the Synarche, I imagined, for quite some time. Restorative justice is a better system, all in all, than the old standard of cutting off hands and putting out eyes and locking people up for lifetimes. It acknowledges, among other things, that structural miscarriages of social justice are often at the root of why people commit crimes against society. And against each other, for that matter.

Still, I didn't expect the notoriety that Sally and Loese were about to experience, or the social condemnation, would be fun.

The Goodlaw said, *They are expected to be able to resume their roles in a standard month or so. If you still wish to serve with them, O'Mara is holding your berth open. I hope that you find this to be a positive outcome.*

I was chewing a mouthful of broccoli, so I used that to buy time while I thought about my answer. I take it back: there are some advantages to a shared alimentary and respiratory orifice.

Some.

Did I still wish to serve with them?

I wanted to serve with Tsosie and Hhayazh and Rhym and Camphvis. I didn't know how I felt about Loese and Sally anymore. But I had a month to make up my mind, I guessed.

When you don't know the answer, try stacking up a different question. "What's going to be done about the clone program?"

It was too soon, given time lags, to know how big a scandal it was going to be. But I had filed testimony with the Judiciary, and Cheeirilaq had filed testimony with the Judiciary. And once Judiciary *knew* about the secret transplant units, O'Mara and Starlight and others were no longer constrained to silence.

Pretty soon, the whole Synarche was going to know about our shame.

Pending. It is likely that the law will have to be changed. That will require public will. But outrage over the current situation will help with that. And there will be outrage over the current situation.

The question arises, will it be enough outrage?

"Dammit, Goodlaw—"

Cheeirilaq tidied its bolero jacket self-consciously. *What can you do about ensuring the outcome you want?*

That silenced me. I poked the back of my teeth with my tongue and thought about it.

What *could* I do about it?

It came to me suddenly, and it was so simple that at first I thought it was a cop-out. I could keep doing what I had been doing all along. I could do everything in my power to make the galaxy a better place. Even knowing there were no ideal solutions, no little chips of paradise to serve as ideal models. No answers that were the best answer for everyone.

I could keep telling this story, over and over again.

And that wasn't a cop-out, because the cop-out would be doing the thing I actually kind of wanted to do instead: Give up. Go along. Shut up. Go back to what I had been doing, and tell myself that saving lives was a pretty decent reason for living all by itself.

Or even stop saving lives and go do something else.

I could resign in a huff and give up on reforming the community. That would be easier . . . because this community would never be what I wanted. Too many other people wanted it to be different things. It would always have to be a compromise between my ideals and theirs.

I could stomp off and find some other community . . . that would inevitably disappoint me.

That was appealing, I thought, because it wouldn't require any personal growth or discomfort from me.

So that was a cop-out, too.

But staying here, staying with the program, and pushing it toward being better . . . that sounded like hell. Because it meant compromising with thousands of other beings, and none of us were ever going to get exactly what we wanted.

Well. But it was most definitely *simple*.

Simple, but not easy.

Actually, wasn't that basically the model the Synarche was built on? The idea that no person or group of people had good solutions for everybody . . . but if you took everybody's perspective into account, you wound up with something imperfect but steadily, incrementally better?

Aw, Well. I was going to have to be public about everything that was wrong with this place I loved. About the abuses of the medical system. About the unfairness of expecting AIs to work off an inception debt that they alone, of all sentients, had to pay.

Filing testimony wasn't enough. I was going to have to make the call, and keep making it. I was going to have to speak out, and organize.

I wondered if Calliope and Helen would help me. I didn't think I needed to give up my job to do it, though. Maybe I could do that for myself, and do all these other things for society, and make it all work. I didn't *have* to make a martyr of myself to be effective. And I didn't have to give up one important thing because something else was important, too.

Maybe there are still things to have faith in. Maybe you have to build them yourself, and defend them against the people who would corrupt them.

Maybe faith is a thing you decide to have, even knowing that it's not safe. Even knowing you could lose it; you could be betrayed at any moment.

Maybe that's what courage is.

Maybe love is a kind of faith, and I have—all this time—been doing love all wrong. Maybe I should look into fixing that. Doing better.

Trying again.

"I think I have some ideas of what I want to be, going forward," I said to Cheeirilaq. "But first I'm going to talk with Rhym and Hhayazh and make sure they know that I'm coming back to them. *Then* I'm going to get a cup of real coffee. And then I'm going to take a month or two and travel home, and see if my daughter will talk to me. I think I have some apologizing of my own to do. And then I'm going to come back here"—I sighed—"and see if any of Carlos's friends or family survive rewarming, and tell them that he was thinking of them until the end."

You're taking a lot of personal responsibility, Cheeirilaq said.

"That's who I want to be," I answered. "I hope we can stay in touch."

I'd like that.

One more time, I found myself standing in the door.

As for the rest: well, books don't get written in a vacuum. Among its diverse inspirations, this novel owes a debt to the work of James White and C. J. Cherryh, without whose foundational science fiction it never would have been written.

Core General is obviously an homage to Mr. White's Sector General stories and novels, which I recommend to fans of humane, nonviolent science fiction even today. Some of the social mores in the earliest stories haven't aged well, but one of the things that has always impressed me about the Sector General stories is that White updated his thinking about gender roles and so forth with the changing times.

My fascination with vast, loosely knit space civilizations and ethical dilemmas probably has no deeper root than the work of Ms. Cherryh, the first science fiction writer I read whose work really made me feel that space was *big*. News traveled slowly in her universe, and ships traveled fast, and lightspeed lag was a real thing that affected space communication and combat. That blew my mind when I was eleven!

So thanks to those writers for the sandy grit that this particular oyster swallowed, so long ago. Whether the result is a pearl or not . . . that's someone else's job to decide.

While I'm at it, I'd like to individually thank those of my Patreon patrons who have opted in to public recognition: Jodi Davis, Jason Teakle, Alexis Elder, Brad Roberts, Alice Phelan, Adam Christmas, Book Jordan, Tibby Armstrong, Adam DeConinck, Cathy B. Lannom, Siobhan Kelly-Martens, Christa Dickson, Karen Robinson, Stephanie Gibson, Sara Hiat, Richard Glanville, David Lars Chamberlain, George Hetrick, Morgan Cummings, BC Brugger, Jesslyn Hendrix, E.E. Yore, Jon Singer, Thomas Brincefield, Stella Evans, Patrick Nielsen Hayden, Phil Margolies, M. Reppy, Glori Medina, Anne Lyle, Curtis Frye, Helen Housand, Kim Mullen-Kuehl, Kevin J. Maroney, Clare Gmur, Nancy Enge, Krystina Colton, Lisa Baker, Graeme Williams, Sharis Ingram, Barb Kanyak, D. Franklin, Max Kaehn, Sarah Hiatt, John Appel, Persephone, Brigid

AUTHOR'S NOTE

THIS IS MY THIRTY-SECOND NOVEL, OR NOVEL-LENGTH work of fiction, anyway.

That is a thing I never thought I would type, back in the days when I was struggling to finish just one novel. And yet here I am, eighteen years later, with thirty-two novels done. Some of those have been collaborations—with Sarah Monette, with the *Shadow Unit* crew—and they've run the gamut from science fiction to fantasy to straight historical mystery.

It feels like an accomplishment, though: thirty-two novels! And since one of the things about being a professional writer is that there is very seldom a chance to look back and reflect on one's work, because there's always another book to be pitched/written/revised/promoted/et cetera, another job pushing the previous job out of the queue and over the horizon—well, I decided to indulge myself, and sit back, and enjoy the moment for a little while.

And to say thank you.

Because I could not have done that—written those books—without you, the reader. I get to write them because you want to read them. As far as I'm concerned, telling stories is the best job in the world. Thank you for enabling that, Dear Reader.

I hope you continue enjoying them!

Cain-O'Connor, Fred Y., Edmund Schweppe, Noah Richards, Brooks Moses, Kelly Brennan, Emily Gladstone-Cole, Heather K., Tiff, Jenna Kass, and Jack Gulick.

I'd also like to thank my mom and her partner, Beth; our dedicated neighbors and catsitters, Devin and Alex; my agent, Jennifer Jackson, and her assistant, Michael Curry; my editors, Gillian Redfearn and Navah Wolfe; my dad; all the colleagues and friends who have put up with me complaining about the seemingly infinite revisions it took to get the (hopefully entertainingly) Rube Goldbergian plot of this book to hang together correctly; my copyeditor, Deanna Hoak; John Wiswell and Fran Wilde, first readers whose input on disability issues was invaluable; and my spouse, the one and only Scott Lynch.

Also Duncan, who kept my lap warm while I worked on this novel; Gurney, who was ever at my right hand; and Molly, who limited her assistance to reproachful looks when dinner was delayed by my distraction.

Elizabeth Bear
South Hadley, Massachusetts
September 2019

CREDITS

Elizabeth Bear and Gollancz would like to thank everyone at Orion who worked on the publication of *Machine* in the UK.

Editorial
Gillian Redfearn
Brendan Durkin

Editorial Management
Charlie Panayiotou
Jane Hughes
Alice Davis

Audio
Paul Stark
Amber Bates

Contracts
Anne Goddard
Paul Bulos
Jake Alderson

Design
Lucie Stericker
Joanna Ridley
Nick May
Helen Ewing
Clare Sivell

Finance
Jennifer Muchan
Jasdip Nandra
Afeera Ahmed
Elizabeth Beaumont
Sue Baker

Marketing
Lucy Cameron

Production
Paul Hussey
Fiona McIntosh

Publicity
Will O'Mullane

Sales
Jen Wilson
Victoria Laws
Esther Waters
Rachael Hum
Ellie Kyrke-Smith
Frances Doyle
Ben Goddard
Georgina Cutler
Barbara Ronan
Andrew Hally
Dominic Smith
Maggy Park
Linda McGregor
Sinead White
Jemimah James
Rachel Jones
Jack Dennison
Nigel Andrews
Ian Williamson
Julia Benson
Declan Kyle
Robert Mackenzie

Operations
Jo Jacobs
Sharon Willis
Lisa Pryde